Wendy Robertson grew up in the North of England, one of four children whose widowed mother, an ex-nurse, worked in a factory. Wendy worked as a teacher, then a lecturer, gaining a Master's degree whilst also at various times writing short stories, articles, a weekly column in the *Northern Echo* and novels for young adults published nationally. A full-time writer since 1989, she also runs a writing group and workshops for new writers. A THIRSTING LAND is her eighth adult novel, the third in a sequence of linked yet independent novels, following KITTY RAINBOW and CHILDREN OF THE STORM – 'stops you in your tracks . . . Wendy's best yet' (*Northern Echo*)

Also by Wendy Robertson

Riches of the Earth
Under a Brighter Sky
Land of Your Possession
A Dark Light Shining
Kitty Rainbow
Children of the Storm

A Thirsting Land

Wendy Robertson

First published in 1998
by HEADLINE BOOK PUBLISHING

First published in paperback in 1998
by HEADLINE BOOK PUBLISHING

10 9 8 7 6 5 4 3 2 1

ISBN 0 7472 5185 1

Typeset by Avon Dataset Ltd, Bidford-on-Avon, Warks

Printed and bound in Great Britain by
Clays Ltd St. Ives plc, Bungay, Suffolk

HEADLINE BOOK PUBLISHING
A division of Hodder Headline PLC
338 Euston Road
London NW1 3BH

In memory of my brother Tom,
who, like my fictional Thomas,
was one of the precious, gentle people

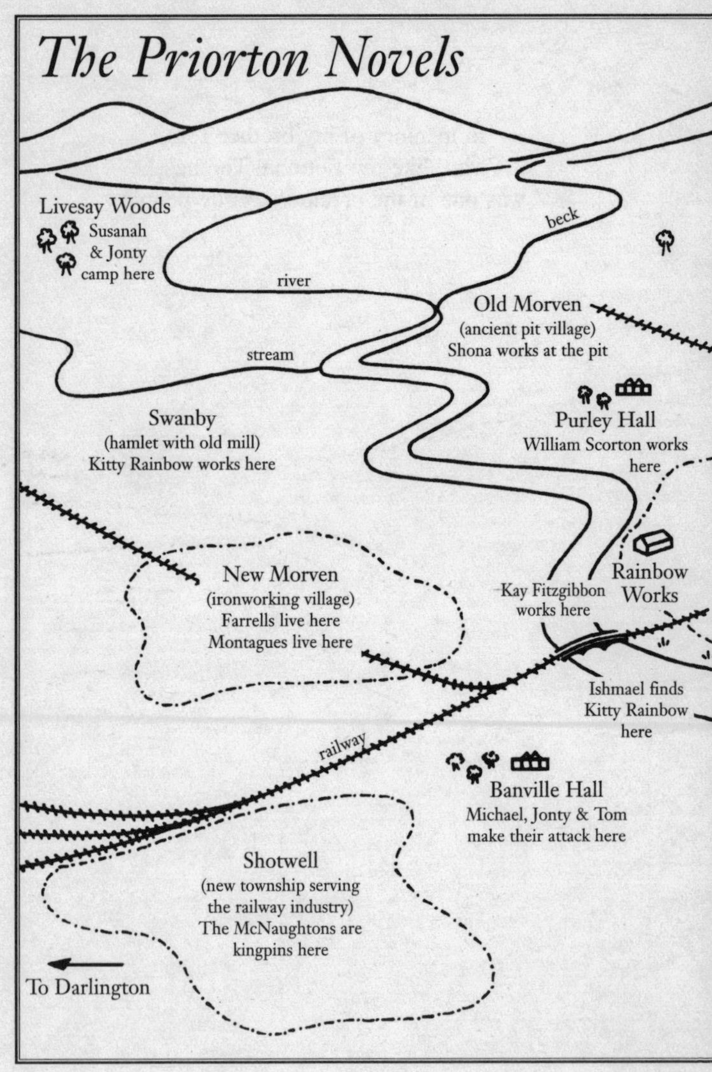

The Priorton Novels
Livesay Woods
Susanah & Jonty camp here
beck
river
Old Morven
(ancient pit village)
Shona works at the pit
stream
Swanby
(hamlet with old mill)
Kitty Rainbow works here
Purley Hall
William Scorton works here
Rainbow Works
New Morven
(ironworking village)
Farrells live here
Montagues live here
Kay Fitzgibbon works here
Ishmael finds Kitty Rainbow here
railway
Banville Hall
Michael, Jonty & Tom make their attack here
Shotwell
(new township serving the railway industry)
The McNaughtons are kingpins here
To Darlington

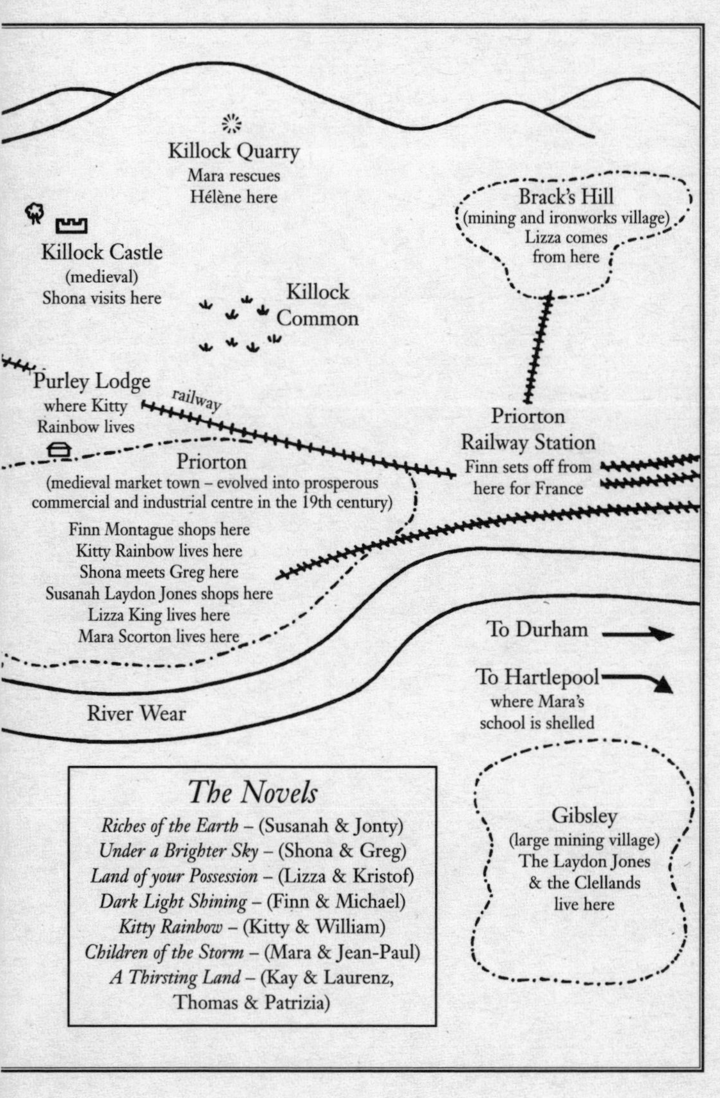

The Novels

Riches of the Earth – (Susanah & Jonty)
Under a Brighter Sky – (Shona & Greg)
Land of your Possession – (Lizza & Kristof)
Dark Light Shining – (Finn & Michael)
Kitty Rainbow – (Kitty & William)
Children of the Storm – (Mara & Jean-Paul)
A Thirsting Land – (Kay & Laurenz, Thomas & Patrizia)

One

Alexandria, 1939

'Dammit, they've gone!' Thomas Scorton lifted the flap of his tiny tent with a trembling hand and peered at the rising column of desert sand which was the only evidence of the truck whose driver had promised him a lift to Cairo. His head throbbed in rhythmic counterpoint to the creak of the harness of the blindfolded water buffalo, already at its day's work walking round and round the well. 'Blighters have left me,' he muttered.

'Fear not, old boy.' Creasing his eyes against the early sun, the thin man beside him smiled down at Thomas and thrust a tin cup of coffee into his hand. 'Here, drink this and be calm. Those blighters have left you here because I told them to. Said I'd wait for you to stir your lazy bones and then give you a lift.'

Thomas took the coffee in his right hand. With his left he scrambled in his breast pocket for his spectacles, put them on his nose and peered at the man. Stephen something. Yes. That was his name. Thomas had spent the whole of yesterday evening with this Stephen something, drinking dusty whisky and talking, talking . . . about what?

About Alexandria of course. Always Alexandria. About his parents who lived there, adopted into the bosom of the family of a merchant who dealt in rugs and exotic feathers. And he had babbled on about his sister, of course; about his ancient grandmother in England: 'Don't tell me there ain't gonna be a war, Stephen, is that your name? Because she knows there is.' He had grasped this Stephen's collar, too tight. 'Her factory's on flat-out production. Shells rattling off the line like hailstones, according to my old grandma.'

The other man had eased away from Thomas's choking grip and filled his glass, smiling faintly. 'No argument from me on that one, old man. I'm dying for it. Sure to need pilots, aren't they?'

And Thomas could remember going on about his Aunt Mara, who was a teacher and wrote the famous 'Tommy' stories for children. Even Stephen had heard of her.

'But you're going in the wrong direction for Alexandria,' he protested now, squeezing his bleary eyes against the penetrating white light. 'That was a proper lift I hitched, you know. To Cairo, I have customers there. Some deals to fix . . .'

'We agreed to travel together last night, old son. You were telling me all about your sister, and those objects you deal in. I told you I thought I knew a buyer. Buyers. I told you I'd fly you back to Alex and we could look at some samples from your store. Then we'll go across to Cairo in the time it'd take you to trundle up there in that truck. We'll get the stuff and you'll have a buyer ready made. And you'd lose no time. You contracted me for the job. Remember?'

'Your aeroplane?' Thomas clapped a hand on his sore head, then pushed his blunt fingers through his tangled black hair. 'An aeroplane, you say?'

The other man nodded. '*The Dragonfly*. My little beauty. I told you all about her.'

'Contracted? Did I say that? Can't remember a thing. To be truthful my sister and I run this little business on a shoestring. I can't see how we could afford the cost of a charter . . .'

'We agreed that too. Subsistence costs and a proportion – say ten per cent – of anything you make on this deal, selling the pots on to those so-called cultured travellers who want to pretend they've dug them up themselves.' Stephen lifted the tin jug and filled Thomas's coffee cup to the brim.

Thomas shook his head. 'I must have talked a lot. Too much,' he groaned. The bitter coffee was clearing his head now and he looked again at the man who seemed to have attached himself to him, wondering if he would count as a 'waif or stray'. His sister Kay was always complaining about him bringing home waifs and strays. But no. This man was no waif. He was softly spoken, a trace of Irish in his voice; respectable; he had quite a bit of charm, in fact. He was the proprietor of an airline . . . well, an aeroplane . . . And neatly turned out, even in his desert dust.

But still, Kay might call him a stray. Thomas could hear himself, as usual, making protesting explanations to his sister, which would sound like apologies.

Kay Scorton closed her eyes and curved her hands round the ancient pot, not quite touching it. She allowed her palms to tingle with the physical sense of the potter who had thrown this pot on his primitive wheel fifteen hundred years before. When she lifted it to her cheek she could smell the old heat and hear the camel-driver's distant cry. She pressed her palms harder on to the old dry clay, sharing with the maker the sense of gladness that the job was finished, as this was the twentieth pot he had thrown that day. Above all now the potter was thirsty and what he wanted most in the world was a drink of cool water.

She blinked and put the pot down, glancing at the closed door. It wouldn't do for Thomas and the others to know that she actually felt the maker of these things. That she could now sense individual potters with unique quirks in the rounded feel of their wares. That she could sense the potter's joy that now he could brighten his creations with this newfangled thing called glaze.

It was sufficient for them to know that she could date them by instinct. This had proved useful, as she and Thomas trawled the bazaars for items they knew they could sell on. The methods of work had changed little over the millennia, so often new pots would be presented as the work of the 'old ones'. But she knew. One of her notes of confirmation had some currency in the shaky world of antiquities dealing. She picked up her pen and wrote neatly on a small piece of cardboard: *1350BC, Suleiman*. She had no way of identifying individual makers so she gave them invented names. Taking a wisp of twine from a crowded shelf she tied the label carefully to the rim of the bowl.

The bead curtain rattled and her mother swept in, bringing with her the dry scents of the market: sandalwood, saltpetre and spice. 'Now then, dear, hard at it?'

Kay sat back and twisted her spine this way and that to ease her aching muscles. Before her were thirty pots and dozens of smaller items of bead and carved jewellery. All of them were neatly labelled.

Leonora sat at the other end of the work-table in a flowing cotton dress which was half Egyptian, half old-fashioned Edwardian day dress, designed by herself to keep her cool and covered in the sometimes oppressive heat of the city. 'Well?' she said. 'And how are you on this sublime morning?'

Kay smiled. 'Stiff and sore with sitting here, but sublime apart from that.'

Leonora touched one of the lines of pots. 'It's a mystery to me how you dig all these up.'

Her daughter frowned. 'We don't dig them up. That's the point, surely? They flow towards us. They're out there, in the houses and the markets. People come to us with them.' Her tone was defensive. Sam, her father, a much more expert archaeologist, had been very critical when she and Thomas started to trade in the flotsam and jetsam of the antiquities market. But the money she made from this trade was important to them all now, more important than ever.

Her mother had always acknowledged this. 'Wherever they come from they're lifesavers.' Leonora stood up. 'Will you come along and see your Poppa, love? Ali is pouring the lemonade.' There was a note of pleading in her voice.

Kay hesitated. 'Well, I . . . Yes. Yes, of course I will.' She linked arms with her mother and they walked out of the narrow house, past the fine wrought-iron door of their friend Mr Kohn, who traded in rugs and exotic feathers, and on to the next small house which was her mother's home and had been her own until a year ago when Mr Kohn, a brisk sharp man, had let her and Thomas have the other house to trade from and live in.

One way or another they were all pensioners of Mr Kohn, who continued to show great kindness to the Scortons. Many years ago Kay's father Sam had done some favour for a relative of his and this was never forgotten. Mr Kohn was very fond of Sam and had been elaborately grief-stricken when his old friend had been struck down so cruelly by a paralysing stroke.

Sam looked up from his long chair in the back courtyard, his first smile as always for Leonora. He held his good hand up in congenial greeting to Kay. Leonora smiled gaily at him. 'You're looking so much better, Sam. The air's a bit fresher today, I think.'

He nodded and made a gesture to Kay who took a stool beside her father and waited while Ali, another product of Mr Kohn's munificence, poured lemonade on to ice which cracked and clicked as the warm liquid surged around it.

Kay endured it as long as she could, then stood up saying abruptly that she had to go. There was much to do. She charged towards the door, her head turned away to hide the tears which had started to flow.

Her mother caught up with her in the alley outside. 'Kay, are you all right?'

Kay pushed the tears off her face with her hand and sniffed. 'Fine. I'm fine. Just got the sneezes in there.'

'Sam sent you a message.' Only Leonora could understand the painfully twisted sounds that came from Sam's mouth. Sometimes, looking at her father's stricken body, Kay thought her mother made it up.

She sniffed. 'Message?'

'He said it's not so bad on the inside as it looks on the outside.'

'Did he?'

'Honestly. That's what he said.' Her mother paused. 'Between you and me, I hope that's true. Perhaps he just said it to be kind. To help you. He's like that.'

'Mmm.'

They avoided looking at each other, focusing on the camel which was making its delicate sponge-footed way down the narrow street, lurching to one side now and then, and catching its load of grass on the rough clay walls mended here and there with scurvy patches of plaster. 'Really. It is our old Sam in there, you know. He still makes the most crass jokes. We still recall the old times.' Leonora's voice was soft in Kay's ear.

'But . . .' Kay left it at that. She still could not reconcile that massive slumped figure with the energetic, robust, surprisingly subtle character of her father. Finally, unable to hold back, she burst out, 'How can you love him? How can you love him, like that?'

They stood with their backs flat against the wall to let the camel through, taking in his extra smell with the stench of the alley. 'Oh, you're such a clever girl, Kay, so shrewd dealing with all those pots, so businesslike.' She laughed. 'Just like your grandma, though that can't be proximity when you think how long it is since you've seen her.' She ducked as the camel's load of grass seemed just about to tip on her. Miraculously, the camel swayed the other way and the danger passed. 'But you don't know about . . . this thing with me and Sam. How it is to love someone for so long. To share so much.

'I've loved him since I was a little girl, you know?' she went on softly. 'We were like brother and sister, Sam and I. But even when we were little he was my knight in shining armour. Then, when we were older, quite old in fact, we conceived such a passion for each other that its heat would have forged all the steel in the world. Of course we lost that time together, when I went to England. Sam always said it was worth while, that he admired me for it, and I try not to regret it. But it is hard.'

'That time' was a period in the late twenties and thirties when Leonora, sickened with the decadence of Alexandrian life and her own uselessness there, had taken Kay and Thomas to England to school. Once there, she became involved in radical politics and stayed on for seven years. Always Sam was going to come home after her, but the fascination with Egypt and archaeology kept him one year and then another. Then, missing him too much, they had all returned, and Leonora resigned herself afresh to the confined, expatriate life which had so frustrated her in earlier years.

'Even with a continent between us, we felt together, Sam and I. Now, the way he is, that thing which has happened to his body, is nothing in comparison. We communicate without speaking. We make love without touching. This thing makes no difference.'

Kay was facing her mother now in the deserted alley. She searched hard in Leonora's face for signs that she was making it all up to comfort them both, to comfort herself. There were none. Kay shook her head. 'I don't understand,' she said.

Leonora touched her cheek. 'You're too young, sweetheart,' she said, looking at her young daughter, sturdy and boyish with her cropped hair and desert trousers. 'You are too young for all that. You have lots of time.'

Later that day, when Kay had tidied her table and entered the details of all the pots, complete with provenance, small drawings and possible values, into her big ledger, she went to sit in the shade of the high-walled courtyard. She took two bites from the melon which Ali had left in a bowl on the rickety little table for her, and put her head against the high back of the chair.

Her father, Sam, danced back into her mind: always burly yet light on his feet; always laughing in those very deep tones. She could see him putting his hand on one cheek as he discussed business with Mr Kohn. Talking energetically about some 'dig' he was helping to 'fix', where some eminent archaeologist was sifting the sands to access more and more of their ancient mystery, slicing flesh off the bones of history with a very fine knife.

Thomas had originally worked alongside their father, fixing trips and locations for the scattering of amateur and semi-professional archaeologists who inhabited this part of the Middle East like leeches. Thomas, though slight, proved to be very strong and could toil alongside Egyptian workmen with ease. Sam prided himself on limiting the damage ham-fisted amateurs might do.

The archaeologists were a mixed bunch, involved in that game for all sorts of reasons. But Sam, the local man, the 'fixer', loved best of all the men who used the objects they found to weave lyrical tales about the lives of the old ones. These men, he would say, were tracing a poetic truth about the importance and dignity of human experience.

Sam had no time for antiquity hunters, tricksy individuals who saw it all as a kind of sport and the objects as trophies. So he was disgusted when Kay and Thomas started to sell the objects coming down from the old ones to travellers, who would later profit greatly from them in their own country.

Thomas, who was too much in awe of Sam to find him comfortable to work with, was pleased these days to be working with his sister, out of his father's burly shadow. In their little business they could make a tidy bit of money.

Kay closed her eyes and smiled slightly. In fact it was this very despised money which, after Sam's stroke, had kept them all afloat and marginally independent of Mr Kohn's admittedly willing charity.

It was hot in the courtyard and she must have fallen asleep because she jumped wildly when a pair of hands clapped themselves over her eyes. She fought to move the intrusive hands – which she knew to be her brother's – away from her face. The night had turned the courtyard pitch dark here and very chilly. She had recognised the feel and shape of her brother's hands, but did not recognise the face of the man before her, standing in the beam of lamplight from the open bead curtain.

He was tall and very slender with the dried, faintly golden skin of a European who has spent a long time around the desert. His eyes were strangely silvery, as was his hair, which, white as torchlight, caught the glow from the open door.

She twisted round to look at her brother. 'Thomas! You're supposed to be in Cairo!'

He grinned and pushed his glasses back up his nose. 'No I'm not. I'm here. And guess what? I came by aeroplane. Stephen here gave me a lift.'

Furiously she jumped up. 'Oh, you! Always bringing home w—' She was stopped by the enigmatic light in the stranger's eye. She blushed. 'Where're your manners, Thomas?'

'Oh, sorry!' Her brother came round from behind the chair. He smiled comfortably at her. 'My sister, Miss Kay Scorton, Stephen, though to be honest you might mistake her for my brother in this light.'

Kay was acutely conscious, then, of her breeches and her cropped hair. She put out her hand. 'How d'you do?' she said stiffly.

'And Kay, this is Stephen . . . er . . . I tell you what, old man, never did hear your name.'

The stranger grasped Kay's hand in his. 'Stephen Fitzgibbon, Miss Scorton. Delighted to make your acquaintance. Haven't I heard so much about you?'

Kay shot a killing glance at her brother. She pulled her hand away from the stranger's. 'There's nothing to know, Mr Fitzgibbon. Nothing at all,' she said stiffly.

For a second the air was filled with the ululating sound of a voice – it was hard to tell whether it was in prayer or mourning – rising above the hubbub of the city. Kay shivered. Stephen Fitzgibbon coughed and turned to Thomas. 'Perhaps we could go in, Thomas? You were telling me about these things you already have to sell?'

Before Kay could stop him, Thomas had bustled the man past her and down the passage into her little workroom, where her pots stood in neat rows on the long table. She stomped past that doorway and into her own little bedroom at the back. She banged the door and put a chair behind it before she sat on the bed.

The sound of their voices murmuring and muttering, the occasional yelp of laughter, made her more and more angry.

After a while Thomas came and rattled at the door, telling

her to come out, to have tea with Stephen. She ignored him. The rattling stopped and the murmuring on the other side was more sedate. Then it stopped. She waited ten minutes then cautiously opened the door and moved down the corridor to the living room. The beads clicked as she pushed through the curtain and even in the pitch dark she knew her twin was sitting there.

'No need to be rude, old girl. What on earth's the matter with you?' He was sitting on the long couch covered with kelims. His voice fluttered across to her in the darkness. She made her way unerringly across the floor and sat beside him, shoulder to shoulder.

'It was the shock. And that man looming up like that. And you've been talking about me again. I can't think what rubbish you were burbling out. And you took him into the workroom.'

'It's my place as well as yours,' he said quietly.

'I know. I know,' she said. 'But it was just . . . Who is he, Thomas?'

'Stephen Fitzgibbon. He hires out this plane, *The Dragonfly*, he calls it, along with himself as pilot, to anyone who has light loads or items to move about the delta. He's offered to buy some of our stuff himself, and transport it for us – you know, this fellow I'm to talk to in Cairo. If I have some pots there with me . . .'

'We can't afford to move them by plane.'

He explained Stephen's profit-sharing idea.

'There might be something in that,' she said reluctantly. 'But if he's so useful, such a good businessman, why does he need to join up with us?'

Thomas chuckled. 'Perhaps he likes the colour of my big blue eyes.' He reached over and squeezed her hand. 'Don't take everything so seriously, Kay. What can we lose? At least it's an idea worth trying.'

'How do you know you can trust him?'

'Come and find out. Talk to him. We're to meet him at the Cecil for a drink in an hour. I promised you'd make up for your . . . shyness then.'

'The Cecil? Oh Thomas, the money! You know we can't—'

He put up his hands as though warding off blows. 'On him, Sis, I promise you. On him.'

She put an arm through his where they sat. 'Anyway, I'm not shy. What makes you say that to people?'

Kay gulped her lemonade and sat back with a certain relish. Stephen Fitzgibbon had not recognised her as he came into the broad mirrored entrance to the hotel. She watched him through the mirrors walking swiftly towards them, a tall gangly figure with a shock of white-silver hair, responding with a raised hand to greetings from various parts of the room.

She also saw herself in the mirrors: a figure of unrecognisable glamour. She had gone to her mother with the problem of what to wear. In the end she chose one of her mother's flowing white Egyptian dresses. On Kay it only reached mid calf. She had clinched it on her small waist with an enamelled silver girdle, tied with tiny silver bells, and topped it with one of her mother's deep fringed Persian shawls. She had brushed her hair hard to flatten it and caught it with a silver slide just above her left eyebrow. Her mother had helped her apply a bit of lip-rouge and made her parade for Sam, evoking a whistle of appreciation from his twisted mouth.

Here at the Cecil Hotel Stephen Fitzgibbon was not whistling, but he was looking at her as though she were made of marshmallow.

She settled back to watch this man whom she had known for a single afternoon. He looked so much younger when he started to laugh. She observed his narrow gawky shoulders, his thick tossed-back hair, his clear silvery gaze which seemed to be seeing you and thinking of quite another thing: far horizons from the cockpit of his bucketing plane, perhaps.

She caught her breath. In her nineteen years, twelve of them in this hot, flotsam-and-jetsam city, she had known quite a few very personable young men. But with her brother always at her side as boon companion and escort, she had been spared the problem of choosing any one person especially, and had never succumbed to the blandishments of men attracted by her strange combination of intelligence, toughness and untouched intensity.

In any case all social life in their family had ground to a halt when two planned digs were cancelled and Sam lost all their money and very soon after had this dreadful attack. In one way she had not been sorry. There had always seemed something ridiculous about bobbing along on the surface of this over-social and threateningly corrupt city. For Kay, the adventure of setting up the little business between her and Thomas was exciting enough. She had had her fill of being sociable.

But the scene here at the Cecil was not 'being sociable'; this was different. The touch of Stephen Fitzgibbon's hand as he shook hers and ushered her into her seat here renewed the sense of shock she had had when they first shook hands in the courtyard. It made her think of the hands of the potters whose bowls she handled every day. It had a familiar feel. It was as though she had known him for a thousand years. She tried to keep her face and body very still, so that she did not betray the strength of her feeling.

Stephen sat back in his fragile seat. 'Can't think why you like this city, Thomas. Too hot, the slimy heat from the water. These blasted insects. Give me Cairo any day.' He flicked long narrow fingers against his own neck, disposing of an inquisitive fly which was replaced in a second by another one.

Thomas Scorton chuckled. 'We grew up here, Kay and I. Anyway, Alexandria has its own . . . charm, shall we say? You know, rich buttressed against poor; Sudanese, Lebanese, Bedouin cheek by jowl with Egyptians, English and French. The way the dawn creeps in from the Eastern Marches . . . amazing dawns, colours that sink into your soul. Then the markets – have you ever seen the match of the fruit stalls, the colour . . .'

'Whoa!' Stephen put up a defensive arm. 'I believe you. I believe you.'

Thomas, relaxed and delighted with his new friend, got up

from his chair to harry the waiter into bringing more ice for their drinks. 'Anyway, can't be the first time you've been in Alexandria, old chap,' he said over his shoulder. 'You must have been here dozens of times, hopping around the dunes on that machine of yours, *Dragonfly*. Isn't that what you call it?'

Stephen stayed silent, watching Thomas weave his way through the tables. Then he leant over towards Kay. 'You have a very nice nose,' he said.

She frowned and touched her nose with her own forefinger. 'Nose?'

'Your brother there said you had this great big nose and it could sniff out real pieces of the old stuff, antiquities, blindfold.'

'I can do that all right. I inherited it from my father who has now retired. Good thing I can, too, or we'd not make a living,' she said calmly. 'But my nose is fairly normal, thank you very much.'

He leant forward even further and laid one of his thin fingers on it. 'It's a very beautiful nose.'

The touch of his fingers shocked her again, a tremor racing up through her hair, down her back and right to her heels. She pulled away. Her pale cheeks reddened. 'He can be a fool, can Thomas.'

She waited for him to disagree, but he didn't. He merely said, 'He is very young, after all. Nineteen, is he? Eighteen? Sure, you couldn't be more unlike. He says you're twins?'

She nodded. 'We might not be like each other but we know each other very well. More than brother and sister might, I think,' she said, instantly regretting her tendency to take everything too seriously. He must think her very dull.

He shrugged. 'I would not know, having neither mother nor father, sister nor brother. And my parents had no sisters or brothers so . . . alone I am in this cruel world. Except for a few Irish second cousins, that is.'

The words were light but they moved her. She couldn't imagine life without Thomas, or without her mother and father carrying on the residue of their antiques trade and their own love story back in their untidy house. She couldn't even imagine life without her grandmother or her Auntie Mara and Uncle Jean-Paul back in England. And these people she only knew now through letters. Her lip trembled, devastated. 'An orphan. I'm sorry . . .'

He gave her a strange look, then coughed. 'They . . . they say you never miss what you never had, Miss Scorton. My people died of influenza just after the Great War. Parents and my sister. I was just a nipper then. Grandparents brought me up in Ireland, out to the West there. Also dead now. Just a bit of money left to buy *The Dragonfly*. Freedom. Can't get enough of it. First flew in India. Now here.' His tone was sober. 'But I envy you your twin, your brother. An alter ego. A friend on this earth. Ah.' He switched on a smile at Thomas who was striding across the floor, a harassed man in a fez hurrying after him, splashes from his dish of ice slopping on to his snow-white djibbah. 'Here's the boy.'

The ice cued a more businesslike tone to their conversation. The talk was all about the transport of the precious cargo of pots and other small antiquities back up to Cairo where there were customers waiting. Kay, watching as Thomas polished his glasses and Stephen started to scribble figures on a notebook, allowed herself to relish the feeling: the shock of meeting this silver-gold man in a city where many of the Europeans were prematurely wrinkled, tired-faced and, at worst, debauched.

Stephen hunched forward now over his freshened drink, his smooth brow wrinkling. She realised they were both staring at her. 'What?' she said.

Thomas tapped her arm with his glasses. 'Here am I telling old Stephen that you're the businesslike one, the clever one, and there are you in a brown study or up a gum tree or something.'

She shook herself. 'What was it?'

He thrust a notebook towards her. 'Stephen reckons he can do the job, on a regular basis, for this much a trip – which we were paying for the truck anyway – and a percentage of our sell.'

She shook her head. 'Don't know that Ma and Pa would countenance it. Selling in such a hurry. They urge us to wait for the prices. Sometimes it takes months.'

Stephen shook his head. 'Short-sighted. You watch. Within those months there'll be all-out war back home and no one'll be buying pots and votive items then. It'll be guns and bombs, tanks and planes, spears and hatchets. Believe me.'

The two men were still staring at her. She shrugged. 'Well, there would be no harm in trying once, would there? Or twice.'

Stephen stood up and pulled her to her feet so that he could shake her hand yet again. 'A wonderful decision, Miss Scorton.'

She could sense him as a child, running the lanes in some village in the West of Ireland, hair yellow-blond then, blowing in the wind off the Atlantic.

'I knew I was fated to work with old Thomas here the minute I saw his spectacles glittering in the light from the campfire.' He paused, his hand tightening on hers. 'And I knew I would work with you the minute he spoke of his very special sister. I might tell you you have no greater advocate.' He paused, then said very slowly, 'In fact, I suddenly feel the whole of my life has led to this moment, here meeting you.'

She stood very still for a moment, then Thomas clapped him on the shoulder. 'Perhaps it was the gleam of my whisky bottle, don't you think, old boy?'

Sam winked at Leonora, a painful screwing up of the side of his face which made her smile. She came and knelt by his side. 'What is it, love?'

'Young Kay and that man.' The words, warped and meaningless to any outsider, were clear to her.

She nodded. 'She is very taken with him. He seems quite charming. I like him.'

'I was thinking of Russia.' The words squeezed out of the stiff mouth.

Her hand tightened on his. In her mind's eye she could see him, dressed in the ridiculous borrowed finery of a Caucasian officer, silver buckles rattling, riding towards her through the pines like some hero in an operetta. She could hear his voice: '*The whole thing's a disaster, Leonie. Idiots running the show . . . thousands of cartridges, none of which fit a Russian rifle . . . using sticks and stones against the Germans.*'

She could feel his body enfolding her there among the pines, loving yet made frustratingly impotent by the tragedy unfolding around them. His voice in her ear, young and strong. '*Even so I have missed you, darling girl.*'

She felt again her own pain the next day when Sam had gone, and she had to return to the drama and the drudgery of nursing an army in full retreat, the cold seeping into her soul.

Now, in the dry heat of Alexandria, his hand turned in hers. 'I have never loved you more than this,' he said. 'Not even in Russia.'

Three weeks later Kay Scorton and Stephen Fitzgibbon were married quietly at the house of the Irish consul, attended by a jubilant Thomas and a shocked, but tentatively pleased, Leonora. They all went back and had a quiet celebration in the courtyard of the little house. Sam sat smiling a twisted smile of delight, the dignified Mr Kohn, their only guest, beside him, smoking a cheroot.

In those three weeks, Stephen Fitzgibbon flew backwards and forwards to Cairo with Thomas, helping him to get good prices for his wares. The rest of the time he spent with Kay; sitting with her in the workroom as she handled and labelled her pots; walking in the streets past the old men playing chess and the water-carrier clashing his cups like cymbals and the boy carrying wild birds in a basket on his head; strolling past the shops in the rue Fuad; drinking rose-scented water in the café by the Goharri Mosque. To her own dawning surprise she felt easy in his presence and her heart leapt each time when she heard his swift light steps in the corridor.

So when Stephen talked of the war and assumed their marriage without asking her directly, Kay accepted the assumption with little question. With this war looming, it was better, surely, to marry now?

Her body told her this also, but she did not submit to his urgency until she had his ring on her finger. Then, properly married, when they made love in the little room behind her workroom she felt a circle click together; the click confirmed that they had done this together before, a thousand years ago. It was good then and was good now.

Those days in Alexandria before the war were lyrical for Kay and Stephen. In the shimmer of green, mauve, and red that hung in the very air they held hands as they strolled amongst the white-robed figures on the curving esplanade. They ate succulent water melon by street stalls. Gasping with the luck of finding each other, they reaped to the full the sensual opportunities of the city.

Kay continued her work with the old pots and objects, and Thomas and Stephen sold them to buyers eager to buy them up before war swept them away. The sense of urgency, of time running out, threaded an eager pattern in the air they breathed. Sometimes Kay flew to Cairo with Stephen, the little plane rattling low over the mountainous sandscape, as the dry desert wind drilled grit into their eyes.

But all of this came to an end suddenly one day when Leonora gathered them together to say she thought that they should return home to England before things got worse there. Kitty, her mother and the twins' grandmother, was back there facing all this war business virtually unsupported. Leonora felt she should be with her. She paused. 'Mind you, Sam says we will be safer here.'

Sam grunted.

'He knows how much I worry about your grandmother. But he says we should stay.'

Sam grunted again.

Thomas said, 'Well, I'm staying. There'll be plenty to do here for the British war effort. The Germans are lurking around all over the place.'

Stephen wrinkled his nose at this. 'Catch me skulking here when the action's bubbling up over there! I told you they would need flyers, Thomas, and they're shouting for them now,' he said gravely. Then he kissed Kay on the nose. 'I'm going, beloved girl. My Irish cousins will never forgive me for fighting for the English, but this I must do.'

She smiled uncertainly. 'They will need pilots, I suppose.'

'You come too. It'll be a lark, darling.'

But in the end they all stayed and Stephen went on his own, leaving Kay struggling in the heat in the first sickening throes of pregnancy. Then the Germans marched into Poland and the seas were no longer safe. So she settled back in the heat with her brother and her parents. Her mother's flowing dresses became very useful, adjusting and expanding over her growing girth. So she waited in her narrow house by the bazaar for the distant war to burn itself out and bring her husband, her silver-gold boy, back to her arms.

Patrizia Zagorski hauled herself back to her feet, brushed down her coat and pulled her hat further down on her head. A cart came trundling along in the narrow Vienna street and charged straight towards her. She leapt out of its way, off the cobbles straight back into the arms of the boy who had just tripped her up.

The boy was shorter than Patrizia but very strong. He gripped her tightly by her upper arms and drew his face close to hers before he hawked up some spit into his mouth and waited a terrible moment before he spat. At the last second she pulled her face hard to one side so the spit clung to her dark hair rather than her cheek.

His friends jeered. 'Stay still, Jew girl.'

'I am not Jewish. I am not,' she wept.

He took her face in one hand then and turned it forcibly to show his three friends one by one. 'Look at that face. What have we here?'

'A Jew!'

'A Jew!'

'A Jew!'

'Now, Jew girl' – he thrust her away from him and she fell again on to the pavement – 'you go home and look in your mirror. See the Jew girl staring out. And go and slit your wrists. That is the easy way.' He took out a cigarette and lit it slowly, taking a very deep drag before he spoke, the smoke pouring out of his mouth with the words. 'Stinks here, comrades, do you not think? Can you smell it? Pig. I cannot stand this. Let us go where the air is sweeter.' He went off and the others followed him, the last two placing their big boots very deliberately on Patrizia's sprawling wrist as they passed.

It took her a long time to get home, travelling ever upwards towards the Judenplatz, dodging down back alleys and over walls to avoid any roving groups of troublemakers. It was not just boys one had to be careful of, these days. Men and even women were enjoying the sport. It had been a group of both men and women who started this torment last year, when they broke all the windows and dragged people out of their homes and shops. Patrizia's own mother was dragged out of her smart millinery shop in her high heels; a small nail-brush was thrown at her and she was made to scrub the cobbles till her polished finger-ends bled.

Her mother was in the room when Patrizia returned. She threw off her blanket and clucked over the state of her daughter, tearing petticoats to make a bandage for her arm, and carrying jugs of water to wash her sticky hair. She did not ask for details. She would ask later. The task now was to calm her daughter down, tend to her wounds.

The little storeroom where they lived these days was at the back of her mother's boarded-up millinery shop. Patrizia had seen a lot of this room since she had finally been forced out of her school. When she first went there the teachers had delighted in her cleverness, and supported her suitability for a career in medicine. Towards the end those same teachers had avoided looking in her direction and had not protested when the other pupils tormented her, threw ink over her copy book and, once, put a rat in her satchel.

The storeroom was like a fortress. There were three bolts on the door and heavy bars at the window. The wide bed, which they shared, and where her mother spent most of her time, was crowded into it. There was a small table and a Primus stove on a window-sill. The corners of the room were piled to the ceiling with goods of every description: folded carpets, rolled tapestry curtains, boxes of silverware and crystal wrapped in fine linen sheets. There were finely worked footstools and elaborately framed pictures. All these things had been much more elegantly accommodated, of course, in their high-ceilinged apartment near the Opera Ring, long since confiscated.

Patrizia brushed her long hair and peered critically into the ornate mirror, a ludicrous object on the stained storeroom wall. It was true that her hair was dark, but her features were sharp, her eyes pale like her father's. 'I told them I was not Jewish, Mama.'

'You are Jewish, child. I am Jewish. Your father's mother was Jewish. So you are Jewish.'

'But my father was—' Her father had been Polish, a traveller selling the exotic feathers from the East which her mother used to such effect in her hats. His mother may have been Jewish but he was Catholic. Patrizia could remember the gold glinting off his crucifix as he swung her around and around so that the leaves on the trees about them blurred into a great green sea in the woods. That was the last day before he returned to Poland and vanished for ever into the East.

'I am Jewish, so you are Jewish,' her mother repeated. 'Your stepfather was Jewish.'

'But we do not go to temple, Mama. The rabbi will not visit us.'

'That is no matter. That does not count.' Her mother fitted a cigarette into her long ebony holder, lit it and took a draw, then narrowed her eyes against the invading swirls of smoke. 'We must get you away from here, my dearest. We must. We have hung on here far too long.'

Patrizia's stepfather and his brothers had been taken just three months ago. First arrested, then transported. So many people had gone, creeping away in the night, or torn from their beds by hard hands.

Patrizia put her hand on her mother's. 'You too, Mama. We will both go.'

Her mother shook her head. 'I would not survive it, *liebchen*.' She was very fragile now, skin and bone. The pneumonia brought on by the terrors of that night of crystal, when all the windows were broken, had broken her health irreparably.

She put down her cigarette and picked up her scissors, to continue the task she was completing when Patrizia came in. Tonight her fingers were busy unpicking the yellow stars from every one of their coats; the yellow stars which were the official endorsement of attacks such as Patrizia had had to endure tonight.

'You will have to go yourself. You are young, you are strong,' her mother repeated.

'You too, Mama. You too,' Patrizia said anxiously.

Her mother shook her head. 'No, dearest. I have a man coming tonight. The nephew of an old customer of mine. His name is Gold.' She laughed quietly and cast her eye over the bleak treasures heaped in the corners. 'There was a scandal, some story about when he was a child. But now he is a scallywag, a greedy young man. That is not a very attractive quality but it can be useful in times of great need. We need such people now, the ones that you can buy.'

[illegible] knew [illegible] came [illegible] as the [illegible] though [illegible] heart beats.

[illegible] hand [illegible] with [illegible]

He [illegible] his head. 'I wouldn't have it otherwise.' [illegible] were [illegible]

[illegible]

'You will [illegible] yourself [illegible]' [illegible]

[illegible] Not the [illegible] Parliament [illegible]

[illegible] shook her head [illegible] thing [illegible] [illegible] and [illegible] people [illegible] dropping [illegible].

Two

Flight, 1943

To celebrate the final defeat of the Germans at Tunis, Sam sent Leonora to secure the services of a photographer. She found a Greek who had run from the Italians as they moved in their comfortable fashion into his country, Mr Menander, who was willing to bring his equipment to the house. He was to take photographs of Kay's child, Florence, now a sparky three-year-old.

Mr Menander made a great fuss about the exact setting for the photograph. He finally decided on a spot in the tiny courtyard beside a cloud of flourishing poinsettias. 'Such exquisite flowers, madame,' he murmured, eyes bulging, 'so delicate and yet so potent, like the child herself.'

Leonora rolled her eyes at Kay and argued weakly that it was too hot outside for the little one. And the air from the water was too full of miasma, laden with who knew what kind of disease.

'The light, the light, madame! The light here is perfect for the artist! It is dark as Hades inside these Arab rabbit hutches of houses, and alas I have no flashing lights with which to take the photographs.' He put his slender, well-manicured hands together at the tips. 'There is the war and alas I am but a poor man.'

From inside their shaded doorway Kay and Leonora laughed at Mr Menander's mannered protest. 'Where does Mr Kohn find them, these oddities?' said Kay.

'Sam said Mr Kohn said this one was very good,' Leonora told her. 'And such oddities are very much at home in Alexandria.'

It had been Sam's idea to have their photographs taken. He was entranced with his little granddaughter. In his opinion Stephen (miraculously still alive and aloft over England and France after twenty sorties) should have a photograph of his daughter and Kay for his wallet.

Sam's point of view was transmitted by Leonora, of course. Kay still didn't know whether her mother was reading Sam's thoughts or actually listening to his speech.

Florence was named after the Englishwoman who had delivered her; a nurse married to Mr de la Valle, a French kinsman of Mr Kohn. Florence's birth had been dramatically simple. Kay had suffered four very powerful pains before her daughter's lusty bellow proclaimed delight on first seeing the world.

Mrs de la Valle told Leonora that the young mothers either had it very easy or very hard and she, Kay, was the lucky one. The midwife leapt at the chance to discuss Leonora's own experience of having her children – and twins at that – at the late age of forty.

Kay had ignored their chatter and gazed at this daughter whose silvery thatch of hair and palest blue eyes made her the very image of Stephen. As she drifted in and out of sleep wriggling a little to relieve her aching body she reflected on the fact that she had only known Stephen for two months, but this silver-haired daughter of his was hers for life. She did not feel old enough to be a mother, not old enough at all.

As time went on a certain thing started to niggle her. She told no one, not even Thomas, but once Florence was born Kay stopped missing Stephen; it was as though her daughter had waylaid all her love, all her passion, so there was none left for her husband. In her wildest moments it was as though the whole object of their chance meeting was for Florence to come into the world.

She found herself unable to write loving letters to Stephen. Instead she wrote long conversational epistles about Florence and the tiny changes that occurred in her every day; about

Leonora, who was taking care of Florence like a mother; about Sam and his friend Mr Kohn; about Thomas and the business. That was much reduced, although they still retained some former customers who pretended there was no war and continued their customary idiosyncratic quests for the old and the strange. Still she loved to work on in the little workroom. She left Florence in the willing hands of her mother and Thomas and vanished in there every day.

From the first time he saw her cocooned in Leonora's arms, Florence was her grandfather's delight. She would lie in the crook of Sam's disabled arm while he crooned and clucked in response to her babble. After only a few weeks the stiff side of his face seemed to soften and he dribbled much less spit from that side of his mouth. Leonora swore that his speech was getting better, but Kay herself could not hear any difference.

As Florence grew stronger Sam would haul himself on to the cool floor so she could climb all over him. He would roll around the great tiles, lifting himself crookedly using one arm and one leg. When Florence started to walk Sam got Mr Kohn to find someone to make up a design of Sam's own: a steel contraption concocted from guide rails taken from a bombed ship in the harbour. This was like two walking sticks, each forked at the bottom for stability, connected by a curved chrome rail which had once done duty keeping the captain steady as he shaved in the morning.

So, as Florence started to totter on two feet, Sam tottered with his walking contraption and the two of them clucked and chattered together in their private language.

'Hem! Hem!' Kay came back to the present to find the photographer waving his hands in front of her. 'Madame will sit here?' Mr Menander had draped one of the kelims over a wicker chair which he had placed carefully to one side of the poinsettias. 'The little one on her knee?'

He took one quick photograph but after this Florence wriggled and clambered about her mother's knee holding her arms out to Sam. 'Gandy! Gandy!' she bubbled.

Sam hauled himself across the courtyard on his contraption and Kay made him sit in the chair with Florence on his knee and his good side to the camera. Mr Menander took one photograph of them, then came from behind his camera waving his arms. 'Now everyone!' he said, beaming. 'Now all people!'

So they all clustered behind the chair: Leonora behind Sam with Kay and Thomas on each side of her, their arms around her.

'Wonderful,' said Mr Menander, vanishing behind his camera again. 'So very exquisite.'

Stephen loved the photographs.

> What a topping idea, [he wrote]. Baby Flo is a star. How did we make her? By God we're clever. And your pa looks wonderful. I can get a glimpse of his old self and know what you mean when you talk of him in the days before. And you, my darling girl. I see you've returned to your desert shirts and trousers, but there's still no hiding just how beautiful you are. And you're letting your hair grow. It looks very nice, but I did like you with your Eton crop. You were very beguiling, dressed as an eager boy. I love, love these photographs. They will never leave my side. I love, love, love you. Being a bit of a self-sufficient chap I never knew I could love or miss someone so much. I thank God I've known you because even if I had not met you I would still be doing this, trying to get rid of these blighters for the sake of what's right. But having you, and now little Flo, makes it so much more worth while. I fly as a man, not an adventuring boy. You ask about what I do. Well, there is a hell of a lot of waiting. Too much. Then there are these huge flurries of activity. Flying with your blood buzzing with the importance of what you're about. And there is fright, even terror, but not wanting to let anyone know. The drudgery of waiting. And there is coming back and counting the heads and keeping the stiff upper lip about the ones who've gone. They tell us we are

heroes to keep us going. I suppose they must do this. I am a bit tired now but am up for a week's leave, so will visit your Auntie Mara as you suggest. There's much talk about the delights of London these days, which is very lively in spite of – or perhaps because of – the bombing. But how I wish I could come back home to you, my darling. I would kiss little Flo and watch her sleep and then I would take you in my arms and, oh, my sweetheart, we would make such love as created the world.

Good night, my darling. S

PS Tell old Thomas I love him and miss him. Can't get a sensible conversation round here.

Kay smoothed the letter on the table with a tender hand. Did all those men writing home to their wives adopt such heroic phrases? Did they mimic the grand assertions of the official propaganda which washed around everywhere these days? She read his words again, looking in vain for her Stephen, silver-haired, soft-tongued Stephen, in this wall of words: the man who had all but faded from her own memory.

At that moment a real sense of loss crashed over her like a wave. Her tears dropped onto the creased letter, smudging the ink, making the grand words bleed helplessly into each other.

Thomas caught her crying with the letter still on the table in front of her. He took her hand. 'What is it, old chum?' he said kindly. 'A letter's a good thing, not a bad thing, surely?'

She smiled through her tears. 'He sounds very cheerful, really. Pleased with the photos. By the way, he misses you. Sends you his love.'

A smile curled Thomas's lips. He had had just a few doubts at first about old Stephen. In this city of many appetites more than one older man had let him know that they could, in their own way, love him. 'Misses me, does he? The old devil. Well, sis, you have my permission to tell him that I don't miss him. Far too busy.'

In the end Thomas had decided to volunteer for the army. He

was sure someone with his strength would be of value to the war effort, but was told at the consulate that he would be turned down flat because of his eyesight. Instead they found him a desk job which involved listing names and locations of German nationals whom he knew were interested in antiquities and were presently in, or likely to come through Alexandria. His good ear for languages had been sustained by tutors and by acquaintances in Alexandria. His war job involved very little actual work but the fact that he got paid for it was a relief to them all. Kay's work had dwindled almost to nothing.

The three years she had been in the refugee camp was a lifetime of drudgery to Patrizia, as it was for hundreds of others around her. Each soul numbly acknowledged its good fortune at still being alive. Better indeed than those incarcerated further East under the iron-segged boot of the SS.

Overwhelmed by the enforced intimacy of living in sight and smell of so many people at such close quarters, Patrizia took refuge in the boring routines of collecting food and water, of washing clothes in a single chipped enamel dish, of clearing their tiny space in the long hut which had been their home for three years. She became a machine for moving and working, with no memory before the long trek West with the man called Gold. She herself willed the memories of before then to fade. Every time an image of her mother, or the milliner's shop, or the apartment near the Opera Ring, rose in her mind she deliberately dismissed it, obliterating it by offering to go for water, or do some cleaning for her neighbour in the next section of the hut, whose left hand was useless, injured during her escape.

In the end it was as though her life had started on that day, the day when she parted from her mother and joined Gold. All memory started there, that time she first met him.

That first evening she had shouted at him: 'Where are we going?'

Patrizia humped her pack on to the opposite shoulder and

tried to stop her voice sounding plaintive. She had to run again to catch up with the man striding on along the darkened road. 'Wait, wait, please wait,' she gasped.

The man called Gold turned round and a dense moonbeam illuminated his thick sweep of hair and his finely cut features, and cast his eyes and mouth into shadow. 'Come on, you stupid girl. Keep up. There's army traffic on this road all the time.'

As if on cue, they heard the roar of an engine to their left. He pulled Patrizia into the shadow of a field gate and forced her to the ground. She stopped breathing while the vehicle roared its presence in front of their noses and then faded away into the distance again. He pulled her to her feet and shook her. 'Now, keep up, *Dummkopf*. You will get us both killed.' He strode on and she scurried after him, her bag bouncing painfully on her back.

She was footsore and dropping with tiredness when, an age later, the moonlight carved out a straggling hamlet against the grey rise of a hill. She noted this: grey not black. The wide sky was lightening very slightly. Here at least was rest, she thought now dully. The morning was nearly upon them. She knew they could not walk during the day. Gold had preached to her about night walking that first evening when he came at dusk to wrest her from the arms of her tearful mother. His manner had been brusque, only softening slightly when her mother handed over the money and the rings, which was the courier price for him rescuing her daughter so late. So very late.

Very deliberately her mother had disentangled Patrizia's hands from her neck. 'Go now!' she said roughly. 'Do not behave like a child. I will be here for you when it is all finished, when it is all over. Remember.'

And she had turned away, not watching as her daughter dodged down the darkened street with this stranger, to be handed into the sidecar of an old motor bike. Laurenz Gold, her courier, rode pillion. Patrizia never saw the face of the driver, who had left them out here somewhere in the great vine district, to begin their long walk.

In this hamlet the houses were low, their roofs almost to the ground. The tiny windows let into the deep walls of the houses were unlit and the little street was deserted. Here and there, beside the house was a tall door, wider than any stable door.

Patrizia flinched suddenly and clutched Gold's resisting arm. From the East came the terrifyingly familiar sound of grinding gears and roaring engine. Simultaneously they dropped back into the shadow of one of the high doors. The vehicle, whatever it was, rumbled nearer. Then it stopped and they could hear people jumping out: the pound of boots; shouting voices; guttural laughter and barked orders.

Patrizia squeezed back against the door and felt it give a little. Her hand brushed against an iron door handle. Behind her was a small door let into the great door. 'In here,' she whispered. She dragged the man called Gold through the small door with her, then pushed it to behind them. The scent of new wood, earth and raw grape hit her senses. Her knees were trembling.

They leant with their backs to the door and listened as the truck-driver put the engine into gear again. They stood stock still as the truck – it must be a truck – came abreast of the door and went straight past.

'Where are we?' she whispered. 'What place is this?' She felt rather than saw Gold remove a heavy torch from his knapsack and click it on.

She caught her breath as the beam of yellow light flashed up over the natural stone-vaulted roof and then down on to great barrels lining the walls. 'We are inside the hill,' he said. 'This is where they store their wine. It can be in here many years.' The echo of his voice reminded her of the one time she had been in the Stephansdom, the great church in the centre of Vienna. Monika, her friend, had taken her to see it. Monika was a great mischief maker; she knew she would be in trouble for taking a Jew in there, but she did not care. Of course, in the end even Monika had changed. Monika was the very last to turn her head away when Patrizia was dismissed from the school, but she did turn away.

'Ssh ssh!' Patrizia said now to this stranger called Gold.

He caught her arm, gripping it painfully. 'Come on. It is nearly light outside. We will stay here.' And he started to pull her deeper and deeper into the cave, along spotless walkways lined by great barrels lying on their sides, their ends like gaping mouths ready to swallow unwary passersby. Here and there a smaller barrel stood upright, before it a stool on which stood an earthenware jug.

After walking nearly half a mile they reached a kind of crossroads. She caught up to him and pulled him along one way. 'This way.' His lamp wavered over tools and dismembered barrels as they walked on. Beneath their feet the hard walkway turned softer, and they were walking on a rock surface deep inside the mountain.

They walked what seemed like another mile and finally reached a dead end. Before them were two great barrels, bigger than houses, lying side by side. Between these great hulking shapes was a deep triangular chasm of darkness. 'Here,' Gold said, pulling her into the shadowy space. 'We can rest here. We will hear them coming, if they come.'

Crouching, she put down her rucksack, pushing it into the far corner.

'Hey, what have you there?' Gold pulled her out of the way and grasped at her heavy bag. She watched while he untied the top and raised his torch to see inside. Then he started to pull them out: watches, lockets, rings, all in gold. This was the essence of the wealth she and her mother had saved from their other life, their life in the apartment near the Opera Ring. Her mother had insisted she take all of it. She had no one left to bribe.

'Ah, your old mother is a wily bird.' His voice was soft yet piercing. 'She pleaded poverty with me, only offered a few trinkets to risk my life like this for you. And all the time there was this.' She could hear his hand chinking through the jewels. 'And what danger she put you in! You will be robbed of such wealth. I shall carry this for you tomorrow.'

'No, I promised her—'

He put a finger on her lips 'Ssh. There is somebody coming.' He shut off his torch.

In the darkness they could see the firefly light of a swinging lantern and hear a man's voice. He chuntered away as he walked along the barrels, but she could not understand his words: the deep country dialect was impenetrable. They could hear the man tapping the barrels, too, and fiddling with the taps.

His footsteps were very near. Then he stopped. She knew he could feel their presence; she imagined that every morning he must come to his barrels here in this great church-like space. He would know his great wine cave as well as he knew his own kitchen. He would feel rather than see their presence.

'Hello. Hello!' His voice was ancient and crackling. Then his lantern lit up their space, picking out Patrizia's expensive leather boot.

'Out, out!' he said. His face, bottom-lit by the lantern, was all silver beard. His shadowy body, thickset and stocky, seemed to take its cue from the mountain around him. In his hand was the heavy knobbed stick with which he had been tapping his barrels.

They crawled out of the shadow and stood before him. He rapped out grunting questions at Gold in his thick dialect, but Gold shook his head and kept saying, 'We mean no harm, sir. We just wish to rest for the night.'

'Please . . . please, sir.' Patrizia spoke for the first time and he lifted his lantern to look at her.

His lip drooped. '*Juden!*' he said and spat his contempt on to the earth floor. '*Haben Sie Geld?*'

'Yes!' she said eagerly. 'No money, but we have gold!' She dived into the shadow, brought back the bag and thrust it towards him.

The old man took the bag from her, already peering into it eagerly. In that second Gold flicked the stick out of the old man's hand, caught it in his own and cracked him over the head with it. The man fell to the ground and Gold continued to hack away at him. Blood spurted on to his coat.

Patrizia pulled him away. 'Stop it. He is an old man.'

The man grasped Gold's knees. '*Mein Herr* . . .' he muttered thickly, then crumpled back to the floor and lay still.

'You've killed him,' said Patrizia.

Gold leant the bloody stick carefully against a barrel. 'He would have killed us.'

'No. The gold. He would have let us go if we gave him that.'

Gold's sharp face blazed; his eyes were bright. 'He would have taken the gold, told the police and we would be on our way East in a cattle wagon. Or more probably dead.'

She looked at him closely then, almost for the first time. She had been deceived by the strands of grey in his hair. He was younger than she first thought, perhaps only thirty. His bullying had made him seem much older. 'What is your first name?' she said.

'Gold,' he said. 'Laurenz Gold. I told your mother.'

'Do you know you have just killed a man, Laurenz Gold?'

A smile lifted his lips a fraction. 'That is nothing. I have killed before,' he said calmly. 'Anyway, perhaps he is not dead.' The words were loud. She could hear them winging down the length of the cave towards the door and echoing back.

'Ssh!' she said. 'It is daytime now. People will come. They will find him and we—'

'You are right. They must not find him. They will not find him.' He took the old man's lantern and walked down the avenue of barrels, tapping and poking them with the old man's stick. Then he called to her and she stumbled towards the light. He was standing on top of a smaller upright barrel with an iron lever in his hand. 'Here,' he said. 'We will put him in here, and even if they come they will not find him. He will be well and truly pickled.' He chuckled. 'They might not find him for years, though. Not until they try to feed this fine vintage to some Prussian grandee who will be the new King of Austria. He will say, "Gentlemen! This wine has very good body!" '

He jumped down lightly. 'Now, we will get our magic ingredient.'

The old man was a dead weight, heavy to move. At one point he seemed to groan, and Patrizia dropped the arm which she was pulling. 'He's still alive!'

'No, no. The last of the air coming out, that is all. Come on, pull! Pull!'

She picked up the arm and pulled. When they got to their destination she looked at the high barrel and shook her head. 'You will not get him in there. We cannot lift him in there.'

He leant the old man, half sitting, against the barrel and came to where she was standing. He took her face in his two hands. 'We have to find a way. There will be a way or we are dead.' Then coldly, as though administering a slap, he kissed her very hard.

No one had ever kissed her on the mouth, except her mother. And even that had stopped when she was twelve.

She wrenched her mouth away.

He tapped her cheek, hard. 'You will learn, little girl. I am very clever and very strong,' he said. 'Wait here.'

In minutes he was back with ropes and curved planks from smashed barrels. Then he set to work and lashed the old man's body to one of the planks, and finally leant it upright against the side of the barrel. He made her stand beside it and hold it upright as he tied another rope to it and threw this rope like a juddering snake over the top of an oak supporting beam above the barrel.

Then he took her shaking hands and placed them at the bottom of the wood plank near the feet of the tethered corpse. 'Now I will be on the other side. I will pull him up and over by hauling on this rope, and he will drop into the barrel, splash! Your job is to guide him so that when I pull him, he will flip – kind of flip – over the edge of the barrel.' He struck her arm with a hard hand. 'Now remember, little girl! If we do not do this, we are dead.'

Then he vanished and soon she could feel him tugging at the

body. Sobbing, she lifted her end of the plank, which got lighter and lighter as Laurenz Gold's grunting efforts were rewarded. At one point, just over the belly of the barrel, he got stuck and Gold whispered hoarsely, 'Push, *Dummkopf*, push!'

She took a deep choking breath and pushed with all her might. The body slipped out of her hands, seemed to wobble slightly on the edge of the barrel then splashed into the deep interior, throwing up a shower of wine which slopped on to her head and shoulders. She looked down at her hands and in the flickering light of the old man's lantern she saw the deep red stain of wine.

'Oh, oh, blood! Blood!' She started to moan and utter short shrieks. Gold bounded round to her side and grasped her by the arm. 'Stop it! Stop it!' he commanded. 'It is over now.'

She didn't stop screaming. And he put his mouth brutally on hers for a second time, but this time he didn't stop. He forced his tongue into her mouth and his hands were in the small of her back pushing her into him. She gulped back her moans and her body began to shake. He stopped kissing and started to stroke her. His hand started on her cheek and moved lightly over her breast to her thigh, as though she were a bolting horse. 'There now, calm down, little girl. Calm. We will tidy up here and make ourselves invisible, high on the great barrels. They will be coming soon, these yokels, looking for the old man.'

He put her away from him and he was all cold efficiency. First he replaced the lid on the barrel, then he cleared up all signs of their activity on the ground, stamping the ruffled soil back into place and taking the wood and tools to their place near the crossroads. When he returned he ushered her stiff body back along to the great barrels at the dead end. He climbed up on top of one barrel, sent a rope down and hauled her up, just as he had hauled the body of the old man.

They made themselves as comfortable as they could on top of the barrel. She lay there like a stone, not thinking, not feeling, for what seemed like hours. He was much more at ease than she was. At one time the sound of his light snores penetrated her wooden senses. Later – it could have been an hour, it could have been half a day – her flesh prickled as she heard the echoes of voices in the tunnels, voices calling: 'Peter! Peter! Are you here? Where are you?'

Laurenz Gold was instantly awake beside her. He put an arm over her body and one hand over her mouth. 'Quietly now, pigeon,' he breathed.

From the voices it seemed there were four or five of them, all men. Their heavy footsteps stamped on the walkway. Patrizia lay rigid and watched as the beam of a lantern flowed like thrown silk over the mountain rock above her. Then she relaxed as she noted the tone of resignation in the voices and heard the footsteps receding. Within three minutes there was silence.

Laurenz Gold was jubilant. 'That's it! They are saying he has wandered off somewhere, that he has gone to look at his vines. That he is a mad old bastard.'

They clambered down from the barrel and stretched their legs. She shivered.

'Are you cold, *liebchen*?' he crooned. He enclosed her with his arms and kissed her again. Ignited by sheer relief, she found herself melting towards him, reaching up to hold him close, to kiss him back. Then she felt him pushing hard against her and there was nothing in her to resist. He scrabbled at her skirt and they slipped together to the dirt floor beside the great barrel. She let him do what he wished, only moaning once at the unbelievable pain as he came inside her. His moans were all delight and pleasure. After it was all over she waited in his arms for him to come back from some rapturous place which had nothing to do with her.

Finally he said softly, 'You are a very plain girl, but I tell you there is something about you.' He stood up and put his clothes right, looking down at her with lazy eyes. 'Come on, *liebchen*. It will be dark outside. Now is the time for our walk.'

She stood up. 'I need to wash,' she said numbly.

'We will find a stream,' he said.

She picked up her heavy bag. Gently he removed it from her

grasp. 'I will take this, *liebchen*. We cannot have you dropping such a precious cargo, can we?'

They darted through the darkened village street and then started to plod on their way towards the horizon. She waited for him to mention it, what they had done. To tell her . . . what? That he loved her? That they would marry? Was that not what people did, when they did that thing? The girls at school had talked of it in dark corners. But Laurenz Gold said nothing about it. He strode on ahead and, as before, turned round and shouted at her, called her an idiot when she dropped behind.

Finally she did ask a question. 'Where do we go, Laurenz?' After what they had done, she could surely call him by his name.

He stopped and waited for her to catch up. 'Well, the plan is changed. Now we go to my uncle's house. He has a small farm near the border. He will hide us. I have papers which are good. We will bribe our way on to a train to Switzerland. Or walk.'

'What do you mean, the plan has changed?'

He put up a finger and outlined her lips. She licked them to stop them tickling. 'Well, *liebchen*, the original plan was to . . . lose you, if you know what I mean? I was going to lose you and go on swiftly myself. For the first time I too am in danger.'

'Lose me?'

He shrugged. 'Once I am paid it is sometimes too tiresome to proceed. People get lost . . .'

'You mean you let them get caught?'

He shrugged again.

'So why is this plan changed, then? Why did you not lose me?'

'Well, now, you are not some schoolkid. There is the old man and what we did to him. We did that together. When you kill you are bound to your fellow killer. To free yourself you must kill them.' His hand tightened on hers. 'Or you must bind them to you.'

'Then why not kill me?' she said wearily.

'Well there was . . . the other thing. I have led a very bad life, *liebchen*. I learnt how to be bad from a great teacher. But there is something about you. You never did that with a man before, did you?'

She shook her head.

'So you are a new beginning. You are my luck. In the times to come I will need my luck. So I take care of you, I do not lose you. We go on together, with your mother's trinkets, and see if my cousin Mikel can get us to Switzerland.'

They plodded on. Patrizia felt entirely blank. Behind her eyelids she could see her own blood caused by that searing contact with Laurenz Gold, mixing with fountains of wine and the death blood of the old man called Peter on the dirt floor of the wine cave.

Poking away at her from the back of her mind was the certainty that the old man had still been alive when they tipped him into the vat of his own wine, to drown.

'Can you tell me how to get to Armistead Road?' Stephen Fitzgibbon deliberately stood in the way of an old man hurrying along the pavement before him.

The man, who was clutching a bulging paper carrier bag and a gramophone with a horn, nodded, jutting his chin towards the left. 'Down to the corner, second on the right, but it ain't no good you going there, chum. Blarsted to kingdom come two nights ago, Armistead Road. Fifteen souls lost, cats howling like banshees.'

'Right. Thank you.' Stephen walked on, ignoring the man whose voice followed him, calling that he was wasting his time, chum, wasting his time.

Armistead Street had indeed been blasted to kingdom come. All that remained of the houses were odd areas displaying the dreadful bunting of ripped wallpaper fluttering in ribbons from wrecked walls. In one place a toilet bowl hung precariously on a wall where there was no toilet floor. In another, curtains fluttered in the breath of wind which raised powdered plaster in puffs, like smoke from a train.

Men and women with broom handles and spades were poking

about in a desultory, hopeless fashion in the heaps of rubble. A youngish woman, her arms heaped with dusty blankets and clothes, watched Stephen with keen eyes. He looked very smart in his RAF uniform with his silvery-white hair. The very image of a hero.

'Good afternoon, miss,' he said, sketching a salute. 'I'm looking for number twenty. Can you direct me?'

'The schoolteacher, is it that one you want?' She pointed with her free hand. 'Second from the corner, down there. Didn't they haul her husband out last night, poor soul. See her there? Sitting on what was her doorstep, once.'

Stephen walked the length of the street and stood before the woman who must be Kay's Aunt Mara. She was crouching on the step of her demolished house, a pile of dusty books in her hand. Crossed by his shadow before she was aware of his presence, she looked up. Her long face was white and there were dark rings under her eyes. An unused brush and dustpan lay beside her. 'Yes?' she said dully.

'I am Stephen Fitzgibbon,' he said. 'Kay, your niece, she's my wife.'

She blinked at him and shook her head. 'Kay lives in Alexandria with my sister Leonora.'

'Kay is my wife,' he repeated. 'I'm in the RAF here. I had some leave. I said I would come to see you.' He stared at her. Even in her distress she looked younger than he had expected. She must be twenty years younger than her sister Leonora.

She looked round at the wrecked house. Then she stood up quite gracefully and shook his hand with a firm grip. 'Well,' she said drily. 'I would ask you to come in, to have a cup of tea. But as you see . . .'

'I am so sorry, Miss . . . Mrs . . .'

'In this road I am Mrs Derancourt. In school I am Miss Scorton. But you can call me Mara, or Auntie Mara, if, as you say, you've done the deed and married my niece.' She flicked the dust off the pile of books in her hands.

He looked around. 'I was sorry . . . The woman on the corner said . . .'

'Jean-Paul? That I lost Jean-Paul? Do you know we would have gone together, both blown to smithereens, but I went off to do my fire-watching? I told him not to stay in the house but he was putting the finishing touches to a table he was French polishing. He said the Boche wouldn't be bothered with him tonight. But the Boche did bother.' She laughed harshly, dabbed her eyes and blew her nose. 'It was far too soon. He was too young. But they're all too young, aren't they? The warden said Jean-Paul would feel nothing. That's a great mercy, I suppose. Then again I suppose they always say that. Such rubbish is talked these days.' She looked around the heap of rubble. 'Do you know Jean-Paul made every single stick of furniture in this place? We drew them together and he made them. Even down to the toilet seat! A life's work. Only good for firewood now.'

He took her hand. 'Didn't I notice a little café before I turned the corner in this road? Why don't we try to squeeze tea and scones out of them?'

'Scones? These days?' she said bitterly.

Gently he pulled her away from the house, then he put an arm round her shoulder and guided her away towards the café. It was crowded, but somehow the sight of the young man in uniform and the dusty, pale woman made the crowd drop back a little. Two sailors stood up and gave them a corner seat.

Mara was right about the unavailability of scones, but there were some strange dried-up little oatcakes for sale, so he bought four, which the waitress put on a very dainty plate.

He poured her tea. 'You can't stay here, Mara. What about going up to County Durham? Kay's grandmother's there, isn't she? It must be safer up there. Can't be many bombs up in Priorton.'

She gulped the tea and shook her head. 'No. No. There is my school here. My pupils.'

'Well, you can't stay at the house.'

‘I’ve been offered a room in the schoolhouse. The infant headmistress has it but she’s alone there. She’s a bit of a trout but she did say she’d welcome the company.’ Mara shook her head at the offer of a second oatcake. ‘There’ve been few enough children at the school latterly. What with the raids, their parents don’t know where they are much of the time. And many are evacuated now.’

‘The children who do come to school will be pleased to see you there, at least. It’ll feel like a safe haven.’

She shrugged. ‘Two teachers were evacuated with the children, one ran off to the Scottish Highlands. If I’m not there, there is no school. It’s been hard enough to keep it open as it is.’

Her voice fell silent and the buzz of talk in the café filled the space between them. Finally Stephen said, ‘Did you manage to get anything at all from the wreck of the house, Mara?’

She touched the pile of dusty books before her. ‘Just these. There are more things, but they’ll take a lot of digging out.’

The one on top was called *Tommy Battles Through*. ‘I read most of the Tommy books when I was young,’ he volunteered, desperate for something to say. ‘I really liked them.’

She bent her head. ‘I’m pleased about that. I started to write them as a tribute to my brother who was killed in the First War. Remembering him when he was a child.’

Then Stephen recalled the photographs. ‘Would you like to see these?’ He took them out of his pocket and spread them out on the stained table.

She took each one and examined it closely. She sang the little girl’s praises and remarked on how well Sam looked, considering. Leonora was looking a little older, but weren’t they all? ‘And young Kay! I haven’t seen her since she was fifteen years old when she was across here at school. What a beauty! She looks like some young Lochinvar.’

‘Her hair has grown. When I first saw her it was as short as a boy’s. She was even more beautiful then.’ His voice was mournful.

'You must miss her.'

He nodded, then said, 'We only really knew each other a couple of months.'

She put her hand on his. 'You can make up for it all after the war,' she said.

He shook his head. 'Time will tell,' he said.

She put the photographs together and carefully put them back in his pocket for him. Such an intimate gesture. 'I think you were sent to me, Stephen. If I believed in God I would think He had sent you.'

He blinked, forcing himself to cheer up. 'What makes you say that?'

'I was sitting on that wall thinking everything had ended. That nothing was worth while and that I should have gone to kingdom come with Jean-Paul. I will feel that again, I'm sure. But you come along and give me a cup of tea and show me it *is* worth while. You show me your photographs. And there is little Florence taking us into a better future. That's what this is all about; it must be. Jean-Paul and I never had children, you know. We looked after his sister Hélène, who was not well. Then I had my teaching and my schools, all my wonderful children there, and my books and my young readers. And Jean-Paul had his wonderful furniture. We had each other. We didn't feel we'd missed anything. But sitting on that doorstep I felt so alone. Then along you came to tell me I was wrong.'

He stood up and picked up his cap. 'Look, Mara, I have a week's leave. We'll keep each other company. I'll help you dig out whatever's left of that lovely house and get you settled in your new home. We'll go to town and have lunch at the Café de Paris and tea at the Ritz. We'll find a show that's still on and see that.' In truth he had looked forward to doing the town himself, or pairing up with some other bloke and relieving the awful tension inside himself with drink, perhaps even girls. This was war, after all . . .

Mara frowned. 'But Jean-Paul . . . I have to . . . He was a Catholic, you know. In the beginning, anyway.'

He pulled her arm through his. 'But first of all we will make sure that everything is right for Jean-Paul. I promise you, I know what to do. I too was a Catholic at the beginning.'

Three

Raiders

Kay and Thomas had come upon a lucky haul. An Egyptian café singer, a man known to Thomas, had died in some knife play at a whorehouse. It seemed the singer had inadvertently placed himself between an American and a Persian in a fight over some boy that each thought they had bought and paid for.

The singer worked in the café of a Mr Hassan who had mentioned to Thomas that there were two boxes of old pots and things in his back room. He had been storing them for the singer who had always slept in elusively temporary places. Now the singer was dead Hassan was intending to redeem his debt for a hundred unpaid meals by selling the boxes. To be on the safe side, in case the singer had other pressing legatees, he had urged Kay and Thomas to come just before dawn, before the harbour was awake.

Thomas brought Kay down to the café to assess the contents of the boxes. Being impressed by some of the pots and two of the enamel bracelets, Kay proposed a price. Mr Hassan forced this up by a third but they still got a bargain. And the café owner was so pleased with his side of the deal that he offered them the services of his donkey and his donkey boy to transport the boxes across the city. 'There are too many, sir, madame, to carry yourselves.'

The three of them, with the scrawny, unwilling donkey in tow, had just made their way up the winding streets from the harbour area when the sirens started to howl, the sound funnelling down the narrow alleyways into the harbour.

'Here we go!' said Thomas.

The donkey boy started to mutter that he must get back to the café. They should take the donkey themselves but he must go back to the café. His master would beat him. No question about it. He would be needed down there at the café. There would be items to save, to lift out from the café into safer places. It was always a problem having a café on the harbour.

Thomas tried to stop the boy, telling him that it was safer up here, where they were going, away from the harbour. 'Look down there, it's the ships they want.' Thomas flapped his hand towards the huge fleet of ships moored in the harbour: the looming liners in their ridiculous camouflage livery, the lines and lines of military ships with their long snouting guns, even the innocent feluccas with their sails of plum and ginger.

'No. No, sir, I must go. My master will need me. Master more bad than bombs.' The boy wrenched his arm from Thomas's grasp and ran, bumping into more sensible people who were streaming up from the harbour, away from the explosions and the fires now breaking out.

Thomas and Kay tucked themselves into a deep doorway, hauling the unwilling donkey close to them. To their right the heavy air balloons bobbed about in a slow drunken dance. Above them the searchlights cut through the air like swords, crossing and recrossing, seeking out the aeroplanes which were wreaking such damage down below.

Then the beams started to catch the planes, insects caught in the amber light. Sure of their prey now, the ground rockets homed in on them. They spat upwards into the sky then, when they failed to hit their targets, they scattered drops of pure light on to the harbour below.

The ears of the crouching Kay and Thomas were assaulted by the phut-phut-phut of shrapnel fanning upwards and the finger-tapping rattle of metal clattering down on to the tin roofs of harbour shops and houses. Here and there, a building weakened by the onslaught crashed to the ground, grinding and writhing like an animal in pain. Fires danced up into the darkness, creating for a split second a chilling beauty in the middle of chaos.

Now they could make out two of the aggressors, hovering like bees in the crosspiece of light. Kay peered upwards, remembering Stephen in the cockpit of his little *Dragonfly*. He too would be doing this. He too would be dicing with death and raining terror on cities in France, in Germany.

Suddenly the shore battery spat upwards and one of the planes turned over almost lazily, then spun down in a spiral on its way to the sea and a watery grave for its crew.

Kay gulped, in her mind's eye seeing Stephen struggling with his straps, desperate to escape the dying plane.

Somewhere from the crowd milling by the harbour there came a cheer, as though this were merely some spectacle put on for them. For a second it seemed to Kay that they were cheering Stephen's death and she shouted, 'No! No!'

Thomas shook himself out of his own mesmerised trance and put an arm round her. 'Steady on, old girl. Feller up there's the enemy, don't forget. Come on. Shall we get these pots home or shan't we? This donkey's scared out of his wits. You push and I'll pull.'

They had to shove the animal in all directions to get it moving. Thomas finally lifted it bodily off the spot so they could join the crowd making its way up the hill, away from the devastation of the harbour and the painful sounds of great ships breaking up. By the time they had reached their own alleyway the 'All Clear' sirens were sounding and they knew that, for now, they were safe.

Leonora met them in her doorway. Florence was asleep in her arms, straddling her outjutting hip like a monkey. Leonora's gaze was steady. 'Oh, good! You're all right. I knew you would be. Knew it. I've been watching from the door. Quite a firework display.' Her gaze dropped to the doleful face of the donkey. 'And what have we here? I expect it's got fleas,' she said resignedly.

Kay grinned. 'We only borrowed the donkey. We bought more pots, and a few other things.' She poked Florence's soft cheek. 'How has she been?'

'Peaceful. She wouldn't settle down after you went and started playing with Sam. I left them to it and went to read a book. When I went back in they were both asleep. She was lying across Sam's stomach stark naked, out like a light. Even all this unholy row didn't disturb them.' Leonora handed the child over. Florence stirred, still fast asleep, and draped herself across Kay. 'So what are you going to do with the donkey? It can't stay here.'

Thomas looked at his mother. 'You look all in. You need some sleep yourself, Ma. Don't worry about the donkey. We'll unload our pots and I'll take him back to Mr Hassan.'

'Down at the harbour? The risk, Thomas, the risk!'

'The "All Clear" has sounded. There'll be no more trouble today, believe me.' He took off his glasses, wiped the sweat from his face, cleaned the glasses and replaced them.

Back in their own house Kay put Florence on her bed, drew a light sheet over her and came through to the workroom to help Thomas unload the pots. She peered at them as she put them in rows on her table. 'Some treasures here, Thomas.'

'More than we have customers for,' he said gloomily.

She touched him on the arm. 'They will come back,' she said.

He shook his head. 'It'll never be the same, sis,' he said firmly.

Full of affection for him, she walked over to where the donkey was tethered and watched as he hauled the animal away shouting and cursing at it with words he had learnt from Mr Hassan.

The headmistress of the infant school, in a flush of patriotic fervour, had offered Mara Scorton her dining room to live in, and the smallest bedroom to sleep in, until she found something more to her liking.

Stephen helped Mara retrieve the few things that had survived unscathed in the bombing and wheeled them to the school house for her in a handcart. He had found her a sympathetic Catholic priest who had seen to it that Jean-Paul had the proper funeral rites of his Church. Such was the pressure on this priest's services, they had had to share the funeral with two other families bereaved by the bombing. Mara did not mind this; unable to cry herself she took comfort in the sobbing of the other wives and mothers. She would save her tears for after the war.

Now, settled right by the school yard, she would find refuge from her misery in her children and her work with them. There was no time to mourn. Now, above all, they needed the discipline and the soothing regularity of Mathematics and English, Geography and Drawing, to remind them that the world could be an ordered place.

She imposed on herself such a pressure of work that she had to refuse an offer from Stephen of a final night out. 'I have work to do. You go out and enjoy yourself in your own way. What kind of a leave has this been for you?'

He shrugged. 'Hasn't it been a pleasure, ma'am, to be a member of your family for just one week? I had no family at all when I went to Alexandria, thought myself free as the air and liked it. Now I have Kay and Florence. And Thomas, don't I love him more than a brother? And Leonora and old Sam. Now you.'

'I'm the lucky one, to have known you. Now go!' she said in her brisk teacher's tone. 'Go and enjoy yourself.'

She watched him saunter down the street, and closed the door behind him with some relief. Then she picked up a dusty box which Jean-Paul had made her when she was just a girl. She took a duster and rubbed its surface, easily retrieving the polish which Jean-Paul had laid into it all those years ago.

Stephen started off in a pub off Compton Street where he made the acquaintance of an army major called John Clamp who worked on tanks down in the West Country, and was also on snatched leave in London. Clamp was fascinated by Stephen's talk of Alexandria, where the major had spent some time before the war. Clamp took him on to a crowded underground club which was low and dark and featured a very striking black singer who imported syncopated rhythms into old love songs in a way which stirred the blood. Stephen and Clamp were squashed on to a table with two men in sober city suits who introduced themselves as Toby and Ed. After three drinks the four of them dropped into an easy intimacy, talking of life in the services and the perils of 'piloting a Foreign Office desk in this war'.

After that Toby insisted on taking them for supper at the Ritz – 'My treat, boys!' – where Stephen marvelled at the delicate chicken and the fresh fruit which were served. He thought of the meagre oatmeal cakes he had had with Mara.

'Now,' said Toby, touching his mouth gently with the snowy napkin. 'I have some very fine brandy at my place. Shall we conclude our evening there?'

Stephen thought of his return tomorrow to his unit, and to the drudgery of risk to which flying had been reduced for him. 'Yes,' he said. 'Don't mind if I do!'

They all laughed at this as though it were the funniest joke in the world and waited while their coats were brought for them.

Toby's apartment was round the corner in James Street. It was rather dingy, but the fire was still in and Ed, hitching his sharp pleated trousers and bending down, soon coaxed it into life.

Toby came and stood so close that Stephen could smell the wine the man had recently downed at the Ritz. He thrust a glass into Stephen's hand. 'There you are, old boy. Make yourself at home. Take off your jacket. I'll put some music on and we could have a little dance.'

Clamp already had his jacket off and his army tie loosened.

'Dance?' Stephen nearly dropped the glass. He looked round at their gently smiling faces and realised what he had got himself into. He was vexed with himself. He was usually sharper with the signs. He put the glass carefully on a stained table. 'Sorry,

Toby, I seem to have got into the wrong party.'

Clamp grinned. 'Loosen up, old boy. We'll all be dead tomorrow.'

'Really I . . .'

'Seems we too've got hold of the wrong end of the stick, old boy,' laughed Ed. 'I'd have sworn you were . . . well, a more understanding type. Anyway, stay and have a drink. No hard feelings?'

'No. No,' said Stephen. 'No hard feelings. But I have to get back to my wife's aunt. She was just bombed out. I promised . . .'

Toby shook his head. 'You go, dear Stephen. I'm sure you have other fish to fry.'

Stephen straightened his jacket and went to the door. From his place lounging in a chair, Clamp toasted him with a sloshing glass. ''Bye, old boy,' he said.

Outside Stephen turned the collar of his coat up against the night air, peering round in the blackout to see which way to go. Bit of a close shave, that, he thought. He smiled to himself as he felt his way along the pavement. He had thought all that stuff was over, a phase he had gone through. But they had spotted it somehow. The ways of such men had suited him at one time. Right from when he left school up till when? When he had met Thomas Scorton and half fallen in love with him, only to be blown away the next day when he fell hook, line and sinker for Thomas's sister. Yes, true love was a funny thing, he thought. Can it change a man for good and all, though?

He touched the photograph in his pocket like a talisman, then turned a corner in the pitch blackness and was ploughed down in the street by a bus, whose lights were shaded downwards like a coy woman's eyelids. He was not conscious to hear the cries of anguish from the driver nor to hear the mutters of the crowd about his youth, his RAF uniform, and his beautiful silvery-blond hair. He was not alive when the ambulance got there ten minutes later.

Patrizia's dramatic night with Laurenz Gold in the wine cave was followed by nights under hedges and the lee side of walls. On what turned out to be her last night in Austria, Patrizia looked blankly into the space which, according to Laurenz, was to be their home until he and his cousin Mikel could organise safe passage into Switzerland. They were to live in a narrow room at the end of a cow byre. Eighteen feet by seven, it contained two beds on makeshift trestles, a rickety chair and a table. The only light was that trickling in through a straggle of misplaced boards in the roof. It had obviously been used before as a hideaway: Laurenz must have done this more than once: move people through Austria into Switzerland for money. Some of them, it appeared, he 'lost'. What was left of her heart, that little grey chip inside her, was heavy at the thought.

'You will not have to stay here all the time,' Laurenz's cousin Mikel told her reassuringly. 'But you must sleep here in case anyone comes by in the night. Visitors. If people come during the day you must run to hide in here till they go away. The farm is quite high so we should see them coming.'

Mikel was as different from Laurenz as a pet cat is from a tiger. He was taller and softer-faced than his cousin; a country lad to Laurenz's sharp town boy, an efficient farmer and a good son. The two men shared a grandfather who had wept for a week when his daughter married the Jewish trader, Hermann Gold; wept for a month when his daughter died in childbirth; rejoiced when his son-in-law was killed in an automobile accident, and given the little boy away to a childless cousin of his who was a butcher in Vienna.

Mikel was both troubled by and fond of his cousin whom his own father had rescued at the age of eight, from the butcher, who turned out to be stark staring mad.

Mikel clapped Laurenz on the shoulder when he arrived. 'Bad times in the city, Lau.'

Laurenz nodded. 'The worst, just now.'

'We hear of it here. We thought you might be dead.' Then he said, 'This must be the last time, Laurenz. Herr Müller down in the village, that craven rascal who mends the shoes and whose son is in the army, told me quite pointedly that the man who brings him the leather saw strangers up here, the last time you came through. And he mentioned the problem of spies.'

Laurenz hunched himself into his coat. 'This is the last time. The man who makes my passports has turned betrayer. I am not safe there. This time I will go on with this one. We will stay together. I will marry her.'

'Marry?' Mikel frowned at Patrizia. 'But this is a child, Lau. And a very plain one at that.'

'I am not a child. I am nearly eighteen,' she said. 'And you're not so pretty yourself.'

'She is not a child now,' growled Laurenz. 'But she has other qualities. In any case this war will go on and we will all die, leaving nothing behind us. No family. No money, no nothing. Well, this child, as you call her, has money, and she is pregnant.'

'What?' said Mikel.

'What? What do you say?' said Patrizia, pulling at his arm.

'Pregnant. I think you are pregnant. I know it.'

On each of the five nights it had taken for them to walk to Mikel's farm on the Austrian border Laurenz had come to her before they set off and pressed himself upon her unwilling body in the shadow of some barn or under some hedge. It was less painful now, so she endured it, accepting it passively as the price of survival. All that filled her mind was walking through the next night and getting to Switzerland without being caught. She had forgotten the apartment near the Opera Ring; she had forgotten the little room behind the milliner's shop. Even the face of her mother had faded from her mind in the numbing progress towards the West. Laurenz's attentions had no tenderness in them to which she could respond. And here at Mikel's farm it was the first she had heard of any baby or any marrying. That her body was capable of having a baby she had no doubt. But it felt old and battered and used. The girl Patrizia was a month ago had vanished, like the memory of her mother's face.

Now Mikel was laughing into her face, pulling her towards

him in a bear hug. 'And what do you feel about all this, little Patrizia?'

She shook her head. 'I do not know about anything of all that. All I want to be is safe.'

Mikel's gaze softened. He took her chin in his hand. 'And so you shall, child. So you shall.' He handed her a thick blanket. 'You look exhausted. You go and have a long sleep and tonight, or tomorrow night, or the night after, we will get you across the border. Do not worry. It will not be so difficult.' He turned to Laurenz. 'And us? We will talk, cousin.'

Wearily Patrizia took off her overcoat, her ears absorbing the voices raised in angry argument outside the cow barn. She closed her eyes and slept, not knowing, not caring about what they said. She cared only for sleep.

She felt rather than heard Laurenz heave himself on to the other bed an hour later. And the fragile, wary side of her waited to see if he would come and to try yet again to attack her. But he didn't. The schnapps must have made him sleepy.

It seemed like a second later there was a clatter as Mikel moved the boards and brought in a basket with milk and bread and a small sack containing more bread. 'Wake, wake, the pair of you. You must move.'

Patrizia shook her head awake and put her feet on the floor. Mikel went across and seized Laurenz's shoulder. Laurenz groaned and turned over. Mikel shook him harder. 'Wake up, you dolt. The road down in the village is alive with soldiers. They are moving through, but only one of those dolts down there needs to mention the possibility of strangers here and it will be me up against a wall as well as you.'

Laurenz leapt up then, pulling on his jersey and his jacket. 'Come on, girl. Eat this, drink this, we must be on our way as soon as it is dark.'

'Sooner,' said Mikel. 'They will not wait for dark before coming up the mountain.'

Mikel vanished and Patrizia ate as much as she could force into herself and Laurenz did the same. She tidied her hair as best she could and gave up any thought for the moment of washing her face.

Without saying anything, Laurenz lifted the panels and went outside, carefully replacing them behind him. She imagined he had gone to relieve himself outside. She wished it was as easy for a woman to do such things. Strange how in the last few days life had become so simple. Such basic priorities. Survive to the next night. A stream to wash in. Privacy to relieve yourself. Something to eat. Human contact, even if it were just with a bullying, predatory egotist like Laurenz. The extra care and kindness brought into their tight little world by Mikel was very strange, a shock almost.

She put on her outer coat and looked down in despair at her wrecked shoes.

At that moment the wall panels moved and she jumped. It was Mikel in his outdoor clothes with a sack on his back and boots in his hand. He laid the boots at Patrizia's feet. 'These were mine when I was eleven years old. Those socks too. They should fit you.'

She threw off her shoes and pulled on the socks and boots eagerly. She nodded at his bag. 'Are you coming to show us the way?' she said.

'Laurenz knows the way,' he said. 'I am coming with you. I have a bad feeling about all that military in the village. I – we – have had great luck so far. I think it is at an end.' He watched Laurenz lift out the panels and enter the narrow space. 'And in any case I think that you might need a little protection from more than those army blockheads, do you not think?'

Three years after Patrizia Zagorski set off on the last stage of her journey to the refugee camp, in Alexandria Kay Fitzgibbon dreamt Stephen's death. In her dream she was walking the desert with people buffeting her on either side, saying, Come, come, you must hurry. It seemed they had found his missing plane at last, on top of a sand dune. The plane was intact. There had been no fire, which was her worst fear for Stephen. The person beside her told her that his body was sixty yards from the plane. She walked towards it across the deeply sucking sand. They let her see him, although a fussy voice said it was against military protocol, against diplomatic protocol. Stephen was unmarked and very dead.

In the dream, the neck of his uniform was caked with sand. There were grains on his lashes, which were long and thick and two shades of blond. Florence had those lashes. She wondered whether, grown, Florence would have that handsome, flawless face: a face which was bland, innocent but which seemed to contain secrets. After the first two months, those wonderful days, Stephen began to change, or show her more of the secret side of himself. Sometimes he had vanished into the stews of Alexandria for a day, two days and come back without an explanation, with his excuse that her feelings should be thus saved. Yes, he had met someone briefly, but acquaintances were ten a penny in Alexandria. Beside her they were nothing. They were ephemeral and she was permanent. She must know that.

In those two months of marriage, still loving him dearly, she had hardened just a little against him. There were times when she had cursed Thomas for bringing him home, irritated for some reason when Stephen clapped Thomas on the back and called him a good fellow. Other times she gave in, wallowed in their living dream, the three of them corners of a privileged triangle.

In this dream of his death she kissed Stephen's sand-rimed face and woke up, feeling the salty gritty rasp on her lips.

That same day she had a letter from her Auntie Mara telling her, with enormous sadness, of Stephen's accident. No aeroplane, no fire, just a London omnibus trundling on in the blackout.

> It has been a terrible week for I lost my own Jean-Paul too; Stephen was such a help over all that, giving up his precious leave to help me. I hope it is all right, Kay, but I have arranged funeral rites of the Catholic Church, which

> was the Church of Stephen's birth. He is laid to rest beside Jean-Paul. These two fine men did not know each other in life but they are companions in death, comrades in their own particular Paradise.

So, not the all-enveloping sand; not the searing terror of explosion and fire in the sky. Stephen had died the almost casual and very unnecessary death by accident in the cold rain of London. She received the news steadily. She felt her dream had told her what she already knew. She had met and loved him in another time, another place. And she had lost him like this in another time, another place. Perhaps this was why she lived so easily without him once he had gone to England to fight. It was an old love, an old loss. But still she grieved.

A day later Kay received the official government wire; she was pleased she had Mara's letter first. After all, it contained the life as well as the death.

Thomas was as grief-stricken over Stephen's death as she was and they cried in each other's arms on and off for days. She had a letter from her grandmother Kitty.

> Mara has written to me of the tragic accident to your husband Stephen. She said he was a wonderful young man and such a support in her own terrible loss. These are dreadful times, full of anonymous wickedness and somehow women are left to hold the skin of things together. I feel for you and wish you were by my side. Once this war's finished you must all come home. It has been far too long. I am sure your mother is a great comfort to you.
>
> Your loving grandma, Kitty R.

Kay told Florence that her daddy had gone to live with Jesus in the stars, but Florence's little face was blank. For her, Stephen was merely a word on other people's lips.

Then, one morning, Kay woke up and the excess of her grief was gone. Stephen himself was almost gone. There was little trace of him in her heart. It was like the tracks of a truck in the sand: they stay a while, then there are faint indentations; then there is nothing.

She felt guilty about this, keeping it from Thomas, who was still gloomy and sometimes tearful about the loss of his friend.

The death of Sam was quite another matter. That also was sudden. He had been so much better, especially in the three years since Florence had been born. One day Florence trotted back round to her own house, saying her Gandy was fast asleep and she could not wake him up. He had sung her a song, laughed and gone fast asleep. Something made Leonora leap from her chair and run from Kay's house.

When Kay caught up with her she was already with Sam, sitting on the arm of his chair, his head cradled in her arms. His eyes were closed. There was a single dribble of blood from the corner of his mouth. Leonora was rocking backwards and forwards saying, 'No-no-no-no.'

Florence looked up at Kay. 'Grandma looks sad, Momma. Why is she sad?'

'She is so very sad –' Kay's face was stiff with the effort not to cry – 'because Gandy Sam is . . . gone . . . He is not with us any more.'

'He is, Momma. He's there in the chair,' Florence chuckled. 'See!'

'No, just his body is there. The inside of him, his spirit, the bit that talked and laughed and played with us, that's gone. D'you understand?'

Florence's face was long now; her lips were trembling. 'Did Gandy Sam go above the stars, Momma? With my daddy? Will they be drinking mint tea and playing with their little cards?'

Kay nodded slowly. 'He's there with Daddy and Uncle Jean-Paul, whom you don't know. And his own daddy and brother and lots of people he knew long ago.'

Leonora had stopped rocking now. The tears were dropping with silent persistence, falling down into the furrows of her cheeks, into her mouth, dripping off her chin. 'Take Florence home, Kay. She wants nothing here,' she said bitterly.

Kay met Thomas outside their own door. 'What is it?' he said, seeing her stricken face. Then, without waiting for an answer he said, 'Sam!' and dashed past her.

She went and sat on the couch holding Florence to her. After five minutes Florence wriggled from her lap and climbed on to a chair to get her teddy from a dresser. Then she came back and sat beside Kay and rocked backwards and forwards clutching him in uncanny resemblance to Leonora. She muttered into teddy's ear, 'Now don't worry, Teddy. Don't worry now.'

The clock on the dresser, made long ago by Sam's father, ticked away one hour. Two hours. Outside the desert dark dropped like a curtain. Then through the open door she could hear a great moaning and sobbing from the courtyard of Mr Kohn.

Thomas appeared through the curtain, pale-faced, blind-looking without his glasses, which were in his hand. 'Kay . . .' he said.

'I know,' she said.

But she didn't know. She had not, like Thomas, been afraid of their father; she had not, like him, perpetually hungered for Sam's approval. Unlike Thomas, she had accepted that Leonora always came first with Sam. That beside Leonora they were of very secondary importance. Now there was no time left for that to change.

'Mr Kohn is shattered,' he said. 'Crying his eyes out. His daughters are crying too. His wife is sitting with Mother.'

'It must be the sisters I can hear. In some ways it must be such a relief to moan and sob like that,' she said, nodding towards the courtyard door.

He shrugged. 'Not our way, is it?' He put a hand on his sister's shoulder. 'It will all have to be very quick, Kay. The funeral, I mean.'

She frowned at him.

'The heat. The doctor has been there. It was a heart attack. After all he has been through! The doctor brought Mrs de la Valle. She's still there.' He paused. 'They'll bury him at dawn tomorrow.'

'Watch Florence,' she said, and sped round to her mother's house.

Leonora was sitting on a couch, her hand being held by Mrs Kohn, whose wide eyes, made blacker with belladonna, were full of unshed tears.

Kay made her way past Sam's empty chair into the bedroom. Mrs de la Valle was there bending over him. On the table beside the bed was a bowl of water and a tray of containers which brought alien, but not unpleasant smells into the room. The nurse stood back from her task leaving the space beside the bed for Kay.

The trickle of blood had gone from Sam's face and his thick springing hair had been combed. Kay leant over and kissed his massive brow which was already icy cold.

'Thank you, Mrs de la Valle,' she said, not knowing what else to say.

The other woman bent her head in acknowledgement. 'He was a great man,' she said. 'A man of principle. Much respected in this city.' Her rough voice softened further. 'And how is the little one these days? She must be three now.'

'Florence? Oh, she is flourishing.' She looked sadly at her father. 'They got on so well, he and she. The very best of friends.'

'That is the blessing: they knew each other. There are exits and there are entrances. The circle goes on.'

'Will she remember him, do you think?'

'Does she talk?'

'She talks very well. All the time.'

'Then she will remember. Seems to me they can remember things from the day they can say the words.'

Comforted by this woman who had supervised innumerable entrances and exits, providing services for people as old as time, Kay went into the other room to her mother. She sat beside her on the opposite side to Mrs Kohn. 'Mrs de la Valle said that Florence will remember him. Isn't that good? Just think, she will talk about him after the year two thousand.'

Leonora looked at her blankly. 'Yes. I suppose so.' She stirred. 'You had better get back to Florence, love. She will need you now.'

'I can't leave you.'

'Send Thomas. Florence will need you.'

But Kay went and collected the sleeping Florence and both she and Thomas came to sit with their mother. Mrs Kohn made a graceful exit reiterating words of comfort in an ancient Hebrew which none of them could understand.

So they sat with Leonora and Sam. They sat with him till dawn. Then, standing in the doorway, Kay watched the pigeons rising over the battered roofs, turning black as they were suddenly silhouetted by the red and yellow streaking sky as, from the East, the dawn made its immaculate, breathtaking progress across the city.

Four

Cool Victory, 1946

It was the heat that she missed most. Of course she didn't miss the flies, nor the fruity, dusty stink of the harbour; not the dry desert wind that made your lips taste of saltpetre, nor the old men spitting as they played chess or backgammon. It was the sheer blissful heat that warmed you to the bone.

The long journey back to England, to what her mother called home, had made Kay realise that those years in Alexandria had over-warmed her blood, thinned it down so it flowed through her veins so lightly that she had always felt insubstantial, floating on life's surface; implicit and explicit tragedy, or public and private loss could not weigh her down. Even the deaths of Stephen and Sam seemed not to have impinged on her as they had on Thomas and her mother.

Here at last in the chill North of England, her blood was thickening, turning to ice, filling her body, freezing and sludging up her brains. This heavy sluggish feeling was compounded by the clothes her grandmother had sent for her to wear against the English winter. There was no doubt these clothes were of good quality; her grandmother had started life as a draper and she knew how to buy quality, even when she had to find coupons to buy clothes at all.

So here was Kay at Darlington Station stamping her feet on this bleak station togged up in woollen stockings, long corset and lisle stockings, thick tweed skirt, layers of jumper and cardigan, topped by a belted coat and bottomed by woollen socks under her best desert boots.

Beside her Florence was similarly ballooned up in layers of clothes, clutching her teddy with mittened hands. Her skin was stark white with cold apart from her nose and the high points of her cheeks which were glowing red. It was hard to think now of Florence under the sun: golden skin plumping on the fair, fragile form underneath. Florence copied Kay and stamped her feet and Kay put an arm round her and hugged her.

Kay's eye lit on a newspaper stall with a poster on the wall proclaiming the coldest winter in living memory. 'Not long now,' she said encouragingly to Florence. Privately she wondered if her grandmother had got their telegram.

Leonora was sitting on their luggage a few feet away smoking a cigarette. She was wearing an old Russian fur hat which quite suited her; her face was lined but tranquil. Her eyes were closed. She too was padded up against the November chill but Kay knew that she was relishing the crisp air, the fine tingle on her skin. She would be recalling her youth, spent tramping these lanes. She had said again on the train that this cold was nothing compared to the cold in Russia. Compared with that, this crisp, freezing November day was mild.

This was her home. She was content to be here. Mara's letter talking about her mother Kitty's eighty-fifth birthday had been a good excuse finally to make the effort to get here.

Kay wondered about roots; about this cold country. With its thirsting for sustenance, could this cold, war-devastated land really call to the blood? Even blood thinned by the desert sun?

Kay had been born here, of course, but her roots were young and frail when they were pulled out of this dark soil. She left here when she was even younger than Florence. For most of that first journey with her parents she had clung to Thomas for comfort. He was her chum, the source of her delight, the object of her childish torments.

The sea at the beginning of that voyage had stretched grey and turbulent right to the horizon. She could remember her delight when it changed, as they sailed through the days and weeks, from gun-metal grey to blue; the sky lost its European marbling and melted to turquoise, then pure sapphire as they chugged south, ever south. The further south they went, the more her frail roots began to float upwards into the hot air, drifting freely, seeking nourishment from the heat and the light, like seaweed as it roots in water.

She had felt that delight again when returning from England to Egypt at the age of fifteen. This turning of the roots to the sun. The relief of the sheer heat.

Their recent long voyage 'home' had reversed the process of the early journeys. Sapphire-blue sea in the beginning; chilling darker and darker to a turbulent gun-metal grey as they got nearer home. The white light, the enveloping heat of Egypt transformed into the dull light of England where the brightest thing is the human face.

Standing shivering here on this dark railway station, she wondered if, without the sun to nourish them, her life-giving roots would shrivel and she herself would dwindle into nothing more than a dried-up fig.

'Well, well, well!' She jumped as a tall elderly man, his silvery hair slicked to one side, came striding on to the station, making for her mother. 'Leonora!'

Her mother leapt up from her nest of luggage and shook his hand, holding his in both of hers. 'Duggie! We thought the telegram had gone missing.'

'Missing? No fear. This is England, Leonora. We win wars and our telegrams arrive on the dot. Ask a thousand mothers and wives and sweethearts. Good news and bad news, the telegrams arrive.' As though that were the perfect explanation. He turned. 'And here's the next generation, if I ain't mistaken, grown up now.' He shook hands heartily with Kay. 'No doubt in the world she favours her dad.' He stood back and half closed his eyes. 'But, if I ain't mistaken, she bears a resemblance to my mate Tommy. She has a look of Tommy.'

Leonora laughed. 'I hadn't seen it.' She turned to Kay. 'Remember? Duggie knew your Uncle Tommy like a brother.

Was with him right through the Great War.' Tommy's unfair execution for cowardice, known to them all, was not mentioned.

Kay knew about Duggie: how he came back from the Great War and took up the role of protector to Kitty and stayed. Though it was years since she had seen Kitty, or Duggie, Kay felt she knew them both as well as she knew anyone except her parents. She had a box full of letters in Kitty's neat draper's hand. That had become a bit shaky lately. *Getting old is no joke*, one of the latest letters had said with typical wryness. Mostly the letters were full of Priorton news. Of Duggie and his friend Mrs MacMahon; of the Rainbow Works which, having been converted to armaments during the war, was now being returned to its more fruitful production of cookers. Kitty's factory was her life, and she still drove there every day in her old Ford motor car.

Duggie was pumping Kay's hand up and down, gripping it too tight in his excitement. 'No finer man . . . well, boy, God rest his soul, than your Uncle Tommy. You could be proud of your Uncle Tommy, Kay. Like you must be proud of your husband, God rest his soul. Ain't that so, Leonora?'

Smiling, Leonora nodded towards Florence who was standing gravely by her mother.

Duggie squatted down in front of the child so they were looking eye to eye. 'And the next generation! Well, I am blessed. Good afternoon, Miss Florence Fitzgibbon, ma'am,' he said, and shook her hand very gravely. 'You must be like your daddy because there ain't been no blondies, as yet, in the Rainbow family. Say hello to your Uncle Duggie, sweetheart.'

'Hello,' she whispered, her voice insubstantial in the heavy northern air.

He stood up and glanced round. 'No Thomas?'

'He went across to London to see Auntie Mara,' said Kay. 'He's travelling north with her for Kitty's party.'

Thomas had thought Kay should come with him to London, to pay respects, as he wished to do, to Stephen in the cemetery where he lay by Mara's husband Jean-Paul. At first she had said she would, but when they landed the darkness of this country gripped her. All she wanted to do was go straight up north with Leonora, to curl up and hibernate somewhere. She wanted to be at her mother's elbow for this short time up till Kitty's birthday. She did not want her mother to settle. Then, after a reasonable time, they could all return to the heat and light of Alexandria.

'We'll get a porter's trolley,' said Duggie. 'Might even get a porter. Only lady porters in the war, it's a fact. And who could let them haul cases? But there's a few more lads out of the khaki now.'

In minutes one such ex-soldier had helped them off the platform to the station yard and helped Duggie load their luggage up on the luggage rack of a well-kept, old-fashioned Ford car.

'Where d'you serve, mate?' said Duggie.

'North Africa,' he said.

'Then you'll know Alexandria,' said Kay. 'We live there, you know.'

He cocked an eye at her. 'Can't think how you stood it, flower. Bliddy terrible place. Too hot, all those flies, beggars in the street.'

Crushed, Kay climbed into the car and settled Florence beside her.

'D'you drive?' Duggie asked Kay, as he finally set it in gear and they were on their way.

She shook her head. 'There was no need, in Alexandria.'

'Watch me. It's as easy as falling off a log. You'll pick it up in no time.'

Florence kneeled up against the window, her breath steaming against the cold glass. Here and there another child looked with interest at the car and she waved at them, eliciting an uncertain wave in return.

Kay looked glumly out of the window at the drab streets which seemed bleached of colour; at the white-faced adults, the pinch-cheeked children. The clothes of the people were sober greys and blacks or sensible greens. The High Street in the winter dusk glittered with a recent fall of rain on top of the heaped-up snow. Tall shops huddled together on the long straight street, where the wide windows displayed scant produce, and fewer goods.

Duggie turned the steering wheel and started to chug up a steep hill which led away from the High Street. 'Ah!' said Leonora. 'I was waiting to go to the old house. I had forgotten Kitty moved.'

'She took a fancy to a new one. Not that it's any smaller than the old house,' he said gloomily. 'Can't get Kitty to realise she's in her eighties. Said she needed it large 'cos you would all come back. Then we had those five evacuees there for two years. It was bedlam, I'm telling you.'

Looking back over the town they could see the rows and rows of narrow streets in grey stone. But the houses were getting larger now. Kay thought of the dusty golden houses of Alexandria with their scabby plaster and greasy bead curtains. They were less substantial than these sturdy dwellings, but they emanated a high-baked warmth which she knew would be missing here.

Raising her eyes she could see beyond the town to two man-made mountains of coal spoil and, further away, the deceptively delicate beauty of a colliery wheel. In her mind she put them against the shifting majesty of the sand dunes and the creaking progress of the blindfolded water buffalo as it made its weary way round and round the well.

Both places were hard on those who sought a living from them but at least in Egypt the sun and the light were free, and people did not have to grub round under the earth for their living.

Kitty's home, in a long row of houses called The Lane, stood at the head of two narrow rising streets facing away from the town. It looked towards the sweeping valley of the Gaunt River and the towering viaduct which carried the trains further up the Gaunt Valley.

The house had a small garden in the front, big double bay

windows and a black door with a brass knocker; above it, painted in neat lettering, was the name: 'Blamire House'. To one side, pushed almost round the back like a child hiding behind its mother's skirts, was another much smaller house. Kay knew from Kitty's letters that Duggie lived in this house with Mrs MacMahon who had come to Priorton as an evacuee from the bombing of Sunderland, and had stayed on. *I do not ask the status of their relationship*, Kitty had written, *but there is no question that they are the best of friends*.

Kitty had seen them from the window and was opening the door as the car came to a stop. She stood there, a diminutive figure leaning slightly on a stick. She wore a twinset in vivid purple and a fashionable longer skirt. Her grey hair was cut short and had been Marcel waved. And she wore rather startling lip rouge. She threw away her stick and opened her arms. 'My dears,' she said.

There was no room in any carriage, so Patrizia piled their boxes into the corner of the corridor, made Peter sit on them and clutched baby Rebeka in her arms. Peter obeyed with an unchild-like resignation. For one so young he had experienced too much walking, too much crowding, too many admonitions to 'be quiet!' to retain the spontaneity and mischief which is every small child's birthright.

Patrizia leant against the partition beside Peter with Rebeka in her arms, making herself as small as possible. She looked longingly at two empty seats in the carriage in front of her, but a notice on the window and on each seat proclaimed irrefutable ownership. Patrizia had been bullied mercilessly by a ticket inspector in Switzerland for trying to put her children in just such empty seats. She would not risk it here.

They had been treated with similar contempt at the refugee hall in the British docks where, before anyone would deal with them, a British soldier, immaculate in his uniform and highly polished boots, had walked up and down the line of refugees spraying them with DDT from a battered red pump.

The train was steaming up when the seats were finally taken by two people who squeezed past Patrizia. As the train started to chug its way north she watched the couple dispose of their parcels and take their seats. The woman, in her late thirties or early forties, was tall and elegant; she wore her hair up in the old-fashioned way: terrifyingly English, like the women on covers of English novels which Patrizia had read in translation.

The young man who accompanied the woman was odd. For a start he was much browner and healthier-looking than all these pale Englishmen. His lightweight suit was criss-crossed with crumples and creases. His tie was half loose and twisted round nearly under one ear. He wore his thick winter coat over his shoulders like a cape and his tortoiseshell glasses kept slipping down his nose.

The man glanced up and caught her stare; she blushed and turned away. He spoke to the woman with him. To her horror Patrizia was aware that he was standing up now and moving to the door of the carriage.

He came into the corridor and spoke to her. She shook her head. '*Ich verstehe nicht*,' she said. '*Ich spreche kein Englisch*.'

The man smiled. 'No problem,' he said in German. The sound of her own language on this man's lips was like balm. 'I said, Would you like to take my seat? The children look exhausted. My aunt will take one on her knee.'

'No – no,' she protested. 'I cannot take it. I . . .'

He took her shoulders with surprisingly strong hands and turned her towards the door. 'Go and sit down. You look all in.'

She collapsed into the window seat beside the woman. The man lifted a quiescent Peter on to the woman's lap. The woman, who did not seem to mind at all about Peter's dusty shoes and stained legs, smiled a broad smile. 'I am Mara Derancourt,' she said slowly.

Patrizia imitated her English. 'I am Patrizia Gold.' Then she retreated into German: '*Hier sind Peter und Rebeka*.'

Mara shook their hands. 'And my nephew out there in the corridor is Thomas Scorton.'

Patrizia nodded then breathed deeply and put her head back on the seat. She wondered how far Laurenz and Mikel had managed to travel. Laurenz had gone off with the very last of their money and bought a battered third-hand motor bike. He and Mikel were making their own way North on that. How they were faring in the blustery cold November winds she shuddered to think. She had no say in the use of her money on the bike. Laurenz went his own way with that, as he did with everything. Over the years the rest of the money from her mother's jewels had gone on surviving in the displaced persons' camp in which they had ended up in Switzerland, and then, finally, on getting out. So much for her mother's life and her fine apartment near the Opera Ring.

Peter laughed, and Patrizia blinked. It was a long time since she had heard her son laugh so openly. The woman called Mara had a notepad and pencil on her knee, and she was drawing a picture of a rather smart bear with big round ears and a checked waistcoat and trousers. Mara pointed at the bear. 'Here is Rupert.'

Peter giggled. '*Hier ist Rupert*,' he repeated.

Patrizia relaxed a little more and closed her eyes again. Laurenz's English, learnt in the camp, and practised obsessively on every English speaker he met, was very good. He had been quite a 'big' man in the camp, wheeling and dealing, making contacts which he said would be useful later. He made enemies too, people he did down on deals who earned his contempt. He was always learning, learning things he said would be useful when they got out.

He had sneered at her suggestion that she should learn the language too. It was sufficient that he knew. Her place, he told her, was simply to take care of the children.

She had got into the habit of doing just what he said. Her physical submission to him during their escape, nothing to do with love, was succeeded by reluctant gratitude in the camp when he married her before Peter was born. The actual marriage surprised her. He did not need to do it. Life in the camp had its own laws; the old rules did not apply. But still he married her and she was grateful. So grateful was she that she closed her eyes to his flirtations with other women, both in the camp and outside of it.

He had soon found work outside the camp, at a toolmakers' shop where his quick brain and skilful hands were appreciated and modestly rewarded. Within eighteen months he was a confident craftsman and something of a credited designer.

She called the first baby Peter after the old man whom they had killed the night the baby was conceived. Laurenz did not make the connection, of course. He was simply pleased to have a son which was, of course, part of his plan for his life after the war. Despite the conditions they lived in he pressured her to have a second child almost straight away, but a woman at the camp called Ruth showed her how to make sure this did not happen. Then Rebeka had come along a year ago; Patrizia was four months' pregnant before she realised it and had felt Rebeka kick inside her. She had not the heart, then, to go through Ruth's procedures. So Rebeka was born.

Laurenz liked to make sure Patrizia was very grateful to him for staying her protector, always reminding her that he had married her when so many more attractive women were his for the taking. He liked her to be grateful to him that he held off from hitting her when she had been, he said, particularly stupid.

The train trundled along for an eternity and finally stopped in Doncaster and the man called Thomas Scorton bought them all tea and biscuits from a booth on the platform. Patrizia stood in the corridor to drink her hot tea, pleased to stretch her stiff legs. Thomas asked her questions about where she had come from and where she was going.

'They gave us tickets to a place in the North, a camp near a place called *Dur-ham* city. A temporary place till we find somewhere to live. There will be work up there, so they say. My husband and brother-in-law sold their tickets and put the money towards a motor bike. They ride up on that.'

'And before?' he said.

She shook her head and her eyes moved to the window, at the telegraph poles which were flying past, marking off the distance to their destination.

'I have read in the newspapers,' he said hesitantly. 'So many terrible things. So much to be ashamed of.'

At that moment the conductor came bustling down the corridor announcing the train's imminent arrival in Darlington and there was a flurry of coat and case as Thomas Scorton and Mara Derancourt alighted from the train. The children waved through the window at them. Peter clutched the notebook which had dozens of pictures in it now, of the adventures of Rupert the Bear.

Stretching her legs and arms before her, Patrizia wondered whether Laurenz would be at Durham Station as he promised. She doubted it. He would have stopped at some café, be flirting with some Englishwoman in his broken English. No doubt she would have to make her own way to this place, this redistribution centre whose address was scribbled on the paper. No matter. She had done harder things.

Florence Fitzgibbon loved her Uncle Thomas, and missed him until he arrived in County Durham the day after they did. She quite liked the Auntie Mara who came with him, who brought her a book of wonderful stories. But she was terrified of the old lady with the stick who smelled of violets. She refused to call her Grandma Kitty and refused to give her a kiss. She even hid behind her mother's skirts when Kitty came into the room.

The third morning at Blamire House, Florence came down to breakfast to find a wonderful contraption by her plate.

'What's this?' she asked her mother. 'What's this thing?'

'I don't know,' said Kay. 'Isn't it a strange thing?'

'What's this?' she asked her Uncle Thomas.

'Haven't got the foggiest idea,' said Thomas gravely. 'What do you think, Mara?'

Auntie Mara shook her head. 'Afraid I haven't a clue either,' She clapped her hands, 'I know! You must ask Grandma Kitty what it is. I think she knows just about everything.'

Florence looked up at Kitty through her eyelashes. 'Do you know what it is?' she said.

Kitty put on her spectacles and peered at the thing. 'I think I might, but I can't quite see it. Perhaps you would bring it here.' She moved her breakfast plate, making a clear space in front of her.

Florence slipped off her chair, lifted the contraption carefully and put it in front of Kitty. Kitty put out a hand and turned the thing round and round, then she stopped it. She pressed a small pin on the top and it flew open. It became a small rostrum on which cavorted painted tigers and lions, elephants and horses. She touched another button and music tinkled into the air, slightly scratchy and faint.

Florence clapped her hands and watched entranced till the mechanism wound down and stopped.

'Do you know who made that?' said Leonora.

'No.'

'Can you remember Mr Kohn, Gandy Sam's friend?'

'Yes.' Of course she could. Had he not given her the very silver bracelet she was wearing today?

'Well, a man from his family, his great-uncle, who used to live with us here, he made it for me when I was a little girl like you.'

'Would you like to make it go?' said Kitty.

Florence nodded her head.

Kitty held out her arms. 'Well, climb on my knee and I'll show you how.'

Eagerly Florence leapt on to her knee, and soon the two of them were so wrapped up in their play, they did not look up when the others stole out of the kitchen and left the pair to themselves.

That night, to assuage her hunger for the heat and light of Egypt, Kay crept into the dining room and unpacked the box which had arrived ahead of her. It was full of her favourite, most treasured old pots. She had left the rest of them with Mr

Kohn who promised to keep them safe. He would show them only to keen and respectable buyers. And if he got her price he would salt away her money for her. Mr Kohn was as anxious as she was that they would all return. Already he was missing his friend Sam Scorton. He wanted the privilege of watching over Sam's widow and her family as they grew.

She had just got the pots into rows on the dining table when Kitty walked in. 'Well I never!' she said. 'What have you got here, love?'

'This is what Thomas and I did in Alexandria. I wrote to you about it. We collected old pots, from markets, from homes, and sold them on. It made us a living. These I could not bear to part with. This one here is more than a thousand years old.' She cupped her hands round it in her own particular fashion. 'And this other one was, I think, made by the same man.'

Kitty touched it with a finger. 'How do you know? Are they marked?'

Kay shook her head. 'I just feel it. I can close my eyes and feel his hands on mine. I know where he is in his working day.' She laughed. 'There! I've told you something I've told no one else in the world.'

'I'm honoured,' said Kitty drily.

Kay went through the pots then, telling Kitty why each was special in its own way. Kitty nodded, her face serious, obviously interested. When Kay came to the end she said abruptly, 'I loved it there, Kitty. The light, the heat, the dust. These pots hold it all for me. I miss it so much.'

Kitty moved restlessly in her seat. 'I looked forward to seeing you all, but there is too much sadness in the house. Apart from Thomas we are a house of widows. We have Leonora and Mara commiserating with each other over their loss. And you are bereft of a land as well as a loved one. And as for me, I too am mourning my dear Sam, always as good as a son to me.'

She paused, and Kay smiled slightly at the thought of her heavily entwined family. Her father Sam would have been Kitty's stepson, had Kitty consented to marry his father William

Scorton, who was her lifelong partner. That Sam went on to marry Leonora, who was not quite his stepsister, added to the complications.

Kitty went on. 'And recently I cannot get the thought of your grandfather, my dear William, out of my head. How long has he been gone? More than twenty years? Then something wonderful. You come and show me, with your pots, that I must not be infected by this mourning. I must make connections.'

'Make connections?' Kay frowned. 'What do you mean?'

'Your grandfather William had just this feeling for old things which you have. Like you he could touch an item and feel its maker. He could feel the lasting story of things. Do you know about the museum?'

Kay shook her head.

'Well, William collected all kinds of things in his lifetime, mostly Roman objects lying on and under the soil in this district. Some earlier. When he died we made a little museum for all his objects and artifacts. This was to be in memory of him and in memory of your Uncle Tommy and Sam's brother Michael. All gone in the first war, one way or another.' She shook her head. 'We didn't think there would be another war, then. Another war. My goodness. The waste.'

Interested, Kay said, 'Does it still exist, this museum?'

Kitty shrugged. 'It's been in dust sheets since the beginning of the war. But it's still all there, in the middle of the town.' Her tone lightened. 'But your pots could go in there, alongside your grandfather's things. What do you think?'

'Would you like that?'

'Yes, yes, I would.' Kitty grasped her stick and hauled herself to her feet. 'I'd like something else as well, Kay.'

'What's that?'

'I would like you to come with me for a ride. Just you and me. I want to show you something. There's heat here, you know, in this land too. But it's a hidden fire. You have to stoke it and feed it but the heat comes forth in ideas and energy.' She made her slow way to the door. 'Would you do that? Come with me on a mystery tour?'

Kay stood up, warmed for the first time since she had been in England. She put her arms round her grandmother's fragile shoulders and held her close. 'I'd like nothing better, Kitty. Nothing better.'

Five
Hidden Fires

The conditions in the resettlement centre were marginally better than those in the Swiss camp. A four-room hut shared by four families here would have had to house eight families at the other camp. And the toilet and washroom here, though also shared, were inside, not across yards of slush.

But the Golds' little room with its single and double bed and its army blankets, was still a prison to Patrizia. Laurenz and Mikel were rarely there. They were always off to Durham City or even Newcastle on private errands. Patrizia did not ask where they got the coupons for petrol or the money for the other things they came back with. She had tried once, but Laurenz said impatiently that they had to go out and about like this. How else would they get money? And wasn't money the key to staying in this godforsaken land?

Patrizia eked out their small allowance as well as she could. She kept the room tidy and read stories and drew pictures for the children all day to keep them quiet and happy. Being seen as German the Golds weren't too popular in the centre; four times she had to endure a superficially mild person spitting the word *Nazi* at her behind her back. She did make friends with an old Dutchman, Willem. Born in Holland, his mother had been German and Willem had worked in Cologne as a florist for ten years after the first war, before returning home, only to have to flee for his life after the German invasion of Holland, when someone discovered his uncle had been a rabbi.

Between his old-fashioned German, spoken with a Dutch accent, and her Austrian accent, it was not always easy to communicate. Even so they had tea together every morning and muddled along, each happy that there was someone to talk to. Sometimes Willem brought her twigs and flowers in jam jars, which she placed in the centre of the table. In the little room Peter played with his few toys on the bed and became more and more silent. Rebeka became worryingly good.

One rare day Laurenz stayed at home, deep in an English grammar book which he had borrowed from the library, cursing the vagaries of this *verdammte* language. There was a knock on the door. She opened the door to a man in a thick navy jerkin and a cap which had earflaps coming down, and a little girl with pale silver hair. The man had a bag in his hand and a bunch of chrysanthemums stuffed under his arm like a swagger stick. The spicy scent of the flowers iced the stale air of the room.

Patrizia did not recognise him at first.

'Frau Gold? Thomas Scorton. Do you remember?' he said in German.

'Ah yes!' She clapped her hands. 'How did you find us?'

'This is the only resettlement centre for twenty miles. So I took a chance.'

'Patrizia!' Laurenz was at her shoulder.

'This is Mr Scorton, Laurenz, whom we met on the train from London. You remember the man who gave us his seat?'

Laurenz pushed past her and shook Thomas heartily by the hand. 'Ah, Mr Scorton. A thousand thank yous for your kindness to my family,' he said in English.

Thomas held up his bag. 'I have toys for the children.' He laid the bag beside Peter, who was sitting wide-eyed on the bed. 'And flowers for Frau Gold.' He handed her the chrysanthemums, rather battered now, with a slight bow.

She took them and stroked them, looking round in vain for somewhere to put them. '*Danke*,' she said. '*Danke sehr*.'

'Thank you!' said Laurenz reprovingly. '*Auf Englisch,*

Patrizia!' He turned to Thomas again. 'I say again and again to my wife that she must learn the language. How bad it is for the children not to speak the language of their new home.'

Patrizia glared at him, despising his hypocrisy.

'I can't think that is important just yet, Herr Gold,' said Thomas, still speaking German. He turned to Patrizia. 'You have a hard task here, Frau Gold.' He glanced round the room. 'My country offers you a welcome which is somewhat austere.'

She smiled faintly. 'It is a welcome, nevertheless, Mr Scorton.'

'Thomas, please call me Thomas.'

'Yes, yes,' said Laurenz eagerly. 'And here is Patrizia. And I am Laurenz, and that fellow on the bed is Mikel.'

Mikel threw down his book, stood to attention and clicked his heels. 'Good afternoon. Pleased to meet you!' he said in English, his lugubrious tones quite comic.

They all laughed at this and the atmosphere lightened.

'Is this your daughter?' asked Patrizia.

'Oh no. This is my niece Florence. She is feeling very cold at present because she has come from Africa.'

'She is out of Africa?' Young Peter's voice, surprisingly deep, came from the corner. 'But she is not black.'

Thomas chuckled. 'We Africans come in all colours,' he said. He pushed Florence forward. 'You go and show Peter and Rebeka the toys in the parcel.'

She bustled across confidently, climbed on the bed, tipped the carrier upside down and spread the toys across the bed. 'Now,' she said. 'The dolly is for you, little girl, and the train is for you, little boy, and the teddy is for you both to share.' Peter reached eagerly for the train, nodding vigorously, the ghost of a smile on his face.

Florence tipped the bag further. 'And there is chocolate. One for you, one for the little girl, and one for me. They are from my own coupons.' She pulled Rebeka's face round so that she was looking directly into it. 'Do you know we had to get two big red buses to here? The man punched the ticket . . . twice!' Her voice was full of awe at this exciting event.

Patrizia held up the flowers. 'I will go to the warden. I will need a very big jar for these.'

Laurenz nodded and pulled out a chair from the table for Thomas. 'Yes, yes, Patrizia. And when you return you will make coffee for Mr . . . for Thomas and me,' he ordered.

'You have coffee?' said Thomas, watching Patrizia vanish through the door.

Laurenz nodded wisely. 'I have coffee. And chocolate. Mikel and I get around. Did you see the motor bike?'

Thomas nodded.

'Well, Mikel and me, we go places. A little work here, a little work there. We find out where to get things in this *ver*— in this country.' He sat back in his chair and put his feet up on the table. 'But what we want, what we want from the heart, is a job, a good job we can get our teeth into. That is a very good English saying. We must make progress. Is that not so, Mikel? We were talking to a man in a public house in Durham. He said there was much work in a town called Coventry, making cars. We may go there. Or we may find a job here. Do you know of any factories here, Thomas? Where they might employ two very hard-working men?'

Kay was surprised that Kitty drove the car herself. She had thought Duggie would drive. Kitty laughed at the thought. 'Duggie's at the factory doing his bits and pieces as usual. I'm not decrepit; you know, love. I like this old car. So long as I can get hold of the petrol coupons it makes me free. Better than limping around with my gammy leg and stick.'

'Where are we going?' said Kay.

'Well, I told you it was a mystery tour: a tour of our lives here in Priorton. Everything you might've learnt bit by bit if you'd lived here all these years, instead of that place with the sun.'

First they drove down to the High Street and parked outside a pub called the Royal George, which stood on the edge of the Market Place. Kitty turned to Kay. 'I stayed in this pub with your mother just after she was born.'

‘With Ishmael.’ Kay had heard the tales of Kitty’s foster father, a boxer of the old school.

‘With Ishmael. Did Leonora tell you she was born in a carriage? No? She forgets. Old age, you know. Well, she was delivered by William Scorton. When he delivered Leonora he was a stranger to me; later he was my lifetime love, though never my husband. You know about that? Well, at least she’s told you something.’ Kitty’s demeanour was pent up; her voice, oiled by excitement, was getting younger by the second. ‘And dear Sam was William’s son, so he and Leonora knew each other all their lives. That means you have a bit of William in you and a bit of me. That makes you very special.’

Then Kitty crashed the car into gear and headed off through the Market Place and down the bank leading to a narrow road by the river. The flat morning sun glittered on the fast-moving water charged with melted snow, brown now with the mud which it had torn from the banks further upstream. One dark tree trunk lay low across the water, sporting glistening green ivy like a cheeky winter jacket.

A moorhen, disturbed by their chugging motor, skimmed the surface of the water in a paddling flying walk, and a big fish betrayed his presence under the water by creating a churning wake. Kay thought of a diving submarine which she had seen on a newsreel at the pictures. Kitty changed down a gear and they chugged past hedgerows and trees, stripped bare of their leaves, which stood out black against the silvery-grey sky.

Kay closed her eyes against it all, wanting to keep her hatred for this cold land fresh, not wanting to see the beauty.

A mile along this road, Kitty took a right turn up a battered avenue of lime trees, on to a high promontory above the river. They continued nearly half a mile in this twiggy tunnel before coming out into the light again.

There before them was a long low house with columns on each side of the door. It was crumbling and decrepit: a picture of forlorn neglect.

Kitty climbed out of the car and Kay followed her. The old

woman stood very still, then put one hand out as though sketching an outline of the length of the building in the air. 'Purley Hall. He lived here, William, your grandfather, with his sons Sam and Michael. And eventually, eventually, we did too, Leonora and me. And then William and me had our own children, Mara and her brother Tommy. Oh, he was a boy! A merry boy, Tommy. A bit like Peter Pan. Do you know about Peter Pan?'

Kay shook her head.

'That's a story – well, a play really – about a boy who never grew up. That was Tommy. They never let him grow up.' She paused. 'Your Stephen is the same, I suppose. You'd think they'd have learnt not to kill their children, wouldn't you?'

'It was the blackout that killed Stephen.' It was hard to talk of Stephen because she could neither feel nor express the deep grief that was expected of her. It was as though she was the river they had just passed and he was a gleaming jewel cast in there. The water had closed over and there was no sign of him. Except for Florence.

'Blackout? Same thing. Accidents galore up here. Old people. Children.'

Kay turned back to Purley House. 'It's all very big. This house and all the gardens.' Even under the snow, with its tangles of black undergrowth, the garden secreted an echo of elegance.

'Do you know who took care of it?'

Kay shook her head.

'Luke, Matthew and John Kohn. They were with William for many years. They worked with him in Egypt once, long before I met him. And came back with him here. They took care of us all, of the garden and the house. Luke made the most wonderful cakes. They were old even when we arrived. Luke was the last. Matthew and John are buried in this garden somewhere.'

Kay looked across the cold, tangled reaches of the neglected winter garden and shivered, welcoming the return of bad feeling. How could those old men bear to spend so many years here in this cold dank land; how could they survive without the bright Mediterranean light, the dry desert heat?

'Of course your parents took old Luke back to Egypt at the very end. He longed to return. I think somehow he was taking the spirit of his brothers home. That's how you came to be there, of course. We couldn't let him go alone, so Leonora and Sam took him. I never thought they . . . you . . . would stay for so long.' Kitty paused, and her shoulders sagged for just a moment. 'Luke was very ancient, you know. A wonderful man. He was some kind of grand-uncle to your neighbour Mr Kohn, the one Leonora mentions in her letters.'

'Mr Kohn's very kind,' said Kay. 'He loved Sam, you know.' She paused. 'So who does Purley Hall belong to?'

Kitty shrugged. 'Dunno. Council? Whoever it is, they've let it run to rack and ruin.'

'Did William sell it?'

Kitty shook her head. 'No.' She paused. 'The whole thing went to another branch of the family when William died. I had to start again from scratch.'

Kay wondered what Kitty was up to. Her grandmother was not a moaner and did not indulge in self-pity. But something was afoot here. 'Where to next then?' she said brightly, wanting to get away from this place.

'Well,' said Kitty, cheerfully, clambering back into the car. 'First we'll go to see William's museum. Then we'll go to my factory. I have more treasures in store for you, believe me.'

Thomas and Florence stayed more than an hour at the Golds'. Patrizia returned from the warden's trim house with a tall fruit-bottling jar, full of water for the flowers. She made coffee for the men and they sat round the table and talked. Or Thomas talked about living in Alexandria, and the other two listened, their dark eyes full of patent respect. The three children on the bed, talking away to each other in their own language, communicated perfectly.

Florence was sad when they had to leave.

'She has only had grown-ups to play with in her life,' said

Thomas. 'It must be great fun for her to play with someone her own size.'

'Uncle Thomas, what are you saying in that funny way to the lady?' Florence was pulling on her mittens.

'I'm telling her that you have enjoyed yourself and I am speaking to her in her own language, which is German.'

'German? Is that like the men in the aeroplanes? The ones who exploded the ships?'

Thomas was pleased Patrizia could not understand this. But Laurenz could. He said curtly, 'No, little girl. Not the same as those men. Not the same at all.'

'Can she come back?' Peter's deep voice came from the bed, where he was still clutching the train. 'Can the little girl come back to play?'

'Yes,' said Patrizia decisively. 'It would be good for the little girl to come back.'

'Peter wants you to come again to play,' said Thomas.

'There!' Laurenz beamed up at him. 'You see, you will be very welcome. You and the little girl.'

Thomas shook hands with them all, including the children, and made Florence do the same. The Golds clustered round the door of their hut to watch their visitors crunch down the cinder path, and waved at them just before they dropped out of sight on their way to the bus stop.

Laurenz closed the door behind them and stood with his back to it. 'Well,' he said through his teeth. 'Are you satisfied?'

Rebeka began to whimper. Patrizia pushed back her hair. 'What now?'

'Our first visitors and this place is like a slum. Shoes hanging round. Clothes hanging round.' He picked the objects up and flung them into the air as he spoke. 'Flowers in jam jars.' He threw the flowers against the wall and the jar smashed, splintering on to the wood floor, ending up in a tangled heap of glass, leaf and spiky frond of chrysanthemum.

He grabbed her and dragged her over to the mirror. 'And look at this, look at you. You look like an old woman. Your hair's filthy, you . . .' his voice drummed in her ears and she looked in the mirror and knew what he said was true. Then she remembered the boys in the street in Vienna, the boys who told her to go home and look in the mirror and call herself Jew, then go and slit her wrists because that was the best that could happen to her. Perhaps they had been right.

Then, with the memory of those boys came the memory of her mother, ripping petticoats to bind her injured arm, and later telling her to leave her; to go with the man called Gold. Suddenly Patrizia felt the wind of anger gusting through her, anger at those cruel boys, anger at her own mother for letting her go, and finally great anger at this man in front of her now, heaping insults on her powerless head just like those boys in the Vienna street.

She let out a great cry and flung herself round and threw him off balance. She leapt at him, scratching his face, grabbing his hair. He finally pulled her off and held her away from him, both her hands in one of his big hands. He was just drawing back his fist to punch her when Mikel stepped in and pulled him off and flung him into a corner. He stood over him where he lay. 'That's enough, Laurenz,' he said quietly. 'It is time you stopped all this. I make allowances for you because of that thing when you were small. But now we have been the victims of barbarians, and you too have transformed yourself into one. Congratulations.'

Laurenz got up on to his knees smiling ingratiatingly into his cousin's eyes. 'You have always been so good, Mikel. You know I wouldn't . . . What do you think you are doing, knocking me down?' He actually managed a rueful chuckle.

'Teaching you some good manners.' Mikel helped him up and dusted him down. 'I have seen enough of this, Lau, do you hear? If you touch one hair of her head, or the heads of those two children, I will kill you. Do you hear this?'

Laurenz sat down and looked into his cousin's eyes. 'Always the great protector, Miki. Once me, now them. You know I would not hurt them, Mikel. Truly. It's such a crowd in here. We need to strike out. Get out of here. Do you have the address of that man in Coventry?' He smiled again. 'Perhaps one of us could go down and investigate? See what the possibilities are there? What do you think?'

Patrizia watched dully as her husband repaired the breach, charming his less clever cousin into leaving them all alone, stripping her of her last defence.

'The worst thing about seeing your little sister as a middle-aged woman is that it makes you feel old,' grumbled Leonora.

'Old? You will never be old, Leo. And anyway, I refuse to be middle-aged.'

'You certainly don't look it,' said Leonora with feeling. This morning the twenty years between them were very evident.

Mara was wearing her hair down, tied loosely in a bow at the nape of her neck. They were working together, sorting out their mother's kitchen and pantry, throwing out jars and bottles which were past using: the cumulated detritus of hoarding imposed by a war in which everyone had been exhorted to dig, bottle, preserve, sew and save for victory.

'It must have slipped Kitty's mind that she was digging and bottling for one, not twenty.'

'She did have those evacuees, remember?'

'Perhaps, but they've been gone nearly two years now.'

They washed the useful bottles and jars and burnt what rubbish they could in the big kitchen fire. 'I had forgotten what a comfort it was, to have a big Durham fire like this,' said Leonora, poking away.

'You must have missed all this – England,' said Mara, wanting her sister to say yes.

Leonora shrugged. 'It was more important that I had Sam and he adored it out there. The twins too, especially Kay. She was like a desert flower, always. But sometimes, yes, I did miss it. Sam wouldn't think of coming home, though. He was at home there. I think all those years he spent with Luke and his brothers as a boy made him an honorary Egyptian from birth.' She shook out her tea towel and hung it over the bar above the fire. 'I did come back for those years in between, when the children went to school, didn't I? I enjoyed all that political stuff then. But without him it had no value. Anyway, I never thought you'd stick it out in London.'

Mara smiled. 'Well, there was little or no work for Jean-Paul up here in the thirties, skilled as he was. Getting a job teaching down there was not so difficult. He sold his furniture, collectors' items, piece by piece. Even in the Depression there was money down there, and a good time you could have if you had enough.' She sighed. 'I miss him so much, Leo, that I get angry. I was devoured with anger for months. But I don't need to tell you . . .'

'I should thank God for the luck of having Sam so long. He survived that stroke and we had five more years together. Sometimes I feel he's still here, inside me. Other times I just want to join him wherever he is. In the week after he died I'd have taken steps to do that. But his friend Mr Kohn stuck to me like a leech. I think he was under orders from Sam himself. And there was Thomas and Kay, and Flo.' She paused. 'Do you ever wish you had children, Mara?'

Mara sat in the chair by the fire. She laughed wrily. 'They didn't come along, did they? I think Jean-Paul and I were so clever at avoiding them in the first place, because of me staying a teacher and not getting married, so good at that that in the end our bodies forgot how to make babies.'

'That's a pity.'

Mara laughed. 'Not at all. We had each other to "baby", and I had the most wonderful children to teach. Do you know I still hear from children I taught twenty years ago?' She frowned. 'Some of them were killed in the war and I felt a fragment of a mother's anger, and grief.'

'But now . . .'

'Now I have you and the twins, I have a family.'

Leonora sighed. 'I wouldn't count on that, Mara. They're talking about going back in the New Year, as soon as we've celebrated Kitty's birthday. Kay's very keen. Thomas too; he always follows her lead.'

‘Are they now? You wait till Kitty’s had her hands on them. Where is Kay now?’

‘With Kitty. They’ve gone for a ride.’

‘See?’ said Mara triumphantly. ‘And Thomas . . .?’

At that moment Thomas marched into the kitchen blowing visible breath against the December cold, his face and nose cherry red. Florence, close behind him, had an equally red nose. ‘Ah, Auntie Mara!’ he said. ‘Just the woman. I want to know the best and fastest way to teach a foreigner English and you’re just the one to give me the best tips.’

The legend ‘RAINBOW WORKS’ was outlined, in shredding, battered paint, on a triumphal arch over the main gateway of the factory. Kay exclaimed at the beauty of the gates, crafted in wrought iron, which depicted the Priorton Viaduct entwined in ivy leaves.

‘Made for me by Geordie McManners the blacksmith in 1928, when he had no work. I only hung on to them by the skin of my teeth during the war. A truckload of workmen came with their chisels to take my gates away to build tanks.’

‘But they didn’t get them?’

Kitty shook her head. ‘They got all the railings round Blamire House, of course, like all the other houses on The Lane. But we were making shells here at the factory, see? So it was easy to argue to keep the gates on security grounds. We had to screw sheet-tin behind them. Then, the minute peace was declared, I had the tin taken off. Now then, love, just jump out and open them for me, will you?’

The gates swung back easily on well-oiled hinges and Kitty drove the car through. She parked it alongside one other car near a high blast wall. Kay helped her grandmother out of the car. Kitty steadied herself with her stick and walked over to a little door which was set in a much bigger one in a long low building. She stepped through and Kay followed her.

They were in a hangar-like space, roofed in grey-painted corrugated iron, with steel girders supporting it like the struts of a bridge. The space beneath was occupied by two long production lines beside which, on continuous rollers, stood cookers in various stages of production. No one was working.

'I might have known it,' said Kitty, striding as fast as her leg and stick would take her to the far end of the line, following the chatter of voices which were echoing up into the void.

At the end of each line a cluster of workers sat on a random collection of chairs and stools, even upturned boxes. Making her royal progress through them was a short, bandy-legged woman, with an urn on a wheeled contraption protected at the sides by cardboard. She stopped at each group and filled cups and mugs, tuppence apiece whatever the size. She raised a hand as she saw the visitors. 'Now, Miss Rainbow, payin' us a visit, are yeh?' Her voice frosted on the cold air.

Faces turned towards them: women of all ages, overalled and turbanned; men in jumpers and work trousers, some of them army fatigues, obsolete now, to the relief of their wearers. From the other line, which also had its clusters of tea-drinkers, people were peering across to see the cause of the disturbance.

'Visiting? So I am, Avril. And what do you lot do when I turn my back? Waste time drinking tea.'

'Now then, Miss Rainbow,' said a red-haired younger woman on their left. 'We're due our tea breaks else you'll never get the sweat you want out of us till five o'clock.'

'D'yer want a cuppa then?' Avril grunted. 'I've some spare cups here. Thruppence, seein' as you didn't bring your own cup, like.'

'Don't mind if I do,' said Kitty cheerfully, fiddling in her purse for a sixpenny piece. 'And no, Ginger, I don't begrudge you your tea breaks.'

'Got us through the war, didn't it?' said the red-haired Ginger. 'Gallons of tea and acres of overtime and a bit o' dancin' on the side.'

'So it did,' said Kitty, leaning her stick against the line and taking her mug of dark brown liquid in two hands. Kay took hers, grateful for its warmth in the cold air. She couldn't understand how it was possible to work in such cold.

'An' who've you brought to see us this time, Miss Rainbow?' said Avril. She turned to Kay without waiting for an answer. 'She was always bringing people to see us in the war, like. Ah wis on the lines then, not hawkin' tea round like some old gypsy. Proper heroines she made us out to be, then.'

'Heroes now, like . . .' piped up a tall gangly boy at the back.

Kitty handed Avril her half-empty cup and grasped her stick again so that she could stand taller. 'Well, girls, this young sprite here is Kay Fitzgibbon, my granddaughter. I'd like you all to meet her.'

'Chip off the old block, eh?' Avril winked and screwed her neck to one side like a questing cockerel.

Kitty grinned up at Kay. 'These terrible girls were with me right through the war and some well before that, when we were last trying with cookers. The noisy one with the tea urn is Avril, and the ginger-top is Ginger, of course. Then Janet. Here's Susannah, and Betty and Ethel and . . .' She came to a strange face.

'I'm Maureen, miss. And these are Sheila and Beryl. And across there is Barry and Colin just back from the army, and—'

'Have you just started then?' Kitty frowned.

The girl shook her head. 'No, miss, been here two months now.'

Kitty frowned. 'So many changes,' she said and for a time seemed lost in her own thoughts.

Avril took Kay's empty mug from her. 'Chip off the old block, eh?' she repeated. 'Come to show us how to do it, like?'

Kay shook her head. 'I'm just visiting. I live in Egypt.'

Avril raised her sparse brows. 'Ah thowt you looked a bit of a blackie, like. Our Lennie was in Egypt. With Monty at El Alamein, you know.'

'That's only sixty miles from where I live.'

'Our Lennie knows the desert, like. He knows the desert like the back of his hand. The desert knows him too. Knows his leg anyway. He lost his leg there . . .' She paused. 'His sense of humour as well, come to think of it. He's a miserable b—bloke.'

'I'm sorry about that,' said Kay.

'Kay's husband was a pilot in the Battle of Britain, you know,' put in Kitty. 'She lost him too.'

'Shot down, was he?' said Janet.

'Not shot down. It was in an accident in London, in the blackout.' Kay hurried the information into the equation, scowling at her grandmother.

'But he flew, what was it, Kay? Thirty or forty operations over France and Germany, didn't he?' insisted Kitty.

'Another bloody hero,' said the gangly lad at the back.

'What was it you did, Tadger?' said Janet. 'Take part in the relief of the Bristol barracks?'

Tadger's riposte was drowned by the brief scream of a siren which had them all standing up, dusting crumbs from their overalls and taking up their stations once again.

Kay and Kitty set off again through the factory. Their presence generated a good deal of interest from the lines, and more than one wolf whistle followed their progress towards the glassed-in section at the end which was the progress office.

Duggie was waiting in the doorway, business-like in a hairy three-piece suit which, when he took it off, must still bear the imprint of his body. He was grinning. 'I heard a kerfuffle down there so gave them another minute on their break. Caused a riot, have you?'

'Not at all,' said Kitty calmly. 'Just introducing Kay to old friends, although there are fewer of those these days, Duggie.'

They looked back down towards the lines, now busy and vibrating with the sound of drills. 'No better sight than that,' said Kitty fondly. 'Warms the cockles of your heart, doesn't it?'

Kay, engaged in spite of herself, looked at Duggie. 'Are you in charge of all this, then?'

Duggie laughed. 'No fear. Always the bottle-washer never the chief cook. Deputy everything, that's me. Just keep an eye on things for Kitty here.' He winked at Kay. 'You should step back across to the admin. block and meet Captain Marshall. We got the Captain in the war, didn't we, Kitty? He's the man the ministry put in, Kay. Took over from Kitty, stayed on after the war to give us the benefit of his . . . er . . . leadership.'

The wind whistled round them as they walked out of the factory and across to the admin. block, another long low building. At the end of a long narrow corridor was a large panelled door. Through this was an outer office where they were watched with interest by three women and a man, anchored behind desks. Duggie led them to a door made obscure by etched glass. He knocked and walked in.

The bearded man at the desk was large, with wide shoulders and a massive head crowned by a tonsure of iron-grey hair. His apparent height melted as he stood up and took off his tortoiseshell glasses. Clearly his upper body held a promise which his legs couldn't deliver.

Kitty looked up at him. 'Kay, this is Captain Marshall, ex RN. Captain, can I present Mrs Kay Fitzgibbon, my granddaughter?'

Captain Marshall came round the desk and shook Kay's hand with a grip which would have melted iron. 'Delighted, Mrs Fitzgibbon, delighted.' He turned to Kitty. 'And Miss Rainbow, you honour us with your presence *again*!'

'If that is sarcasm I can hear in your voice I shall be very cross, Captain Marshall.'

He smiled. 'It is always a pleasure to see you, Miss Rainbow,' he repeated. 'But what can such a beautiful young lady want here, in this dark satanic mill?'

'Places like this breed tigers, Captain. Forge steel. Nothing dark and satanic about that. The factory is hers as much as mine, and she should know what's hers,' said Kitty brusquely. She sat down on a chair that Duggie was holding out for her. 'Now, Captain, tell me just what kind of mess we're in at the moment!'

Six

Rope-learning

'So what do you think?' Kitty looked over the teapot at Kay as she poured her a cup. They were in the smart café in the Priorton Cooperative Society, being watched very closely by a rather grand young woman in a black dress and white apron.

'Of what?' said Kay, eyeing the rather drab cakes on the perfect glass cake stand. 'What do I think of what?'

'The factory. The Rainbow Works.'

Kay blinked. At the factory she had been ignored by Kitty, once the formidable Captain was presenting his report. Later, outside the factory, Kitty had suggested a cup of tea.

'Are we not going home then?'

Kitty had shaken her head. 'Your mother and Aunt Mara will be deep into the problems of widowhood and the post-war world, and just what they are going to do about me in my dotage. We'll see to ourselves, shall we?'

Now, in the café, Kay asked quite crossly, 'What about the factory?' The factory was a paradox. On the one hand she had thought the place grimly cold and felt revolted by the smell of petrol, and of something else like burnt plastic that had been hard to pin down. On the other hand, she'd been warmed by the intense energy of the people with their baskets of nuts and screws, by the way that machine skeletons at the beginning of a line ended up as gleaming, complete objects at the end. She could not contain it all within her hands like she could the old Egyptian bowls, but inside her, ringing like an interior bell, was a similar response to that buzz of creation.

'Do you like it?' persisted Kitty.

'The factory was like another planet to me, Kitty. I'm used to one-legged beggars, water-carriers with ancient faces, turbanned heads, tinselled whores . . .' But they had something too, these factory women with their pale faces, their quick tongues; the drawn men decked out in the faded detritus of war; the great bull of a man who sat at the helm of it all, as though he were still piloting a minesweeper in the channel . . . 'It was interesting,' she said cautiously.

'Would you like it?'

'What?'

'I said, Would you like it?'

'What?'

'The factory, for yourself.'

'When?'

'Now.'

'Why?'

'If you hadn't noticed, I'm getting on a bit. Reduced to taking what that puffing billy of a captain says as gospel.'

Kay mashed at her cake with her fork. 'I'm going back to Alexandria in the New Year.'

'Are you?' said Kitty, looking her straight in the eye. 'Do you need to?'

'I want to,' said Kay vehemently. 'It's where I grew up. Where I belong. I can't stand this dark and this cold, thirsting land.'

'I know Alexandria is where you grew up, Kay, but your roots are here,' said Kitty firmly. 'Now then. I had the sense that you liked the factory. What did you think was interesting?'

'I like to be where people are making things. I always liked to see the potters at work. They would start with clay and end with a useful, enduring object. In your factory it's about taking something from sheets of steel to become a very complicated object. Although I don't think your cookers'll last a hundred years, never mind a thousand, like some of my pots. Still, it has its excitement.'

'How do you know that? That they won't last?' said Kitty defensively. 'My cookers are works of art in their own way.'

'There's a buzz about the place,' Kay said slowly. 'And from what the Captain said, once you get on top of the shortage of materials you'll be racing ahead.'

'Ah. You were listening. *We* will be racing ahead,' Kitty corrected her.

'And those people, Kitty. I liked them. The women . . .'

'The powers that be want me to replace them with men now, you know, with men back from the war. But they're skilled, my girls . . .' Kitty's voice sharpened. 'You'd better eat that cake instead of mashing it to a pulp. The waitress'll have a sour face if she has to clear that plate. The waste, my dear!' She watched Kay clear up the cake and eat it, careful forkful by careful forkful. 'So what do you think?'

'About what?' Surely they didn't have to go through it again.

'About the factory.' Kitty's bland voice hid her impatience.

'I told you, I liked it. It's interesting.'

'Well, as I told you, it's yours.'

Kay frowned. 'Are you telling me you'll leave it to me?'

'It's yours. Now! The papers are already drawn up. But I'll only sign them if you promise to stay here for – say – two years. Work there every day. Get good at it. Then after two years if you still want to go back East you can sell up and get on with your life there.' Kitty put her knife neatly by her fork. 'Think about it.'

'Sell up? What about Duggie?'

'I'll see that he's all right.'

'What about Florence? How could I work full time?'

'Leonora'll see to Florence. Doesn't she do that already? And there's Mrs MacMahon. And me, as long as I am spared.'

'What about Thomas?'

'I did think about him, but Leonora said that you were the one with the business head.'

Kay laughed. 'It wasn't much of a business. Those pots.'

'You didn't have much to work on. Even so, it kept you and

the rest of them after Sam's stroke. I myself started by sewing scraps of material into aprons and selling them. It's the attitude that counts.'

'But what about Thomas? There's no way I would do this without talking to him.'

Kitty shrugged. 'He could work with you. Or do something else. He'll know what he wants to do.'

'You've got an answer for everything, Kitty.'

'That's what you do in business, love. Think of all the possibilities and choose the best one. The most profitable, in terms of people as well as money.'

Kay stood up, picked up their umbrellas and pulled out the chair so Kitty could grasp the table to stand up. 'Do I have to say now?'

Kitty shook her head. 'No. But you can tell me in the morning. You'll know one way or the other. Big decisions are better made quickly.'

'Do the others need to know?'

Kitty shook her head. 'Not until you've made your mind up. If you decide not to, I'm going to give it to Duggie.' She grinned mischievously. 'Either way, the Captain's going to get a bit of a surprise.'

When they got back to the house Thomas and Leonora were toasting their toes by the fire and Mara and Florence were playing Snap at the kitchen table. Florence jumped down from her stool and started dancing around in front of Kay, desperate to communicate her big secret. 'Guess what Momma? Uncle Thomas took me on a visit and I have two new friends! One called Rebeka, she's only little. But Peter, he's nearly as big as me and we've got a secret.'

'A secret? What's that?'

Florence folded her arms in disgust. 'Don't you know what a secret is, Momma? Gandy Sam told me all about secrets. They are things you must not tell a single soul. Well, me and my new friend Peter have a secret.'

From the table Thomas grinned. 'Can't think how they

cooked up any secret, Kay, one talking in German, the other in English.' He went on to describe their visit to the Golds. 'Conditions not much better than their DP camp, I shouldn't think. Intelligent people too.'

'*Persecution falleth like the rain on the just and the unjust*,' said Kitty. 'I read that somewhere. Or did I make it up?'

'They must be quite bewildered.'

'The wife looks like a hunted deer, but the men, Mr Gold and his cousin, are quite perky, surprisingly enough. They speak quite good English, but the wife and the children speak none. I've been picking up some tips from Mara here about teaching them English.'

'Teaching them English?'

'It's a big job – there are others in the camp too, but I'm going to have a stab at it. Didn't do much for the war effort except pinpoint a few Nazis for the security chaps in Alexandria. Call this my war reparation if you like.'

Kitty exchanged a glance with Kay. 'And will you get paid for this?'

He shrugged. 'I don't know. The ones who are working might pay me something. That reminds me. These chaps seem very intelligent, Kitty, and handy. Any chance of a job for them at your factory? That would help the whole caboodle no end.'

The next morning, Kay negotiated a 'wait and see' option with Kitty. She would work in the factory. See what it was like. So she spent the few days leading up to Kitty's birthday at the factory. She survived very well under Duggie's wing, an overall pulled over her dress while he gave her her instructions. Her first job was to count stock in the stores. He showed her how many items actually went into making a single cooker. She counted hundreds of screws, washers, elements, handles, control knobs, and thermostats, noting them carefully on the stock sheet.

From time to time a tall boy would come with a trolley and, referring to a list in his hand, would load it from the shelves. He spotted her up a ladder and winked at her, clicking his teeth as you do to a dog or cat to try and get its attention. After that he wolf-whistled her every time he came into the stores but she firmly ignored him.

When Duggie came for her at twelve o'clock she stuck her pencil in her hair, flexed her aching fingers and stamped her aching legs. 'I'm just about dead, Duggie.'

'Sorry about that. At least it'll have given you an idea of the stock,' he said.

'What next?' she said.

'Dinnertime!' he said. 'Now then, Mrs Fitzgibbon, you've a whole half-hour to sit down.'

She looked round. 'Is there a café?'

He laughed. 'There is a canteen of sorts,' he said, 'but it'll take you five minutes to get down there, twenty minutes to queue for food. No. Kitty sent some sandwiches for you.'

With polite nods and half-smiles the women in the outer office cleared a space at a desk for Kay, and found her a chair so that she could eat her sandwiches in comfort. Their demeanour was polite but they said very little. Munching her way through her corned-beef sandwich, Kay wondered if they were always so quiet, or whether they chatted and gossiped about things. About their lives: husbands, mothers, families; about Mr Attlee and all the new moves in the government; about Princess Elizabeth and this Greek she now had in tow; about the Captain and the way he ran the factory. As it was, when they had gulped their sandwiches, the women got out their knitting, or copies of the *Daily Mirror* or *Woman's Weekly*, and kept their heads down over them.

It was a relief when Duggie came back for her. 'Girls all right?' he said as they made their way down line one.

She shrugged. 'Can't tell,' she said. 'Never said a word to me once they'd got me a chair.'

Duggie nodded. 'One of two things,' he said. 'Either they were too frightened to talk to you because of Kitty and the Captain, or they didn't like an overall girl sitting in their sanctum.'

'An overall girl?'

'They think they're a real cut above the shop-floor girls, those office girls. Give me the shop-floor lasses any day.'

He stopped at the line where Janet and Ginger were sitting on hard plastic stools, wiring up the back of two cookers which were standing on the rollers to one side of them. Duggie hauled up an extra stool for her. 'Let Kay watch you first, girls, and when there's a bit of slack, give her a go.' Then he strode off, to head off the Captain who was standing looking down the line with a speculative eye.

Without stopping working Ginger turned to Kay and said, 'Any good with yer hands, lass?'

Kay spread her hands with their neat fingernails and turned them over to her soft palms. 'Well, I can sew, and I can throw pots.'

'Throw pots? What kind of pots?' said Janet. 'Where d'you throw pots to?'

Kay watched their swift fingers. 'You make them with your hands. Bowls, and things for cooking in. Out in Alexandria where I come from they make them with a kind of spinning wheel which they kick with their feet.'

'They would, I suppose, a backward country like that. We make'm with machines here in England, being more advanced, like,' said Ginger.

'Anyway, that's about all I can do with my hands.'

Ginger sniffed. 'Mebbe you'll do,' she said. 'Hey, Ralph,' she shouted at a boy who was passing with a trolley filled with coloured wires. 'We'll be needing filling here in no time, mind!'

Ralph turned out to be the boy who had wolf-whistled at Kay in the stores. At this distance he was quite good-looking, with brown eyes and a shock of mousy hair falling down over his brow. He came over and looked Kay up and down and winked at her. 'Change yer on to the lines did he, flower? New starter, that it? You want to watch yer step. Wouldn't trust these two as far as I could throw them.'

Kay grinned at him. 'I'm learning a lot.'

'Oh!' he said, picking up on her different speech. '*I'm learning a lot, am I?* From down South are we?'

'Yes,' she said, deciding not to tell him from just how far down South she had really come.

'Well, I'd have nowt to do with this riffraff if I was you, flower. They'll lead you astray, sure as shot. Tell yer what, love. Come to the pictures with me tonight an' I'll give you the lowdown on this place, the job, the folks, the lot. Boss, every last jack of 'em.'

'So who's the boss round here, then?' she asked demurely.

'Well, Captain ruddy Marshall waddles round this place like some ruddy Hitler. But it really belongs to old Kitty Rainbow. Me father worked for her before the war, and his father worked for her before that. Blacksmith, he was. But they say she's past it. Gaga. Bonkers.'

Ginger called across, 'You want to keep your gob shut, Ralph.'

Kay cut across her: 'Do they say that, Ralph? That she's gaga? Have you ever seen her?'

He shook his head. 'I just been here two months, since me demob, like. I have seen her from a distance. She walks with a stick. Like I said, past it.'

Ginger put up a hand and grabbed him, pulling him to her side. 'D'yer want to hear a really great secret, Ralph?'

He giggled. 'Nothing like your secrets, Ginger.'

She whispered in his ear. He leapt away as though she had burnt him and he went bright red. He shot a glance across at Kay, jumped over to his trolley and raced away with it down the line.

Ginger and Janet roared with laughter and Kay joined in.

'Not much bloody use, men,' said Ginger, 'not much use at all. 'Cept for one thing.' And they all laughed again.

Kay watched her work a little longer and said, 'So how do you get to be called Ginger, then?'

Ginger giggled. 'Mebbe you didn't notice the hair. Me and Rita Hayworth.'

'Yes, but all redheads aren't called Ginger.'

'Well, Miss Nosy Parker, before the war I was called Mavis. Then in the war I used to go out dancing with this lot of lasses. We all went out in a gang with these two Canadian lads and one of them called me Ginger and it kind of stuck. Even me dad calls me that now.'

After a while, when she had finished one lot of wiring extra quickly, Janet let Kay have a go. What had looked so simple, so swiftly executed when Janet did it, Kay found almost impossible. She didn't screw in the screws tight enough; she omitted one wire and it took her ten goes to redo it. Even then it was wrong.

Janet laughed and retrieved her screwdriver. 'Give us it here, lass. Mebbe them pots in Egypt is easier. No screws in pots, eh?'

'How long does it take,' said Kay, 'to get as quick as you two?'

'Let's see,' said Janet. 'Ginger here was all fingers and thumbs when she started. Couple of weeks? Three? Before you stopped being a liability, Ginger.'

'That's about it,' said Ginger. 'But that was on the shells. Different thing.'

'Aye, that's when you were called Mavis. All fingers and thumbs you were then, like I said.'

'But I soon learnt.'

'This is harder than the shells,' put in Janet.

'I suppose it is,' said Ginger. She turned to Kay. 'But it's more interesting. Not that it matters for you, like. You won't end up on the line like us poor sods.'

'I'd like to get good at it, though,' said Kay. 'Seems to me that this end of it, making the things, is what it's all about.'

'Attagirl!' said Ginger. 'You get old Duggie to put you down here properly for three weeks and we'll knock you into shape. That right, Janet?'

'*Durn* sure we will,' said Janet and they all laughed uproariously. Kay was not sure whether the hilarity was at the thought of her being any good at all at this very difficult task, or just Janet's Roy Rogers accent. Still, she laughed along with them.

Duggie was amazed when, later that day, she asked to be put on the line with Ginger and Janet for a longer time. 'Above and beyond the call of duty, I'd say, Kay.'

'I want to. Gives a better sense of what it's about.'

He pursed his lips. 'I suppose so. Don't know what Kitty'll say. You'll have to close your ears to all the language. That Ginger is a good worker but she has a mouth like a sewer.'

'I've heard worse in four languages in Alexandria.'

He rubbed his bristly chin. 'You know, you stand there looking sixteen and it's easy to forget you're a grown woman with a daughter of your own.'

'You'd better tell that to your . . . er . . . progress lad. He obviously thought I was on the market.'

'Ralph? Has the cheeky blighter been setting up to you?'

She laughed. 'Not his fault. Didn't know who I was. Obviously didn't know I was a respectable widow with a six-year-old daughter.'

In the end Mara actually went with Thomas to the resettlement camp to help him teach Patrizia and the others. They borrowed Kitty's car, loaded it with paper and pencils filched from the factory stock, and sat Florence in the back, assuring her that she would be playing with her friend Peter again.

After Mara had greeted Patrizia and the children, she made her way to the warden's office to explain what she and Thomas intended to do. 'We thought we would gather any people together who had little to do during the day, and teach them English. It will be hard for them to get work, to settle at all, unless they know English, and a little about England.'

The warden, a rather tired-looking ex-Navy CPO, scratched his head. 'Don't know about that, ma'am. No orders regarding that. Not from the government, not from the council. There was some talk about that kind of thing, but nothing's happened so far.'

'But do you need orders?' she said. 'Here we are. Volunteers. We don't need paying.'

'How do I know you can do it? There is the issue of qualifications.'

Mara pulled herself to her full height, which was only just short of his. 'Well, Mr MacAlister, I am a qualified teacher, trained in Durham and with further diplomas from the University of London. Do you wish to see my certificates?'

'No. No, ma'am.' He scratched his head again. She could smell the faintest touch of rum on his breath, although it was only eleven o'clock in the morning. 'Can't see that it'd do any harm.'

'Marvellous. Marvellous. So, is there a larger space? There is so little room in the huts. Beds, chairs and bodies and all that seem to fill them.'

'Well, there is an empty hut. Used as a sort of social, recreational place when the prisoners were here.'

'Prisoners?'

'Didn't you know? This was a prisoner-of-war camp before. During the war. Italians mostly. A rum lot, but no harm. A lot of them are still around, married Durham girls and stayed.'

She glanced at his coal fire, roaring in the grate. 'Do you think there'd be any chance of a fire in there? If it's been empty it'll be freezing. It's cold enough outside.'

He threw up his hands. 'I'll see what I can do. Is there anything else you need, ma'am?' The tone just avoided sarcasm.

She smiled brilliantly at him. 'How kind of you to say. Could you just make sure that there are plenty of chairs and tables in this hut? That, and the fire, will be wonderful.'

He sighed, thinking of the small square bottle under his desk that he had bought at a very cheap price from the Austrian fellow, Laurenz Gold. All he wanted now was to be rid of this gently persistent woman, although she was rather a looker, he had to admit. Once she'd gone he could nurse his bottle by his fire; sit there and think of his last trip to Rio where he'd palled up with a rather mature dancer for three glorious days of self-indulgence. That was the last of his great adventures: the last freedom before his ship was torpedoed on its way back across the Atlantic; three days in an open boat before they came for him.

Of course that was all before he'd somehow been washed up here with this shipload of misfits and miscreants who were more intent on messing around with the black market than on being properly grateful to the country and its citizens who had given them succour.

Later that day, Kitty cackled with pleasure when she heard of Kay's request to work with the girls on the lines for a couple of weeks. 'You've got hold of the right end of it, love. Anybody who's had an education can write in a few ledgers or add up a few sums. But those girls: the very life-blood of the factory, they are. If you find out what makes those girls tick you'll know how to manage them.'

'It's not just girls, Kitty. There are boys and men there; plenty of them now.'

'Well, I suppose they'll be all right,' said Kitty doubtfully. 'But . . . Anyway, does this mean you'll take me up on my offer?'

Kay shook her head. 'Wait! I'm just starting. And at present I'm still intending to go back, remember! I simply can't get warm in this place.'

Kitty laughed. 'Put another layer of vest and drawers on, and get nearer the fire. You'll soon be so used to it, you won't even notice it.'

But Kay did not believe her. For a while today, laughing and joking with Ginger and Janet, she had forgotten about how hard it all was in this dark land. But she was forced to remember it again as soon as she walked out of the factory, when she was nearly blown off her feet with a cold wind which chilled her to the marrow. How much longer she would last here she really did not know.

Seven

Something to Celebrate

Twelve people gathered in the room where Italian prisoners had once played cards and listened to scratchy records of extracts from *Il Trovatore*. Mr MacAlister, the warden, had set a fire roaring in the hearth making the cobwebby ice patterns on the windows melt into streaming water. The warden had also found two trestle tables and an assortment of pockmarked chairs. The bare wooden boards rang with the clatter of heavy boots as the men, women and children found a place at a table.

Among the twelve people who turned up were Patrizia Gold and her children, and the old Dutchman Willem who had befriended Patrizia. Laurenz and Mikel, she explained to Thomas, had not come because their English was so good they did not need lessons. 'In any case Mikel is packing his bag. He is going to Coventry to look for jobs. Perhaps for both of them.' Her voice was weary and resigned.

The truth was that Laurenz had laughed and said the people at the camp who had anything about them could already speak decent English. Only the old women and the deadbeats were still hanging on, he said, gabbling in their mother tongue.

Mara handed out sheets of paper and black crayons. She wrote on one sheet herself, pinned it up on the wall and read it out loud. '*My name is Mara. I am a teacher.*'

Thomas did the same. '*My name is Thomas. I am an archaeologist.*'

Then he translated his and Mara's words into German,

French, Italian and Dutch, generating smiles of relief all round. Busily the people at the tables checked their words in English with Thomas, and painstakingly wrote them down in large letters on the pieces of paper. Then, one by one, with many blushes and stumbles, they read out:

'My name is Judith. I am a dressmaker.'
'My name is Willem. I am a flower-seller.'
'My name is Walter. I am a silversmith.'
'My name is Jan. I am a hat-maker.'
'My name is Patrizia. I am a mother . . .'

Patrizia wished with all her heart that she could say she was *something*: a dressmaker like old Judith here; a milliner, like her mother. But she'd had no time to *be* anything, as she explained earnestly to Thomas. Just a schoolgirl, then, after *Kristallnacht*, a much maligned Jew. Then Laurenz, then nothing.

Thomas took Peter on his knee and taught him to say out loud: 'I am Peter. I am a boy. This is Rebeka. She is a girl.'

Everyone in the room repeated and repeated their sentences. They said who they were, then said who other people were: 'You are Judith. You are a dressmaker,' said Patrizia to the old woman.

People relaxed; the inner as well as the outer atmosphere of the room warmed up, giggles accompanied the words as they were repeated and repeated with varying accuracy. Those who had worried so long about the awful wall of sound around them, which they could not penetrate, began to relax.

Then they all watched as Mara the teacher pinned up a very strange picture of a large egg with spindly legs and arms and rolling eyes. It was sitting on a wall. Behind it were men with long moustaches wearing red uniforms and high hats. They were all riding high-stepping horses.

'Now,' Mara said, with Thomas translating, 'Thomas will teach Peter a nursery rhyme. A children's poem.'

Line by line, with everyone watching closely, Peter's deep

little voice chanted the rhyme. Thomas did a little work getting Peter to say toge*th*er instead of toge*zz*er, making everyone in the room try as well, with their tongues firmly clamped between their teeth. Then he made Peter say the verse all through. When Peter got round to chanting it a second time, the others were chiming in with individual words, engaged by the punching rhythm. The third time they all joined in together, tapping in time on the trestle tables and finishing by applauding themselves.

Mara clapped her hands. 'That is wonderful. Wonderful.' She glanced at her watch. 'Now that is our hour over.'

Thomas translated. There were groans all round.

'But tomorrow there will be another hour. Then the next day another.'

'And more children's poems?' demanded old Judith, glancing at Thomas. 'Peter should know more poems for when he starts the English school.'

Thomas translated.

Mara laughed. 'Lots more children's poems. One called "I had a little nut tree" tomorrow, I think.' She took down her poster and gave it to Patrizia. 'Would you take charge of this, Patrizia?'

Patrizia glanced at Thomas. 'Tell her I will write it out many times and everyone can have a copy, so they can read it themselves.' She looked around the bare room. 'But can I keep it in here? I could do the copying in here. Laurenz can be so . . .' she paused. 'He takes up so much room.'

Thomas frowned. 'Of course you can. We'll fix it up with Mr MacAlister.'

When they left the hut they found Laurenz lounging around outside. With his polished, slightly sallow skin, Brylcreemed hair and brilliant eyes he had the aura of a film star. He shook Thomas heartily by the hand, then turned, took Mara's hand in his, clicked his heels and touched his lips to her knuckles. 'Madame Derancourt!' he said. 'Such a kindness to teach these poor foreign peasants.'

Mara removed her hand. 'Kind of you to say so,' she said, not meaning that at all.

Laurenz turned to Patrizia, a much sharper note in his voice. 'The water is boiling, Patrizia. Go make the coffee.' She scuttled past him, Rebeka in her arms, holding Peter by the hand.

Laurenz smiled at Thomas and Mara. 'I have Brazilian coffee for our guests.'

Thomas whistled. 'Brazilian!' he said.

They followed behind Patrizia, Laurenz with his arm through Thomas's. 'You are well, Thomas?'

'Very well.'

'Forgive me, won't you, if this is too soon, but I wondered whether you perhaps had had a moment to ask about a job for me? Not Mikel because he has gone off to Coventry today to look for work down there.'

'He went?' said Patrizia, turning sharply. 'He did not say goodbye.'

Laurenz shrugged. 'I took him into Priorton for the long-distance bus. He would have missed it.'

Thomas nodded. 'A job, Laurenz? Well, to be honest it seems as though it's my sister who has the say on that side of things now. But she's been out so much at the dratted factory I've hardly seen her.'

'But perhaps she will find a place?' Laurenz persisted.

'I promise you, I will talk to her tonight.'

'Tell her I can make anything from anything. I can solve problems. I have served time with a Swiss toolmaker though I have no papers. We both do this, both Mikel and me. Though I am the best. Mikel will acknowledge that. Mikel has so much of the slow farmer in him, though he is a good man.'

Thomas and Mara only stayed the time it took to gulp their coffee. They mentioned the darkness settling in and left as soon as they could.

Laurenz sat down at the table and poured the last of the coffee from the jug. 'Well, Patrizia,' he said, 'I think between us we have snared that one.'

Patrizia frowned at him. 'That is a terrible thing to say.'

'Don't you think he is terribly attractive, in that tousled

professor fashion? Surely you are not such a log of wood as to miss that?' He leant over and ran an immaculate finger down her cheek.

She pulled herself away from his touch. 'You are ridiculous.' She glanced round uneasily, missing Mikel.

He laughed. 'Perhaps you are right. There is something very soft about him. Too much time amongst women. How strange he allowed that sister of his to go to the grandmother's factory rather than himself. It is obvious that it is the factory where the fortune is to be made.'

Patrizia stood, picked Rebeka up and held out her hand to Peter.

'Where are you going now?' he said.

'Back to the recreation hut. It will still be warm there. I have some writing to do for tomorrow. For Mara Derancourt.'

'Writing for Mara Derancourt!' he mocked and burst into laughter. He followed her to the door and bawled after her: 'You enjoy your writing, Patrizia. I am off to Durham to do some business. I will be very late, you can be sure of that.'

Mr MacAlister smelt of rum when he came to the door, but he chucked Peter under the chin and gave Patrizia the hut key willingly enough. Inside the hut, she stoked the fire vigorously to enliven the flame. She was boiling up inside and she didn't quite know why. Her years with Laurenz had numbed her to all his bullying, but now, day by day, she was getting more angry. And with Mikel gone she had cause to be more frightened. It had been such fun today in Mara Derancourt's class. Peter had enjoyed it, his pale eyes gleaming as he chanted that ridiculous Humpty Dumpty poem. Thomas had been so kind. Perhaps, yes, with a woman's kindness. And she had liked that, that womanish quality. Seven years with Laurenz had inured her to the powerful attractions of a very male man.

> Humpty Dumpty sat on a wall,
> Humpty Dumpty had a great fall . . .

Peter's voice pierced her reflections and she laughed, joining in with his rhyme, encouraged that English of a sort was pouring from her lips.

Kitty looked up as Leonora peered through the sitting-room window.

Kay was sitting at the table trying to make some kind of sense out of a pile of production schedule books she had wrested from the grasp of the unwilling Captain, who was daily more alarmed at the interest she was showing in the Works.

Florence was on the floor playing with the train set which Kitty had asked Mrs MacMahon to rake out of the loft. Some parts of the train set were broken but Kitty and Florence had managed to mend it, after finding the stray pieces in the boxes. They had sat on the floor for an hour about this intricate task.

Leonora closed the curtains, shutting out the dark. 'Another bad night, I'm afraid. Doesn't that howling wind make you shudder?'

Kitty sighed. 'You're just like young Kay here, hungering always for the sun.'

Leonora shook her head. 'No. Not me. I was the one over there who was always escaping from the sun. I never seemed to manage to cool down. Sometimes I spent the whole day looking for the deepest, coolest shadow.' She smiled faintly. 'But mostly, of course, I didn't notice the heat because I was talking, or working, with Sam. And the last years were very busy, keeping things right for him. Even the simplest things.'

Kitty stared into the fire. Her own husband William had been frail in his last years, but not cast down, like Sam. A coal dropped and the fire leapt. Now she could make out William's face, forming and dissolving as the flames danced and spurted. He was smiling and nodding in that way he had.

'I see him all the time, you know,' she said abruptly.

Leonora frowned. 'Sam?'

Kitty shook her head. 'William. In the fire, in the clouds in the sky. In the river as it swirls away. I sometimes take the car down the road just near the viaduct. And I see him in the water.'

'Does it worry you?'

'No, no. William was my lifelong friend. He'll do me no harm.'

'Have you always seen him?'

Kitty shook her head. 'Just recently. Just since . . . I suppose since I knew you were coming. No, since just after I wrote you the letter, telling you about the party.' She paused. 'To be honest I only thought up the party to get you here.'

Leonora clapped her hand to her head. 'We should get on with that! Thursday! Party on Sunday, and nothing's done.'

Kitty waved a hand as fragile as a bunch of twigs. 'Don't worry your head about any of that. Duggie's friend Mrs MacMahon's seeing to it. It will be a Durham delight. Home-baked ham, leek pies, egg-and-bacon pies, queen cakes and her special cream horns.' She grinned. 'You can see why Duggie is putting on weight. His work suit hardly fits him any more. Mrs MacMahon's always complaining about it but she's to blame.'

'Well, will there be just us there?' said Kay. 'At the party?'

'Just the family. And Duggie and Mrs MacMahon. Which is family really. I don't usually make being too old an excuse, as you know, but I think I am too old to bother with those things where you have to sit around, not knowing who half the people are.'

Leonora nodded. 'I think I must be too old for that too. But I never liked it anyway. Even when I was young.'

'In that case I'm too old too,' chimed in Kay.

'Me too,' echoed Florence, making them all laugh.

Kitty looked at the clock on the mantelpiece. 'Thomas and Mara have been quite a time.'

Leonora laughed. 'Thick as thieves, those two. Off to their refugees again. That's three times this week.'

'It keeps Mara's mind off Jean-Paul,' said Kitty. 'She's missing him, though she doesn't make a song and dance about it.'

'And it keeps Thomas out of my hair,' said Kay. She closed the ledger and took a breath. 'He doesn't want to come to the factory but he moans about me vanishing across there every day. Sometimes he seems so young.' She paused. 'Kitty?' she said.

'Yes, dear?'

'I've decided to do it.'

'Do what? What?'

'I'll work at the factory for two years and see . . . well, I'll see.'

Kitty was smiling broadly. 'What? And miss all that sunshine? All those flies?'

Kay picked up the heavy ledger. 'Kitty Rainbow, if you start to mock I'll throw this book at your head!'

'No!' Florence leapt towards Kitty and stood protectively beside her knee. 'She's my Grandma Kitty and no one is to hurt her.'

The Captain was less than happy to be told the new proprietor would be the young girl from Alexandria. He had spent most of the war politely keeping the old woman Kitty out of his hair and now here he had a slip of a girl to whom he must kowtow.

Kitty had collected her from the production line on her way to the office to communicate the news to the Captain. So, Kay was still in her work overall when she sat facing the Captain in his sparse office. She watched his grim face as he took in the news from her grandmother. Taking effect immediately, Kay Fitzgibbon, her granddaughter, was owner of the Rainbow Works.

'Well, I am sure I must congratulate you, Miss . . . Mrs Fitzgibbon,' he said stiffly. 'I think Miss Rainbow will have told you that the Works have been running very smoothly indeed, production is up, though there is some problem with sales. Profit is very tidy even in these bleak days. And this is so even though Miss Rainbow's own experienced hand has been off the tiller for some time.'

'I've no intention of getting in your hair, Captain Marshall,' Kay said, then coloured as she remembered his bald dome. 'I thought what I might do, for a while at least, was work my way through the departments. On the lines at first, then production control, then planning, then wages . . . Duggie will slot me in. I won't interfere.'

He shook his massive head. 'You won't be able to resist it, Mrs Fitzgibbon, getting your fingers into the pie. Any more than I could.'

'Anyway,' she said reassuringly, 'it would take me ten years to get the kind of grip on the whole thing which you have now.'

'Kind of you to say so, ma'am,' he said drily.

She went red. 'And, although the papers are drawn up, we want no one to know this until I am ready. As far as anyone will know I am simply Kitty's granddaughter who happens to be working here during her stay in England.'

He picked up a pen. 'Very well. Now if you good ladies would excuse me, I have a scheduling meeting to prepare.'

They were dismissed.

Kitty stood back and watched Kay take a step towards the desk. 'There is one thing.' Kay put her hands on the desk and leant towards him. 'There is an Austrian, a refugee protégé of my brother. I would like work found here for him.'

The picture of patient, enduring control, the Captain placed his pen back on the desk and shrugged his shoulders. 'It's your factory, Mrs Fitzgibbon. If you drop into Personnel on your way out and give them your instructions . . .?'

She was already shaking her head. 'No, Captain. I'll inform this man he should attend here on Monday. Perhaps you would inform the Personnel department yourself.'

'Attagirl!' said Kitty as they came away from the admin. block and made their way towards the car. 'Don't let him walk all over you. Even so, Kay, he's a very good manager. Hard – even rather harsh – but the place works. It ticks over. You should think carefully before you change anything.'

'Change? That's a joke. It's taking me all my time screwing the wires into the wiring harness. Ginger's getting madder at me by the minute because I'm losing her her bonus. How can I think I could run a factory?'

'You made him take on that Austrian.'

'That was just because he was dismissing us like naughty girls. I'd forgotten about him. Thomas asked about it again last night. He just popped into my mind.'

'Still, it's not a bad start, Kay. Not bad at all.'

Back at home that Friday night Thomas was delighted with Kay's news. But his delight was swept away amid the hubbub in the kitchen where preparations for Kitty's birthday were under way. Normally he would have joined in, helping his mother to mix the pastry or decorate the cakes. But with Mara and Kitty and Mrs MacMahon as well as Leonora working away the place felt too full of women. So when Kitty told him not to worry, they could manage, he put on his cap and made his way out of the house and down into the town.

There was a Friday night buzz about the place: women standing in drizzle at the bus-stops, their shopping bags at their feet; men in twos and threes, elbow to elbow, walking the length of the street, stopping and greeting first one man then another, then strolling back and dropping into one of the pubs.

Thomas followed their progress and counted twenty-nine pubs, ranging from the battered grandeur of the Gaunt Valley Hotel to the steamed windows and greasy door of the Royal George, where he knew his own mother had been born. Or was it that she was there just after she was born? Something like that.

He went in and through a door with 'Public Bar' etched on the window. Heads swivelled as he found himself a seat on a velour-covered bench which was bald with age. Most of the men wore suits and caps. Some had ties, some had silk neckerchieves round their throats. The suit jackets on the young men strained over muscles more used to pit shirts than the constraints of shiny serge.

The man behind the bar, whose braces were showing below

a waistcoat which didn't quite meet the trousers hoisted up over his smoothly round belly, shouted across to Thomas. 'What's it to be, lad?'

'Do you have red wine?'

More heads turned at this and the barman cackled. 'No, son, seems like we've run out of red wine.'

'Beer, then.'

'Pint or half-pint?'

He looked at the men standing by and leaning on the bar. They had pint glasses in front of them. 'Pint,' he said.

The barman drew a pint into a straight glass and pushed it on to the bar. 'That'll be fourpence,' he said.

Thomas lay his belted raincoat over the back of his chair and walked across to pick up his drink. The barman, drawing another pint for the next man, looked up. 'New round here, are ye?'

'Yes. Yes.' He put down a sixpence.

'Been in the army then?'

He shook his head. 'No, I lived abroad.'

'Thowt yer looked a bit of a blackie, like.' There was a snigger round the bar.

'Well actually . . .'

The *actually* was whispered after him, behind him, near the window.

'. . . actually I come from round here originally,' he said. He put his foot on the bar rail, took a gulp of the beer which nearly made him retch with its bitterness. 'I was born in this town. My parents and grandparents came from here.'

Parents and grandparents . . . another mocking echo.

'What they ca-al them, your muther an' fa-ather then,' said the man beside him, winking at the barman. 'Fauntleroy?'

'Scorton. My father was called Scorton. And my mother was Rainbow.'

He felt rather than saw the ripple of interest along the bar. 'There's an old woman Rainbow has the Works down back of Priors' Way. Her name's Rainbow.'

'So it is,' said Thomas.

'Proper old crow,' said his neighbour.

'They do say she never got married. Lived tally all her life. Had a family and everything,' said the barman.

'Factory got prizes in the war, for output. All them weapons and shells, like.'

'Factories!' A heavily built man at the end of the bar put on his glasses and peered at Thomas, then spat into a conveniently placed spittoon. 'Give us the pit every time. Man's work.'

'You work at the pit?' asked Thomas.

'Work at it?' said his neighbour. 'He lives it, breathes it. He'll own it soon if his Labour marrahs have their day!'

'Aye,' said the pitman with satisfaction. 'Nationalisation. NCB. Nee mair bosses.'

'My mother's father was a miner . . . a pitman,' volunteered Thomas.

'Where'd he work, then?' Interest sparkled in the man's deep-set eyes.

'White Leas. I believe it was White Leas Pit.'

'What was his name?'

'Freddie Longstaffe. He was killed, way back. Before even my mother was born. Even she never knew him. He was killed, trapped by tubs. That's the story, anyway.'

'Well, I'll be buggered. Had an inkling, like, when yer mentioned being a Rainbow,' said the man. He heaved himself from the bar stool and walked round to where Thomas was standing. Before Thomas could stop him he had grasped his hand and was pumping it up and down. 'Hugh Longstaffe, son. My father was another Hugh and he was brother to Freddie Longstaffe.' He stood back and peered at Thomas with half-closed eyes. 'An' the Rainbow woman at the factory is your grandma then? 'Cause she was Freddie's . . . like . . . girl then. Years ago, like. Dark Ages.'

'Married no other, never after,' supplied the barman.

'But you know about all this?' Thomas asked the man.

'Me da often telt us. He liked old Kitty.'

'Kitty never mentions him.'

Hugh Longstaffe shrugged. 'Time goes by. When Kitty got so up in the world, shops she had, then factories.'

'Capitalists in Hugh's book,' said the barman. 'Him being a bloody Communist, like.'

Hugh didn't deny this. 'Me dad'd never bothered her, so why should I?' He was still staring at Thomas. 'Here, let's get yer a pint, son.'

Thomas swallowed the last of the bitter liquid and pushed his stained glass towards the barman. He was charmed by the thought of this little hidden bit of his own history, and the big man with his wide good-humoured face was part of that. 'I'll buy this one,' he said, pushing Hugh's hand away from his pocket. Then Hugh gave him a look.

'No,' he said. 'Let a man buy you a drink, will yer?'

They went to sit back on the bench seat and Hugh started to question Thomas carefully about himself. Thomas explained his work on the fringes of archaeology.

Hugh laughed. 'Diggin' things up? I could tell you a few things about digging things up. Only the things I dig up are millions of years old, not thousands. Fishes, plants, animals, petrified in the stone. Got a box full in my house. I'll let yer see them sometime.'

It was ten o'clock when the peace of the kitchen at Blamire House was interrupted by a raucous rendering at the door of 'Lili Marlene'.

Underneath the lamplight, by the barrack gate . . .

Leonora picked up a kitchen broom and opened the broad door. On a gale of laughter, old beer, tobacco and damp dust, Thomas fell in, followed by a massive figure with very broad shoulders and a shock of grey hair.

'Thomas! What in heaven . . .'

'Mother,' he said, putting an arm round her shoulders. 'I have a s-surprise for you. Guess who this is?'

Leonora frowned up at the big man with the deep sharp eyes. She shook her head. 'I'm sorry I . . .' she turned to

Thomas. 'Thomas, what are you up to?'

'Mother, this is your f-f-first cousin, Mr Hugh Longstaffe.'

'Well!' Kitty was coming into the kitchen in her dressing-gown, a poker in her hand; Kay was fighting to get in front in a vain attempt to defend her. The old woman went and stood before the stranger, peering up at him. 'Hughie Longstaffe, is it you?'

'Yes it is, but not the one you think. Hughie Longstaffe, who was brother to Freddie, was my father. They call me Hugh.'

Kitty put the poker in the hearth. 'You're very like him. He was a big strong man.'

'Hewer in the pit,' said Hugh. 'Just like me.'

'Tell me about Freddie Longstaffe,' said Kay later as she and her mother washed up the dishes after the late supper they had put on for their unexpected guest.

'History really. Back in the last century. Do I go that far back? He and Kitty were childhood sweethearts and were about to marry when he was killed in this terrible accident at the pit. Of course I was on the way by then.'

'That must have been hard on Kitty. A child . . .'

'Out of wedlock? Well, when you think of it, we were all born out of wedlock. Mara and Tommy as well as me. She never did marry William Scorton, although they took his name.'

'Didn't people say anything?'

'Well, it was a funny thing. She did things in her own way and people respected her in the end. They called her a "one off". It's a term they use round here.'

'So what about Freddie Longstaffe?'

Leonora shrugged. 'I never asked, really. I always took William as my father.' She smiled suddenly. 'She did tell me they only did the deed once, on a gravestone in Priorton cemetery, and I am the result.'

Kay found herself blushing. 'Think of it!'

'Anyway,' said Leonora briskly, 'you should thank goodness it happened or you and Thomas, and I, wouldn't be here.'

'Funny, though,' said Kay, folding up the tea towel. 'To think that you and Florence are the same. Growing up without your father, never really knowing him.'

The next morning Kay came down early for her seven-thirty start to find Kitty in the kitchen, sitting staring into the already flaring fire.

'Early bird, Kitty?'

'Couldn't sleep, love. Thinking about Freddie and recalling those old times. I've been sitting here trying to see him in the flames, but do you know I can't quite recall the face? Now I'm worried in case I won't recognise him.'

'Won't recognise him when?'

'On the other side, when I move over.'

'You think that, believe that? That there is a Heaven? Another side as you call it?' Kay and Thomas had been brought up without religion. In Alexandria they had been surrounded by Muslims; even Mr Kohn, whilst very Egyptian, was of the Jewish faith.

'I don't know about Heaven, Kay, but I know they're waiting in some place beyond. All of them. Duggie told me that William came in a vision to your Uncle Tommy just before the execution. Tommy saw him. If William was waiting for Tommy, he will be waiting for me.' She laughed. 'And now I'm being reminded that Freddie Longstaffe'll be waiting too. And Ishmael. It's going to be a bit crowded there.'

Kay knew about Ishmael: how he had found the baby Kitty. Thrown by her distraught mother, she came hurtling from the great Priorton railway viaduct right into his arms. That day a triple rainbow hung over the viaduct: an inspiration to Ishmael when he named his new foster daughter.

'Tell me about Freddie,' said Kay now.

'Well, let me see. We were in the same class at school. He was very bonny, I think, a great mischief but very clever. Won a scholarship. Worked in a chemist's shop, then went down the pit with his brothers. Man's work, you see?' A short laugh barked out. 'Man's death.'

'Did you love him?'

Kitty's eyes, bright as an old bird's, settled on her. 'Did you love Stephen?'

Kay hesitated. 'To be honest, I can't remember.'

'So how do you think I can remember? We're talking seventy years back. And in between there has been so much.' She stood up. 'Now have some breakfast and I'll make you some sandwiches. Are you on the Saturday shift?'

'Yes, I'm at work today. Ginger calls it her bait. She's always wanting to share hers.'

That Sunday, by invitation, Hugh Longstaffe came to Kitty's birthday party and was introduced to everyone as Leonora's first cousin. He sat at the table beside Leonora, and their heads stayed close together as they talked of the Longstaffe family and compared identical birthmarks on their forearms. Touched and inspired by their interest, Hugh talked to them of the pit where he worked. 'I was a hewer, like. But always getting kicked upstairs, that's my problem. Then I got mixed up in a strike and now I'm back at the coal face.'

He talked of the mystery and the danger down below. Of the deep blackness which is the heart of a mine, where, open or closed, your eyes cannot see. 'Thomas here was telling of the opening of an ancient grave untouched for two thousand years. Well, down there we see what no human eye has seen before, the very fold of the earth from the beginning of time.'

He spoke of the way the earth revealed its riches, bit by grudging bit, to the miners. How a miner used more than his strength painfully to abstract this amazing stuff for the hearth and the anvil of the world. How he needed high skill to know just where to rake away and pull the coal down, where to tickle it off the face with just the right amount of force.

'Have you ever worked these very narrow seams one reads about?' asked Mara.

He nodded. 'Twenty-two, twenty-four inches deep down here in South Durham.'

'It must be physically impossible to get into them,' said Thomas disbelievingly.

'How do you do it?' said Mara.

'Do you really want to know?' he said.

'I do.'

'You lie down on your back with your tools on your chest and hitch backwards, ever backwards, until you reach the place where you're to work. Then you kind of turn on your side and pull your pick up and start to work. Some lads use a kind of shoulder sledge. But sometimes there's not even room for that.'

Thomas shook his head. 'Amazing!' he said.

'You should try it,' said Hugh. 'My da and Uncle Albert were good'ns down there. And Freddie, your granda' – he glanced at Kitty, who was watching him very closely – 'died down there, o'course.'

Kay thought of Freddie, dying young, crushed underground; of her Uncle Tommy dying young, shot by his own fellow soldiers on a muddy battlefield; and of Stephen whose face she could not conjure up now, mown down in a blackened London street.

Hugh went on: 'Our Freddie would have gone on, been a hewer, been good too, if the pit had left him alone.'

Leonora shuddered. 'What a way to earn a living.'

Hugh shot her a sharp glance. 'It's a great craft. Dinnet forget it's the coal that was the driving engine for the war and further back the factories and ironworks and the ships which made the country great. Always at the behest of the owners, like. Always to line their pockets with gold. But not for long,' he finished proudly. 'Soon it'll all belong to the people.'

Leonora regarded him. 'Our Thomas says you're a Communist.'

'Nowt wrong with that, or why did we fight the war against the Fascists?'

'I didn't say anything was wrong, Hugh. I knew Communists myself, during the Great War. I was in Russia during the revolution.'

His face lit up. 'Were you? A privilege, like, to be there at that time.'

'It was in turmoil. Hard to see what was really happening. Some terrible things have gone on there since, they say.'

'The capitalist press has its prejudices.'

'Will it make any difference, the mines being run like this?' put in Thomas, more interested in the here and now.

'It'll be a sight safer down there at the very least. Allus cutting corners, the owners, their job being to screw out as much profit as they can. As an overman once, before I got cast down again, safety is what I had to deal with. Never liked kowtowing to the owners over safety. Stuck in my craw, that did. Gorrus into trouble.'

Florence, who had been sitting at Kitty's right-hand side, announced she was full and asked if she could get down.

Kitty took her hand and stood up herself. 'I think I've had enough as well.'

'Kitty, I was going to do a speech,' said Duggie.

'No you won't,' said Kitty, 'I'm too tired for all that. You all stay and have a nice chat and Flo and me will go into the sitting room and play trains.'

They watched the oldest and the youngest member of the family leave, then returned their attention to Hugh. 'How did you start in the pit, then?' asked Mara.

It was an hour before they finally rose from the table and trickled, one by one, into the sitting room where Florence was playing on her own with the train set on the floor.

'Where's Grandma Kitty, Flo?' said Leonora, glancing around.

Florence wound up her train. 'She's gone to see William,' she said.

Mara frowned. 'William?'

Florence nodded. 'She said to say to Momma that she had gone to see William and . . . and F—Freddie.'

Kay put her hand on Leonora's arm. 'We'll search the house.'

Kitty was nowhere to be found. Duggie came in from out the

back to say the car had gone. 'She's gone in the car somewhere?' said Mara. 'Where would she go?'

'The river,' said Kay. 'She said she saw William in the fire, and in the sky and the river. She's taken the car to the viaduct.'

They pulled on their coats and started to run. It took ten minutes to get to the viaduct. Mara, on her long legs, passed Duggie and Hugh Longstaffe to lead the way and Kay trailed behind, pulling Florence along as fast as she could.

The car was parked at the head of the path which cut down through the water meadow to the great stone feet of the viaduct. Mara led the way, her long legs crashing through the high grass, slipping and sliding on the slope. Kay stopped at the head of the path and lifted the sobbing Florence in her arms. She watched blankly as the others reached the edge of the water, where Kitty was lying face down, her body half in, half out of the water.

'What is it, Momma? What is it?' cried Florence. 'Why did Grandma Kitty go to sleep in the water?'

It was the big pitman, Hugh Longstaffe, who lifted Kitty's body up the bank and insisted on walking back with her in his arms all the way up The Lane to Blamire House. Leonora and Mara walked alongside and the rest rode in the car. The procession drew curious glances from children, slicked down in their Sunday best, on their way to Sunday School at the Central Methodist Church.

Hugh placed Kitty on her bed, and Leonora, set-faced, started to tidy her up, dry her face, push back her sodden hair, trying in vain to make her look her normal self. Duggie had run for the doctor, but Leonora knew that Kitty wouldn't like even the doctor to see her in such disarray.

The rest of them sat in the kitchen, Kay with Florence on her knee looking into the flames of the fire; Hugh Longstaffe leaning on the wide window-sill and Mara beside him, staring out of the window. Thomas, thoroughly agitated, was walking up and down between the table and the door.

'I know what she did! What she tried to do,' announced Kay.

'Don't t-talk nonsense,' said Thomas bitterly. 'We all know what she did. She d-drowned herself.'

'I'm not talking nonsense, I . . .' Kay's voice faded and her glassy eyes returned to the fire.

Mara cast an agonised glance at Hugh, who went across and put a hand on Thomas's shoulder. 'What say you an' me go out for a bit of a walk, son? Nothing we can do here.'

The door clicked behind them and Mara went and lifted Florence from Kay's lap and hoisted her to show her her own reflection in the overmantel mirror.

Mara glanced down at her niece. 'Now then, love, what do you think Kitty was doing?'

'Can you remember her telling us she was always seeing William? In the fire, in the clouds, in the water, she said.'

'Yes. I remember that.'

'Well, she talked again to me about it. That William was waiting there for her. And Freddie. And Ishmael.'

'Well?'

'I think she went to them. Isn't that the place where Ishmael first caught her? In the water? Where she came into his world?'

'Yes, it is.'

'Well, I think she went there to join them. To go out of this world where she came in.'

'Nonsense. That can't be. She was just having her dinner with us. No thought of committing . . .'

Kay shook her head. 'I don't think she committed suicide. I just think she went to be with them. Nothing else.'

The tension went out of Mara. 'I hope you're right. I never pray, but I pray you're right.'

At that moment Leonora came through the door, an enamel dish in her hand, a towel over her arm. Kay took them from her and made her sit down. 'Are you all right?' she said.

Leonora brushed her hair back from her face with the back of her hand. 'She looks sweet up there,' she said. 'Her real self. But d'you know what I was thinking up there, just as I was finishing off?'

Kay shook her head.

'I was thinking that now I am the oldest woman in our family and just now I feel very, very old. And I don't feel wise enough to be that old. Not wise enough at all.'

Later, in bed with the reflected light from a street lamp streaming through the window, Kay lay thinking about Kitty who had been so full of life, despite her gammy leg and growing frailty. Just look how she knew how to engage Florence's interest, dissipate her fear. How she had plotted to get Kay herself in place at the factory. How she had plotted to get them back, halfway across the world on the pretext of a party. They should have known. The last thing Kitty would be interested in was a party to celebrate herself, her own birthday.

It was just her managing things. And now she had managed her own death. Not by drowning herself; such a negative thing, suicide. No, Kitty was not 'giving up', she was 'going towards'. Kay closed her eyes and for a split second she was Kitty, treading the edges of the water, arms out, walking towards shadowy figures shining with light, all with their arms open, waiting.

Kay opened her eyes, herself again. She turned over and stretched out, ready to sleep, certain that she had shared that last second with Kitty. Just as certain as she had been in Alexandria, about the identity of the potters who had made the pots those thousands of years ago.

[illegible]

[illegible]

[illegible]

Eight

The Idea of Working in the Pit

Hugh walked with Thomas out of the town through the fields to Bracks' Hill village, which lay under the shadow of a great spoil heap alongside the massive double pit wheel which, like its human co-workers, was having its eerie Sunday rest.

'There we are, son, White Leas Pit,' said Hugh. 'Your grandfather, Kitty's man, worked there just a short time. My dad Hugh and Uncle Albert worked there all their lives. It's an old pit, no baths there yet, like there is at some pits. So the men has to go home in their muck. I've worked there all my life, bar that time in twenty-six when we stuck it out on strike till November. Much good it did us. My son Harry worked there straight from school. Got his deputy's tickets real early and trained up as an engineer. Then he signed up with the DLI to fight for King and Country. Western desert with Monty, and in Germany. All that stuff. Never came back here, like.'

Thomas held his breath. He did not want to ask the obvious question and find out about another death. Not today.

'Some people say you shouldn't blame him. South Durham pits're hard cheese. Low seams; plodging in water half the time. No, our Harry got a taste for it, that war shenanigans. Stayed a soldier. Bomb disposal at first. Used to facing death in the pit, no problem with danger above ground. Took a commission in the end. Quite the toff now, with his swagger stick. Training other lads down South.'

Thomas looked at the pit wheel and the grimy buildings.

'How can you bear it, Hugh? Being down there out of the light, all day long?'

'Bear it? Why man, it's bloody wonderful.'

'Wonderful?'

'Grant you it's bloody hard. Heartbreaking, sometimes. But just think. You're down there at the heart of it. It's a secret place with its silver walls of coal, a place only few gets to share. Beside that, the petty ways of man fall into place. A feller from the office comes and tells yer "what for" and you look at him and you know he'd never fill a tub in a thousand years. He'd never know what to do in a two-foot seam; he's never sat with his marrahs in the deep earth and worked out a plan for a brave new world. On the other hand, like, I know I can do his job, pen-pushing. I was top of my school before I left to go in the pit, just like our Harry – but could that pen-pusher as hell do my job? That's why pitmen never give quarter, son. That's why we're called bolshy, and mostly are.' Hugh stopped and leant on a fence and Thomas followed suit.

'But you'll get no finer lot of men, I'm tellin' yer. It stood our Harry in good stead in the army. Place to recognise a real man there. They say Monty liked the miners' battalions; it was nothing new to them, depending on each other; facing death each day.' Hugh lit his pipe, fiddling with it a while before he got it to a satisfying glow.

'Me wife used to say otherwise, like. Clubby, clannish, she called us, hated the pit, she did. Didn't care for pitmen, even. But women don't know about these things, son. They've no idea.'

'Used to?' Another death.

'She died. Nineteen-thirty. Poliomyelitis. It was going round just then. Bad times. But then I brought the lad up meself. Little team, we was, our Harry and me. Till that devil Hitler raked him away from me hearth, like.'

Down in the town the church bells started to ring for evening service. 'I have to get back,' said Thomas, uneasy suddenly at the thought of the women back in the house, and Kitty lying more than asleep on her bed in the front bedroom.

'Right, son. We'll get yer back.'

They turned and walked in a companionable silence towards the town with its Church at one end and its castellated priory at the other, sitting neatly within the coils of the River Gaunt. 'Canny town, this,' said Hugh. 'Decent place for a man to live. Good market. Good pubs. Canny people.'

They stopped near some short pit rows just on the edge of the town. 'I'll peel off now, son,' said Hugh. 'I'll try me best to get to the old girl's funeral. An' I'm sorry it turned out like this. Though at her age, for Kitty Rainbow to make such a choice has, like, a bit of tone to it. I'm glad I knew her even for a bit. Seems to me now me Uncle Freddie knew just what Kitty Rainbow was about, lad that he was. Younger than you when he died, come to think of it. Less than twenty.'

Thomas digested the thought that the man who had fathered his mother never reached beyond the age of twenty, while he himself had never indulged in or even achieved the act that would father anybody. His close relationship with Kay, which had its hugs and affectionate side, had always seemed enough.

He shook the other man heartily by the hand. 'Funny thing, meeting you like that, Hugh. But I'm glad I did.'

Hugh nodded. 'Let's know about the funeral, son. I'd like to pay my respects, like.'

Kay went to the Works on the Monday because she decided that that was what Kitty would have wanted. Captain Marshall came down on to the line to offer his condolences. He was clearly surprised to see her. 'Perhaps it will be seen as a little indelicate, your being here, Mrs Fitzgibbon?'

'Kitty wouldn't think so. Perhaps you mean *you* think it is indelicate, Captain Marshall? To be honest, it has been an awful effort to come today but I came because I thought Kitty would think it right. Now she's gone, perhaps more than ever I need to be here.'

The Captain nodded curtly and walked off the line.

'Good kid,' said Ginger approvingly. 'You show the old bugger.'

That morning both Ginger and Janet helped her to reach her minimum score. Just for once they did not curse her for the fumble-fingered beginner that she was.

It was after their breakfast break that she looked up to see Ralph, the progress lad, wheeling his trolley of oven knobs, wire and washers down the line. Today he had the assistance of a newcomer whose brown skin and oily, dark, slicked-back hair reminded her of the market boys in Alexandria. But this was no boy: a man, rather. Perhaps even as old as Mara. He walked with a swagger; everything about him marked him out as different. As he unloaded wires into the basket beside her and Ginger's bench he looked up at her, caught her glance and winked.

'Oh, Kay, we've got a cocky one here,' said Ginger. 'And what's your name, little boy?'

He swept off an imaginary hat and bowed. 'Laurenz Gold, madame. Perhaps you would introduce me to your beautiful assistant here?'

'Ooh, get him,' called Janet from the other side of the line. 'Buggerlugs with a side parting. What are yeh, a Frenchie?'

Ralph stood back, arms folded, watching the performance with narrow eyes.

The man clicked his heels and bowed. 'I am from Vienna, madame, the most romantic city in the world. Where they invented the cream cake and the waltz. So!' He waltzed around in the space between the lines, an imaginary partner in his arms.

'Give over, will yer?' said Ralph.

'He's a bleedin' Nazzy,' said Ginger, suddenly frosty.

'No, no, madame. I am the *bleedin' Nazi's* enemy. I shoot them, I blow them up. Pouf! Like this. They chase me out. So I come here.' He knelt down in the dust beside Kay. 'And what is your name, o beautiful, silent one?'

Ginger shoved him with her high heel. 'Her name's Kay, you bliddy Don Juan.'

'Kay? A strange name. I never heard that name.'

'Short for Katherine,' said Kay.

'Now get lost,' said Ginger, 'or our Ralph here'll have your guts for garters.'

'Aye, gerron!' said Ralph sulkily. 'You'll gerrus both the sack at this rate.'

Laurenz stood up, dusted his knees and smiled dazzlingly at Ralph. 'Of course, of course you're right. Now we gotta work twice as fast to make it up.'

Still busy with her wiring Ginger watched the two men progress down the line. She said to Kay, 'Well, what do you think, flower? Nice bit o' goods, that? Wouldn't mind meeting him on a dance night? That what yer thinkin'?'

Kay coloured, but she realised that this was Ginger trying to help her keep her chin up, keep her cheerful on this difficult day. She entered into the spirit of it. 'He's quite . . . attractive.'

'Quite attractive, quite attractive? He's a bloody Nazzy spiv, that one, flower. I'd watch my step with him if I were you.'

That night the Austrian was waiting for her at the gate as she came out of work. He was leaning on a motor bike smoking a cigarette. He whistled. 'Hey, Kathee!'

She kept her head down. He jerked the bike off its stand and walked it alongside her. 'How about a lift home, Kathee? I take you, you save bus fare.'

'No thanks,' she said. She nodded across the road, to where Thomas was sitting scowling in Kitty's car. Angry with her for coming to the factory under the circumstances, he had insisted that he would take her to work and bring her back.

'I've got a lift,' she said now to Laurenz Gold.

He blinked across at Thomas; his face cleared and he beamed. 'What? What? Is Thomas your boyfriend?' He shunted his bike across to the car. 'Thomas, my friend, you are a lucky dog. This beautiful girl—'

'Is my sister.' Thomas pushed the door open for Kay. 'Get in, will you? Now, Laurenz old boy, will you just go home? Today is not the day for any fooling round. We have a bereavement.

Our grandmother has died. Would you kindly tell Patrizia and the others that Mara and I will not manage to attend the classes this week? Of course we'll be there again next week.'

When they got away from the factory Kay said, 'Is that your Austrian?'

'So it is. Didn't you know? It was you who put a good word in for him.'

'He's very pushy.'

'You'd have to be, I imagine, to survive what they have, that family.'

Behind them, Laurenz Gold stood astride his bike, watching them with a smile on his face. Better and better, he thought.

When Laurenz reached home Patrizia was sitting half asleep in a chair with the baby in her arms. Her mind was many miles away.

> *It is a hot summer day in a pavement café on the Kärntnerstrasse. I am sitting with my friend Liesl wearing my pale lilac silk dress and the frothy hat Mama made me for my sixteenth birthday. Liesl and I are sharing a* Sachertorte, *spooning the cream into each other's mouths . . .*

Laurenz crashed through the door and Patrizia jumped, instinctively fearful. But Laurenz was in a very good mood: he picked up baby Rebeka and tossed her into the air until her giggles had just about melted into tears. Peter watched carefully, wary that it might be his turn next to experience such joy.

But his father turned to his mother. 'And what progress have we made today with our English baby-rhymes?'

'We can say six of them now,' said Patrizia.

He turned to Peter. 'Come here, Peter, and say these rhymes for Papa,' he said. Slowly Peter made his way across the room and Laurenz pulled him between his knees and held him there tightly. With much nodding and mouthing from Patrizia, Peter stumbled through 'Humpty Dumpty', and 'I had a little nut tree', then he stalled on 'Baa baa, black sheep'. Hurriedly Patrizia joined in, nodding hard at him as he mumbled wordlessly with her.

Laurenz pushed Peter away from him, so hard that he fell to the ground. 'The child is an imbecile,' he said. 'Takes after his mother.'

Patrizia lay the baby on the bed, drew Peter to his feet and brushed the dust from his legs. 'Don't fret, little one, don't fret.'

Laurenz lit a cigarette and stared at them both through the smoke. Then he stood up. 'You must be a good boy and take care of your sister for a little while,' he said abruptly. 'Mama and Papa will go to the classroom where Papa will teach Mama a nice English love song called "The Foggy Dew".' He held a hand out to Patrizia. 'Come!' he said.

She looked around the bare hut which she had tried to make homely with cloths and cushions. She knew better than to resist Laurenz. She lifted Peter on to the bed. 'Now sit still, and mind your sister, *liebling*. Mama will be back soon.'

The warden, sick of being interrupted, had allowed Patrizia to keep one of the keys. He said as she seemed to be in charge of the class she might as well have the key and he'd be left in peace.

There in the dusty dark, Laurenz pulled her to the floor, underneath the tables where she had helped Willem and Judith with their writing of English. She did not protest as he fumbled with her clothes and forced his way into her. She had learnt long ago that the less protest she made the shorter the pain. If she resisted he seemed to enjoy it more and she wished to deny him that.

But today she had anger to deal with as well. She was angry that he had brought her here for this, instead of waiting till the early part of the morning, when the children were asleep, as he usually did. But she knew exactly why he had done so – he wanted to destroy her pleasure in the classes, in the contact with the teacher, Mara Derancourt, and her brother Thomas. She was not a sentient, intelligent human being. She was his property and if she had forgotten he would make sure that this was a lesson she would relearn.

* * *

It seemed as though all the tradespeople of Priorton made an effort to be at Kitty Rainbow's funeral. The church was full to overflowing. The mourners ranged from Ginger and her friends from the shop floor of the Rainbow Works, to a very elderly lady called Miss Aunger, who tottered up to Kay and told her of the days when she worked for Miss Rainbow in her draper's shop; from the Captain in a greening black suit, to a rather portly type who monopolised Mara. This was, they whispered, the Welsh Labour MP, Dewi Wilson, who knew the family from wa-ay back.

Hugh attended, wearing what he called his 'dark black suit': it had pleats across the back to accommodate his broad shoulders. At the funeral and at the burial he located himself somewhere near Thomas's elbow. He confided that he had taken a shift off the pit for the funeral. 'After all, as I said to my marrah, it's a case of close family, man, close family.'

At the house Mara tracked Hugh down in the dining room where he sat looking huge and out of place on a dining chair, one of a line placed around the wall. She thanked him for being so kind the day Kitty died.

His cheeks coloured slightly, and he wished he was back in the bar at the Royal George. 'Nothing, Mrs Derancourt, nothing. Any man would do it.'

She swept some sheet music from the piano stool and sat down beside him, her flowing black skirt swirling before it settled around her trim ankles. 'I thought we were cousins, Hugh. Or more properly my sister's your cousin. So if you don't call me Mara I'll think you don't like me. Or, worse, you'll think I'm this stuck-up person from down South who has her nose in the air. Kitty wouldn't have stood for any of that.'

He sensed rather than saw the woman beside him, elegant in black, her hair swept up and pinned with a plain black bow. 'I'm sorry I didn't know her better, like, old Kitty,' he said, offering Mara a cigarette. 'Look at all these people! The town must be empty. Shops must be shut; pubs must be empty.'

She drew on her cigarette and watched Duggie, who was moving through the crowds carrying a tray of sherry and whisky with a suave deftness which reminded her that once, aeons ago, before the Great War, he had been a gentleman's gentleman. 'Yes,' she said with satisfaction. 'She was an exceptional woman. I was very proud of her.'

'I'd think she'd be very proud of you. A schoolteacher and all that,' he said carefully. 'And a book writer, Thomas tells me.'

She laughed out loud and the people nearest to them turned to evaluate such hilarity on such an occasion. 'Only a schoolteacher, Hugh. Not a missionary. Not even as adventurous as Leonora, out there in foreign climes half her life, getting involved with politics here.'

'Important thing, schoolteaching. Hope for the future. Only way out of the cage,' he said gruffly.

They sat silently for a moment.

'Do you have family, Hugh?'

'Just Harry. He's a captain in the army.'

'Not a miner?'

'That's how he started out, like. But the war has changed everything. Not just for him and me. Would yer have ever thought we'd have a Labour Government so fast? I'd a thought it'd take us ten years, they were all so busy licking Mr Churchill's boots.' He paused. 'I saw you across there with Dewi Wilson.'

She raised her brow. 'You know him?'

He shook his head. 'I know of him. Seen him speak at the Big Meeting in Durham once. Heart's in the right place, but like the rest of them, too comfortable these days. Your Leonora Scorton was a staunch Labourite herself, wasn't she, when it was a real movement? In the thirties, before she lit back off to Egypt? I know of them both, from those times, though I'd never met them.'

'You knew that? You knew she was your cousin but you didn't let on?'

He shrugged. 'The connection was all in the past. No point in pushing meself forward.'

'And now?'

'Just took a fancy to young Thomas. He reminded me of someone. He was standing in the bar of the Royal George asking for a glass of wine. A glass of wine, bigod! A lamb to the slaughter!'

She smiled at that. 'I take it you must be Labour, then, Hugh?'

He shook his head again. 'Once I was a great follower of Ellen Wilkinson, MP for Jarrow, God rest her soul. A proper Socialist, that one. Then one day I heard her talk to some journalist, outside a meeting, about "my" miners. Like we was pet budgerigars! That finished me with her. But the party didn't do right even by her in the end. Now they're all compromising. No more'n capitalist lackeys.'

'But look at the moves in Education, the Health Service, now the mines! Look what they're doing!'

'Not enough. Too frightened for the status quo. In power they become the status quo and forget their roots.'

'But . . .' To her acute discomfort tears started to stream down Mara's face, tears which had nothing to do with politics. 'I'm sorry, my mother . . .'

Hugh was all contrition. 'Don't take on, flower. Kitty was a good age and she knew where she was going, like, according to young Thomas.' He plucked a snowy handkerchief from the pocket of his dark black suit and started to dab at her cheeks. She took it from him but the tears gushed further and she was obliged to press the whole thing to her face to stop the tears as they came out. She was conscious that her hand was being held very tightly in his large rough-skinned one.

The tears stopped as quickly as they had started. She offered him his handkerchief, and he had to let go of her hand to retrieve it. She stared at him red-eyed. 'I'm sorry about that,' she said.

'Kitty's in a better place,' he said. 'Be sure of that.'

She shook her head. 'I don't think it's Kitty,' she said. 'I think it's about my husband, Jean-Paul. Three years, and I never cried till today.'

'He died too?'

'We were bombed in London. He was in the house. Hugh, the war has so much to answer for. We lost young Stephen, too. Kay's husband. He died in the blackout.' She sniffed. 'Ironic. No medals for any of that, Hugh.'

'Young Thomas seemed to think a lot of him. Pilot, wasn't he? Some guts, those lads. An' that's a compliment, from a pitman.'

She blinked. 'You and Thomas have hit it off.' She smiled through the last of the tears.

'I like the lad. Can't think why, 'cos he's a weedy kid, but I have to say I have a bit of time for him.'

'He's not weedy. He's, well, slender. But Kay's the really tough one, according to their mother.'

'I can't take her down the pit, though, can I?'

'What? What are you about, Hugh Longstaffe?'

'I'm gunna see if he'd like to work at White Leas. They're looking for men. They're just losing all the Bevin Boys, those lads conscripted into the mines, you know? Left, right and centre, they're falling off. I'll put a word in for him. Make a man of him.'

Mara chuckled. 'I can't think what Leonora'll think of that. And Kay'll have something to say about it, you bet your boots.'

'*Am I my brother's keeper*? It'll make a man of him, Mara,' said Hugh. 'You watch me.'

Thomas, intrigued by the idea of working in the pit, finally decided to ask Hugh if he would indeed 'put in a good word' for him. If he could, he would start soon. He told Kay of his decision in the car as he gave her a lift to work and she was furious. 'What do you think you're up to? Mines are terrible places: no sun, no daylight, just dark spaces.'

'I'll do what you're doing at the factory. Work hard. Learn about something. The pit. Ourselves. Our mother's father, Freddie, he worked there. Hugh says Freddie was supposed to be lean but very strong, like me. I'll find out something about him, working like he did.'

Kay looked at her twin and suddenly saw he was changing. The little brother had gone. The slender figure and the soft eyes which blinked through their glasses were the same. But there was a steel about him now, which she didn't recognise. The soft desert air had kept him young, pliable, always ready to fall in with her plans and schemes. The hard chill of the North-East of England had thickened her blood and made her party to Kitty's schemes to put down tentative roots of commitment and intent. That same chill had flipped Thomas into adulthood without her noticing. It had driven a hard wedge between them.

'What about your work with those refugees?' she said. 'I thought you enjoyed it. You'll have to give all that up.'

He shrugged. Missing Patrizia had been one of his concerns. 'Mother says she'll help Mara, and carry on herself after Christmas when Mara goes back South, and Florence starts school. She needs to get her teeth into something now Kitty's gone. Her Labour committees aren't enough. They were talking about the problem of naturalisation when I came out. The refugees need an advocate; and our little mother's old political antennae are quivering. Haven't seen her so alive in a long time.'

'Still, you'll have to give up the refugees on your own behalf.'

The haunted kitten face of Patrizia Gold seemed for a moment to dance on the lenses of his glasses. 'I'll be on shifts anyway. I can get across there sometimes during the day.'

'But you don't need to go down the pit, Thomas. Don't even need to work in the factory. You could get in touch with archaeologists here; do that again. The work you know. There must be digs all over England. They would welcome your help.'

He laughed. 'All my expertise was arrived at out there in the desert. Fetching and carrying for Sam's customers. Or grubbing around for your beloved pots. I have no college diploma or degree. No experience of Roman, British, or Pre-British artifacts, of digging conditions, nothing. Calling myself an archaeologist was always a vanity, anyway.'

She was struggling, she couldn't deny any of that. 'You could go to college, get some qualifications . . .' she floundered.

He was shaking his head. 'This is what I want to do, to go to the pit with Hugh,' he said.

'It is ridiculous. Those men are hard, they'll laugh at you,' she said. 'You can't do that kind of work.'

The more she objected the more determined he became. 'Fetching and carrying all those pots was not light work you know.' He flexed a muscle. 'A couple of jars of spinach and I'll be fine.'

'It's not a joke. It's not right for you to do that kind of work.'

'Ah,' he said. 'Here we have it. The Scortons are too good for the pit, are they? Good enough for our grandfather but not good enough for me?'

She put her hands over her ears, 'No, no,' she said. Then she looked him in the eye. 'All this is because Kitty left the factory to me, isn't it? You can't bring yourself to work with me there, can you?'

Kitty had indeed left the whole of the business to her in a complicated trust which said that if after two years she abandoned her hands-on work at the factory, she had to hand over the whole thing to Duggie. Lock, stock and barrel. That would be on top of the lump of money and Kitty's car, which he was to receive directly.

Thomas was shaking his head. 'I'm not in the least bit interested in the factory. And I'm not interested in working for you. Time all that stopped, don't you think?' He leant over and opened the car door.

Kay jumped out, waving at Ginger who was just wheeling her battered bicycle through the arched gate. 'Well, Thomas, it's not up to me to tell you what you do. But I think you'll rue this.'

'I think I won't. But thank you for caring.'

'And do you intend to drive the car to the pit?'

'Bit tactless? You're probably right. Anyway, it's Duggie's car not ours now.' But Thomas didn't smile at her as he went off and it gnawed at her heart to know that the intimacy between them had somehow frozen to a much diminished thing in this cold country.

She raced to catch up with Ginger who had parked her bike and was bouncing along on her high heels, taking a last drag on her cigarette. They walked along in silence for a while.

'Gave old Miss Rainbow a hell of a funeral, there,' said Ginger cheerfully. 'She'll be a big miss in this town, I'm telling yer.'

Kay walked on in silence.

Ginger picked up her mood. 'No need to be down, kid. She had a good innings, and was never ill and wailing, was she?'

'It's not quite her,' said Kay slowly. She couldn't tell Ginger that she was feeling down because her own brother was going down the pit and was too good for it. She knew Ginger's three brothers and father worked down the mines and were proud of it. As well as that, there was the fact that next Monday she herself would be coming off the line and going into the Captain's office. It would be public knowledge then, that the factory was hers. 'I'm just a bit down, really. This foggy weather is getting on my nerves, as well as everything else.'

'Tell yer what, Kay – dance on tonight at the Gaiety! You come down with me and Janet. Bit of a dance'll cheer you up. Not as good as when the soldier boys were around, but a bit of a jitterbug don't half iron out the creases, I can tell you.'

Kay started to refuse then changed her mind. 'Yes. Yes, Ginger, I wouldn't mind a bit of a dance. Don't mind if I do!'

Nine
Dancing in the Dark

From the outside, the Gaiety Dance-Hall was a seamy, ramshackle building; its prefabricated walls were dotted here and there with crumbling wartime bricks laid in to reinforce the rotting substructure. In a bold attempt to draw the eye away from this, the double doorways were painted a cheerful red and the row of bulbs above them shone like radiant white teeth.

Ginger and Janet, with Kay in tow, greeted the girl in the kiosk like an old friend. They bought their tickets, then walked in behind other chattering women (some as old as thirty) and passed through more swinging double doors into the long dance-hall. The bright lights and clean bright colours made Kay blink; her ears were assailed by scrapes and rattles as people moved about, finding tables and pulling up chairs.

She watched as individuals marked their place with a strategically placed glove or handbag and made their way to the little counter where they could buy tea, coffee or different kinds of pop.

The dance-hall was, this early in the evening, mostly inhabited by women and girls. Here and there at the tables were very smartly dressed couples; some of those men even wore black bow ties. Apart from that it was mainly women in pairs and clusters, giggling and chattering, pulling at their belts and touching their hair.

Runs and trills of music meandered towards Kay and the others from the central bandstand where the band, a collection of a dozen or so men in evening dress, were just about to start.

A hand yanked Kay from behind. 'Come on, Kay,' said Janet. 'An't you ever seen a dance-floor before? Come on, we've got to hang our coats up.' She led Kay up a broad shallow staircase which veered off to make a long balcony down one side of the hall. There were tables up here as well, overlooking the dance-floor.

They went through yet more double doors into a brilliantly lit space: the cloakroom. Behind a counter a patient woman in black was handing out tickets and hanging up coats. On the opposite side of the room was a floor-length mirror, lit Hollywood-style by theatrical bulbs. In front of it stood dozens of girls, peering, preening and commenting on each others' clothes and hair.

Ginger took Kay's coat, grandly paid for her cloakroom ticket, then dragged her before the mirror, dislodging two weaker souls in the process. 'There!' she said. 'Now, flower, we can set about gilding the lily.'

She leant forward and dragged an extra layer of brilliant red lipstick across her lips. 'Right, Kay, who am I?' she said into the mirror.

Kay shook her head.

Ginger pulled her hair down over one side of her face and peered through the tangle. 'Rita Hayworth. The lily is gilded. Get it?'

Kay laughed. 'Oh yes,' she said. 'Rita Hayworth to the life.' In fact Ginger looked more like a chrysanthemum than a lily; her bright hair was too curly to resemble the lank sultry brilliance of the film star. But there was something, perhaps the mirror, perhaps this brilliant light, which did make the claim to film-star glamour credible.

Janet borrowed Ginger's lipstick, applied it, and treated them to a brilliant toothy smile. 'An' jes' who d'you think I am, little Kay?' she drawled in a menacing fashion through the mirror.

Kay got that one. 'Barbara Stanwyck!' she said triumphantly.

'Now you,' she handed Kay the lipstick.

Kay hesitated, then leant towards the mirror and applied it to her mouth. She had never worn lipstick before. In Alexandria such bright colours were part of the whore's armoury: alien, sticky stuff. On her lips now it felt and looked like jam.

'Stand back. Let's see,' ordered Ginger.

They all stared at Kay through the mirror. The girls around them looked on with interest at a game they had all played in their time. The floor-length mirrors at the Gaiety were part of their Friday treat. The largest in their own homes were shaving mirrors where their dads shaved, or the looking-glass over the mantelpiece where their mothers tucked unpaid bills and letters of condolence for sons lost in the war.

'I know!' said someone behind her, a stout girl with a broad black fringe. 'Merle Oberon!'

'That's it!' said Ginger, scrabbling in her bag for a comb and hair grips. 'You just need your hair pulling back and up a bit, right off your face. Like so. And a bit of eye black.' She spat on a little brush and carefully tidied Kay's eyebrows and touched her eyelashes. 'There. Merle Oberon to the life.'

And so it seemed, even to Kay. The smooth, faintly brown skin, the pulled-back hair which made her bones look fine and high, the dramatic eyes. She looked five years older, nearer her real age. And she did look more like the film star Merle Oberon than the Kay Fitzgibbon she knew.

'Can't do much about the clothes, of course,' said Janet sadly, looking at the swirling black skirt and white blouse Kay had borrowed from her Aunt Mara. Janet and Ginger were both dressed in blouses cut slightly low at the front, and skirts which reached below the knee revealing a lot of leg sheathed in precious nylon.

Outside in the hall, the band was surging forth with a foxtrot version of 'I don't want to set the world on fire'. 'Well,' said Kay, 'now we've decided who we are, shall we go and see the dancing?'

Ginger led them out on to the balcony and along to a table where they could look down on the proceedings. Janet went off for some lemonade. 'We'll sit and watch a bit,' said Ginger. 'No point in going down yet.'

'Why's that?' said Kay, who would rather have been nearer the dancing. The band had an exciting big-swing style which she had only heard before on gramophone records.

'No lads as yet,' said Ginger briefly, nodding towards the floor. Three of the older couples were making use of the space, dancing the foxtrot with sweeping, ducking style. Darting in and out between them were girls and women dancing together, their movements equally expert, but much less sweeping and dramatic. It was a modest display. 'Some lasses only get to dance with each other,' said Ginger contemptuously.

'They seem to be enjoying it,' said Kay, 'so what does it matter?'

Ginger shrugged. 'Depends what you're here for, I suppose.'

Janet returned with lemonade and Kay sipped it, relaxing, entertained by her companions' sometime acid comments on the scene below. They seemed to know, or know of, half the dancers.

'Ah, here they are,' Ginger said finally with some satisfaction. As they watched an assortment of boys and young men started to trickle through the double doors in ones and twos, casting glances around the hall, ending up in clusters, lighting up their cigarettes, offering laconic comments to their mates on the band and the 'talent': the girls present with whom they might, with a bit of luck, 'click' tonight . . .

'Do the boys always come in after the girls?'

'Always,' said Ginger. 'They go to the pubs first. Poor dears need a bit of Dutch courage.'

'Don't the girls need Dutch courage?'

'Pubs? Wouldn't see me dead in the pubs that lot get into.' For all Ginger's contempt she was interested in the boys, her glance darting to and fro from the hovering clusters already in, back to the swinging doors through which newcomers were still trickling in a perpetual stream. The girls were now standing in clusters themselves near to, but apparently ignoring, the boys.

'Right.' Ginger picked up her bag. 'I think I'll go down and view the scene.' Janet was already gathering her own bag. 'You coming?' she said to Kay. 'The lads'll be snapped up in no time.'

Kay shook her head. 'No. I wouldn't dare. I'll just sit up here and pick up some tips.'

'Sure?' said Ginger.

'Sure,' said Kay.

She sat watching as Ginger and Janet positioned themselves just to the left of the band and appeared to become engrossed in deep conversation, ignoring the groups of boys close at hand. Then, one by one, boys came up and asked them to dance, only to be sent away.

After a time which made the watching Kay tense, Ginger consented to dance with one of them; after that, Janet said yes to the next one who asked her. She watched her two work-mates dance then, clutched in the arms of strangers, laughing and talking with them as though they were real friends.

Some boys were strolling along the balcony eyeing the girls who were sitting there. One of them stopped and asked Kay, 'Are you gettin' up then?'

She shook her head. 'Sorry, I don't dance.' That was a lie, of course, she could dance quite well. She and Thomas had danced to records since they were quite young. She had danced once or twice with Stephen before he went away. Thomas had danced quite regularly in cafés and dance-halls, but Kay never would, avoiding as always the shallow social life of Alexandria.

On the balcony one keen passerby did not want to take no for an answer. 'Can I get you a drink then?'

She shook her head firmly. 'No. I'm waiting for my friends. They'll be back soon.'

'Waiting for your friend, are you?' She winced as he mimicked her uncommon accent. He stared at her, then shrugged. 'Suit yourself,' he said.

Kay sat back to enjoy the music. Ginger and Janet showed no sign of coming back up to the balcony. They returned to their hovering spot and were asked to dance again and again, some boys coming back for a second dance and being turned down.

The seat beside her scraped and someone sat down heavily. Her head whipped round. 'I'm sorry, I'm saving these seats for . . .' Then she recognised him. It was the Austrian, immaculate in a dark suit and a snowy shirt, his hair parted and brilliantined like a shining cap. 'Oh, it's you,' she said weakly.

'And here are you, Cinderella at the ball.'

'I don't want to dance,' she said, surprised at how flustered she felt. 'What made you come up here?'

'I saw your friends from work and my heart told me you must be here. I have walked round downstairs twice and then came up here.'

Her embarrassed glance drifted back to the dance-floor where the dance had ended and Ginger and Janet were sitting on chairs set against the wall, deep in laughing conversation with their most recent partners.

The band struck up again. Laurenz Gold stood up, clicked his heels, bowed his head and held out his hand. 'Ah. A waltz. May I have the pleasure of this dance, *Fräulein*?'

She found herself putting her hand in his. They walked along the balcony hand in hand. She could feel his finger running over her wedding ring. 'So, you are married?' There was a world of disappointment and sorrow in his voice.

'I was,' she said quietly. 'My husband was killed. Three years ago now.'

'Oh dear. I am so sorry. And you are here to cheer up? The waltz will cheer you up!'

The way he danced the waltz would have cheered anyone up. They swung round and round the floor, clearing space as they did so. Her long skirt swirled around his legs and the music, perfectly in time, clicked its rhythm into their very muscles. She danced better than she had ever danced before. In the end there was a small circle standing watching them as they did their final swirls. When the music came to a rest, there was a patter of applause at their efforts.

Ginger came and put an arm round her. 'Trust you to get the best dancer in the room,' she said. Then she looked at Laurenz. 'Oh, it's the Nazzy boy. Blown up any Germans lately, have yer?'

He smiled sweetly at her. 'You are looking very glamorous tonight, Ginger. I do not recognise you. Kay and I will get lemonade. Will you join us?'

Ginger shook her head. 'Nah. The next set's jitterbug and me and Janet's got our hooks into the best two jitterbuggers in Priorton. You watch us.'

The dance-hall was now packed and a small ensemble from the band set the frenzied rhythmic pace. Laurenz and Kay watched the frantic leaping for a minute or two and made their way back up to the balcony.

'Phew!' Laurenz said. 'Is it too warm up here for you, Kay?'

Kay laughed. 'Warm? It's the first time I've been warm since I came to England.'

They sat down, quite at ease with each other. Laurenz turned his back to the hall and gave her his full attention. He asked her about Alexandria and her family; about little Florence and the business with the ancient pottery.

Gradually, she relaxed. Perhaps, after all, he was not really pushy. Just a bit more confident. She asked him about himself and he told her about his dreadful experiences escaping from Vienna and the grim years in the displaced persons' camp. He told her about his children, and his poor wife who had suffered so much in this process that she was entirely changed from the girl he once knew. 'Poor Patrizia,' he said sadly. 'Sometimes I think she is quite insane.'

It was all Kay could do not to put a sympathetic hand on his. She was just resisting this impulse when Ginger came bouncing up. 'We've got a couple of lads keen to walk us home and are setting out now. D'you want to come, Kay? No problem, you know. We can walk you home first.'

Kay laughed. 'I can walk myself home, thanks. I'm a grown woman, you know.'

Ginger leant down to hug her, putting her lips close to Kay's ear. 'Don't you trust this one, mind. He's poison,' she murmured. She stood up. 'See you at work on Monday, then,' she said loudly, and pranced off, her high heels clicking.

Laurenz watched her go. 'She is a strange girl,' he said. 'So very different from you.'

'I like her,' Kay said.

He nodded. 'Oh yes, she is very easy to like.'

They talked on. He told her about the toolmaker for whom he had worked in Switzerland, how clever he was, and how much he had learnt from him. And she told him about her very special grandmother who had died just this week. And her mother who had been quite famous in politics for a time in the thirties. And her father who had been a spy in Russia in the Great War. It seemed she would never stop talking. She could not remember when she had talked so much.

Finally, incredibly, the band was playing 'God Save The King' and the evening was at an end. She made her way back to the cloakroom to collect her coat. When she came down the wide sweeping stairs Laurenz was at the bottom, waiting for her. He was wearing a leather flying jacket over his suit. 'Can I escort you home, Kay? Perhaps it will be safer.'

She nodded very slightly. He took her arm and they walked out through the swinging double doors. Outside the pavement was thronged with people, standing talking or shouting to each other. The dank December air hit her and she shivered.

Laurenz led her to an alleyway alongside the building where his motor bike stood in the deep shadow. She looked at it doubtfully. 'I don't think . . .' she said.

'You will be fine, fine,' he said. 'Jump on behind. Tuck your skirt right in.'

The drive up to The Lane was very short, but when Kay alighted from the bike her hands were shaking and her teeth were chattering. Laurenz took one of her hands in both of his and rubbed it till it was warm again. Then he took the other one and did the same. She looked up at him in the light of the streetlamp. 'Well, good night, Laurenz,' she said.

He shook her hand heartily and carefully let it go. He nodded. 'Good night, Kay. It was wonderful to dance with you.' Then he clicked his heels, bowed very formally and turned away.

She walked to the door and watched him get back on his bike. As she felt in her bag for her key he roared away on the bike and she fought down a feeling of profound disappointment that the evening had not ended in some other more intimate way. The man was married, after all. She knew that, didn't she?

When the first knock on the door came, Patrizia did not answer it. Mr MacAlister had turned up the previous night, smelling of rum, asking her if she wanted a fire in the recreation room tomorrow as the class hadn't been on for a couple of days and had her teachers deserted her? He had tried to push the door open and come in but she had leant hard against it until he had gone away.

Now a voice whispered through the worn wood. 'Patrizia, Patrizia. *Hier ist Thomas*. I need to see you.'

She unbolted the door, let him in, then put her fingers at her lips, glancing to the corner where the children were in bed. She went over and pulled round the rough blanket curtain which served to separate their sleeping and their living areas. She pulled out one of the chairs at the table for him and sat on the other herself.

He put a bottle on the table and smiled at her. 'I would like to say that it was wine, but where can you get wine in this sunless place?' He whipped off the brown paper covering. 'Dandelion and burdock! A local delicacy, I believe. Regrettably, no alcohol.'

She brought cups from the table in the corner and they tried it. She wrinkled her nose. 'It is like cough mixture.'

'Then it's bound to do us good.' He beamed, raising his cup. 'Your health,' he said, then looked round. 'Is Laurenz about?'

She shook her head. 'He is in Priorton,' she said. 'He got some pay from his work at the factory. I do not think he will drink dandelion and burdock tonight. What is that, dandelion and burdock?' she frowned. 'What do the words say?'

'They are weeds, growing in the hedgerows. The dandelion is like the golden sun, and the burdock, well, I don't know what that is. They grow wild.'

She smiled. 'Wild. I like that.' She wondered why he had come, but was too polite to ask.

He said, 'I have come to speak English to you because from Monday I start work and will not come in the day.'

'You work at the factory?'

He shook his head. 'No, I will work in a coal mine. There are many in this area.' To her relief, he continued to speak in German.

'I notice this when we arrive. It makes it very dirty.'

He laughed. 'It's not dirty everywhere, you know. I suppose Vienna is a very beautiful city?'

Her face lit up. 'Oh yes. Wide streets. Such great buildings. The river, the trams, the cafés. Do you know in the cafés you can get cream cakes this big?' She made a mountain with her hands, and Thomas noted how small they were, and how neat her nails, in spite of having to live in this terrible place.

He was puzzled. 'I don't know how you can love a city so much where . . . where . . .'

'Those terrible things happened?'

'Mmm. I suppose so.'

Her dark hair fell across her face as she leant forward eagerly. 'But I was born there. My mother and stepfather, uncles, my grandparents were born there. My stepfather and uncles fought in the Great War for Austria. They were all Austrians through and through. And Vienna. Vienna was so gay, so smart. My mother made hats and my stepfather made suits. We could sit in a café out on the Kärntnerstrasse and watch the people go by. We would spot the hats my mother had made, the suits my father had made.'

'Your mother and father, they . . . ?'

She looked at him blankly.

It was a stupid question. He cursed himself for asking it.

'It was my stepfather. My father went back to Poland many years before. But there was only my mother left at the end, and she was ill. My stepfather and his brothers had gone. Been taken. We thought they'd killed them straight away. But we saw my stepfather, days later, in the street in a line of others. He did not look like himself. He was always such an immaculate man. And here he was, his clothes and body so filthy. They did that, you know, so they would be seen and spat upon in that state.' She paused. 'I had a letter in the DP camp from Elisabet, who had been our maid. She said they took my mother, ill as she was, to Theresienstadt. She did not live long enough to make the next journey to Auschwitz.'

He reached across and put his hand on hers, where it lay on the table, and they sat there for a long time in silence. He could find no words, and she was back with her mother in the small back room of the shop which on its front window had a large star of David painted on the window in dripping red paint. Finally she looked at him. 'I should have stayed with her.'

'No. No,' he said with awkward gentleness. 'Then we would have no Peter. No Rebeka. Think what they may do in the world! They are the hope. Surely they are the hope.'

She nodded slowly and gently removed her hand from his. She stood up. 'I will make you some coffee, Thomas.' Her face was grey.

He nodded, relieved at the slight break in tension. 'And I have something in the car for you.'

When he returned with his bulky parcel the coffee was steaming on the Primus and Peter was sitting up, bleary-eyed, drinking milk from a cup. His eyes sparkled when he saw the parcel. They sparkled even more when Thomas whipped off the paper to reveal the knobs and the gleaming veneer of a small wireless set.

Patrizia watched without expression.

Thomas placed the wireless on the floor and plugged it into the one socket in the room. Then he tuned it into the Light Programme; music from the operetta *Maritza* filled the room and both Peter and Patrizia clapped their hands.

'I will not be here all the time for the lessons. And I don't know whether Mara will be able to manage it. She has to go back to her own school soon. Her leave of absence is up. So I thought we could still do lessons to fit in with my shifts. And in the meantime you are to listen to the wireless. It will be good for your English.'

She nodded. 'We will like it. It will be good for Peter.' Her voice hardened. 'Peter will not be Austrian, like his father and grandfathers. He will be English after all.' She paused. 'One bit of me says we should not keep it. Laurenz will be angry. He will break it.' She rubbed her eyes, tired suddenly. She was not used to so much talk, so much listening.

Thomas stood up. 'I will go.' He laughed. 'We forgot to speak English. Next time, Patrizia, we speak English all the time.'

He waited outside for more than an hour before he saw the lights of Laurenz's motor bike. Laurenz shook his hand heartily, apparently delighted to see him. 'Come in, come in! Patrizia will make us coffee.'

Thomas shook his head. 'No. I have been and had a word with her. I brought you a present, Laurenz. A wireless which we bought my grandmother for her birthday. She does not need it now, of course . . .'

'I was sad to hear about her,' murmured Laurenz.

'I thought it might entertain the children.'

Laurenz shook his hand all over again.

'Very good, Thomas, very kind. We will treasure it.'

Thomas hung on to his hand. 'I expect nothing will happen to that wireless, Laurenz. If it did I would be obliged to give somebody a good beating. A very good beating.'

Laurenz pulled his hand away. 'How would we let anything happen, Thomas? We will treasure it.'

Thomas jumped back into his car and signalled his farewell. Laurenz went into the house to admire the radio and declare that he was a little worried about their friend Thomas. In fact it was dawning on him that he was . . . well, more of an Oscar

Wilde than a Don Juan. The English called them pansies. That was it. Pansy boy! He twiddled with the tuning knob of the wireless and the squealing sounds woke up Rebeka. 'So, dearest, do not cast soulful eyes in Thomas's direction. It's not just that you're ugly, which you are. But even if you were less ugly to look at, it is me to whom he is drawn. Don't you see that? Why else would he stay so long just to see me? Why?'

Ten

The Matter of the Last Witness

Thomas had had, despite his assurances to Kay, more than one misgiving in finally taking up Hugh's offer to 'put a good word in' for him at the pit. But after only a few more days he had become very engaged by Hugh's talk and felt in his bones that the pit was for him. This intuition was fed by the desire to separate himself from what seemed increasingly to be a bubbling household of women. He felt drained by the very energy of his mother, the elegance of Mara, the intensity of Kay, the charm of little Florence, even the delicate aura of Kitty, still hovering in a ghostly fashion about the house. Worse, he'd had to endure a kind of amused uneasiness about his enterprise from both Leonora and Mara, as well as the barely suppressed anger on Kay's part.

He was sick of all that. He could not understand why his sister was so critical. And for the first time in his whole life he started to feel truly angry with her, even to like her less. She had become so cool since she had come to England: as though the chill air had entered her veins and hardened to crystal. Even worse, in Thomas's book, she had been barely civil to Hugh the couple of times he had called at Blamire House.

While he felt estranged from Kay he was much more drawn, he had to admit it, to the strained, haunted quiet of Patrizia Gold, as well as the robust energy, the masculine certainties, of Hugh Longstaffe.

This, then, was how he came to be knocking on Hugh's door

at half past three in the morning, facing who knew what horror beneath the dark earth. Hugh opened the door, already dressed in his thick jacket, collarless shirt and neckerchief. 'Come in, come in, lad. Let's see yer.'

Thomas came within the glow of the gas mantle to one side of the fireplace and Hugh examined him top to toe, from his well-brushed hair, over his thick tweed jacket down to his heavy brogue shoes. 'Hey, that'll not do, lad. Tha'll stand out ower much. The lads'll kill 'mselves laughing. Tha'll stand out enough with how tha speaks, although they're used to different tongues now, with these Bevin Boys in the war.' He nodded towards the settle by the fire range, which was strewn with dark clothes, lumpy with the shadow of the body they had once encased. 'I put some of our Harry's stuff out foh yeh. He's no use for them now, like, in the army.'

Obediently Thomas stripped off and put on the thick undershorts, the heavy trousers, the collarless shirt and the thick jacket. He sat down on the settle to pull on the long pit socks and to lace up the heavy boots. He turned round and saw his new self reflected against the night outside, in the curtainless window. The man reflected there could have been any man, any miner. And Thomas was glad of it.

'And here's a cap.' Hugh threw it at him. 'No self-respecting pitman goes to work without his cap. A few of them still even work in them. No time for helmets, silly sods.'

They set out in silence, their boots thudding companionably as they walked on the packed earth of the back street, which served as a *cordon sanitaire* between the houses and the privies, which stood like pitch-black sentinels against the more luminous black of the sky.

Half an hour later Thomas was undergoing the thrill of pure fear as he stood shoulder to shoulder with twenty other men in the cage as it ground down the shaft through the layers of the earth. His nostrils flared, his stomach wrenched at the mingling smells of dried sweat and coal dust on old serge, made wet and dry again innumerable times.

Up there at the bank top the faces of each of these men had been differentiated by character: sombre, mirthful, distracted, thoughtful. Here in the crowded cage these same faces bore the stigmata of grim resignation: held back, folded in, tightly controlled. The custom of a lifetime, of generations, of brave endurance, of waiting eight hours for light had etched their terrible mark on these faces: an unspoken requiem for a life lived in the sunlight with its freedom of movement, its setting among flowers and women.

Hugh, wanting Thomas to like the pit, had prepared him for those first days when he would be consumed by a feeling of entrapment, of revolt, but these feelings, said Hugh, had to be gulped down, incorporated, if the pitman was to go on to meet the heroic challenges of his daily task with any dignity.

In the months to come, as his life went forward, Thomas was to see that first trip down in the cage as a watershed. Those first weeks when, despite his light frame, he was put to inferior jobs like hauling and filling, were for him days replete with exhaustion and pain. At the same time they were days full of wonder at what he was witnessing.

One time he was given the job of scooping up the sloshing water which gathered on sections of the way, where the steam pump could not reach. Bucket by bucket he filled the tubs which he then pushed along the rail to be pumped away. Water ran down the walls, dripped off the ceiling; it gathered between the rails of the wagon way. The sloshing of ponies' hooves through the water mingled in the dark with the creaking of wooden pit props and the murmur of men, the only clue that you were in the real world, not locked in some dark dream.

The coal was prime quality but it was hard won. The pitmen walked doubled up in the low walkway for half a mile before they reached the face which they were working. Hugh told Thomas that across at the East coast there were seams as high as ten, even fifteen feet. But here in the south-west the seams were low, some as low as a foot and a half, often inches deep in water, in parts too narrow for the conveyor to function.

After some days Hugh had wangled Thomas the job of filling for him; his own mate had been put in hospital with back-strain so there was a place for Thomas. His job was, at first sight, impossible. He was supposed to fill the tubs with the coal which Hugh had brought down from the face. Above the lip of the tub there was only twelve inches for him to squeeze his coal-laden shovel and slide the coal in. At the end of every shift Thomas would nurse hands which were blistered on the palm with the shovel and bruised on the knuckle from the times his hand hit the stone roof, trying to manoeuvre the coal into the tub.

Watching Hugh work he would admire the settled assurance of this man who knew just what he was about: the neat efficiency with which he removed all his clothes except baggy shorts, called pithoggers, and heavy boots, and folded himself into such a shallow space, turning his shoulder to act as a kind of support to the tense, focused power of the pick in his hand. Thomas marvelled that such a large man could fit into the space at all.

Previously, Thomas had imagined that hewing depended on brute strength; here he was to witness the much more controlled power, even the delicacy of the operation: the way in which neat holes were drilled, then the fine, sharp pick struck, eased, teased the coal away from its primeval fastness to send it on its way to heat homes and generate power out there above, in the world of women and flowers.

But all that was in the future, unseen by Thomas as, with Hugh at his shoulder, he felt the cage jerk and clang as it reached the bottom, and, stepping out, gulped his first lungful of sour, used, dust-laden air.

'I can't believe it.' Leonora surveyed her daughter. 'You look ten years older.'

'I *am* twenty-six, you know,' said Kay, pushing in another kirby-grip to anchor the Merle Oberon hairdo more firmly in place.

'You always looked sixteen.'

Florence, sitting on her grandmother's lap fingering a story about a rather naughty red fox, examined her mother closely. 'Momma looks like Auntie Mara,' she announced.

Mara laughed.

Kay glanced down at her clothes. 'That's hardly surprising, Flo, seeing as this is Auntie Mara's frock and her shoes. And this is her lipstick.' She smoothed down the fine brown worsted skirt, touched the white collar.

'Mara has very good taste,' said Leonora thoughtfully. 'But if you're to go to the factory properly dressed you should buy yourself some clothes. There are some very decent dress shops in Priorton. Or you could take a trip to Darlington.'

Kay sighed. 'It does seem so settled, to buy heavy English clothes.'

Leonora laughed. 'It is very settled, you clot, you've taken Kitty's challenge, haven't you? You didn't turn down her inheritance. Two years, was it? You can't manage without proper clothes for two years.'

Kay peered at herself in the mirror above the fireplace. 'Going to the factory dressed properly' was a consequence of the Friday night dance. When she had shut the door of Blamire House behind her, after saying good night to Laurenz Gold, she had decided it was time she grew up. Her own image in the ballroom mirror; the time on the balcony watching the dancers whirl below, all busy on their own odyssey from childhood to parenthood, many of them workers in her own factory; hearing Laurenz Gold's tale of what he had endured to end up with the privilege of sweeping floors and pushing trolleys in that same dirty northern factory; listening to Thomas jawing on with such evident stupidity about working in the pit: all these combined to make her embrace now what Leonora called Kitty's Challenge. She would grow up and run the factory, to the best of her ability. Anything less would be to remain in the hothouse of childhood which she had for too long been so reluctant to leave.

'And what are you going to do today?' she said to Florence.

'Me and Mrs MacMahon do baking today,' said Florence. 'Then I go and play with Peter.' She glanced at Mara.

Mara nodded. 'Yes. We're going across there to do the language class. Your mother's coming too, with some information she's gleaned from the local politicians about the Labour Party and naturalisation.'

'What?' said Kay. 'Politics? Language? You'll be setting up a college soon.'

Mara shrugged. 'I'd like nothing better. But this will be my last visit. I have to get back to London. My school board has been very tolerant, giving me this extended leave, but it can't go on for ever.'

'But you don't want to go?' said Kay.

Mara shook her head. 'I love this place. Always have. And there's so much to do here.'

'Come back, then,' urged Leonora. 'Live here. Work here. As you say, there's so much you could do.'

Kay left them arguing about whether Mara should stay or go and went to call on Duggie to catch a lift to the factory. Even though Kitty had left the car to Duggie, if any of them needed it and the petrol coupons had not run out, they got it.

'My goodness,' said Duggie when he saw her, 'we are smart.' He winked. 'Taking over the reins proper, are we?'

She grinned. 'How did you guess?'

The Captain was not so sanguine. As she came through the door of his office he got to his feet, thinking her a stranger. 'Ah, Mrs Fitzgibbon, I didn't recognise you.'

She smiled and nodded. 'Ah, Captain Marshall, I have thrown off my disguise.'

'Well. What can I do for you?' His impatient eye turned to his desk which was piled with papers.

She sat down and pulled off her gloves and he was obliged to sit down too. 'To be honest I'm a little bit ashamed of not taking the factory on wholeheartedly. Playing here, if you like. But since my grandmother's death I've been thinking that I should do it properly.'

'I assure you, there's no need . . .'

She smiled and went on as though he had not spoken. 'So from today I am on your side of things, Captain. I'd like you to call a head of departments' meeting for two o'clock this afternoon. There we will tell them that I am the new proprietor and intend to be a *working* proprietor. Would you be kind enough to ask them to be prepared to speak at the meeting about the working of their own department for, say, five minutes?' She looked round. 'Perhaps you would arrange for some kind of desk in here for me for the time being?' She laughed. 'Don't look so shaken, Captain. I'll not be here long. There's a ramshackle storeroom by the big stores on the shop floor. I'll have that cleared out and make that my permanent office.'

His red face developed a fine purple hue. 'On the shop floor? Mrs Fitzgibbon! Here in the admin. block would be much more—'

She shook her head. 'I'm new here. Where will I learn more about how things tick? The factory floor's the place.'

'When she ran the factory Miss Rainbow had her office here,' he said sulkily.

'But she knew so much already, didn't she? Hadn't she been in business since she was thirteen? And was a skilled clock-maker herself. Knew what made things tick in more ways than one. All I've been doing is selling pots in Alexandria. I have so much to learn.' She picked up her gloves. 'First, though, I wonder if you'd show me the tool room. Isn't that where your most skilled workers are?'

He looked longingly at the papers on his desk again.

'You're too busy?' She stood up. 'Then perhaps you'd ring down and tell them I'm coming. Duggie O'Hare can show me round.'

Duggie took her to his cubbyhole off the shop floor where he made her hang up her coat and hat and discard her gloves. He poked about in a cluttered cupboard till he found a brown paper parcel with a new white dust-coat in it. He shook this out and held it while she put it on. Then he gave her a clipboard and pencil. 'Now then,' he instructed. 'As we go round, look hard at everything and write something down. It don't matter what you put, but write something. That'll make them sit up. You might think afterwards what you've got is all gibberish, but you might find one or two bright ideas. It don't matter really. It's just that you must look like you mean business. You're not some lady bountiful visiting the yokels.'

He continued his instructions as they walked down the edge of the lines towards the penned-off area which was the tool room. 'Now, you have to give respect to toolmakers. They're the top of the heap here. The cocks of the walk. A toolmaker is the prince of workers. Like the hewers in the pit. Five years time-served apprenticeships and they can get a job in any factory in Britain.'

A bubble of silence enclosed them as they made their way down the shop floor. She smiled briefly at Ginger who returned an icy stare in her direction, and nodded briefly at Ralph and Laurenz Gold who were pushing a trolley of wires and washers towards the line.

The tool-room foreman, a big man, whose shiny red face came to a shark-like point at his nose, met them at the chicken-wire gate. He said sourly, 'The Captain rang down. Dinnet knaa what you're hoping to see here, like. With no warning.'

He pulled the door open and they walked in. The men nearest them lifted their heads from their lathes and looked coldly at the invader. A wave of reluctant interest rippled though the enclosure. Challenge and mistrust were in the air.

Kay smiled with deceptive meekness up at the red-faced foreman. 'I am here to learn, Mr Harkness, that's all. Here to learn.'

The wireless, with its wall of talk and its sprightly, sometimes swinging music, contributed with the daily class in English in the reconstruction of Patrizia Gold. She was eager that her Peter and Rebeka should know English, so the growing list of English words and nursery rhymes was repeated hourly in their dingy room. Peter, sensing the lightening of his mother's spirit, smiled more, played more and spoke more not only in this new stumbling English, but in his own language.

Patrizia's time was now liberated by the predictability of Laurenz's absence every day from seven in the morning until six at night at his job in the factory. Every afternoon she entertained Willem the Dutchman and old Judith. She invited them to drink Laurenz's Brazilian coffee and to listen to her wireless.

Judith hobbled down into the village to buy crude off-coupon sweets for the children. In the hut she took Rebeka on her knee and acted as willing audience for Peter's practise in English. Willem brought pictures to show Patrizia of his sons and their children who had all been 'taken'. He knew, from the trickle of hearsay, what had happened to them. And they both knew that their own raw times in the DP camp and here in the resettlement camp were nothing to the horror of the German camps.

Willem told Patrizia his story again and again, eloquent in his role as the 'last witness' of his family. Patrizia, full of her own misery, had heard many such stories in the camp in Switzerland, her mind resisting, stunned by how commonplace this evil seemed to be.

Now somehow there was proper space in her mind for the old man's grief. She noted down the places and the names of which he spoke and made him place her notes with his photographs.

Mara Derancourt turned up unexpectedly late in the afternoon, with Thomas in tow, and a small round woman whom Patrizia didn't recognise. Using Thomas as translator, Mara introduced her sister Leonora, Thomas's mother. 'Leonora has volunteered to continue the lessons, Patrizia. She has great knowledge of your rights here. She will help you. I'm afraid I must return to London.'

Patrizia's face, so long trained to betray no emotion, crumpled with disappointment.

'I'm sorry, Patrizia. I've a class of children waiting for me down there. An old colleague has been teaching them while I was away but she has fallen ill, so I must go to them now.'

Patrizia froze. First Thomas had deserted her, now Mara was leaving. That would teach her to become optimistic, to imagine things could really change. She looked despairingly at this Leonora, this older sister. This mother. This dumpy, even elderly figure. In her Patrizia could discern nothing of Mara's style, of Thomas's intense concern. 'You will not return, Mara?' she said.

Mara shook her head. 'I have a school down there. Children. A life,' she said slowly.

Then Patrizia surprised herself by feeling angry. First Laurenz, now Mara and Thomas. Not since she had flared up at her mother for refusing to leave Vienna had she felt so angry. 'How can you do this to me, Mara? Come here and be the saviour, then decide for your own reasons that this should end? How dare you?' She gagged then, at the stricken look on Mara's face as Thomas faithfully translated word for word. 'Don't worry, I didn't mean . . .'

The hand of the other woman, the one called Leonora, was on her arm. 'Mara has not really left you,' she said quietly. 'She is my sister. She is in me. I am here. *Ich bin hier*,' she said with difficulty.

Patrizia looked at her and saw through the old woman to the person. Lively, bright eyes. The serene face. '*Nicht Deutsch*,' she said slowly. 'Not German. We will speak only English, then I will learn. Peter and Rebeka will learn. In January Peter goes to the school here.'

Leonora shook her head. 'You will learn, but perhaps you will also teach me some German so there is an exchange. We will have to do lessons without Thomas to translate, so you will have to teach me something of German.'

Later that night the class in the recreation hut went very well. Leonora sat very quietly and watched as Mara switched from old man to child to woman with exquisite appropriateness. At the end Leonora herself stood up and explained how important it would be for them to become naturalised British citizens. Then they and their families would be protected from the kind of persecution which had dogged them half their lifetime. A ripple of excitement buzzed round the room, but the excitement had an undertow of caution. There had been so many promises, so much spurious optimism after the recession of pure terror. Gratitude for being alive was the threadbare reality that many of them had had to live with for a very long time.

Thomas stayed on after his mother and Mara had gone, making an excuse of Florence's eager plea to play some more with Peter. They all stayed together in the learning hut, reluctant to abandon its neutrality for the room which reeked of Laurenz's brilliantine and the lesser scent of Patrizia's perpetual fear.

'I wondered if you should help me with something?' Patrizia said.

'What is it?' he said, eager to help. 'Anything.' He resisted the desire to take her hand again.

From a cupboard in the corner of the room she produced a pile of sheets which they had been using for the lessons. They were covered in her neat schoolgirlish hand. 'I have been listening to old Willem. He called himself the "last witness". I thought I should write his things down. What he says. Then I thought that I too am the last witness of my family. And I thought I should write that down too. About my mother and my stepfather. About the Vienna we loved. It is in German, of course. But I have left spaces between the lines. I thought you might write it in English for me. In years to come Peter will not speak German. There will be no need. Why should he? It is the language which articulated his oppression. But he will need to know who he is . . . Why do you laugh?'

'I am sorry. I am sorry. Patrizia, you are like a ticking bomb. Who are you? First you are the oppressed refugee, then the craven wife. And now here you are talking about a language articulating someone's oppression.'

'But that was their trick, wasn't it?' she said despairingly. 'I told you how they took my stepfather and did not allow him to wash or shave for a week, then when they parade him in the street he truly looks like the killer Jew of their cartoons. And he was so particular, you know. The barber came every day to shave him, to dress his hair.' She stood up and looked Thomas in the eye. 'I am the best student in my year at the *Gymnasium*, before they ejected me, the best student they ever knew in that year. But here you see me as this . . . mendicant Jewess who should be so grateful for the safety of your shores, for the smallest attention from charitable English souls.'

He held his hands over his ears. 'No. No. I suppose I need to know . . . need to know what? Your suffering? I can never know that. I know I have had this soft life. And I have things to say to you. But not now, not now.' Then he was on his knees before her, looking into her eyes. 'It's not the time.' He kissed her hand and pressed it to his face. 'There'll be a time for you and me, Patrizia. Count on it.'

A hand rattled the door then banged it with three crashing knocks. Patrizia went pale and Thomas stood up. The children playing in the corner looked up.

'Mrs Gold! Mrs Gold! There's a light still on. Do you realise how much electricity this place takes?' It was the slurred voice of the warden. 'Let us in, let us in, Mrs Gold. I have to see that all is safe and locked up for the night.'

Eleven

Discovery Learning

'Florence Fitzgibbon!'

Florence's head went up in alarm at the sound of her name hedged about with the rasping tone of the teacher.

'Come out here.'

The child beside her nudged her shoulder hard, so she nearly fell off the bench before she righted herself. She approached the large square-faced woman, avoiding her eyes, concentrating on the long lips which turned in on themselves, creating a hard line.

The children who watched Florence now with such eager eyes were strangers to her. That is, all except Peter Gold who was sitting at the far end of her row, looking wild-eyed and even more scared than she was.

Miss Plumstead, whose name was richer and rounder than the woman herself would ever be, pushed a battered book towards her which had 'Beacon Reader Book One' on the cover, barely visible through the finger marks. 'Read!' she said.

Florence read quickly through the first ten pages and the last ten pages. After that Miss Plumstead pushed Beacons Two, Three, Four and Five in turn under her anxious eyes before she started to stumble. The teacher inserted a paper bookmark at page eleven of Book Six and thrust the book at Florence's chest. 'You will start here, Florence Fitzgibbon, and continue.' She held on to the book. 'Which school were you at previously?'

Florence shook her head. 'I didn't go to school before.'

Miss Plumstead scowled. 'I didn't go to school before, *miss*,' she corrected.

'I didn't go to school before, *miss*,' Florence repeated humbly.

'Rubbish! How could you read to this level without going to school?'

'My granny showed me, and, in Alexandria, I read every day to my Granda Sam.'

'You live with your grandparents?'

Florence was flustered. 'Yes. No. My granny, yes, she's there, and my momma.' She blushed at sniggers from behind her, and the mocking echoes of *Momma, Momma*.

'And where is your grandfather?'

'Granda Sam?' Her eyes filled with tears. 'He's not there any more. They say he's behind the clouds but I look and look and don't see him.'

Miss Plumstead, well used to the sight of a child's tears, was unmoved. 'Very well, Florence Fitzgibbon, I will expect you to make progress through this book on your own. Please ensure I hear you read every ten pages, eleven, twenty-one, thirty-one and forty-one, and so on. You will sit in Section One. Clara Bell!'

A tall girl with black pigtails jumped at the sound of her name.

'You move down to Section Two and give Florence Fitzgibbon your seat.'

Clara did as she was told, treating Florence to a murderous look in the process.

Miss Plumstead lowered her hooded eyes back to her list. 'Peter Gold!' she announced.

He looked up in fear and then stood up slowly in his seat.

'Come here!'

That was easy enough. In his young life, '*Komm hier*,' had been barked at him many times with varying degrees of authority. He walked forward slowly. The woman thrust Beacon Book One at him. He opened it at page one.

'Read!' she said.

He looked wildly down the page of hieroglyphs. 'Er . . . boy!' he said triumphantly. The woman was glowering at him, no encouraging smile such as that Mara or Thomas had bestowed on him when he had made out an English word. The woman's horny fingernail came down first on one word, then the next. He shook his head at each one. Then he sighed and closed the book over her finger. '*Ich verstehe nicht*,' he said sadly.

For some reason this seemed to enrage Miss Plumstead. She went the colour of ants' blood and drew herself up to her full five feet seven. 'Speak English, will you, boy!'

He shook his head and turned to go. Her hand grasped his shoulder. 'Stop, will you! Stay where you are. Stand still. I don't know what they think they're doing, sending your sort here, mouthing words in that disgusting language. Your people bombed our cities, killed our families . . . Stand still, boy!' There was a ripple of keen interest across the class: sufferers delighting in the suffering of others. 'Hold out your hand!'

He stood still. She grabbed his hand and held it out in front of him. 'There, keep it there!' She turned round and reached for a small cane which nestled permanently in her pen tray. Then she took the tips of his fingers in hers, measuring her distance. When the cane slashed down a groan, a catharsis of personal relief, passed around the class. Peter said nothing but tears stood unshed in his eyes and his jaw trembled.

'Now!' instructed Miss Plumstead. 'Say this! *I must not speak in German*.' She shook the fingers of his still extended sore hand. 'I must not speak German.'

'*Ich* . . .'

Titters fluttered round the room like a wasp trying to escape a closing jar.

'His dad's a Nazzy,' John Armitage said.

The cane slashed down again. 'I must not speak German.'

'I must not . . .' His brow wrinkled, fear and pain making his memory flee.

'. . . speak German,' said Miss Plumstead through gritted teeth. 'I must not speak German.'

'I must not speak German,' he stuttered, the silent tears wetting his cheeks now.

The cane slashed down again. 'Again!'

Peter did not get a chance to say it again because Miss Plumstead had dropped her stick, knocked nearly off her balance by a small figure which had run down the whole of Section One and launched herself at the teacher's stomach. After several minutes Miss Plumstead managed to get her hands on her assailant's shoulders and push the child off. 'Florence Fitzgibbon, what do you think you're doing?'

'Stop it! Stop it! Leave Peter alone.' The young voice was shrill. 'He can't understand. He's not done anything wrong!'

Miss Plumstead raised her eyes to the stricken Peter who was standing clutching his sore hand. 'Sit down, Peter Gold! See what trouble you've caused!' Then she hauled Florence out of the classroom and stood her in the corridor. 'You will stand there till you cool down, young lady. Do you hear?'

She returned to the classroom, retrieved her stick and cracked it hard on to her desk. She asked for absolute silence and got it. So Miss Plumstead's class proceeded with the reading lesson which had been so regrettably interrupted.

'I stood outside for two lessons,' announced Florence to Leonora later that day. 'Miss Plumstead only let me back in for Arithmetic and that was after playtime. I couldn't even go out to play.' She showed her reddened hand. 'And she gave me three strokes of the cane when I came back into the classroom. But that wasn't too bad. You should've seen Peter's hand, Granny.'

Leonora listened in silence, then made Florence put on her coat and hat again and they went out to get the bus to the camp. When they reached the Golds' hut they found Peter with his hand in a bowl of cold water and Patrizia white with anger. 'Bad woman,' she stumbled over the word. 'Bad woman teacher.'

Leonora shook her head decisively. 'It won't happen again. Not again, Patrizia.' She put her hands on the Austrian woman's shoulders. 'I'm here to apologise, to say sorry. Sorry? You understand? The teacher should be ashamed of herself. You must complain. Go to the school. Tell them . . .'

Patrizia shook her head. '*Nein*, *nein* . . .' How could she tell this woman? 'In Vienna, many times beating. Teachers, police, other schoolchildren.'

'This is not Vienna, Patrizia,' said Leonora firmly. 'I assure you this is not Vienna.' She relaxed then, the anger going out of her. 'Now then, I've brought some sweets and lemonade. We have lots of spare coupons in our house one way or another. Why don't we give these to the children? You and I will have coffee and talk.'

They went into school together first thing the next morning and were obliged to wait half an hour outside the headmaster's office before he opened the door and instructed Leonora to enter. 'I will see you first, Mrs Scorton, then Mrs Gold.'

Leonora shook her head. 'No. I'm sure you won't mind if we speak to you together, Mr Hudson. Mrs Gold's English, though improving, will not meet the demands of this situation.'

The headmaster's craggy brown eyebrows shot up into his low hairline. 'Well, come in then, come in!' he said crossly. Once inside his small crowded study he kept them standing, the children close behind them, while they made their complaints. He sat behind his desk and shaded his eyes as Leonora spoke. He left a long silence before he responded. 'Miss Plumstead is one of my very best teachers,' he said abruptly. 'She is known throughout the county for her effective teaching and her discipline. Forty-six children in her class across two age ranges, and she has them at a word.'

Patrizia, understanding very little of this, looked desperately at Leonora.

Mr Hudson proceeded to talk about the necessity of assessing children who came in the spring term, halfway through the school year. Leonora nodded vigorously as he made each particular point.

His flow of rhetoric now extended to the shortage of materials in this post-war period, the problems they had had with the blackout and evacuees and bomb scares that had rendered real education impossible during the war. Then, of course, there was the indiscipline engendered by the post-war euphoria of parties and celebrations and the hubris of victory.

Leonora finally managed to stop him mid-flow by waving a hand under his considerable nose. 'This is all very well, Mr Hudson. I sympathise with your many difficulties. I see the weight of responsibilities laid on the shoulders of teachers like Miss Plumstead. But that is not why we are here. Come here, Peter!'

Peter stood before her.

'Show Mr Hudson your hand.'

The child held out his badly bruised hand.

'Mr Hudson. This child was hit viciously with a stick, because, having no words in our language, he spoke in his own.'

'Miss Plumstead tells me he swore at her in German.'

'He told her he did not understand her.' Leonora glanced at Patrizia. 'What did he say to the teacher, Patrizia?'

'*Ich verstehe nicht*,' said Patrizia. 'Peter this to teacher says, "I do not understand." '

Mr Hudson stroked his long jaw. 'Perhaps . . . I understand Miss Plumstead's brother was taken prisoner in the North African campaign. Died in a prisoner-of-war camp, so I understand.'

Leonora gripped Peter's shoulders, making him squirm with discomfort. 'No doubt you read your newspapers, Mr Hudson? This boy's grandmother and grandfather, his uncles and aunts, all citizens of Vienna for three generations, whose language too was German, they also died in a camp. Peter was born in a displaced persons' camp. He has come to England to find his first permanent home.' She took a deep breath to contain her anger. 'That woman should be ashamed of herself. She beat this child in a fashion which was no better than those other oppressors who beat his grandfather senseless in the streets of the city where he was born.' Her tirade dissolved into prickly silence.

Mr Hudson coughed. 'Perhaps there has been a degree of hastiness on Miss Plumstead's part. But that does not excuse your granddaughter here launching an assault on the teacher. If all the children did that, with or without cause, there'd be anarchy and no learning would go on at all.'

Leonora pulled Florence in front of her and kept a hand on her shoulder. 'This child has never been inside a school before yesterday, so she has yet to learn the unassailability of one's teacher. But yesterday she went to the aid of her little friend. The pity is that Peter's grandfather and uncles did not have a friend such as she.'

Mr Hudson turned his back on them and went to the window to stare out at the school caretaker who was shovelling coal from a heap into the buckets which he used to fill the classroom stoves. The headteacher stayed with his back to the women for several minutes, then he turned round. 'It will be impossible for these children to be in school today. I will talk with my staff. Then I will send a message to you before the end of the school day.' He glanced first at Patrizia, then at Leonora. 'Will you be at home?'

Leonora said, 'Mrs Gold will spend the day with me. Blamire House on The Lane. We'll wait there for your message.'

At Blamire House Peter followed Florence to the kitchen to raid the biscuit jar. Leonora led Patrizia into the shabby sitting room and invited her to make herself at home. Patrizia put Rebeka down at her feet and wriggled her own aching shoulders. She closed her eyes for a second, relaxing finally in this cluttered space. She absorbed the warm atmosphere, touched the fine old fabric, the worn embroidered cushions. '*Sehr gemütlich*,' she said.

Leonora smiled. 'My mother was a gifted needlewoman, a very fine sewer, even in old age.'

Then Patrizia tried out some English. 'Mother die? It makes me sad for you.'

Leonora smiled. 'My mother was like Florence. She fought for her friends.'

'Pretty house,' Patrizia said. She put her hand to her breast. 'The house of my mother, before eight years, very pretty also.'

Leonora nodded.

Then Patrizia frowned and shook her head. 'But not since then. Only huts. Only camps.'

Leonora threw up her hands in despair. 'Oh, Patrizia. There's so much to do. But first you and Peter, and the baby here, must learn English. And we'll get your naturalisation. After that the rest will follow. You watch.'

At five o'clock a child delivered a message in Mr Hudson's fine cursive hand. The children were to attend school the next day. Peter Gold would be taken to the first class, where he would get help with the language. Florence Fitzgibbon was to return to Miss Plumstead's class and was on her honour to be on her best behaviour or else she too would be removed to the lower class.

The next day Miss Plumstead was subdued: so restrained with her class that twice Mr Hudson had to come in to quell the noise. Florence sought out Peter to play with at playtime and showed him how to shout back at boys like John Armitage who called him *Nazzy*. When the bell went she watched Peter march in with his baby-class line, looking like a blond Gulliver among snub-nosed Lilliputians.

Kay had joined with her mother in voicing her disgust at the teacher's actions, but, preoccupied with the factory, had left those matters in her mother's capable hands.

She had used the few days leading up to the short Christmas break as 'settling-in time' at the factory under the wary eye of Captain Marshall. She said, and did, very little, just wandered around in her white dust-coat, writing notes on her clipboard. Her meanderings took her on to the shop floor, into the machine shop, the tool room and the paint shop. She also made her way across the yard into the admin. block to production meetings, planning meetings and financial meetings.

The atmosphere in the Captain's office was so oppressive

that as soon as she could she moved in to the little storeroom which was being transformed into an office for her. Duggie came to tell her as soon as the whitewashing was finished. She went down, put her clipboard dead centre on the battered deal table and screwed her own coat hook into her own door.

After suffering the chilly glares of Ginger and Janet for days, she finally stopped beside Ginger on one of her journeys down the line. A minute ticked by before Ginger looked up from her screwdriver. 'Can Ah do anythin' foh yeh, Mrs Fitzgibbon?' Each syllable dripped with sarcasm.

'Not really, Ginger. I was just wondering about this cold shoulder stuff.'

Ginger threw down her screwdriver. 'What d'yer expect? Yeh come down here like a simpering schoolgirl, weaselling your way in. Then suddenly you're Miss Glory Be, white coat and all. Word on the line is that you're the boss, now. That your gran give yer the lot.'

Kay hesitated. 'Word on the line's right, Ginger.'

'Get on, will yer, Ginger,' said Janet grimly from across the line. 'Ye'll lose us our bonus, sure as shot.'

Ginger picked up her screwdriver and started to attack the wiring again.

'It's your fault,' said Kay.

Ginger glared at her. 'Dinnet talk bloody soft,' she grunted.

'It is! That night at the dance-hall. When you did me up as Merle Oberon. I'd been wondering whether I could take all this on. I thought I couldn't, to be honest. Hardly been anywhere, never done anything. Then I looked in the mirror and thought perhaps she could, that Merle Oberon type that you invented.'

'Dinnet talk soft,' repeated Ginger.

'No. I swear to you. You gave me the courage to do this, that night at the Gaiety.'

'Well,' said Ginger, mollified. 'I've heard of clickin' with a lad at the Gaiety, but never thought I'd know a lass that "clicked" with a bloody factory.' Her eyes narrowed. 'It wasn't that Nazzy did it, was it? He's been after you since he clapped eyes on you.'

Kay laughed. 'What rubbish, Ginger! Laurenz is married. He's got two children. Anyway he's no Nazi. He's Austrian. Jewish. The Nazis were their enemies.'

'Me dad always says he wished them no harm but he'd never trust a Jew. As for being married, niver stopped any lad round here before,' grunted Ginger. 'They want watching, all of them.'

In fact Kay had seen Laurenz Gold most days since assuming her new role. But apart from a melting smile and a nod he had said nothing. Somehow the smile was a signal of their conversation in the Gaiety, of the warmth of their parting. But there was nothing else. No presumption. His behaviour had been exemplary.

After what turned out to be a very quiet Christmas Kay stopped hovering round the offices and shop floor like a white shadow and started to ask questions at the meetings: about the organisation and distribution of materials; about the shortness of the toilet breaks for the girls on the line, finally about the practice of hidden surveillance in the timing of jobs.

She listened to explanations that the stores and the progress of materials through production had always worked very well; that the women loitered far too long in the toilets anyway; and the hidden timing was justified by the time engineer who claimed people slowed down during timing to enhance their bonus. She listened carefully to what was said, writing it all on her clipboard. When they had finished she allowed the silence to hold for a second longer than was comfortable.

Finally the Captain, forcing a genial smile, said, 'Does that assist you, Mrs Fitzgibbon?'

'Yes. It does.'

The Captain picked up his folder. 'Well, then. Gentlemen . . . Mrs Fitzgibbon?'

The others started to gather up their papers and push back their chairs.

'If I could have your attention for just one more minute?' ventured Kay.

They all sat down again.

'I have one or two proposals. I would like to see a full audit and check on materials. This would incorporate a redesign of the stores to make them more efficient. At present they're a shambles. I would like to double the toilet break provision for the women, and I would also like us to abandon the practice of secret timing. It reeks of spying and I'd have thought we had enough of that during the war.' She stood up, picked up her clipboard and smiled around at the men. 'Now, why don't I leave you to discuss just how you will do that?'

She was trembling as she heard the buzz of outrage as soon as she had shut the door. She made her way rather weakly to her little office on the shop floor. The only thing to cheer her on her way was a wink from Ginger as she passed her work station. She shut her office door and leant on it, wondering whether she had the strength to do all this.

She thought about Kitty, who had set these Works up. It was all right for her, she had been there from the beginning, in here with the fixtures and fittings, so to speak. She didn't have to overcome disbelief, patronage, her own lack of knowledge and experience. Kitty wouldn't have to countenance knowing looks and sniggers from the men. Kay smiled at that thought. Perhaps that wasn't an issue with women of eighty-odd.

It would all have been different if she had been a man. Even a soft young man like Thomas. She sat down at the table angry again at her brother. How dare Thomas flounce around playing pitman when she needed all the help she could get down here? What was he trying to prove, anyway? The previous night, after putting Florence to bed and listening yet again to the tale of how she had saved Peter Gold from the wrath of her teacher, Kay had blown up in anger at the sight and the smell of Thomas in the kitchen, displaying his blisters and bruises. 'Nobody forces you to do all that, you know!'

'I have to make a living. And this is a living our grandfather made. It's an honourable profession.'

'Honourable!' she scoffed. 'Honourable? It's dirty and damp. It gives you blisters and bruises and you come in here ingrained in coal dust and smelling of the sewer. Honourable!'

'I make a living,' he said quietly. 'It's my choice.'

'Choice?' she had shouted. 'Choice? You mean you're choosing not to come and work with me. That's the choice you're making.'

He chuckled. 'Work with you? Work *for* you, you mean. Just like I did in Alexandria? Messenger boy and carrier pigeon.'

She simmered down. 'It seemed to suit you out there,' she grumbled. 'We worked well together.'

'As long as I did what I was told.'

'You didn't like it?'

'I didn't know. I didn't realise . . .'

'You mean you hadn't met Hugh Longstaffe then, and found out what it was to be . . . well, to be a man.'

'Hugh's a good man.'

'A good man? A paragon. A colossus! It's a wonder you don't go and live with him.'

'Well, I've not been asked. Then again' – he looked round the table – 'I'd miss Mother here and our Florence.' The firelight reflected in his glasses as he turned his head to look Kay in the eye. 'I might even miss you if you stopped once in a while to remember who you are. Who you really are.'

She stood up. 'I just cannot understand why you want to do it. It's a dirty, disgusting job.'

He stood up to face her. 'It is a very necessary and very honourable job. And if you're telling me that the Scortons are too superior to be doing such a thing, I hold you in contempt.'

'Thomas!' Leonora, sitting at the kitchen table writing up the minutes of a Women's Labour group she had got involved with, had kept silent up till this moment. Now she sounded the warning.

'Oh, Mother!' He glared at them both then bounded off, his feet pounding on the stairs in their heavy pit stockings.

Kay flung herself back into her chair, the tension of the day finally trickling out of her, leaving her trembling. 'He's changed so much, has Thomas,' she said sadly.

Leonora smiled slightly. 'So he has. Don't you think you have changed in these last months?'

'Me? I've been doing something so hard, so difficult . . .'

'Duggie O'Hare tells me you've been cutting a swathe through the factory,' said Leonora.

'. . . and I've been doing it alone,' said Kay.

'So you don't think what Thomas is doing is hard? That he is doing it alone?'

'What? He's just playing.'

'And are you not, in some ways, playing? How real is it to you, Kay, what you're doing?'

Peter Gold, a child to whom caution had become second nature, sat warily on his father's lap, stumbling in English through a story about the Merman of Fowey. He picked his way through the words about the Merman looking at the world above the sea; how he watched in amazement as the earth people opened and shut their mouths without the swirl of bubbles; how their words, prickly as angel fish, assaulted the Merman's ears; how harsh the earth sounds grated without the soothing sibilance of the sea, the tender wash of the waves. Peter thought how much he himself was like the Merman. '*Uns auch*,' he said to his father, a smile breaking on his lips.

Laurenz's hand clasped his wrist. '*Auf Englisch, Peter. Auf Englisch*. In English! How many times must I urge you?'

Peter tried his best. 'He like me, Papa! The Merman. Come out of water and all different. Words different. What things mean. All different.'

Patrizia clapped her hands, eager to break in before Laurenz poured scorn on Peter's brave attempt. 'Well done, Peter. Good English. It is a very clever idea.' She looked at Laurenz. 'Is that not so, Papa?'

Laurenz stared at her for a moment. 'Yes. Yes,' he said. 'Good boy, Peter. The trick, though, is to learn to swim on land. To be the shark and not the codling, gasping for the fisherman's hook.'

Peter looked flustered at the flurry of English words. His

mother translated for him. His face cleared. 'Yes, yes, Papa. I understand.'

'Not a shark, Laurenz,' said Patrizia. 'Peter should not be a shark.'

'Then he will not survive,' said Laurenz crisply. He stood up, tipping Peter from his knee. 'Is that a letter I see on the bed?' he said frowning.

'I forgot,' said Patrizia. 'It is from Mikel. He likes the car factory, though all the time he has to tell them he is not German. They have short memories there. The Blitz fills their mind. Oh, and he has met some people. Austrians called Goldfarb, they . . .'

Laurenz picked up the letter and peered at Mikel's neat, squared-off script.

> They have come back from the East. From the camps. They have met young Heini Goldfarb and his father at the council office here, where I went to register. It seems they did get away. They asked for news of you, cousin, but I was vague, saying you had left me here and gone straight to America. I thought you would wish this.

'Why would he say that, Laurenz, that you are in America?' frowned Patrizia, leaning over his shoulder to read.

He threw down the letter and turned on her 'You had no right to open this letter.' He pushed her shoulder so that she fell awkwardly on the bed. 'You had no right to read my letter.'

She sat up. 'It simply said *Gold* on the envelope. It did not say your name or mine.'

'Who would be writing to you?' he sneered. 'You know no one.' He pushed her back on the bed and leapt so that he was sitting astride her. 'No one.' He slapped her hard. 'All letters for me, do you hear? Or I will beat you.' He raised his hand to hit her again to drive home his lesson, but did not land the blow. Peter had launched himself across the room and butted him with his small head so Laurenz fell off balance and sprawled across the bed. He clutched the boy as he fell and held the child's flailing hands away from him. 'Well, we have a shark here, Patrizia. No codling but a shark!' He laughed then set Peter down beside the bed quite gently. 'Now where did you learn that, Peter? Not from your marshmallow mother here, I think. When I was your age . . .' His eyes went blank then and he stood staring out of the window breathing short sharp breaths.

Peter stayed silent. He could not talk to his father about Florence Fitzgibbon and her flying tackle which had saved him from Miss Plumstead's wrath. He had no way of sharing his feelings about that with him: the bewildering experience of the weak attacking the strong and actually surviving.

Patrizia read his thoughts. 'In school he has to learn how to defend himself, Laurenz,' she said. 'He has been beaten three times in the playground, and remember even the teacher hit him. You saw his hands.'

Laurenz looked at her blankly then seemed to shake himself. 'He must be an idiot, though. Didn't they put him in the lower class?'

'That is just for the language,' protested Patrizia. 'The head-teacher said once he was speaking English he would go back in the higher class.'

'And has Florence Fitzgibbon gone down a class?'

'Well, no,' said Patrizia uncertainly. 'She reads well. She does not need to go down a class.'

Patrizia had hidden from Leonora Scorton her disappointment at the headmaster's judgement, which had separated Peter from his only ally, had punished him for what had been the teacher's transgression. There was no justice. There could never be justice. Peter would always have to work harder for the smallest recognition. She would have to resign herself to that.

In the meantime she had another thing to worry about. What had these Goldfarbs to do with Laurenz? Just why did Mikel need to protect his cousin from them?

'I always wanted to travel meself, but never had the chance.' Hugh took a bite at his bread and cheese. 'Our Harry wrote in his letters about the desert. Twelve hundred miles long, he said. Not just sand but great fields and crags of rock. Said the desert was an ideal place to fight a war. No people, see? But then war in the desert was impossible, he said, because the desert always won.'

'We won at El Alamein, didn't we?' Thomas poured the cold tea down his throat allowing it to wash down the thin layer of coal dust which had settled in his windpipe during the first part of the shift.

'Tenacity. That's what won that battle, our Harry says. Tenacity. Rommel was pretty tenacious himself, like. That's why he won at first.'

They had turned off their lamps to give their eyes a rest and were sitting in the dark having their bait. Their seat was a trestle made from a plank and two blocks of cut prop. Their boots were on another plank to keep them out of the water.

'Alexandria didn't seem like "travelling" when we were there,' said Thomas thoughtfully. 'It was just home.'

'Home? Among all those foreigners?'

'We'd lived there longer than we'd lived anywhere else. And they didn't seem like foreigners. When I came back here, those lads in the Royal George, even you, then, seemed more like foreigners to me. Alexandrians were just people to me. Some were friends. Some we just dealt with. Some cheated us. Some went out of their way to find pots for us, for Kay and me, for our little business.'

Hugh took out a pouch from his sack, tore off some tobacco and pushed it in his mouth, concentrating a bit until he had it in a chewable state. Then he said, 'What about marrahs, friends, mates? Did yeh have those?'

Thomas shook his head. 'I was friendly with Stephen, my sister's husband. But then he went to war.' He shut his bait tin with a click. 'Then there was only my sister. We were great friends then. Not so much now. The cold here's made her a cross patch.'

Hugh shook his head. 'Women! Not the same. Even the wife,

and she was a good'n. Not the same.' He clicked his own bait tin shut and tucked it into his canvas sack. Then with some creaking of joints he hauled himself up to the crouching position which was all the seam would allow. 'Now, marrah, I've got coal to get and you've got coal to fill. Let's gerron, shall wuh?'

Later, at the end of the shift, they walked 'out-bye', the beams of their helmet lamps darting and wandering over rough-hewn timber struts and props, which they marked off one by weary one as they walked to the bottom of the shaft. Hugh grunted to Thomas, 'Yer wanter get down the club on Satdah. Good crack down there. Call for us at six o'clock and I'll tek yer down.'

It was a royal command. Thomas could not dissent. He did not. 'Yes,' he said. 'I'll do that.'

The blessing of early shift was that, despite hauling yourself from bed and trudging to the pit in the pitch dark, you got your release in the mid-afternoon. For Thomas, as he came out of the cage, the light was blinding, a wild benediction. He turned his face this way and that, bent his neck so the light would hit his nape where he could feel it. The tired tufts of grass just waiting for spring seemed brilliant green to him. The pale sky took on an iridescent hue. The very wood on the fences, the bricks on the walls, seemed to throb with colour.

They stopped at the end of Hugh's street. 'I'm just down the allotments to feed me rabbits and hens,' said Hugh.

Thomas hesitated.

'You want to come?' said Hugh. 'Nowt to see, like.'

'Yeah. Yes, I'll have a walk down with you,' said Thomas, not showing too much enthusiasm, learning swiftly now the oblique demeanour which being marrahs demanded.

The beaten-earth pathways between the high, clapboard fences of the allotments were narrow. The smell of chickweed and the faintly fruity stench of pigswill sat in the air. Here and there a cockerel held lordly court on a fence post, ignoring his clucking harem down below.

Hugh untied the string which fastened his gate and pushed it inwards. His allotment was neat: beds turned over like dark velvet, buckets and tools in neat piles and rows. Four chickens scratched their way through the cores of old cabbages which were lumpy like bleached white spines.

He opened another wire-netting gate leading into a shed in which were stacked a dozen rabbit hutches. From a bin in the corner he took up handfuls of greens and one by one he opened the hutches and thrust them inside, muttering and talking to the animals as though Thomas were not there. The last cage he opened wide and lifted the rabbit out by the ears. He held it to his chest and stroked it with long firm strokes, ears to tail, ears to tail. At last he looked up at Thomas, and held out the rabbit. 'Give'm a stroke, lad,' he said.

Nervously Thomas took the trembling animal and held it in the same fashion.

'Nice and firm,' said Hugh, 'that's it. Nice and firm.'

The little body felt warm under his hand and Thomas felt real satisfaction when the animal settled down and stopped trembling. 'He's beautiful,' he said.

'He'll do,' said Hugh, the satisfaction in his voice belying the dry reserve of his words.

When the time came to go Thomas felt sorry that he had to relinquish the little creature. He was compensated when they went from the rabbit hut to the chicken cree where Hugh thrust four warm, musty eggs into his pocket. 'Take them home for our Leonora,' said Hugh. 'I bet it's a while since she had a fresh egg.'

Walking on home alone, the eggs safely stowed in separate pockets, Thomas mused at his mother being called 'our Leonora', and the way that Hugh had somehow, whatever Kay thought, become part of his family.

He mused also about his father, whom he had loved and respected and feared too. The truth was that Sam's preoccupation with their mother had left both Kay and Thomas on the outside, warmly dealt with but of secondary importance. That was of course how the two of them had become so close themselves. It was not just about being twins. He thought now he had never felt as close to his father as he had to Hugh in the musty rabbit hut, stroking the animal with Hugh proudly looking on.

Leonora was delighted with the eggs and touched by the gesture. When Thomas told Florence about the allotment with the hens and rabbits her eyes shone. 'Can I go and see the rabbits, Uncle Thomas? Will you take me?'

'We-ell . . .'

'And Peter! We could take Peter.'

Thomas thought of the small anxious face of Patrizia Gold. 'Yes,' he said. 'We could take Peter. I tell you what,' he went on. 'Just let me have my bath and we can both go and ask Peter if he would like to come. We can go now.'

'The boiler's full,' said his mother, who was laying the table for his meal. 'You make sure you wash all that scum away afterwards. You left a real mess there yesterday. Kay had to make do with a wash.'

He grinned at her. 'Count your lucky stars, Ma! I might have been bathing in a tin bath by the fire. What trouble would that have caused? You'd have had to ladle the water in and out by hand.'

'A bath by the fire, Granny! Can we do that?' said Florence. 'That would be lovely.'

Leonora pointed at Thomas with a fork. 'I didn't sign on as a miner's wife, or a miner's mother, Thomas, so you can draw your own bath from my very sophisticated boiler upstairs and you can wash the bath out afterwards. Or else!'

'The Old Man wants you.' Duggie O'Hare put his nose round Kay's door. 'He ain't half in a sweat about something.'

She looked up at him as they walked across to the admin. block together. 'You've been keeping a low profile, Duggie, while I've been cutting my swathe here,' she said.

He shrugged. 'I'm on a hiding to nothing here, Kay. I work for them but they all know I'm your man. Just as I used to be Kitty's man. They've always been wary, let me get on with my own thing. But I'm wary of them too. They know a hang of a sight more about what they're doing than I do. Or you do, for that matter.'

'What're they saying?'

'If I told you that I would be a spy, wouldn't I?'

'Go on, tell me, Duggie.'

He opened the door for her and they hunched themselves up against the cold February drizzle. 'They're saying you don't know your ace from your apex, Kay. That you'll create havoc then run away. Already production time lost on this toilet breaks thing is increasing. They're doing their sums. They say the toilet rule'll have to come back.'

She laughed. 'We'll see about that.'

They stopped at the Captain's door. Duggie winked at her, gave her a military-style salute, turned smartly on his heel and left her.

The Captain stood up as she came in, making her think briefly that at least his manners if not his attitude were changing a bit. 'Ah, Mrs Fitzgibbon! Sit down, sit down.' He waited until she was seated before he sat down himself.

'Is there a problem, Captain Marshall?'

'Well, in a manner of speaking. I've been having mayday signals all week from our sales section in the South. Put simply, our stocks are piling up and our sales are down. There's not much money around; there are more competitors coming out of the armaments game and splitting this market. Miss Rainbow got in very fast after the war, d'you see, but they're catching up. We have insufficient cash from sales to underpin our purchase of materials. Next, it'll be wages. I don't wish to alarm you but this could mean closure. To be honest, Mrs Fitzgibbon, we are at something of an impasse.' He harrumphed. 'So much energy spent on trivia . . .'

'It's not trivial for a woman to wish to go to the toilet and not be allowed to go, Captain.'

He flourished a hand, dismissing her interpolation. '. . . and not enough on the product.' He nodded towards the bulky, gleaming Rainbow cooker standing in the corner of his office. 'Nobody's buying 'em.'

She walked over and squatted down in front of the cooker. She turned the switches on and off and turned the door this way and that. She knew very little about cookers, never having used one. Cooks – and very good ones at that – were cheap in Alexandria. And at Blamire House Duggie's friend Mrs MacMahon seemed to be a bit of a wizard, alongside Leonora.

'We've got to make people buy ours and not theirs. Who designs the cookers?' She flushed, suddenly aware of the depths of her ignorance. Perhaps she had indeed been too absorbed with trivia.

'We have a small design team in London. Miss Rainbow recruited them. They know the market. They do that end of things.'

'And are there any women there? Any women involved in the designs?'

'Women?' He shook his head too quickly. 'No. No. Designers are men.'

'Captain Marshall! When was the last time you cooked a meal?' In some ways she was thinking of herself as well.

A laugh rumbled somewhere near his belly. 'I'm afraid you have me there, Mrs Fitzgibbon. I've lived most of my life aboard ship at the mercy of ships' cooks, some of whom were excellent, some abysmal. Now I have a housekeeper, Mrs Hunter. She cooks fine traditional fare. Her Yorkshire puddings are, I must say, excellent.'

'Does she cook them on a Rainbow cooker?'

He shook his head. 'No. She favours the more traditional form of cooking. There is a big black range in the kitchen. A veritable monster. How she manages it I don't know.'

'Well then! Number one. You should have a Rainbow cooker installed for Mrs Hunter to use. Better in your house than languishing in our warehouse. Then she can try it and tell you how it works.' She paused. 'Whether it works.' She laughed. 'I'm as guilty as you, Captain. I've hardly noticed the Rainbow cooker in our house. I'll check with Mrs MacMahon. See what she thinks of it.'

'You don't cook yourself, Mrs Fitzgibbon?' She thought there was some justice in the thread of contempt in his voice.

She shook her head. 'I haven't lived my life aboard ship, Captain, but in Egypt we always had wonderful cooks. Men. They could cook in the Eastern or the Western way with great skill.' She sat down on the chair opposite him. 'I tell you what we should do, Captain. We should get your Mrs Hunter and my Mrs MacMahon down here. And some of the older women off the line. Family women. Bring some cookers here in your office. Those of our rivals. What have they got that we don't have? Get the women to take a look at them and make practical suggestions.'

The Captain ran his fingers through his beard. 'I can't think the designers would take kindly to suggestions from such people. They are not aware of the engineering implications.'

Kay shrugged. 'Well, we can tell the designers they must take notice or we will find new designers. We have the whip hand here, Captain. Don't you see that? We have the whip hand and we should use it.'

Twelve
Rabbits

As he alighted from the bus with Florence dancing alongside him, Thomas had misgivings about his promise that Peter should see Hugh's rabbits. But Florence was pleased to be going to see her friend Peter away from the surreal constraints of the school, where the jeering children and the chillingly focused glare of Miss Plumstead made things very difficult.

On his part Thomas was feeling guilty because he had not made time to go and see Patrizia Gold as he had promised. The translations remained undone on his bedside table. Perplexed as he was by his attraction to Patrizia, in recent days he had left the journeys to the camp to his mother. The work at the pit had proved to be more than physically exhausting. Adjusting to the heavy life underground sapped all his mental energy, filled his waking and dreaming life with images of enclosure and entombment, with the gruff murmur of miners' voices and the threatening creak of timbers as they held the weight of the earth off the shoulders of living men.

He saw now why the miners put their home life at great distance from themselves. The talk of 'our lass' or 'the bairns' gave it an anonymity which neutralised its significance in this world of men; it allowed them to concentrate on the dangerous job in hand.

In his exhaustion every evening he had begun to listen to his mother's tales of 'her' refugees with a similar abstraction. All that business – the trouble at school with the head and teacher

– had become a world of women, little to do with him or his work where life and death was the daily preoccupation.

Peter answered their knock on the door of the hut. 'Mama! Here are Florence and Thomas.' He threw the words behind him, gulping with excitement.

Patrizia came to the door, Rebeka on her hip. She beamed her welcome. 'Come in! Come in!' she said. 'I will make coffee.'

Thomas shook hands with her, enfolding her small hand in his. He thought she looked better, much better than before. Her eyes were brighter, her gaze more steady. This combat with the teachers must suit her.

'No coffee,' he said. 'We have come to take you to see some rabbits.'

'Rabbits!' Florence nodded vigorously. 'Rabbits, Peter!'

Peter glanced at his mother.

'*Die Kaninchen*,' she said.

The child frowned.

She glanced up at Thomas. 'No rabbits. Peter has not seen a rabbit.' She smiled slightly. 'But I have seen a rabbit. In the Vienna woods when I was a child. Picnics with my mother. Wild earthberries and bread and cheese. And wine in a little glass specially for me.' She sighed. 'Such warm dry summers.'

'Then put your coat on and I will show you and Peter some more rabbits!' said Thomas urgently, regretting that he had raised in her such a mood of mournful nostalgia.

Later, roused by their knock, Hugh came to the door of his house in his braces, the traces of coal imperfectly erased from the creases and crevices in his skin. These days he did not have the privilege of a wife with the bath tin put out before a blazing fire, and a ready hand with a soapy flannel. He looked in bewilderment at the clutch of people standing at his back door. 'Now, marrah, what can Ah dee for yuh?' he said to Thomas uneasily.

Thomas realised he had overstepped some mark. Some protocol about not visiting your marrah with a horde of women and children in tow. 'Well, Hugh, it doesn't really matter, but

Florence here . . . I told her about your rabbits and she wanted to see them . . . and her friend Peter . . . She thought . . .' he floundered.

Hugh peered past them into the gathering dusk. 'We'll need a lamp,' he said. 'Nee streetlamps down there. Nothing.'

Thomas put a restraining hand on Florence. 'No, no, Hugh. We won't bother. Really. I was carried away, I forgot about the hour.'

'Just wait there,' said Hugh gruffly, then vanished.

Patrizia moved closer to Thomas. 'The man is not pleased. We should go.'

But Hugh was back at the door in a second, his cap on his head, his muffler round his neck. In his hand he held a lit miner's lamp which leaked a restricted pool of light, illuminating their shoes and the bleached clumps of tired grass which broke through the concrete of his yard.

He lifted the lamp so his face was underlit, throwing his craggy brows into dark relief. 'My da's lamp, this, Thomas,' he said. 'Took it underground forty year.' Then he led the way down the yard and along the back lane.

They clustered after him like ducklings tracking a mother duck. When they reached them, the allotments were sunk into even greater darkness than the back lane. Here and there, though, the windows of the makeshift huts gleamed with faint light; behind them men were still tending their livestock, or smoking a last cigarette before returning home to get ready for the club, or to turn in early to get some proper sleep before a very early shift the next day.

They held on to each others' shoulders in the dark as they shuffled in single file along the little path which bisected Hugh's allotment. Thomas thought of a picture he had once seen in the paper, of blind soldiers making their way off the ship which had brought them home from the battlefields of the Great War.

'Stop here!' Hugh went into the shed and hung the lamp high on a hook. 'Now, you first.' He drew Patrizia inside and sat her, with Rebeka on her knee, in a little broken chair in the corner.

'Now we'll have the bairns on these crackets.' He put the two small stools side by side and Peter and Florence sat there, wide-eyed with interest, their eyes fixed on the hutches where the light from the pit lamp reflected fine points of light in the eyes of invisible creatures.

Then from the far hutch Hugh lifted a rabbit out by its ears, settled it on his forearm and squatted on his haunches before Peter and Florence. 'Now this is Joey, son. Gan on, stroke'm.'

Peter could not understand a single guttural word which came out of the man's mouth but he understood everything he said. He put out a timid hand to stroke the dense fur. The old man's hand, hard and leathery, pressed down on his. 'Nice and firm, son. He'll like that, will old Joey. He's scared himself and if he knows you're scared he's even more frit.' Peter stroked the rabbit harder and harder. The trembling body settled under his touch, and the thick fur warmed his chill hand.

'His name's Joey!' commanded Hugh.

'His name's Joey!' repeated Peter. 'Joey.'

'Here, sit still, son. I'll lie him on your knee. Take hold, firm now. That's it. Face away from you, stroke towards you. Now gan on, give him a nice stroke.'

Then Hugh took down another rabbit, this time a white female called Belle. Very carefully he placed her in Florence's lap. 'There now, flower, see Belle's nice pink eyes, the way she twitches her whiskers? A bolder lass she is, than old Joey here.'

Thomas watched him intently, moved by the exquisite tenderness which he had never seen in his friend before. He glanced down at Patrizia, who was sitting stroking Rebeka's arm as though her baby daughter were a little rabbit herself. She felt his gaze and glanced up, giving him a radiant smile. Through him there rippled a glimpse of the woman she might have been, a woman who might have gone on having carefree picnics with her mother in the Vienna woods, playing with the rabbits and eating earthberries. He vowed he would start on the translation for her the next day, the minute he got back from work.

'Here y'are, Thomas,' said Hugh sharply. 'This is yours. He's blue. Called Lenin, he is.'

The shift at the factory was well over when Kay finally made her way, in the car she had borrowed from Duggie, through the big gates on her way home. She had spent the last two hours rushing round hardware shops in the district acquiring other brands of cooker for their comparison exercise the next day. And she had gone along the lines, promising some of the women overtime if they would come in on Saturday morning for a special job.

Ginger had been mad that she wasn't asked. Overtime was a useful perk. Kay asked her if she cooked the dinners in her house.

'Cook? That's a joke. Me mother does the cooking. You should taste her meat and potato pie. Bloody marvellous.'

'Well, bring her along here and she can do your overtime for you.'

Now Jim Murton, the gateman, waved as he shut the gates behind her and went back to his hut to have the second half of his sandwiches and go on reading his Zane Grey, which had reached a crucial bit where the Blue Circle Ranch was surrounded by a horde of shrieking Comanches.

The road outside the factory was narrow and ill lit and she was forced to drive very slowly. Her headlights bounced along a row of windows illuminated against the encroaching dark, open doors with women standing at them. On the corners children clustered like moths magnetised by the glow of yellow light from the streetlamp. After the punitive years of blackout, to stand on your own threshold on a winter evening was still a bit of a privilege. She edged her way past waiting butcher's and greengrocer's carts lit by storm lanterns. These narrow streets were lucrative locations on pay nights.

She turned up into the long road leading towards The Lane. On her right were the larger houses built by affluent citizens of Priorton at the turn of the century, when the town was booming, and the High Street boasted three furriers and two fine jewellers. On her left as she drove were the broad reaches of the Gaunt Valley and the bulky architecture of the viaduct, which was so entwined now in the Rainbow family legend. Kitty had made such a great life for herself after that strange beginning, coming almost out of nowhere as she had done.

Kay was so busy thinking about Kitty that she had to jump on the brakes to stop the car running into a motor bike which was pulled up nearly in the middle of the road. She leapt from her car to berate the driver, only to find herself looking into a familiar face. 'Laurenz!' she said. 'What the blazes are you doing here?'

His handsome face was pinched; he looked frozen. 'The *verdammte* bike behaves very badly. I have a flat tyre,' he said. 'You say flat as a pancake.' They both looked down at his tyre which was, as he had said, flat as a pancake.

'And no one has stopped to help you?'

'I have been here only a little time.' An experienced liar, he was comfortable with this statement. In fact he had been here for more than an hour, watching for her car to start its long haul up The Lane.

'So what will you do? Can I help you?'

He scratched his head, disturbing his immaculate curls and sending one of them snaking down his white forehead.

'Can I take you somewhere? A garage?' she persisted.

He shook his head. 'I can mend it. I have a spare wheel back at the camp.'

'I'll take you there. Push the bike up the road and we'll put it in the back yard at Blamire House. Then we'll go and get your tyre.'

He shook his head again. 'I cannot ask you to go to the camp, Kay. It is a nasty place.'

'Of course you can, Laurenz.' She was suddenly determined to go there. She found herself curious about where he lived, about Patrizia. Funny that she had heard so much about Laurenz's wife from her mother and Thomas, but had never seen her. And there was young Peter, whose name was often on Florence's lips. 'I'll drive up to the house and open the gates,' she said firmly. 'You push the bike along.'

Mrs MacMahon met her in the hall. She said Kay had just missed Leonora who was off to a Labour Party meeting, and Thomas and Florence had rushed off out somewhere. Kay's own supper, a nice plate of panacklety, was in the oven and she, Mrs MacMahon, was off to give Duggie his meal. 'Not panacklety, like. He has no fancy for that, never had. A nice bit of liver and bacon, I've got him.'

Kay told her she wanted to take her to the factory in the morning.

'Factory? Me? I don't need no factory job, thank you very much. Me and Duggie has this worked out. He takes care of me, an' I take care of him. In a manner of speaking, like.'

Kay shook her head. 'I don't want you to work. It's advice I want. About the Rainbow cooker.'

'Advice? You've come to the right place then, Mrs Fitzgibbon. I don't know much, but what I do know, I know, if you see what I mean?'

They went out of the back of the house together and Mrs MacMahon strolled to her little cottage across the yard. She stood at the door and watched as Kay opened the big gates and a man in his thirties, with brilliantined hair, pushed in a gleaming motor cycle.

'We're leaving it here,' Kay explained to Mrs MacMahon. 'Then going to get a tyre so Laurenz can mend it. Will you close the gates behind us?'

Mrs MacMahon did as she was bid, then went in to tell Duggie all about it. 'I don't know what she wants with that one. Proper Dago, if you ask me. You wouldn't trust him as far as you could throw him. You mark my words.'

'Leave it, Mary, leave it,' said Duggie, tucking into his liver and bacon; he didn't care for panacklety. In his opinion that favoured northern dish was good food spoiled. 'Laurenz, you say? It'll be the Austrian. Not a bad sort, to tell you the truth. A bit greasy but certainly a hard worker. I'll give him that.'

Laurenz lounged easily in his seat as Kay drove along, not betraying his pleasure that his stratagem had worked. He had waited there at the bottom of The Lane twice before, but his timing had been wrong. This time he had judged it just right.

In the car the silence wrapped itself round Kay like a deliciously warm cloak which threatened to choke her. She had to break it. 'How are you liking it at the factory, Laurenz?'

She felt rather than saw him shrug. 'It is a job. But carrying things around for people, I do not think that is a lifetime's career. And the pay is poor. My cousin Mikel earns twice as much in the Jaguar factory in Coventry.'

She was defensive. 'Jaguar is a very big operation. It will be years before we . . .'

He put a hand on her arm, all contrition. She could feel the sinewy heat of his body through her thick jacket. 'I do not criticise, Kay. We newcomers have to be grateful for what we can get. Is that not so?'

'No. No,' she protested. 'Why should you? You should try for the best. There'll be more chances there, you wait.'

'Do you go in the tool shop when you walk round your factory?'

'Mmm. Yes, I do.'

'I go in there to deliver materials. It is a mess. A chaos. Filthy. In Switzerland that would not be tolerated.'

'I thought they were good toolmakers in there. Clever. Though they didn't care for me,' she laughed.

'You are very philosophical about this.'

'To be fair, I had thought, with all the women in there during the war – there's a photo in Captain Marshall's office – you'd think they'd have some respect for women.'

She could feel him shaking his head. 'You must see the men would want their place back, returning from the war. *Hail the conquering hero comes*. Is that not a song?'

'Do you think it's right? The men taking the jobs back from the women?'

This time she could see him shrug. 'It's the way of the world.'

She took a breath. 'So what do you think of having a woman in charge? What do you think they think?'

'I think, and I know they will think, that you are different. I knew when I saw you, when you were just a girl on the line with Ginger. How do you say it? The exception that proves the rule.'

She was uneasy at this, feeling that it was meant as a compliment, but saying all the wrong things.

'Next left.'

She was surprised at her own reaction to the camp, near derelict now, with only half the huts occupied and last year's pathetic attempts at gardening showing only whiskery relics of flowers and vegetables. She had seen much worse shanty areas in Alexandria which shocked her less.

Laurenz sensed her reaction. 'It is a dump, do you not think?'

She brought the car to a stop. 'Hard to think people actually live here.'

'Not many left. They go to the cities, or they get council houses in the area.'

'And you?'

He shrugged again. 'I wait. I think perhaps I go to Coventry where is my cousin Mikel. He makes big money.'

The door was locked. He frowned and fished out a key. 'Patrizia should be here,' he said.

The room was empty. The bare bulb illuminated a room with a large and a small bed, a table with four chairs, a bookshelf, a military-style clothes locker and a small cupboard on which stood a small Primus stove, a kettle and a water jug.

'It's very neat,' she said helplessly.

'It is a slum,' he said. 'But only for now. Till I find my way.'

She noticed he said 'I', not 'we'.

He pulled out one of the chairs. 'Now, you will sit down while I get the tyre?'

She sat down obediently and watched in amazement as he

went to the larger bed and heaved at it until it was vertical. Underneath were boxes and parcels and metal containers – a world of possessions: here was the reassurance of a wealth which was lacking in the bleak room. From a far corner he lifted a brand-new motor-bike tyre and rolled it towards her. The rubber was black as liquorice and she could detect the sweet sickly smell of the Malayan tree.

Slowly he lowered the bed and straightened the woven rug. He turned to her, his face closed. 'You are surprised at my treasure trove?'

'I don't know. This hut . . .'

'It is all contrasts, Kay. This hut is a fine place, compared to the one in Switzerland. There were eight families there. Only four here. And I learn what I always knew, what my forefathers distilled into my blood. Our treasure is not in bricks and mortar, it is here.' He tapped his head. 'And is there under the bed. Goods for barter. What we can hoist on to our backs. We made our mistakes in Vienna, building grand houses and water gardens, imagining, even after five generations, that we belonged, that we could put down genuine roots. Ha! What fools!'

She felt like a pampered, helpless idiot.

He laughed. 'Do not be so sad, dear Kay! It is foolish to look backwards. There is only today and tomorrow.' He went to the cupboard and pulled out a bottle of fine brandy and two glasses. 'We will drink to tomorrow!'

He poured the brandy with respectful care and presented it to her as though the simple glass were a silver chalice. The liquor burnt her mouth and as it fired its way down her throat she remembered she had not eaten since breakfast. 'We should go,' she said abruptly. 'Put the tyre on your bike.'

He came and stood before her. He took the glass from her fingers and took her shoulders and drew her to him. 'Since the first day, Kay,' he said. 'This.'

Then he kissed her, his lips making a play of searching her face till they found her mouth. The brandy on his breath, his lips, mingled with the brandy on hers. His tongue was inside her lips, playing with the soft flesh there. It was then that she raised her hands to the back of his head, to press him to her.

The brandy, or this kissing, was making her feel very drunk. She wanted to kiss him for ever to reinforce the heat which was flooding through her in waves. She had never known such kissing. With Stephen the kissing, even the lovemaking, had been jolly, but clinical and perfunctory, a mere part of the fun of being together. He had never kissed her with an open mouth. She had not known of such things.

Laurenz drew back and pushed her hair back from her face. 'You are very young,' he said with involuntary tenderness.

She stood back, freeing herself from his touch. 'Don't be silly.'

'How old are you?'

'Twenty-six. How old are you?'

He laughed. 'I am very old. Thirty-seven.'

That did seem old to her. She wondered what she was doing. Here. With him. Now he was walking away from her and she wished he wouldn't. He looked across at her. 'We should go dancing together,' he said. 'Would that not be very nice?'

She flushed. 'We can't do that. People . . .'

'We could go to Darlington. Do you know there is a very good dance-hall there?'

She shook her head. 'Really I . . .'

But now there were voices outside and she was relieved that there was distance between them. The door burst open and Florence raced in dragging Peter behind her. 'Momma! We saw the car. Did you come to take us home?' Her cheeks were rosy and her eyes sparkling. 'We've been to see the rabbits and Uncle Hugh. He says if there are babies he will call them Peter and Florence. Can you believe it?'

Kay raised her eyes to the small dark-haired woman who walked in behind them, whose eyes also sparkled. This woman who must be Patrizia Gold. She was rather plain, her features being just a bit too large for her face. But she didn't look anything like the worn, half-mad woman Kay had imagined. For one thing she too must be ten years younger than her husband.

Thomas brought up the rear. He was carrying a toddler who lolled in his arms fast asleep. 'Everything all right, Kay?' he said, frowning slightly.

She smiled. 'No emergency,' she said. 'I just brought Laurenz here to collect a tyre. He had a puncture on his motor bike.'

Thomas was relieved. 'I thought something was up,' he said. 'But now you're here that's our good fortune. You can give us a lift home.'

Laurenz was pulling on his flying jacket. 'Yes, we have to get this tyre on the bike,' he said. He patted Peter on the head. 'So you have had a jolly time with the little girl, Peter?'

'Name is Florence,' said Peter sullenly.

'Ah, Florence! A pretty name!'

Florence scowled at him, taking her cue from Peter.

'We really should go,' said Kay hurriedly.

He rolled the tyre out of the hut and down the pathway.

Kay took Florence's hand. 'Are you coming, Thomas?' she said quite sharply. 'School tomorrow.'

Patrizia smiled at Thomas. 'Peter also.'

Thomas returned her smile. 'Thomas also. I have to be up for the pit at three in the morning.'

Thomas sat beside Kay in the front of the car and Laurenz sat in the back, nursing the tyre, with a silent sleepy Florence beside him.

Back at Blamire House, by the time Kay had given Florence her supper, Laurenz was at the door saying, with Thomas's very kind help, the tyre was now exchanged and he must go home. 'I come to thank you, *gnädige Frau*, for rescuing me.' He clicked his heels, took her hand, and kissed it. As his head came up he whispered, 'Darlington,' turned on his heel and left.

Thomas, leaning on the doorpost, chuckled. 'The old dog!' he said. 'If I'm not mistaken you've made a hit there, sis.'

She pushed past him. 'Don't be ridiculous,' she said, and

bounded up the stairs to be away from those mocking eyes.

'Momma!' Florence was sitting up in bed in her nightdress. 'Do you know any stories about rabbits?'

Later that night, lying in bed, Kay contemplated doing wrong for the first time in her life. Living in Alexandria with Thomas and her mother and Sam had been exciting and challenging but more or less virtuous. She had fallen for Stephen but had not made love to him till they married. After he had gone, working with Thomas, running the business and bringing up Florence had been excitement enough.

But here she was, weak at the knees at the thought of going dancing with a penniless refugee who was ancient – ten years older than herself – and who was married with two children, and who was, she was quite sure, on the make in one way or another. And she must not kid herself. What she was contemplating was wrong, a bad thing.

That night she dreamt of the dance. They were whirling round and round in the waltz, her skirt wrapping round his legs. Through her brain whirled the thought: There can't be anything wrong with this. This is so good, so fine. But when she looked up at her partner it was not Laurenz Gold. It was Thomas and on his face was the scowl, then it was Florence scowling, just as she'd scowled so rudely at Laurenz Gold when he had spoken kindly to her.

Thirteen

Improving the Model

The next morning when Kay walked into the factory, Ginger was waiting at the top of the line with a cluster of women. She introduced Kay to her mother, Mona, who was a hennaed, miniaturised version of Ginger herself.

The other women preened themselves, relishing the difference of being in the factory dressed in their Saturday best. Still they were not really sure what was going on. 'D'yer say we've gotta go to the Captain's office?' said one of them uneasily.

'He's dying to see you,' said Kay firmly. 'Now come on.' She walked along with Ginger who was wearing high heels and full make-up. As they made their way across the yard to the long low hut which called itself the admin. block Ginger linked her arm. 'So how are things with Miss Merle Oberon, then?'

Kay laughed. 'Miss Merle Oberon is working too hard.'

'Yer should get down the dance. Swing yer troubles away. Isn't that a song? If it isn't it should be.'

'I'd love to, Ginger. But the girls off the lines, men too, they'd tear my hair out if I went to the Gaiety again. Think how mad you were at me when you realised. Took me a week to unfreeze you.'

'You could go to Darlington. Two dances there. There's a dance bus practically door to door, you know.'

This was so in tune with what Kay had been thinking, in relation to Laurenz Gold, that she almost flinched from the arm which was clinging to hers. 'Darlington?' she said.

'Tell yer what! Janet's buggered off to Doncaster today. Her dad has a dog that's racing there and the stupid animal won't stay anywhere overnight if she's not around. Can you believe it? So why don't you and me go to Darlington? I won't let on down here. Cross my heart and hope to die. You can say you work on the line alongside me. For Gossake don't say you're a boss. It'll send the lads skittling.'

'I could drive us!' said Kay, too eagerly.

'What? Car? That's a joke. That'd give the game away like a shot. No. We'll get the service bus. Goes round the world to get there, but that'll be a laugh too.'

At the Captain's door the women all hung back like shy schoolgirls. Kay strode in first and Ginger hustled the others in like a lively sheepdog. They all stopped short at the sight of the Captain sitting behind his great desk looking like the epitome of the British bulldog. 'Now, ladies,' he growled, 'don't be shy.' He turned to Kay. 'Well, Mrs Fitzgibbon, the floor is yours.'

Kay stood in front of the desk and turned to speak to them. 'There's not much to it, really. Just look at these cookers and tell us what you think of them.'

An older woman looked at her. 'Ah dinnet knaa what yer want us ter say. Ah cook on a range meself, like me mother. Never felt the need to change. Never stumped for anything.'

'But you make modern cookers every day of your life.'

'That's work, but, isn't it?'

Kay took up her clipboard and gradually, very gradually she wormed some views out of them. But they came. What a bind it was to wait for a fire to get to the right heat. How it was all right for those women whose husbands were pitmen, who got their coal free, but the iron ranges ate coal. Using the electric would be an advantage there, wouldn't it?

One woman, Bridget, said she had bought an electric cooker and had her range changed for a nice little tile fireplace. No Friday blackleading for her. There was a ripple of envy at this. 'But,' she said, 'this cooker's a nasty job to clean. Food splashes over and goes right down into the cooker and it burns on. Very hard to get off.'

Gathering courage, the women forgot about the Captain and crowded round the cookers in the corner. Bridget moved from cooker to cooker, poking at the solid rings. 'See? There's nowhere for the spillage to go on any of them.'

Kay peered underneath. 'What if there was a kind of enamel tray here, that you could slide out and stick in the sink? That could catch all the spills.'

'Worth a try,' said the woman slowly. 'Could make all the difference.'

A murmur of approval went round the group then.

Kay had an inspiration. 'What if all of you had a cooker to try? What if we let you have one, say, at half price . . .'

'Careful, Mrs Fitzgibbon,' growled Captain Marshall.

'. . . and you come here and tell us every month just where we're going right and where we're going wrong?'

'Even half price'd be a pull out,' said Ginger's mother. 'Where would we get that money? We live from hand to mouth as it is.'

'Mother!' said Ginger, mortified.

'We could take it bit by bit, off your pay,' said Kay.

'Mrs Fitzgibbon, the accountant!' said the Captain.

She smiled at him sweetly. 'Surely it's better the cookers being tried out by practitioners than cluttering up the warehouse?'

He shrugged and started to doodle on his blotting pad.

She looked round the women. 'Anything else?' she said.

Ginger's mother spoke up. 'Well, they're miles better than the ranges, just a wipe over, like, instead of all that blackleading. But that green colour just makes me seasick, I can tell you.'

Kay glanced behind her. 'Captain Marshall?'

'Colour is coming. It's there in America. Just a matter of time.'

'There you are then. Those who want them in blue or yellow will have to wait a while. But anyone who wants to try one of these at a cheap rate, just put your name on my list. And I'll check with the accountant on Monday just how we should do this. Not,' she glanced at the Captain, 'whether we will do it. Then we'll get back together in a month and you can tell me whether they're any good. And for this morning's work you will get two hour's overtime in next week's pay packet.'

Four people put their names on her list requesting cookers, including Ginger as her mother's surrogate. Kay counted it a good morning's work for all of them.

Buzzing herself to the buzz of excitement around her, a thought darted into Kay's mind about the cooker they had been discussing all morning and the simple Egyptian pots and bowls, also useful domestic implements, which had so absorbed her in Alexandria. Here at the Works the magic was not a single pair of hands, but the subtle interaction of people and materials, the leaven of traditional craft skill and design, the energy of accidental insight which is the essence of invention. Each cooker depended on the touch of many people, not so easily traced as the feel of a potter who worked a thousand years ago. But the excitement she had felt this morning was no less than those feelings she had in Alexandria, when she knew she had found a good pot.

On their way out of the building Ginger linked her arm again. 'So what're you lookin' so serious about?'

Kay shook her head. 'Just thoughts,' she said. 'Just thoughts.'

They were at the gates. Ginger tugged at her arm. 'So what about this dance at Darlington, Merle Oberon?'

Kay thought a second before she said, 'Yes. I think I'd like to go.'

'Right! Six o'clock bus, Number One out of the Market Place. If you're not on it I'll throttle you. That's a promise!' She wobbled away on her high heels, her red curls glinting in the white morning light. Kay wished she was just going to an ordinary dance with her, not this one where all the fibres of her being would be on the lookout for a too-slick Austrian with curly hair.

The long entrance hall of Priorton Working Men's Club buzzed with the guttural burr of male voices; the room was heavy with pipe smoke, raw yeasty beer fumes and the smell of crude green soap battling with the grit and sweat of a week's work.

'Now then, son,' said Hugh. 'I'll give you the tour.' He led the way through the long bar which was not yet full, to the games room where the dominoes laid out their own logic on tables and where dark, half-drunk beer stood in straight-sided glasses. One or two of the players looked up and made a gesture which was half sideways tic, half wink. 'Now, Hughie!'

'Now, Tadger!'

'Now, Hugh!'

'Now, Walter!'

Their glances slid over Thomas in powerful dismissal, and not for the first time he felt the rejection of the outsider. He did not resent this. He had learnt that these men were no comic-cut rustics ready to display their hearts of gold at the drop of a coin or a cut-glass accent. They were powerful, often intelligent men who defended their own by asserting their brotherhood and suspecting outsiders. Their respect had to be earned and even then was not always forthcoming. Thomas, the humble outsider, did not find this arrogance attractive. Yet he could not help but respect it.

'Now the library.' Hugh led on.

They had to mount a narrow staircase and walk down an equally narrow corridor to get there, but when Hugh opened the door Thomas blinked at the sight of a big room which must take up the top floor of the building. Lights blazed from the ceiling and the sloping desks even had brass-shaded reading lights set above them. The room had the holy hush common to every library, broken only by the rustle of newspaper as one of the readers turned a page.

The readers, indistinguishable in demeanour from the drinkers down below, were reading books and pamphlets, newspapers and bulky tomes. Some were writing furiously, pencils squeaking against hard paper. Hugh and Thomas walked quietly down to the end of the room where a great fire burnt in a marble hearth. Around it were four more comfortable chairs in which sat very old men. Two of these were fast asleep, snoring slightly. The other two were reading: one Gibbon's *Decline and Fall of the Roman Empire*, the other a Zane Grey novel called *Showdown at Drystone Gulch*. The Zane Grey reader looked up and treated Hugh to the twitching wink which had been the comradely greeting downstairs.

Hugh nudged Thomas and nodded at the two great mahogany bookshelves on either side of the fireplace. Thomas took that as permission to look closer and spent a few minutes reading titles while Hugh carried on a whispered conversation with the Zane Grey reader.

Thomas scanned the titles which ranged from Gibbon to Karl Marx, Shakespeare to Robert Burns, Darwin to Engels, and well-used copies of Charles Dickens, Mrs Gaskell, Trollope, and Thackeray. There were even translations of Zola and Dostoevsky.

Hugh came behind him and lifted a book from a low shelf. 'And this one's one of our own.'

Thomas read the title. *The Gate of a Strange Field* by Harold Heslop. It was very well thumbed. 'Big Communist, he was,' said Hugh.

'Sssh!' came from one of the tables.

Thomas put the book back and they made their way out of the room.

'He was a very clever feller, that Harold Heslop. So they say. Worked in White Leas at one time in the twenties. Union sent him to college where they turned him into a Communist. Came back to the pit, then went off again. Wrote novels, stories of pit life. They say his books sold millions in Russia. Blacklisted him here in the end. No jobs. Books not published by London publishers. Truest account of pit life I ever read.'

Thomas looked back at the closed door. 'Could I borrow that book?'

'Aye. But only in the library. You read it in there. Open all day every day, you know. Some of those lads spend hours in there. Nice and warm. Quiet. Not a lot of peace and quiet at home for some of'm.' He laughed. 'Not like me.'

'Does everyone here use the library?'

He laughed again. 'Why no, man! Hundreds of'm never seen the inside of the library. Dog men, rabbit men, pigeon men, leek men. Not interested in books. Why should they be?'

They spent the rest of the evening in the corner of the bar, drinking dark, bitter beer and listening to desultory talk about Priorton United's chances in the Amateur Cup, about the men who went to race their dogs at Stockton and forgot the dog, about the Union's changes in compensation rules, about the checkweighman who got a Union scholarship to Ruskin College, and lit off to Australia afterwards. There was great disgust at this betrayal.

The effect of five pints of beer, steadily drunk, only hit Thomas when he came out of the club. Outside his legs turned to cotton wool. He had to sit on a wall till the world stopped swirling.

'You all right, son?' said Hugh calmly, not unused to the effect on newcomers of the strong ale.

'Yeah, yeah,' said Thomas groggily.

'D'yer want me to take you home?'

'Nah. Just leave me here to get my breath. It'll only take me ten minutes. The air'll freshen me up.'

They walked to the corner and then parted company. Thomas's head did clear – enough to make him think of the small, serious face of Patrizia Gold. He was suddenly consumed with the need to see her, to talk to her. He had to tell her he would do the translation for her soon. Very soon. The alcohol still colonising his flesh clarified the issue instantly. It was no problem really. All he had to do was go to the bus stop, catch the bus and go to the camp. No more than ten minutes. Then he and Patrizia could talk and he could tell her whatever . . . whatever . . .

He grasped a railing to steady himself.

. . . whatever she needed he would find for her. He would be her knight. She could give him her favour and he would ride into combat for her.

'You all right, marrah?' An old man had his elbow.

He shook the hand off. 'Fine, fine,' he said. 'I just need to get to the bus stop.'

Later he knocked on the wrong door at the camp, finding himself staring into the eyes of the old Dutchman before he collapsed to the floor. Willem ran for Patrizia and between them they hauled Thomas across to the Golds' hut and laid him on the rug in front of the stove.

Patrizia nodded at Willem. 'Just leave him now. I will watch him.'

'Mr Gold . . . ?' the old man said, an unspoken question in the air.

'Do not worry,' she said. 'Mr Gold will understand.'

She put a pillow under Thomas's head and put extra strong coffee to brew. Thomas started to mutter. She knelt beside him. 'What is it, Thomas?'

He grasped her hand. 'Sorry . . . the beer. Your favour. I want your favour.' He pulled her hand to his cheek and kept it there.

She did not remove it. 'Favour? What is this favour, Thomas?'

Sitting in two chairs behind a plaster column Kay and Ginger reviewed the heaving mass of bodies at the Darlington dance. 'It looks different to Priorton!' Kay shouted above the music.

Ginger nodded. 'More men. They can get beer inside the dance here,' she called back. 'And lads here're taller and fitter. Army blokes from Catterick.' The soldiers were very visible. They were out of uniform but their neat haircuts and sports jackets made them stand out.

'We're used to shorter men up home. Need to be shorter to cut coal in the pit.' Ginger clutched Kay's arm and brought her closer. 'It was even better during the war, Merle. Canadians, milk-fed and nearly seven foot tall. Talk about bonny!'

Just then the music changed to a foxtrot and a blond-haired boy with a soldier's swagger came and asked Ginger to dance.

She glanced at Kay. 'You go,' Kay said. 'I'm all right here.'

Then a short squarish boy in a tweed jacket came and asked Kay to dance. She didn't know how to say no, so she said yes. It was very strange, whirling in the arms of a total stranger.

'I haven't seen you here before.' It was a Scottish accent. He was holding her too close. She could smell toothpaste.

'I've never been here before. Do you come every week?' She pulled herself away from him.

'Yes. Since I've been at Catterick.'

'You're in the army?'

He laughed. 'How did you guess?'

'Your big blue eyes.'

He laughed again and held her closer.

She pulled away. 'What do you do in the army?'

'I'm a cook. I feed the brutes.'

She laughed at this. 'Hard to imagine a man making pastry.'

'Pastry? It's a detail. A mere detail.' He swung expertly on a corner. 'So what do you do when you're not grilling soldiers?'

'I work in a cooker factory.'

He laughed again and tried to pull her closer again. 'Now there's a coincidence,' he said. 'You make'm, I cook on'm.'

The music stopped and she made to go but he pulled her back. 'No. Hang on. There's a waltz next.'

They were only four bars into the waltz when someone tapped him on the shoulder and he stopped. 'What the . . . ?'

The interrupter said, 'Excuse me.'

The Scotsman held on to her.

'Excuse me! It's an excuse me!' Around them other exchanges were being made.

The Scotsman relinquished her. 'See you later, then,' he said sulkily.

Kay turned and slipped into Laurenz Gold's arms with something akin to relief. They danced the waltz and another foxtrot without speaking. Kay could not take exception to the way Laurenz held her. Unlike the soldier he held her lightly. She gave herself up to the moment, feeling the slight pressure from

Laurenz's arms and thighs to swerve this way and that, synchronising their four-step turn into the corners of the hall. She could smell his brilliantine, watch his neatly manicured hand as it held hers.

When the set ended he led her back to where Ginger was sitting, clicked his heels, bowed and took his leave. Ginger shuffled along the seat so that her shoulder was touching Kay's. 'Did you know?' she said.

'Know what?'

'That the Nazzy'd be here?'

'I told you. He's not a Nazzy . . . *Nazi*.'

'D'you know he'd be here?'

Kay hesitated. 'How could I? You mentioned it first.'

Ginger contemplated that for a second. 'So I did. Well, you wanter keep off that one. You're out of the egg. He's seen you coming.'

Kay laughed. 'Just because he's foreign, Ginger.'

The other girl shook her head. 'Nah, flower. Look at me! I'm the one that got off with dozens of foreigners in the war – Poles, Canadians, Frenchies. Blimey, I even like you and you're just about a foreigner. I'm known for it. But this Nazzy's something different. I can smell it on him.'

'He's all right, I tell you. What do you know about him?'

Just then Ginger's blond soldier came to claim her again. As he was swinging her on to the floor she shouted over his shoulder, 'You watch it, Kay. I'm tellin' yer.'

Three more soldiers came to ask Kay to dance and, taking her courage in both hands, she turned them down. A full, slow ten minutes passed by before Laurenz came back and slid into the seat beside her. 'So you find your way to Darlington, little Kay.' The thread of satisfaction purring in his voice was undeniable. She knew he had been watching her with the soldiers.

'I am not little,' she said crossly.

'Kay. Such a hard name,' he said. 'It does not fit. But still you are here, as I suggested.'

'It was Ginger who suggested coming here,' she said defensively.

'Why not the Gaiety in Priorton, as the other night?'

She shook her head. 'There is a problem there now.'

'Aah! Now you are the boss lady. Is that it? But here they won't know, will they?'

'That's about it.' She smiled. 'I told that soldier I worked in a factory making cookers. I suppose that, strictly, is true.'

'Surely there are grand places to dance? Where boss ladies can dance?' he said. 'In Vienna there were many such places.'

She shrugged. 'I would be as out of place there as I am here. I've lived outside it all, all these years. In the cafés in Alexandria . . . I was too young for that. The grand hotels, we hadn't the money.'

'But you like to dance.'

She grinned. 'I love it.'

So they danced all evening. Laurenz was the exemplary partner, ignoring Ginger's scowl as they waltzed past. There was a cheer when the bandleader announced the last dance as a waltz: 'Who's taking you home tonight?' A further cheer when the lights went down very low. A certain purring satisfaction settled in the hall and for the first time in the evening Laurenz pulled Kay very close to him so their bodies were lined up together like the landscape and the sky.

He put his face close to hers and turned to kiss her hard on the cheek as the movement of the dance presented the opportunity. Kay loved it. The closeness; the sinuous danger of this man. He *was* dangerous; she did not need Ginger to tell her that. He was playing her like a fisherman plays a fish. She knew it and a hidden part of her was revelling in it. She had never recognised that side of herself before. Certainly never in her marriage to Stephen, a marriage consummated in the joyous play of children, no more.

In the cloakroom Ginger said she had the offer of a lift from her soldier and his friend who had possession of a Jeep, legal or illegal she didn't know which and cared less. 'We can take you too.'

'No thanks. I can manage.'

'We can see you on to the bus.'

Kay smiled. 'Don't worry about me. Laurenz will give me a lift.'

'You'll freeze on the back of that bike,' said Ginger crossly. She paused. 'It's not right, Kay. The lad's married. You know that. He has bairns.'

'Don't worry, Ginger. There's no threat to anyone. It's just a lift. Laurenz is the perfect gentleman.'

'And I'm the Duchess of Windsor.' Ginger pulled up her skirt and blotted her lipstick on her petticoat. She raised a brown painted eyebrow at Kay in the mirror. 'You're kidding yourself, flower. But anyroads I give you full permission to cry on your Auntie Ginger's shoulder when it all goes wrong.'

Kay laughed back at Ginger's reflection. 'It'll be the other way round, Ginger. You watch it yourself. How you haven't ended up in bother I don't know.'

Ginger winked at her. 'I might know how to get into trouble, Kay, but I sure know how to get out of it too.'

Laurenz was standing outside in his flying jacket waiting for Kay. He had another flying jacket over his arm. 'You're sure of yourself,' she said.

'You didn't say no.'

'I thought Ginger'd be going home on her own.'

He smiled. 'Ginger will never go home on her own. You know that.' He held out the coat.

'What's this?'

'It's mine. The one I'm wearing is Mikel's. It was in the pannier on the bike. You must wear mine. It is the best one.' He looked up at the sky which was blackout blue pierced by pinpoint stars. 'It is freezing. I cannot let you freeze.'

She slipped into his coat, letting its warmth enclose her, with its smell of engine grease and brilliantine. He pulled the collar under her chin and zipped up the zip. 'Now we find the bike.' He took her hand. 'I think I know where it is.'

They made their way through the crowd who were still

hovering, not wanting to leave the warmth and the bright lights of the dance-hall behind, with its buzz of new contacts and hard dancing.

In a few minutes the crowds and the glitter were behind them and Laurenz was leading Kay along a narrow road of houses whose deep bay windows were dark, all life inside them being confined to the back. Then they turned down another road which had houses on the left; on the right snaked a long straight river whose flat stretches reflected the occasional blue streetlight.

Kay suddenly could not believe what she was doing. She did not know this man. She had been warned against him. She had been seduced by his dancing, charmed by his attention. For two pins he could attack her, strangle her and drop her in the river. No one would know.

No.

Ginger would know.

Then his quiet voice came from beside her. 'My dear Kay, you will be quite safe with me, you know.'

'Can't think what you mean.' In the dark she blushed at his prescience.

Then the bike was there, parked neatly by a park wall, in the deep shadow. 'Here we are. I take care of my bike. I do not wish it stolen by drunken soldiers.' He turned her to face him. 'Would you like me to kiss you again, Kay?' he said quietly.

'I . . .' She was gasping now, like the fish on the hook.

'Because I will not kiss you until you tell me to.'

'Oh . . .' She was so tempted. 'Oh, get on the bike, you're a world-champion teaser, Laurenz Gold.' She was pleased that she managed a lighthearted tone.

He cocked a leg over the bike and pulled it off its stand so that it bounced slightly. Then he stood astride while she climbed on behind him. They sat down together and she grasped his leather belt. Then he took her hands and pulled them round his waist, tight. He turned on the engine and the bike trembled under them as it roared into life. Then he set off at such speed that her head jerked back and she had to cling on to him tightly to stop herself falling off.

They raced away. The cold wind cut into her face and picked away at her Merle Oberon hair, pulling strands loose and slapping them across her eyes, her mouth. Soon they left the town behind and were speeding along country roads where the only illumination was the fragile beam of their headlight flickering over fences and rearing trees set like black corduroy against the night sky.

The machine underneath her laboured as they went ever upwards. Then he stopped and the engine cut out. A prickling dense silence took possession of the night.

'What now?' she said, wary about the next step, at the same time wanting it.

'Get off the bike,' he said over his shoulder.

She did so and he followed suit.

'Now look around.'

They must have been at a very high point. The velvet blackness of the land rolled away from them in every direction, punctuated by clusters of yellow light which must have been small villages or farms. Far, far into the distance the bulky blackness of the land gave way to the more luminous blackness of the night sky whose white clusters of stars reflected the villages down below.

'If you drive out of Vienna, if you do this there, if you drive way beyond the woods, do you know what you see?'

'No.'

'You see the great eastern plains and beyond that Russia.' He laughed. 'The Russians came all that way to save us from Hitler. But who will save us from the Russians?' He put an arm round her waist. 'There, little Kay. I lie the earth at your feet and the Heavens above you.'

She turned to him. 'Kiss me!' she said.

He drew her along the grass verge towards a tree and she stood with her back to it. Then he kissed her on the cheeks, on the forehead, on the lips. Her hands went out to pull him to her and his hands went to unzip her sheepskin and move inside, pressing, pummelling her skin through her jacket. She could feel the bark of the tree digging into her back.

He kissed her ear and throat, then came back to her mouth, showing her again how to use her tongue to tease more feeling from him and herself. Then suddenly he stood away from her, zipped up the jacket and pulled the collar up round her ears.

'Laurenz, I . . .'

He put a finger to her lips. 'Thank you, Kay,' he said. Then he went and stood astride the bike and waited for her to climb on behind him. In ten minutes they were outside Blamire House. 'Thank you,' she said. 'Thank you for bringing me home.'

His white teeth gleamed in the dark. 'How do you say it? The pleasure is all mine.'

She watched him drive away and let herself into the house. The hall light was on and her mother was sitting there in her coat and hat. 'Thank heavens you're here, Kay. I'm worried about Thomas. He wanted to see Hugh. He should have been back hours ago.'

Kay came down to earth with a bump. 'They'll be clucking away like a pair of old men. Don't worry.'

'Something must have happened. He's always scrupulous, Thomas, scrupulous. He said he would only be gone an hour.'

Kay put her coat back on. 'You relax, Mother. I'll take the car and go to Hugh's.'

'I don't know where Hugh lives.'

'Then how can we find him? You can't go trawling the streets of Priorton on a Saturday night. You don't know what might happen.'

'Something's wrong,' said Leonora stubbornly.

'Come on. We'll make some tea. He'll turn up soon. He's twenty-six, Mother! Now then, how was Florence?'

'She was fine. She had a great big supper, then we played nurses till bedtime.' Leonora took a drink. 'And how about you? Did you enjoy the dancing? Seems as though that Ginger girl has taken you right under her wing.'

* * *

It took four cups of strong coffee to get Thomas to sit upright without falling sideways again. 'Sorry. I am so sorry,' he kept mumbling to Patrizia. He had no idea how he had got here. No memory of the bus ride, of knocking on the Dutchman's door, of being dragged across here, of being out cold for a full hour before Patrizia could rouse him.

'Don't worry,' she said. 'Just drink.'

Looking at her concerned face some cloudy strands of reason floated into his head to remind him. 'I came to see you.'

She nodded. 'This I understand. Do you want something?'

He frowned. 'Just to see you, I think. Want to say sorry about that translation . . .'

In the corner Peter stirred in his bed. Rebeka whimpered.

'You must not come like this. Laurenz has a very bad temper.'

He leant back in the chair and closed his eyes. 'Tell me about when you were a little girl, Patrizia. Tell me about the picnics in the woods.' He spoke to her in German.

She sat quietly before him. 'Well, we lived in the centre of the city in an apartment. Not a palace, you understand, but quite fine. My mother and stepfather and myself. They were always at business and Elisabet lived with us. She was a maid, you know? A housekeeper? She looked after the apartment and me. But I was mostly at school. I loved to go to school.'

He felt for her hand and she put hers in his. 'Then on holidays my stepfather and his brothers would hire motor cars and we would all go out of the city and have such picnics. They would strap bicycles to the roofs of the cars and my cousins and I would cycle through the woods and out into the countryside. We would stop at a cottage and they would sell us their own wine from a cellar which was really a kind of shed out the back. At some times of the year you would see their little row of vines, heavy with grapes, blue-black, the bloom of freshness on them like a grey veil. Then we would take the grapes back for the others. My mother would have the picnic set on a white cloth. Her picnics always looked so perfect, so artistic, do you know? Like her hats. She would handle the grapes just so, place them in just the right place on the cloth to create the perfect picnic.' Her voice started to tremble. 'She should have come with me, Thomas. I wanted her to, but she wouldn't. She had been ill with pneumonia, you see . . .' Her voice tailed away.

Thomas opened his eyes and took her other hand in his. 'Remember her at the picnic,' he said. 'Only remember her at the picnic, Patrizia.'

The door opened then and Thomas dropped her hands as Laurenz bowled in, bringing a gust of cold winter air in with him. He glanced from one to the other and left it a second too long before he spoke. 'I see we have a late visitor,' he said. 'Good evening, Thomas.' He even smiled.

Thomas stood up, swayed slightly, and came across to shake his hand. 'Must apologise, old boy. Got into an awful pickle here.'

Laurenz took off his jacket. 'It is an awful something, Thomas.'

'Listen, listen. I went drinking in the town with an . . . a kind of uncle. Well, I drank a lot of this strong ale they have here. Then, to be honest, that's all I can remember until I was here, unconscious. Absolutely out of it. Your good lady has been feeding me strong coffee for a good hour. The Dutchman was here.'

Laurenz relaxed, let out a short bark of laughter, and clapped Thomas on the shoulder. 'Well, Thomas, if you were not the good man you are, and she' – he didn't use her name – 'were not the stupid *Hausfrau* she is, I would have been a very suspicious husband. As it is, I am honoured that you came to my house when you needed help. That you know me to be your friend.'

Patrizia turned away and adjusted the bedclothes over the muttering Peter.

'Really I . . .' protested Thomas.

'No! Do not thank me.'

Thomas looked for his coat. 'I must go.'

'Where?'

'Home.'

'The last bus went an hour ago.'

Thomas buckled his mackintosh belt tightly. 'Then I'll walk. The fresh air will heal my head.'

'Wouldn't think of it, *old boy*. You can ride on my pillion.'

'No, no. You've just come in.'

'I insist,' said Laurenz firmly, grabbing his own coat. 'Come on.'

Thomas cast a helpless look towards Patrizia and followed Laurenz out of the hut. A second later Laurenz popped his head back round the door. 'Make coffee for when I return,' he said briefly. 'We will talk then.'

Thomas's mother and sister were in the kitchen when Thomas let himself in. 'Where on earth have you been?' demanded Leonora. 'I nearly went to the police . . .'

'It's a long story,' said Thomas wearily. 'Hugh took me to the working men's club and I drank some of their ale and somehow I ended up at the camp with Patrizia pouring coffee down my throat. I think I wanted to tell her I was sorry I hadn't done her translation.'

'Hugh!' said Kay in disgust. 'I've told you about spending time with that Hugh Longstaffe.'

'How d'you manage to get back here at this time?' said Leonora drily. 'By flying horse? There're no buses this late.'

'As a matter of fact,' said Thomas, glancing at Kay, 'I was lucky enough to get a lift home from Laurenz. He had been out doing some business in Darlington.'

'What are these things, this business Laurenz Gold gets up to?' said Leonora. 'If I didn't know Patrizia so well I'd think her husband's what Mrs MacMahon calls a spiv. He is too well turned out. Too smooth.'

Laurenz, driving slowly back to the camp through the dark lanes, reflected with some satisfaction on his very fruitful day. Thinking carefully, he decided he would not discourage this thing with Thomas and Patrizia. It was not impossible that it could provide some very useful ammunition for another day, some time in the future. Very useful indeed. In his life he had learnt that nothing, information or insight, was wasted. It was all currency of one kind or another.

Fourteen
Transformations

Captain Marshall ran his eye down Kay's list of design suggestions and sucked his teeth a little before speaking. 'Well, in many ways, Mrs Fitzgibbon, these are practical suggestions. But what the designers might make of them I don't know.'

Kay laughed. 'Captain Marshall. Wouldn't it be engineering designers that designed the internal combustion engine, the atomic bomb? They shouldn't quail at the thought of a spillage tray for a cooker, or some kind of cooking ring that would stop spillages in the first place.'

'I imagine they could come up with something.'

'How long would it take them?'

'Six months? A year?'

'What? You should have examples made . . .'

'The word is prototypes, Mrs Fitzgibbon.'

'Whatever the word is, you should have them. And you should advertise them, so that the ones you make are already sold. Make them desirable. Better than those others. Colours . . .'

'Ah, colours. Raw materials are the problem there. Simply unobtainable,' he said with some satisfaction.

'Well then, if that's impossible let's concentrate on the spillage tray and the special ring.'

'I'll have to go down and talk to the designers myself,' grumbled Captain Marshall.

'I'll go,' said Kay. 'I'll go to London. I need to see what they do and how they do it, anyway.'

Captain Marshall blew out like a porpoise expelling air. 'As you wish, Mrs Fitzgibbon.' He glanced down at his folder, longing for her to leave. Then he looked up at her. 'I have come to a point of reluctant admiration for the . . . er . . . industry with which you pursue this task. I must admit I thought you would devolve into a kind of sleeping partner.'

'But I didn't?'

'No. Well, not yet. And I must admit your insights have something to offer. The outsider sees much of the game.'

She smiled. 'Fools rush in where angels fear to tread?'

A bare smile lit his countenance. 'That as well. But I must remind you that I and my senior colleagues keep this company on its feet, more than ticking over.'

'You told me there was a crisis.'

'We have dealt with crises before. And survived.'

'Are you telling me to keep my nose out of it?'

'No. It is your company. I think you have useful insights. But you must respect the insights of the professionals who run this company.'

'I do. I do.'

He smiled his dismissal. 'Enjoy your trip,' he said.

She went out of the room and came back in. 'There is one other thing.'

His head shot up. 'Yes?'

'I want Laurenz Gold to spend some time in the toolmakers' shop, evaluating the production there, and developing retraining programmes for the existing engineers and a fast training programme for the new ones.'

'What?' he rapped out, his goodwill shot to pieces. 'Laurenz Gold? Who's he?'

'He's working on progress now but he has significant experience in Swiss toolmaking factories . . .'

'One of the refugees, you mean?'

'. . . and we need that experience passed on. I want him to be promoted to supervisor status to do this job and I want him and his family to have some kind of house in the town. Don't you have some sort of arrangement with the council?'

'As a matter of fact, we have. But, if I may be allowed to ask, how do you know so much about this man? Has he papers, certificates, recommendations?'

'I know the man because my family has contact with his family. And no, he has no papers. He is a refugee; he was an exploited worker. I wish to try him in this capacity.'

'There'll be trouble,' said the Captain gloomily. 'Tool room is as bolshy as they come.'

'It'll be to everyone's advantage. Better tools will make things easier.'

'You won't get any tools at all if the tool room goes on strike.'

'I want this done,' said Kay stubbornly.

He shrugged. 'It's your funeral, Mrs Fitzgibbon.'

She stood up. 'That will happen this morning?'

He shook his head in resignation. 'This morning.'

'Have you files on the current cooker design?'

'Well, naturally.'

'Can you have them sent down to my office?'

'My secretary Joan in the outer office will raise them for you. You want them today? She can give them to you on your way out.'

'I'll look them over before I go down to London to see the designers.'

'You really are going to get them to do it, aren't you?'

'Yes. Tomorrow, if I can. There's been too much waiting around, don't you think, Captain?'

On her way back to her office, laden with files, she passed Laurenz Gold.

He nodded. 'Morning, Mrs Fitzgibbon.'

'Morning, Laurenz,' she said, and walked on.

That night, over dinner, she told Leonora and Thomas what she'd done about Laurenz. Thomas whistled. 'Very sweeping, that, sis.'

She paused over a forkful of leek pie. 'I'd have thought you'd be pleased. He's your friend. And it will get – what's her name?

– Patrizia out of that camp once and for all. The Captain can arrange a house for them with the council, because he is a key worker.'

'There'll be furniture to find,' said Leonora worriedly.

'Take her to Wilkinson's, choose the stuff for their house and get them to make out the bill to us,' said Kay. 'Our contribution to the refugee situation.'

Thomas glanced at his mother, torn between his delight at Patrizia's rescue and his dislike of his sister's high-handed way of going about it. 'It seems like a very good thing to do,' said Leonora slowly, 'and if we can't afford it we ought to be able to.'

'Right. That's fixed.' Kay dug into her pie.

'And what does the Captain think about all this?' said Leonora.

'He's not pleased.'

'Shouldn't you take notice of that?'

'Kitty told me not to let him ride roughshod over me and I'm not.' She pushed her plate away. 'How was Florence today?' Florence had been in bed fast asleep when she got home.

'Fine. Miss Plumstead praised her composition: last night she went down to Hugh's allotment to see the rabbits; she wrote about that.'

'She fed the chickens as well,' said Thomas, 'and brought six eggs home for Mother.'

At last Kay smiled at her brother, a rare thing these days. 'You're so good with her, Thomas. I don't know what she'd do without you.'

'Well, sis, without Stephen . . . and you're so tied up with things . . . it's a pleasure anyway.' He stumbled through the words. 'Between Mother and me she's well taken care of. You don't have to worry about her.'

It was a kindness. He could have taken her admission and turned it on her as a weapon. She looked at him closely, suddenly mourning the loss of warmth and mutuality which had kept them united, two against the world, since the day they were born. 'Thank you . . . you know I appreciate it, Thomas.' She bit her lip. It was all so very clumsy. The very formality of the thanks showed the distance which had grown up between them in these last weeks.

Thomas stood up. 'Well I'll have to turn in. These early shifts give you your afternoons but take away your nights.'

'I won't see you tomorrow,' said Kay. She told him about getting the women in to advise them on the cooker design.

'You can get away to London? So you haven't quite made yourself indispensable, then?'

'Well,' she said evenly, 'I don't flatter myself that I'm more than a gnat worrying away at the hide of a rhinoceros at the moment. But I'm learning. And I'm enjoying it like I enjoyed the work with the pots. At least I'm not some lady bountiful going down there in a big car to cream off the profits.'

'I'll give you that,' said Thomas softly, 'if you stop looking down your nose at me working in the pit.'

Leonora broke in. 'Stop it, the pair of you. You'll both be accused of "playing at it" until you've been doing what you're doing for five years, even ten years. So for goodness' sake stop sniping at each other.'

Kay felt the heat go out of her. 'I was thinking I might stay with Auntie Mara for an extra day or two. I've only ever been in London in transit. I'd like to see a few things.'

Thomas laughed. 'At least you'll give the poor Captain a rest.'

'Oh no. I've told him I expect to see these changes in place when I get back.'

It was Leonora's turn to laugh. 'Poor Captain!' she said, not a little proud of her daughter's firm stand. 'Do you know every day you remind me more and more of Kitty?'

In fact Kay was pleased with her plan to go to London for more than one reason. She needed some distance, some time to think about her feelings for Laurenz Gold. One part of her longed to let the business – you could hardly call it an affair – between them run headlong on its course. The other part of her, not entirely under his spell, urged caution.

The city of London, busy and bustling, still battered from the war, raced by Kay's taxi window. She had forgotten the press of cities in her months in Priorton: how people and buildings wove around each other into a tight fabric impenetrable to the outsider.

Everywhere there were hoardings and picket fences that protected the public against gaping bomb holes. Forests of rose-bay willow-herb and tangles of bramble embroidered the detritus of cast-down buildings. In the gaps between some surviving buildings the rubble had been flattened in a rough and ready manner to make open spaces. Here children were refighting the war or playing football. The traffic held up her taxi by one bombed site where a man was allowing his friend to tie him up in chains in preparation for a miraculous escape. Leaving him wriggling like an armoured, chinking eel, the friend came to the window of Kay's taxi, rattling a coin-filled hat which had a card sticking to the front saying, *Ex-servicemen*. She wound down the window and put a shilling in it.

The recipient was unsmiling. 'Thanks, miss,' he growled as he strode on to the next car.

'Didn't oughter do that, love,' said the taxi-driver over his shoulder.

'Why not?'

'Beggin'! Ain't right.'

She thought of the beggars in Alexandria, a rational business. 'They do no harm,' she said.

'Spiv. They ain't nothing but spivs.'

'The ticket said "Ex-servicemen".'

'Well, it would, wouldn't it?'

'Were you in the services?'

'Not 'xactly, miss. Merchant Navy. In convoys.'

'That must have been frightening.'

'It was no picnic, I can tell you.'

He stayed silent as he wove his way through thinning traffic, finally drawing up in front of Mara's narrow house in Islington, rented from another teacher who had been evacuated to the Lake District, and had stayed on. The door opened straight from the street, but the narrowness of the house was deceptive: it was several rooms deep and its long unkempt garden at the back led right down to the canal.

Mara pulled her into the cosy back room and set her by the fire. 'Wonderful to have you here, love. Leonora tells me you're going great guns up there. Kitty incarnate!'

Kay took off her hat and shook her head to loosen her hair. 'I didn't think I'd like it, Auntie Mara, but it's fascinating. I can hear – feel – the factory ticking like a great clock. If all the bits work, it's a wonderful mechanism; if one bit doesn't the whole thing breaks down. There were three total stoppages on one line last week because they ran out of red fuse wire.'

Mara laughed. 'Just think, Kitty made watches, and of course the great watchmaker was my father – now here you are making a whole factory into a ticking watch.' Her voice became disembodied as she made her way to the little door which connected the back room to the kitchen.

'Something in the blood, then.'

Mara returned and placed a tea tray on the little table beside Kay. 'Now tell me about sweet little Thomas going down the pit.'

Kay grimaced. 'Some kind of game of his. He won't really admit it but he's finding it hard going.'

'Anyone would. I think it's very courageous.'

'Courageous?' Kay sipped her tea. 'I think he's stupid. He doesn't need to get filthy and strain his muscles down that hole.'

Mara shrugged. 'Someone has to do it. Leonora's father lost his life doing it.'

'Why should Thomas do it? There are other things he could do.'

'Don't you think he's proving something?'

'What?'

'Isn't it the first time he's done anything separate from you? Leonora mentions how inseparable you have been. Even Stephen . . .'

'Stephen made the third,' said Kay. 'It was fine . . .'

'Now just . . . just to . . . He's picked the hardest thing he can think of. Isn't that courageous?'

'Why?'

'To prove something to you? I don't know. I still think it takes guts.' She stood up and smoothed down her narrow skirt. 'Now, Kay. I've asked someone to join us for supper tonight, I hope you don't mind.'

Kay smiled. 'Why should I mind?'

'Good. It's an old friend, a friend from my childhood. I think you met him at Kitty's funeral.'

Kay remembered Dewi Thomas when he busted through Mara's narrow door: the big bluff Welshman whom they said was an MP. His broad face beamed when he saw her. He shook her hand warmly. 'Well, Kay, a chip off the old block, I see. One way or another you look like all of them. Thought so at the funeral.'

They had a lighthearted, jolly evening. They had supper. They listened to *Dick Barton, Special Agent* on the radio. They listened to Dewi's tales of the difference between the people in his Welsh constituency and the characters in the House. How, now at last in government, high ideals were rapidly being changed for practical possibilities.

They played cards for ha'pennies and Mara won a pile. Kay relaxed for the first time in weeks and as she watched these two she knew the warmth between them was more than just friendship. At nine o'clock she pleaded the exhaustion of a long journey, made her excuses and went to bed. She was exhausted and was asleep almost as soon as her head hit the pillow. It must have been much later that she turned over in bed awkwardly and woke up to hear voices and suppressed laughter in the bedroom next door. She smiled as she turned over and went back into a dreamless sleep.

Next morning, at the table, crisp and businesslike in her school-teacher's outfit, Mara smiled across at her niece. 'So what do you think about Dewi?'

There was no sign nor sound of Dewi in the house. He must have gone off very early.

'Loved him. Thought he was a treat.'

'Do you want to know a secret?'

'Yes.'

'I'm going to marry him.'

Kay rushed round the table to hug her aunt.

Mara struggled out of her embrace. 'Do you want to know a bigger secret?'

'Is there one?'

'We're expecting a baby!'

'What?'

'Don't sound so shocked. There's a custom of late babies in this family. Aren't I younger than Kitty was when she had me? And aren't I as young, or as old, as your mother was when she had you and Thomas?'

'Well I'll be blowed. You'll have to stop work.'

'Yes. I thought I would mind, but I don't. I've been at it more than twenty years. If I had a mark to make I've made it. Now I'll just enjoy this baby, write some more stories, and help Dewi across in the constituency and here in London. Enjoy him and enjoy the baby. That's what I'll do.'

'I'm pleased for you, Mara. So pleased.'

'To be honest I'm pleased for myself. Do you know what I keep thinking?'

Kay shook her head. 'I keep thinking that Jean-Paul would be pleased too. He wouldn't want me to be on my own. Dewi and I have decided that if the baby is a boy, we'll call him John-Paul. And if it is a girl we'll call her Hélène after Jean-Paul's sister.'

'What if you have one of each, like my mother had?'

'God forbid. One will be quite enough, thank you. I've written to your mother to tell her all about this, but because you happen to be here, you're the first to know.' Mara folded her napkin. 'Now I must get to school. Standard Three'll be untamable if I'm late.'

* * *

Kay met the designers in a dusty London restaurant, which had incorporated wartime shortages into its ethos: it was short on colour, short on light, short on manners. But Kay relished its fuggy warmth after the freezing street and was given a breezy welcome from Tadek, the chief designer, and Rob Fawcett, his young assistant.

They were enthusiastic about the spillage tray and wondered why no one had thought of that before. She forbore to tell them that it was their job to think up new ideas. 'Perhaps it was a fluke. I knew nothing about cookers. Nothing about cooking. The stranger's eye.' They backed up the Captain's view that coloured cookers were out of the question for the time being owing to the shortage of materials. 'But it will come in time,' said Tadek reassuringly.

'That's my point, Tadek, things don't just "come" to you. They happen if you hunt them.'

Tadek exchanged a glance with Rob Fawcett who was making notes in what looked like an army pay book.

After a pause Kay said, 'Can you get catalogues, brochures for American cookers?'

Tadek nodded. 'That will not be difficult.'

'Get those and see how they source the coloured ones.'

'Easier said than done, Mrs Fitzgibbon,' Rob piped up.

'It's more likely to be done if you try to do it, than if you sit back and wait for it to come, like next spring's swallows.'

Tadek leant across and poured her some wine. 'I can see we will get things done, Mrs Fitzgibbon. You remind me of someone I worked for in Germany in 1932. Not that you look like him: he was sixty, had a walrus moustache and was called, if I remember rightly, Mr Pompleburger. He got things done. Before they carted him away, of course.'

Kay walked away from that meeting more than satisfied. They were a bit cocky but she liked them. She had set them up with the task of the spillage trays and got under their skin about coloured cookers. Moreover, she had made friends with them, neither losing her temper nor making them lose theirs.

After that she went to Oxford Street and bought herself a flame-coloured silk blouse, a brown New Look skirt and high-heeled brown ankle-strap shoes. Wonderful, madam, the assistant said, for dancing in.

Then she made her way to the place in the city where she knew Stephen had died. Buses like the one which killed him were trundling along with their load of shoppers and office-workers setting out for home. A bombed site spanning the corner was crawling with children, just let out of school, jumping from stone to broken wall, dragging scrap wood from one place to another, kicking a ball across the open space, climbing a tree which was poking its way through the remains of a well. She tried to imagine the area veiled in the unrelentingly efficient blackout which had effectively caused Stephen's death. She failed. The streetlights were on. There was nothing of him here. Nothing.

She bought some flowers from a street-side stall and, holding them too tightly, walked through the crowds to the cemetery. Mara was waiting for her at the ornate gates. She was carrying flowers in one hand and a shopping bag in the other. She led the way down the narrow paths, round corners crowded with headstones which varied from pill-like modesty to soaring sensual Victorian extravagance.

Their two graves stood side by side, in the shelter of a small wall, which held the land where it rose a little. They were well tended, adorned with vases containing chrysanthemums only a week old. The lettering was identical; the message slightly different:

> Here lies Jean-Paul Derancourt, of France,
> Beloved husband of Mara Scorton Derancourt,
> And brother of the late Hélène.
> A life well lived.
> 1888–1943

* * *

Here lies Stephen Fitzgibbon, of Alexandria,
Beloved husband of Kay, and father of Florence.
A young life, a great loss.
1917–1943

Silently the two woman set to work clearing the old flowers, throwing out the old water and replacing it with the water from bottles Mara had brought in her heavy bag. Then they arranged the fresh flowers and stood side by side, surveying the effect.

Mara put her arm through Kay's. 'He was a fine young man, Kay. Such a help to me in the matter of Jean-Paul's death. Being a Catholic Stephen knew how to do the right thing. That in turn helped me to do the right thing for Stephen himself.'

Kay breathed in very deeply, drenched at last by a complete feeling of loss, not just of Stephen but of her own sunny childhood, which now seemed to be at an end here in this damp, cold cemetery. 'I didn't know that, you know,' she murmured.

'Didn't know what?'

'That Stephen was a Catholic. I knew so little about him. We were like children together with no future, no past.'

'You loved him?'

'Yes, I think I did. It was a kind of recognition. As though I had known him before. But once Florence was here, I think he kind of went from me. But I must have loved him, mustn't I?'

Mara squeezed her arm. 'We have this in common, my love. Don't worry. We'll always love them. We'll never forget.'

They walked slowly back along the path. 'I'll be happy again with Dewi. And I know you will be happy. You'll find someone.'

Kay said nothing. Her thoughts moved to Laurenz Gold, whom, like Stephen, she hardly knew. In some ways he reminded her of Stephen. There was danger about him, an unknown side. She had not known that about Stephen in the first place – but she had known it from the start with Laurenz Gold.

Kay's journey back from London was long and weary and, having forgotten to send a telegram asking Leonora to meet her, she had had to take a taxi all the way from Darlington. Leonora made her tea and demanded Mara's news. They had just shared their delight at Mara's forthcoming marriage to Dewi Wilson when Duggie O'Hare walked into the kitchen.

Kay took one look at his face and said, 'Now what, Duggie? Trouble at the Works, at a guess.'

He sat down and stretched his feet before the fire, his hands in his pockets. 'First the good thing. The Captain says there'll be no problem over the council house for the Austrian. Some feller's just done a bunk to Canada. They'll release his house from Saturday. Apart from that, well, it ain't a party down there at the Works. Tool room downed tools for two hours this morning when the J— the Austrian went in prancing around in his white coat. The Captain himself had to come down on to the shop floor with his sword of Solomon.'

'Must have been bad.'

'Anyway, the toolmakers only started up again when the Captain took him away, white coat and all, and put him in his office. To look at training manuals, the legend is. He told me to pass the word on when you got back.' Duggie offered her a cigarette and she shook her head. He took one out, snapped the case shut and tapped it on the silvered surface before he lit it. 'There was bound to be ructions. They're the skilled men, toolmakers. Don't like their territory invaded.'

'The problem is, it's my territory, not theirs.'

He looked at her carefully through the smoke which was drifting up over his old, lined face. 'Yes, that is the problem, isn't it?'

Thomas looked up from the paper he was reading. 'But it *is* their territory too. They've worked there, invested their skill.'

Leonora was sitting at the table marking up the minutes of a meeting. She smiled. 'Our Thomas has been reading his Marx. The owners of capital with the owners of labour in their Faustian clasp.'

Kay shook her head impatiently. 'I don't know anything about all that. All I want to do is what Kitty did in her day; keep going with the times. Change the way they tackle the work into the modern age so we can all survive. Not just us, but the town. If the Works flourish there could be hundreds more jobs. Thousands.'

Thomas laughed. 'Now you're dreaming.'

'How do you know that?' said Kay crossly.

Duggie stood up. 'Anyway, I thought you would like to know, Kay. Forewarned for the battle is forearmed for it.'

'You make it sound like a war, Duggie. Bad as Thomas's Karl Marx. But he's got it wrong. All it is is a clock. If the bits work the whole thing will tick over for ever. Not battles, but adjustments. That's all we need.' She stood up. 'Apropos of that, I think I'll go and see Laurenz Gold. Get his side of the picture tonight.'

Thomas was putting on his coat. 'You can drop me by the club.'

'You going out at this time of night?' said Kay. 'What about your beauty sleep?'

'You're going out yourself at this time of night.'

'It's work.'

'This is just a drink.'

'Don't drink more than one,' said Leonora.

'I drink it in half-pints. I might tell you that has caused much hilarity, and the steward has had to get a half-pint glass in specially,' Thomas said, smiling slightly.

'Why go out on a work night?' persisted Kay. 'You'll have to get up at three o'clock in the morning.'

'Hugh asked me to go. He said he had a surprise for me.'

'Hugh!' said Kay.

'Please, please don't bring home any rabbits,' said Leonora.

'Or pigeons,' said Kay.

'Or chickens,' said Leonora.

'Oh no, it's nothing like that,' said Thomas, 'I'm sure.' He was not so sure really, but after all, *sufficient unto the day is the evil thereof.*

* * *

The club was quiet, the murmur of men's voices broken only by the tinkle of glasses and the click of dominoes and the whirring of the overhead fan which swirled the dense cigarette and pipe smoke upwards so that it settled again like an interior skyline above the bent heads of the men underneath.

One or two of the men knew Thomas now, from the pit, or from other nights here in the club with Hugh. He was warmed by their greeting.

'Now, young'n!'

'Hello, Gerald.'

'Now, young Thomas!'

'Markie!'

'What cheer, Thomas!'

'Evenin', Mr Gray.'

He spotted Hugh sitting with his back to him. Beside him was the surprise: a slim erect figure, sleek in officer's khaki, who stood up as Thomas joined them. Thomas knew the face, he knew it very well. This face looked back at him every morning in the mirror before he put on his glasses to face the day. Harry Longstaffe, Hugh's son, was neater, and was not burdened by spectacles, but he was Thomas's double.

Hugh introduced them and Harry shook hands enthusiastically. 'Thomas Scorton! Dad tells me he has discovered me a cousin. Looking at you, there's no mistake, no mistake at all.' His voice was deep and his accent was only perceptible in the slightest stretching of his vowels. The army had certainly done its work on him, thought Thomas. And in turn the pit was doing the reverse on himself. Words and phrases which had been alien, almost Scandinavian in timbre, tripped off his tongue quite easily now.

'Aye,' said Hugh contentedly. 'Yeh two's the pot model of each other.'

Thomas wondered why the old boy hadn't reacted more when they first met. He was a rum one, old Hugh. Harry stayed standing. 'Now then, shall I get you a drink?'

Hugh chuckled. 'In the Royal George, when I first met this one, Harry, he asked for wine!'

Harry grinned. 'Now there's a brave man! Can I get you a pint?'

Thomas shook his head. 'Half-pint please. This stuff knocks me for sixpence.'

'See?' said Hugh. 'The lad has no pride. Walked down the High Street the other day hand in hand with two bairns. Three separate lads telt us about that.'

'As I said, a brave man,' said Harry. He nodded and half smiled. They both watched him as he made his way to the bar, shaking hands and chatting left and right as old friends greeted him.

'So what d'you think?' said Hugh.

'Good man. You must be proud.'

'So I am, lad. So I am.'

Thomas wondered about his own father, Sam. Whether he had been proud of him. He could remember love and affection, he could remember warmth. He could remember the occasional feeling of threat. But he could not remember pride.

The camp was lit by a single lamp at the entrance when Kay drove through the gates to park beside the Golds' hut. Around them, doors opened and people, back-lit by interior light, peeped outside, openly curious to see the rare visitor. Patrizia answered her knock, carrying Rebeka on her hip. 'Oh, hello. It is Thomas's sister, is it not? Come in.'

Inside Peter was lying on the bed copying words from a book of English fairy stories. By the lamp on the central table a copy of Lamb's *Tales from Shakespear* was open beside a battered English–German dictionary. Patrizia put her hand on it. 'I loved the plays translated into German when I was a student. The plays in English are very difficult. So Thomas says I should try with this easy one.'

So much for the little *Hausfrau*. Kay glanced around. 'I wondered if I might have a word with Laurenz?'

Patrizia shook her head. 'I am sorry. He has not come in from work.'

Kay glanced at her watch. 'It's nine-thirty.' He would be in some dance-hall, no doubt, dancing with some girl and flashing those eyes at her. She frowned. On whose behalf was she being jealous? This little dark woman in front of her, who was not, after all, a lunatic?

Patrizia swung Rebeka over to the other hip. 'Sometimes Laurenz, he is very late. He goes into Durham, sometimes even Gateshead. There is some business. He buys things and sells things.'

Kay frowned again, remembering someone – was it Duggie? – describing Laurenz as a spiv.

Patrizia smiled faintly. 'This barter, Mrs Fitzgibbon, this buying and selling things, Laurenz is good at it. This has helped us survive many bad times. We must make money, save money. He wishes to make a business here in England.'

Kay looked round the bleak room and thought of Laurenz's gleaming motor bike. 'Did he tell you he had been promoted at work? At the factory?'

Patrizia shook her head. 'He does not speak to me very much; he is here so little.'

'Did he tell you about the council house that he has got for you?'

'What council house?'

'That you have been given a key worker's council house down in Priorton?'

Patrizia looked blank.

'Laurenz has been given a better job at the factory so you will get a house.' She glanced round.

Patrizia frowned. 'That is good.'

'I would think so.'

Patrizia's eyes followed Kay's round the spartan room. 'We have so little to put into a house.'

'Er . . . there is a fund which takes care of that. When people need furniture and that kind of thing.'

Patrizia thought of the great armoire against the wall in the apartment near the Opera Ring. Laden with fine silver and old

Porzellan. 'Oh. That is very good, Mrs Fitzgibbon.'

Kay was irritated by Patrizia's lack of reaction, even her lack of gratitude. 'Aren't you glad to get away from here, Mrs Gold?' she said briskly. 'To get your family away from here?'

Patrizia pushed her hair back from her face. 'I am sorry. I am sorry. I am very rude. Won't you sit down?' She hesitated. 'We are thankful, you know? Sit down, I will make you coffee.'

'No. I'll go. I needed to speak with Laurenz. About work.' She turned to go. 'But he is not here.'

'Mrs Fitzgibbon?' Kay turned back.

'You must know I am grateful. For the sake of Peter and Rebeka. But I cannot think what Laurenz will think of all this. He is such a man. You don't know which way he will turn. See how he has not even told me of these things?'

'Why not? Perhaps he was protecting you?'

'Protecting me?' Patrizia laughed bitterly. 'No, Mrs Fitzgibbon, he would not be doing that.'

Kay pulled on her long gauntlets. 'Well, I'll go now. If you would just tell Laurenz I'll see him first thing at the factory. In my office.'

'In your office.' Patrizia held the door open and watched Kay walk through. 'I will tell my husband.'

As she drove away Kay thought about Patrizia, who didn't seem anything like the woman that Laurenz had described. She passed Laurenz in the road riding his motor bike, head down, leather jacket shining. Kay quelled her instinct to stop the car and turn round; it was far too late to go back and knock again on that peeling door.

She had only driven a mile further along the narrow road when Laurenz was passing her on his bike, then weaving from side to side in front of her. She pulled into the side of the road and turned off the engine. He turned off his own engine, pulled his bike on to its stand, walked back and climbed into the car beside her. He took her hands from the wheel, put them round his neck and kissed her. She took in his kisses like a parched land takes in rain. It was minutes before he pulled away, making her feel cold and dry. He tucked her curls back over her ears. 'Now, tell me why you ran away to London, Kay, and left me, not a word. And all these changes. You were not there and they gave me a new job, a new white coat, a new house . . .'

'You didn't tell Patrizia about the new house or any of this?'

She could feel his shrug. 'She will know soon enough. She is a stupid woman. She would not understand.' He stopped her protest with his mouth. 'Forget about her. Why do you go off for three days and not say a word? Things between us . . .'

'I had to get to grips with the designers. I also thought your . . . er . . . elevation should happen when I wasn't there.'

'I will tell you that makes no difference. Captain Marshall is keen to tell me that the responsibility was entirely yours and he let the foreman of the tool room know that too. There was nearly a riot in there. Dirty Jew was the kindest thing I was called.'

'And they downed tools?'

'Yes. They only started work again when I was banished to Marshall's office to look at the training manuals.'

'Well,' said Kay, pulling his head down towards hers. 'We'll see to that tomorrow. Don't worry. You'll keep your job.'

He pulled away angrily for a moment. 'I do not need you like this,' he said. Then he kissed her and loosened her jacket and blouse and ran his hands over her bare flesh. 'Such warm skin,' he whispered.

She removed his hand and buttoned her blouse and jacket. 'No, not now. Not here.'

He flung himself back in his seat. 'Where? When?' he said sulkily, folding his arms.

'I'm not some tuppeny-ha'penny dance-hall girl, Laurenz.'

'I would not be here if you were.'

'Why are you here, Laurenz?'

'I am here because you are a special woman different to others, and I want you like a drowning man wants water.'

'Is that all?'

'What do you mean?'

She stared out of the car window which was rapidly steaming

up. 'You're a very ambitious man, Laurenz. I know that. Patrizia says so.'

'She is a fool. Ambition. Such a terrible word, this ambition?'

'And you'll do anything to get what you want. Walk on anybody. I know that in my bones.'

'How do you think I survived before the war? In the war? In Vienna? In Switzerland? How do you think even Patrizia survived? And the children were born? There's survival for you.'

'It was more than that. You were like this before. You did not just become this thing.'

He stared at the window drawing zig-zags with one finger. 'How would I know what I was like before? How would you know?'

'What were you like when you were Peter's age?'

'I don't remember.'

'Don't be silly. Of course you do.'

He pulled himself away from her and there was a chasm between them.

'You must remember.'

'I don't. I went to live with Mikel and his family when I was eight. Before that, nothing.'

'It can't be.'

'It is.'

'What was Patrizia like, before?'

'This has nothing to do with Patrizia.'

'No?' She leant over and opened his door. 'It has everything to do with Patrizia, don't you think?'

Laurenz entered into the removal from the resettlement camp to the council house with great zest. He went with Leonora and Patrizia to choose furniture, paying his wife graceful compliments for her taste and showing gratitude without being obsequious to Leonora. For Patrizia the house, red brick and unprepossessing, was like a palace. The bathroom and toilet, the sink unit with two taps, the kitchen cupboards, all these were beacons of civilisation. The utility furniture, the simple carpet squares, the curtains retrieved from the Scorton attics, were for her the new beginning. She still thought of the apartment by the Opera Ring, but she embraced this ugly little house as a new beginning.

One wonder of the house for her was that at long last she would not have to sit or work under Laurenz's critical eye. The luxury of the kitchen, the little dining room and the sitting room meant there would be space enough to lose herself, away from him. And outside the kitchen, where the council builders had carefully skirted it, a mature oak tree was shooting its spring growth.

The council estate was only a short walk from the centre of Priorton so she would be able to walk to the busy High Street each day, pushing Rebeka in the pushchair obtained for her second-hand by Leonora on the afternoon of the day the Golds moved in.

Thomas took Rebeka in the pushchair to collect Peter and Florence from school. He went into the building to notify the headmaster of Peter's new address. 'Are you Mr Gold?' asked Mr Hudson, his voice betraying the edge of pleading he always used with men. His bullying demeanour, practised on women teachers and children through a lifetime, did not extend to men of whom he himself was always just a little frightened.

Thomas shook his head. 'No, I'm Florence Fitzgibbon's uncle, Thomas Scorton. I've come to collect her and take Peter back to his new house. He will not know the way.'

'Well, perhaps you will inform Mrs Gold that we will be moving her son back up a class. His teacher tells me he is making enormous strides in his language.'

'We have been working very hard on it.'

'You help Mrs Gold? Very commendable.'

'He is a very intelligent boy. Theirs was a leading family in Vienna, you know.'

Mr Hudson raised his brows. 'Is that so? Well, we have such bad material to work on here, sons of miners and such . . .'

'Funny that you should say that, Mr Hudson. I work underground myself and some of the men there are the most intelligent I've ever met, as well as the hardest working.'

Mr Hudson went beetroot red. 'Well, Mr Scorton, I will enter the change of address.' He put his head down over his ledger. 'There.' He closed the book. When he looked up his gaze was bland. 'I must say I am full of admiration for the work you people do with these refugees. Now shall I show you to Peter's classroom?'

Thomas took the children straight to Hugh's house and introduced them to Harry who looked much less intimidating in his 'civvies' of collarless shirt, flannels and Fair Isle pullover. Hugh busied around, giving the children tea and bread and jam. While they were occupied Harry, his eyes on Peter, said to Thomas, 'I was there, you know, at the end of the war.'

'Where?'

'Vienna, and . . . well, another place. An unspeakable place.'

Peter's head went up. Harry tousled his hair. 'You're a lucky boy, Peter. Enjoy your life.'

Peter grinned up at him, a smear of jam on his cheek. 'Yes, sir,' he said. 'Yes, sir.'

After that, they all went down to help Hugh feed the hens and the rabbits. Peter gathered a handful of stringy coltsfoot to take home for his mother and Hugh took them all to the allotment of a neighbour, who had a pond, to show them two frogs, lizard-eyed, which were sitting at its edge. 'See these fellers? Sure sign that spring's on its way. Waiting for their lady friends, they are.'

In the end Thomas was forced to drag the children away. The regret he felt at coming away from Harry, and from Hugh, was alleviated by an arrangement to meet that night for a drink in the Royal George. As he pushed the pushchair down the path with a child hanging on either side, Hugh called after him, 'Hey, Thomas!'

'Yes?' said Thomas, looking round.

'Tha looks like a real family man today. Dinnet go down the High Street with that pushchair or the lads'll call tha a pansy.'

Later, as he trudged up the High Street, ignoring the strange looks he was getting from men and women alike, he thought he liked the sound of that. A family man. It had a good ring to it.

Peter was wide-eyed as Patrizia showed him round the house, touching the gleaming furniture and the bright cushions with a nervous hand. When he reached his bedroom with its little bed his face grew grave. 'I have to sleep here on my own?'

'Rebeka will be here in the other little bed.'

He sighed a great sigh.

'What is it?'

'How will I know that you live, Mama, if I cannot hear you breathe?'

She smiled and stroked his hair. 'You call out, *liebling*, and I will answer. I will always be there.'

When she got back downstairs Laurenz had just shown Thomas out. He sat back and put his feet up on the kitchen table. 'So, Patrizia, we make good progress? I find you a nice house; I have a good job. You have Thomas Scorton wound around your little finger and I' – he took out a nail file and started to file his nails – 'have his sister wound around mine.'

'Thomas is not wound around my little finger.'

He rubbed his nails on his shirt. 'I saw the way he looked at you.'

'He is kind to Peter, that is all,' she said stubbornly.

'Do not worry. It will have its uses.'

'I will not use people!'

He caught her wrist. 'You use me. I work and slave for you. I bring you to this country, Godforsaken though it is. I find you a house.'

'I cannot believe you say this.' She wrenched her hand away. 'Without us, Laurenz, you would be a cork bobbing on the tide. We are your family, Laurenz. Like it or not, we make you human.'

He went very still then, and she braced herself for a blow. But he shrugged. 'I have never understood why I have towed you along. Should have got rid of you years ago.'

She was chilled by his tone. 'All of us? Your son and daughter too?'

He smiled. 'But I have only your word that Rebeka is mine. That camp was crowded, was it not?'

She held herself very still. If she struck him he would probably strangle her. Peter and Rebeka were playing upstairs, happily running through what seemed like endless space in the bedrooms. 'Laurenz, I have been thinking.'

'How wonderful.' He took up his nail file again, disappointed that he hadn't got the rise he had hoped for. 'What amazing thought has struck that little mind of yours?'

'I would like to get a job. Are there not jobs at that factory that women can do?'

'Women? The place is full of women!'

'I can do a job there then. Judith can come down from the camp and she will take care of Rebeka.'

'A job! You are too stupid to get a job.'

'My English is much better now. Thomas has been very helpful.'

He threw the nail file on the floor. 'Then Thomas can get you a job. I'm going out.'

'Where?' She was hugging to herself the fact that he had not vetoed the idea of a job outright.

He pulled on his jacket. 'I'll know where when I get there.'

He was halfway through the door when she called him back. 'Laurenz?'

'What is it?'

'I thought I would write to Mikel and tell him our new address.'

'Yes. Yes. He should know, I suppose.' The door clicked behind him and she was left in her new kitchen in her new house, gloriously, wonderfully alone.

Fifteen
Thin Ice

It took Kay one month and two strikes to sort out the tool room. Adjustments had to be made on both sides. She created a new title of manager for the tool-room foreman, John Harkness. She topped up his wages and got him grudgingly on her side. She made the Captain find some capital to buy a much-needed lathe and let the tool room know that Laurenz Gold had advised its purchase.

She conceded, in deference to the toolmakers' sensitivities, that Laurenz would only take the apprentices through short training sequences to familiarise them with some of the processes he had learnt in Switzerland. These would take place in a partitioned section at the end of the tool room which acquired the name of the Pen. Here Laurenz Gold would also have a small tool-development facility separate to the tool room.

In return she could insist that the tool room itself was made and kept immaculate. She did not tell them of Laurenz's comment that no self-respecting Swiss engineer would work in such a filthy environment. They put her insistence on order down to a woman's fussiness.

At first the apprentices borrowed the contempt of the toolmakers as they swaggered into the Pen. However, Laurenz's energy, quickwittedness and charm won him their grudging respect, if not liking. The value of what they had learnt trickled back into the tool room and the working atmosphere settled down again. Grudgingly the Captain noted the improvement.

Apart from Ginger, who had her suspicions, nobody in the factory knew that Kay and Laurenz had anything more than a professional relationship. In fact, there hardly was a relationship. Very occasionally they would meet at some distance outside Priorton and go on to some hall to dance, or have a drink. On the way back they would stop and kiss, but that was all. Laurenz moaned his frustration but Kay was quite aware that once she had given herself to this man she would be lost.

Laurenz got his revenge by flirting openly with girls on the shop floor, and, according to Ginger, who took malicious delight in telling Kay about it, demonstrating the full extent of his Austrian charm. His success with the girls brought sour looks from the men; Ralph, the progress boy, wouldn't talk to him at all.

The apprentices, on the other hand, admired and imitated his swagger and sniggered at his tales of female conquest while they followed his precise instructions on the construction of a particular tool.

Patrizia sent a message with Leonora, asking if there might be a job at the factory for her. Kay could only agree. She arranged for Patrizia to start, as she had done, working with Ginger. Ginger, disliking Laurenz as she did, took to Patrizia and was very patient in showing her the ropes. Patrizia, having left Rebeka at the house with old Judith, and dropped Peter off at Blamire House to go to school with Florence, caught the bus to the factory.

On the third day, wheeling her bike through the arch, Ginger saw Patrizia get off the bus. She caught up with her. 'No lift off Buggerlugs with his shining bike, then?'

Patrizia shook her head. 'He comes in early, goes home late. He says it is not appropriate for me to come with him.'

'He would, wouldn't he?'

Patrizia had only been there a week when Kay, passing down the line with her clipboard, noted Patrizia now had her own work station; her deft hands were flying nearly as quickly as

Ginger's. Kay stopped beside Ginger. 'Star pupil?' She raised her brows.

Ginger nodded. 'Janet's off with German measles and the foreman says to put the new lass on. She's mustard. Good hands. Born for it.'

'Better than me?'

'Now that's not too hard, is it?'

Kay looked down at Patrizia's bent head. Only last night she had been sitting in a pub with this woman's husband, laughing and joking; drinking in flattery which she knew in her heart to be insincere. She stifled her pangs of guilt, nodded pleasantly at Patrizia and strode on.

The next visitor on the line was Laurenz himself, bustling along in his white coat, a roll of designs under his arm. He stopped and watched Patrizia for a few minutes. Under his eye her hands started to fumble. She dropped a wire on the floor and had to slip off her stool to retrieve it. He shook his head, smiling slightly. 'I told you, Patrizia, you would be no good at this. You do not need to do this . . . this menial work.'

'She was managing fine till you came along and pushed your nose in,' said Ginger. 'So you can get lost!'

He put a hand on Ginger's forearm and his thumb moved over her flesh. 'Now then, Ginger, you know you love me.'

Her hand came up as she wrenched her arm away, and the back of it cracked against his face. He leapt back and dropped his roll of designs on the dusty floor. There was a leap of laughter from some of the operators. Ralph, who was delivering a basket of wires, grinned. Patrizia kept her head down over her work.

As he scrabbled for the papers, Laurenz looked up at Ginger. 'Bitch!' he said through clenched teeth.

Ginger's hands were busy again with her job. 'Well, mate, you shouldn't go grabbing folks when you're not invited.'

He strode off, not stopping until he came to Kay's little office. He strode in without knocking and slammed the door behind him. 'You must sack that woman. Sack her!'

She looked up at him from her desk. 'Sack who?'

'Ginger.' He fingered his bruised cheek. 'She attacked me.'

Kay grinned. 'You've been lucky there. A bit higher and you'd have had a black eye.'

'There is no joke. You must sack her. She is violent. She is a bad influence on Patrizia.'

'She is one of our best operators. There is no question of getting rid of her.'

He threw himself on to a chair. 'You care nothing about me. You allow me to be insulted.'

She shook her head. 'Where's your sense of humour? She's just a joker. That's all.'

'You care nothing about me. Nothing.'

She came round the desk and put her hands on his shoulders. He reached up and pulled her face to his and kissed it. 'Sack her,' he said.

'No,' she said, drawing back from him. 'It's not your business to say that, Laurenz. You know it isn't.'

There was a knock on the door and she returned swiftly behind her desk. Duggie strode in, 'Kay, I—' He stopped at the sight of Laurenz. 'Oh, you've got a meeting?'

'That's all right. Laurenz is going, aren't you, Laurenz?' She smiled sweetly at him, ignoring his thunderous scowl as he thumped away. 'Now then, Duggie, what can I do for you?'

That night Laurenz was waiting for her on his bike at the bottom of The Lane where the woodland butted on to the town. She rolled down the car window. 'Hello, Laurenz.'

'I have to see you,' he said curtly. 'Come for a drink. We will drive out of town, and . . .'

She shook her head. 'I'm sorry, Laurenz. It's Friday, I promised to take Florence and your Peter to the skating rink in Durham. Thomas too.'

He stared at her for a second, his eyes hard as agate. Then he shrugged. 'You have better things to do, of course.'

She struggled, then gave in. 'Tomorrow. We can do something

tomorrow night. Drive to Darlington, Newcastle perhaps. We can get lost in the crowd.'

'Not tonight?'

'No. Not tonight.'

'What will you tell them?'

'I'll tell them I'm going to the Saturday dance with Ginger.'

He wrenched hard at his handlebar and the motor bike blared into action. 'Seven o'clock. Here,' he said and roared away without waiting for an answer.

Ginger turned down another offer of a dance and hunched, glumly dissatisfied, over her cup of frothy coffee. Perhaps she was just getting too old for these Friday-night dances. The lads seemed to be getting younger and younger and the band, which had been so swinging, seemed to be settling into a grim syncopated routine. On top of that Janet was still recovering from German measles and Ginger had been obliged to come on her own. Normally that wouldn't bother her as she knew lots of the lasses and she was always asked to dance anyway.

The chair beside her scraped back and she looked sourly at its new occupant. 'What do you want?' she snapped.

'I want to talk with you.' Laurenz offered her a cigarette.

She took it and, leaning forward, allowed him to light it with his flashy aluminium lighter. She drew on it hard then spoke, letting the smoke drift from her mouth, Rita Hayworth style. 'Can't think what you've got to say,' she drawled.

He leant back in his chair. 'You and me, Ginger, we are off on the wrong foot. I speak like that with Patrizia because I think she should be at home taking care of my children.' He removed a tiny shred of tobacco from his lip and dropped it delicately to the floor. 'And I am sorry I take hold of you, but this is just because I am mad at Patrizia.'

'Well,' said Ginger, 'if you're apologising, like . . .'

The light from the spinning globe gleamed on his teeth as he smiled. 'I am apologising. And I wish to be on the right foot.'

'OK,' she said slowly. 'Where does that leave us?'

'Well, Ginger. Would you like another cup of coffee? Or would you like to dance?'

Kay was surprised to see Patrizia, all wrapped up, waiting with Thomas and the children to be taken to the ice rink. The sight of the other woman made Kay become all bustling and efficient, checking Florence's gloves and tucking her woolly scarf round her neck a further time. Leonora had said she would take care of baby Rebeka who, by common consent, was felt to be too small to fall about on the ice.

The journey to the ice rink was easy enough. Thomas drove with Kay beside him and Patrizia sat on the back seat with the children.

'Mama is good skater,' announced Peter.

'You can skate?' said Thomas, his head half turned.

'Since I am a little girl, every winter the river freezes. We skate on the river. We have parties on the river. Schnitzel and hot wine with spices.' She stirred in her seat as the car chugged along. 'In those days I have skating boots in green kid. A birthday present from my stepfather.'

Thomas laughed. 'Well, according to a fellow at the pit, all you get at the ice rink here are these nasty black things. Lucky if you can find ones to fit you.'

In the event they were all kitted out very well, if not elegantly. Kay wobbled on to the ice shuddering already as the freezing air found its way into her nostrils and her eyes. She slithered about, clutched the barrier and watched as Peter and Florence, after a few tumbles, got the hang of it.

Across the other side of the rink Patrizia was towing Thomas along with gliding expertise. Hanging on to her, he managed quite well. Then after three circuits he cried for mercy, leant against the barrier and let Patrizia go. She whirled off: pushing and gliding, turning and spinning, sweeping high and sweeping low. Other skaters stopped to watch her and applauded when she finally spun back to the barrier where Thomas was standing. Her eyes shone brightly, her cheeks were red. She had lost the mousy scared look and seemed ten years younger.

As Kay watched the cold seeped into the back of her knees and neck. Thomas leant down and whispered something into Patrizia's ear which made her blush even more and smile shyly up at him. Kay felt annoyed then, excluded, and shouted angrily to Florence not to race too fast.

With a gritty scrape of their blades on the ice, Thomas and Patrizia came skating up to Kay. Patrizia put her hands out towards her. 'Now you come and try, Kay.'

Kay clung to the barrier and shook her head. 'No, I'll never do it. My hands are frozen, my legs are frozen. I'm sure my nose is blue.'

'Red, actually,' said Thomas. 'Come on, old girl, give it a go. Patrizia will show you.'

Reluctantly she put her gloved hands into those of Patrizia and clung nervously as Patrizia skated backwards and pulled her into the centre of the rink, towing her like a sack of potatoes. 'Come on now, Kay. Open your legs a little and close them. Again. Again. Now relax. Now try pushing with the left foot, now the right foot. That's better . . .'

Kay began to stand up straighter; the ice was less like a moving slippery carpet beneath her. As they moved around her frantic grip on Patrizia's small hands loosened and her brain took command of the ratio of effort required in relation to the movement of her feet. Then Patrizia gently disentangled one hand and turned so that they were skating side by side around the rink. Finally they came to a stop again beside Thomas.

He clapped his hands. 'Bravo!' he said. 'Well done, Kay.'

Kay revelled in the rush of heat which was colonising her body, from the tips of her toes to the roots of her hair. She nodded towards Patrizia, who was smiling up at her. 'Patrizia is a good teacher, a very good teacher.'

Inwardly she thanked God that her dalliance with Laurenz had gone no further than a few flirtatious conversations and clandestine caresses. All that had been possible when Patrizia was this shadowy *Hausfrau* at home, boring and stupid. But now, when it was clear she was neither of these, and had shown Kay how to become warm in this palace of ice, such a betrayal was impossible. She saw it for the cheap thing it was. And she would tell Laurenz so tomorrow night.

Later they warmed their hands on mugs of hot cocoa at the ramshackle stall just inside the door of the rink. Patrizia insisted on paying for this. She flashed her purse which rattled with silver. 'Now I am a working girl,' she said proudly, 'I pay for cocoa.'

Thomas dropped Kay and Florence at Blamire House. Patrizia gathered a sleepy Rebeka into her arms in the car. Florence waved enthusiastically at Peter then raced inside to tell Leonora how good she was at skating, but how Momma had taken a little time to learn.

Kay followed more slowly, aware of embryonic aches in her arms and legs which would probably take over her whole body tomorrow. Poking the fire in the kitchen to a high blaze she reflected on the shallowness of her own morality. It had been all right gallivanting around the county with Laurenz with Patrizia deep in the background, a shadowy insubstantial figure. But now . . . now . . .

'Patrizia is such a nice young woman, Kay.' Her mother's voice came to her from the doorway. 'So intelligent. Her English is coming on in leaps and bounds and she's picking up all this naturalisation stuff with such acuity.' Leonora came into the room a little. 'But to be a bit honest I'm wondering just what there is between her and Thomas. Any trouble from that husband of hers and the naturalisation thing would be in jeopardy. I'm sure getting mixed up there would be a problem.'

Kay looked up at her mother through the overmantel mirror. 'Are you?'

'I'm not one to take a moral stance, as you know.' Leonora paused. 'But it is a worry where there are children, don't you think?'

Kay put back the fireguard and turned to look at her mother, silver-haired and pretty, with one of her Egyptian gowns over a thick wool dress. 'You're a very wise woman, you know.'

Leonora laughed heartily. 'I don't know about that, love. I came down to tell you that your daughter wants you to read to her. I think she has "The Snow Queen" in mind. You know the Hans Andersen story?'

Patrizia put Peter and Rebeka to bed as soon as they had had a supper of warm milk and ginger snaps. Thomas moved to leave. He had promised to meet Hugh in the club. Patrizia shook her head. 'Please stay. Will you light the fire? It is all ready to light.' She spoke in her own language and instantly there was intimacy between them. 'I did not think it safe to leave a fire on when I am at work.'

He found a shovel and put a newspaper across it to fan the flames. By the time he heard her footsteps on the stairs the fire was blazing but the room was still quite cold.

Patrizia had changed her clothes. She was wearing a neat housecoat, obviously home-made but of pretty flowered material. She had loosened out her hair. Freed from its tight plaits, it caught the firelight as it rippled down to her shoulders.

He blushed. She took him by the hand and sat him beside her on the sofa. Then she turned to him. 'What did you say to me there on the ice? I am not sure that I heard it right. My English . . .'

'You looked so beautiful there at the rink. Swirling and turning.'

'That is not what you said.'

He sighed. 'I said that I loved you. *Ich liebe dich.*'

'*I love you.* It sounds best in English.' She stroked his wrist. 'Thomas?'

'Yes, Patrizia?'

'I love you.'

He was aware that his whole body was gooseflesh, the hair standing erect in every pore. 'Patrizia, I . . .'

'You have never told anyone you love them before?'

'No.'

'Have you ever made love with anyone before?'

He hesitated. 'No. It never seemed . . . I never knew anyone who . . .'

She reached up and loosened his tie. He caught her hand, glancing at the door. 'Patrizia, what about . . .'

'Laurenz? He will not return before one or two in the morning. He has gone dancing. He has these special shoes. He always wears them.' She pulled at Thomas's tie so that it snaked away from his neck and then laid it carefully on the back of the couch. 'This is our time. We will learn together how to do it right.' She laughed nervously. 'Doing it right! That will be new for me also.'

Despite herself, Ginger was enjoying the ride. She had never been on the back of a motor bike before. Jeeps, ramshackle cars of various kinds, yes. But never a motorbike. They raced round a long curve and she was forced backwards. She bent forward and clung onto his waist, the wind cutting her cheeks, her red curls whipping away behind her. She remembered a film where Margaret Lockwood rode pillion on a horse behind her highwayman lover, her hair flying free behind her.

He slowed down slightly as they approached the lights of Priorton, and she sat upright again, loosening her hold on his waist. Now he was turning off the road. 'What the heck?' she shouted. 'What the heck are you doing?'

He had veered off into the woodland at the bottom of The Lane. The bike was bumping over tussocks of grass and the soft new growth of the trees was whipping her face. The roar of the engine still didn't drown the rumble of the river, swollen in its first spring flood, pregnant with melting winter snow.

He swerved the bike round suddenly and she shot off the back, landing awkwardly in a small clearing. No light from the streetlamps filtered into this place. The dark was intense. She could feel the grass beneath her as she struggled to get up. She could feel rather than see him get off the bike, the leather of his jacket creaking. Then he was astride her, pushing her back into the earth. And he growled at her in a language she could not understand.

The battering at the door woke Kay from her first deep slumber. Florence's reedy voice called that there was someone at the door and Kay went and tucked her in again before going downstairs. The big grandfather clock showed eleven o'clock in the reflected light from the streetlamp. She blinked as another hail of blows made the door shake. Thomas! It must be Thomas, drunk again on that strong ale.

She turned the big key. 'Thomas, I . . .' She stopped. There on the step, looking like a bedraggled cat in her mock fur coat, was Ginger. Her eyes were wide, clown-like where the tears had spread the eye-black in incongruous lines. Incredibly, she laughed; a high-pitched, mirthless sound. 'I wondered if yeh'd be in like.'

Kay reached out, pulled her into the hall and locked the door behind her. Then she guided her into the kitchen, sat her in Leonora's rocking chair and knelt beside her. 'What on earth is it, Ginger?'

Ginger started to roar then, her mouth wide open like a child's. Kay put her arms round her and rocked her backwards and forwards as though she were Florence. 'Now then, now then don't cry. It's all right. You're all right now. Ssh, ssh.'

It was a very long time before Ginger calmed down enough for Kay to leave her so she could make some tea. She made it very strong and put three spoonfuls of sugar in it. Then she wrapped Ginger's fingers round the cup and guided it towards her mouth. After two or three gulps the shuddering stopped. To Kay's surprise a weak smile crossed her face. 'I knew you had a bairn, but I'd never had you taken for a mother,' she said.

'Multi-talented,' said Kay gravely. 'Now, Ginger, do you want to tell me . . . ?'

Ginger shook her head vigorously.

'Well, what do you want?'

Ginger looked at her, then round the spacious kitchen. 'You'll have one of those proper bathrooms in this house, with a boiler and all that?'

Kay nodded.

'Well, I could do with a bath, to be honest. And some clothes.' She let her coat gape.

'Ginger!' Kay drew a sharp breath as she saw the skirt torn almost to the waist and the blouse ripped at the neck. Worse, there was bruising on her upper chest, angry red now, which would be very black later. 'Who on earth . . . ?'

Ginger shook her head. 'No one you know. Some lad . . . didn't know him from Adam, but' – the bitter laugh again – 'seems he thought he was due for a field day.'

'We should get the police.'

'That's a joke. Ouch!' She touched her lip which was swollen on one side. 'All I want, Kay, is a bath an' some clean clothes, skin out, knickers and things. If I go home like this me brothers'll give me a good hiding before they go off and kill the bloke. Our Ed might have been all right but the others . . .' She stretched out her legs in front of her. 'And I just can't be bothered with that.'

Kay left her with her tea and went up to light the boiler and dig out some clothes which would go anywhere near Ginger's voluptuous shape. In the end she went into her mother's room, whispered an explanation and borrowed a petticoat and one of the accommodating Egyptian dresses.

She peered in on Florence, who was fast asleep, and finally came back to Ginger who was sitting with her eyes closed. Kay put a hand on her shoulder and she shook with shock. 'Kay, oh, Kay!' Then she stood up. 'Do you have a carrier bag or sommat like that? Yeah? Well I want you to burn everything I give you. Burn it, mind. In this fire. Promise?'

Kay nodded, put her arm round her and led her up to the bathroom. She turned on the taps. 'I'll get a carrier,' she said. When she returned the bathroom was filling up with steam and Ginger was standing in the middle of it, stark naked. Without even glancing directly Kay took in the magnificent body and the blotches all over it which could only be bruises. She sprinkled some soap flakes in the water and swirled it round with one hand.

'That the carrier? Give us it here.' Ginger snatched the carrier off her and stuffed it full of items which Kay could not see. Then she rolled it over, tight. 'Now you go and burn that. Just burn it, promise?'

'Of course I promise.' Kay said this almost crossly. 'Now you get in the bath, will you?'

Downstairs she put the parcel on the fire and it flared and sizzled. The smell told her there was blood there and she sat in the rocker herself, tears falling down her cheeks for Ginger.

Ginger came down twenty minutes later, shining faced, her newly washed hair pulled back into a tight topknot, and Leonora's dress pulled in at the waist and gracefully looped over the belt so that it only reached her knees.

Kay smiled up at her. 'That's better.'

Ginger smiled faintly. 'You said it, kidder. Any tea left in that pot?'

Kay emptied the teapot in the sink and made some fresh tea. 'So. What're you going to do about all this, Ginger?'

The other girl took the teapot from Kay and poured her own. 'Nothing. And if you say anything to anyone I'll slit your gizzard.'

'But you should tell someone. Your family. The police . . .'

Ginger shook her head. 'Nah. I've gotta live in that family, in this rabbit hutch of a town, probably for the rest of my life. If I tell anyone now, I'll always be the girl who . . . you know. I wouldn't give them the satisfaction.'

'You're very brave, Ginger.'

'Brave? Bloody brave? You should have seen me two hours ago. Blubbering in the bushes like a bairn for her mother.'

'That's what I mean. Brave.' Kay frowned. 'But this . . . person shouldn't get away with it, Ginger, it's not right.'

Ginger stood up, reached into her bag and pulled out a lipstick. Then she peered in the overmantel mirror and applied it to her mouth, wincing a bit as she smeared over the bruise. 'Oh, he won't get away with it, flower. Don't you worry about that.' She turned and smiled brightly at Kay. 'Now then, if you lend me a scarf to cover this wet hair I'll be on my way.'

'Oh, wait, wait for Thomas. He has the car – well, it's Duggie's car really. He'll take you home.' Kay took her own silk scarf from the back of the door and tied it under Ginger's chin. 'You shouldn't go home by yourself.'

'No thank you, little mother.' She kissed Kay on the cheek and Kay could feel the sticky smear of lipstick. 'I'll walk home on my own two feet. I won't give them the satisfaction. Not him. Not any of them.' Kay closed the door behind her and came back to the mirror again, to wipe off the smear of lipstick with her handkerchief. Its red stain on the snowy surface looked like blood.

Hugh was not at the club when Thomas arrived and the old men shook their heads and said it wasn't like Hugh to miss a Friday night. Thomas set off again and called at Hugh's house. He knocked hard on the front door and got no reply. He made his way round the end of the street and down the back lane. He lifted the sneck on Hugh's back gate but could not make it open. Something was stopping it. He hauled himself onto the top of the wall. 'Hugh!' he said. The old man was lying stiffly inside the back gate, his eyes rolled back, his face still ingrained with pit dirt. He must have been lying there for hours, since they both came off shift.

Thomas jumped down and knelt beside his friend, pulling his head onto his lap. Hugh's eyes closed, then half opened and he started muttering, flailing out his hand as though shooing away a fly. 'Bliddy spade!' The words came painfully from swollen lips. His spade was lying where it had fallen when, Thomas surmised, it must have tripped him up.

Thomas got to his feet and braced himself to pick up the old man. 'Let's get you inside, Hugh. Too cold to be lying around out here.' Thomas staggered under the bulk of him, and had to manoeuvre awkwardly to get Hugh through the narrow scullery door.

He got him settled in his fireside chair. Hugh put his head back and seemed to go to sleep. Thomas turned up the gaslight and poked the fire to warm the chilly room. His glasses, cold from the outside air, steamed up, so he put them on the mantelpiece.

'Me bliddy foot,' the growl came from behind him. 'Hurts like hell.'

He knelt down, lifted High's foot onto a low wooden stool and eased off his boot, ignoring the old man's yelps of pain. The ankle was badly swollen and, even under the black grime of coal dust, looked dangerously pink. 'Have you got a towel?' Thomas said.

'Bottom drawer of the press,' said Hugh through gritted teeth. 'Ah'd a thought you'd remember that, Harry.'

Thomas found the towel. 'It's not Harry,' he said over his shoulder. 'It's Thomas, Thomas Scorton.'

'Ah knaa nee Thomas Scorton,' said Hugh, wincing again. 'Dinnet mak gam, Harry.'

Thomas went through to the scullery and wrung the towel out under the single tap. He came back and laid it carefully across the injured ankle. Then he retrieved his glasses from the mantelpiece and put them on. 'I'm not Harry, Hugh,' he said.

Hugh squinted up at him. 'Aye, you're right. But there's a canny resemblance. What did yer say yer name was?'

'I am Thomas Scorton. My grandmother was Kitty Rainbow,' he said gently. The old boy must have had a crack on the head as well as the ankle.

'Ah know of her,' said Hugh, easing his ankle and wincing again. 'My Uncle Freddie . . .'

'I know about that,' said Thomas. He pulled a chair up beside Hugh's and looked him in the eye. 'We're friends, Hugh, you and me. We've been friends for months. We work together.'

Hugh put a massive fist and knocked his forehead. 'Am I cracked, or what?'

Thomas laughed. 'No. You've had a fall that's winded you. It'll all come back soon. I'm going to run for the doctor.'

'Ah need nee doctor,' said Hugh firmly.

'Yes, you do,' said Thomas equally firmly. He stood up. 'Now don't move. I'll be back soon.'

'Move?' grunted Hugh. 'Fat chance! Before you go, gerrus a bowl of water so I can get off a bit of this pit dirt before the doctor comes. We dinnet want the feller to think he's in the house of barbarians, do we?'

Thomas washed the old man's hands and face as though he were a child; then knelt awkwardly at his feet, and washed the worst of the grime off the injured foot.

Later, running down the back street Thomas thought of the strange and wonderful time he had just spent with Patrizia on the floor before her fire. All that time Hugh must have been lying there in his back yard, in his pit dirt.

The doctor, a squint-eyed man, younger than Thomas, was having a late meal, but came willingly enough when Thomas told his tale. He renewed Thomas's cold compress on the foot and peered into Hugh's eyes and ears, took his temperature and felt his pulse. Then he beckoned Thomas into the scullery.

'It's more than just a fall,' he said briefly. 'He's had some kind of seizure. Can't say whether the fall caused the seizure, or the seizure caused the fall. Either way he won't be back down the pit for some while. If at all.' He squinted up at Thomas. 'You'll be his son?' he said.

Thomas found himself blushing. 'No. He's a kind of uncle. We work together.'

'Then you will have to find another workmate, Mr . . . er . . .'

'Scorton. Thomas Scorton.'

The little man nodded. 'Mr Scorton. I will be back with an ambulance in . . .' he looked at his watch, 'about twenty minutes. He will be better off in hospital. There is the danger of poison setting in in the foot, and the question of this seizure.'

Thomas went back into the kitchen and explained about the hospital. Hugh looked at him. 'It is Thomas, isn't it? I remember now. Sorry to be such a bliddy fool.' He wriggled in his chair. 'Ferget about the hospital. What about me hens? Me rabbits? They need feedin'.'

'I'll feed the lot. Don't worry about that.'

'There's a sack of greens outside the back door,' muttered Hugh. 'I was carrying that when I fell over the blasted shovel.' Then he put back his head and closed his eyes.

As soon as they heard the gate open the chickens flew down from their perches and set up a raucous squawking. Thomas fed them very quickly and went into the rabbit hut. The rabbits made no noise, but as Thomas held up the old pit lamp their eyes gleamed at him in the darkness. He hung the lamp up on a nail and set about heaping the greens into the hutches. Unlike the chickens the rabbits did not leap on their food. They waited until their hutches were locked again. Thomas stood perfectly still for quite a few minutes before they crept from their corners and started to nibble.

The jobs done, Thomas made his way back to Hugh's house. The door was open, but Hugh was gone and the gaslights were tiny tongues of flame. The doctor must have been as good as his word. Thomas stood by the mantelpiece and turned up the lamp to look at Harry's photograph on the mantelpiece. Stuffed behind it, higgledy piggledy, were Harry's most recent letters.

Thomas hesitated. He did need to get Harry's address to tell him about Hugh's accident. He pulled out the letters and placed them beside his cap on the table. He noted Harry's address in his own diary, then, almost without thinking, found himself sitting down and reading the letters. Once he had read one, the offence was committed, so he read a second, then a third. Then he read them all. They were ordinary enough letters: about the vagaries of the recruits Harry had to deal with, the contrariness of Major Barham Smyth, the unexpected kindness of Colonel Jock Johnson, who had been a hero in the Italian campaign. There were some angry paragraphs about the proposal to divide Palestine and about this over-hasty proposal to partition India. There was a comical description of a regimental dinner which ended in a battle involving bread rolls. *So you can contemplate, Da, that great event, when you're fathoms underground, on your hunkers eating your bait.*

The tone of the letters was more that of a friend than a son. Thomas knew now that after Harry's mother died, the two of them had always been together here in this house. There was little they did not know about each other. Thomas sighed as he carefully placed the letters back in the correct envelopes and tucked them back behind the photograph. He wished suddenly that Harry had been here in the room. They could have taken care of Hugh together and perhaps shared a cup of tea. And he could have told Harry about Patrizia. Harry would know what it was like, the first time a man made love. The wonder of it. They could have shared that.

Back at home Leonora came downstairs when she heard Thomas come in. She moved around the kitchen, making him and herself a cup of cocoa, listening to his tale of Hugh's accident. 'He'll hate it, won't he, being stuck in plaster? Such an active man.' She shook her head.

'I'll send a letter to Harry tomorrow. He'll need to know.'

Leonora frowned. 'Harry?'

'Hugh's son. He brought him up on his own. I told you. He's an army captain.'

'Yes. I remember. What's he like?'

'Everything like Hugh, and nothing like him.'

'Now that's a good answer.'

'I will tell you something strange about him.'

'What's that?'

'He looks like me.'

'What?'

'I know. It's weird.'

'It does go to show something.'

'What's that?'

'That you must be like Freddie, my father. Kitty's first . . . well . . . love.'

He grinned. 'A nice thought, that.'

She sipped her cocoa and started to tell him about Kay's visitor. 'Ginger something. Can you remember her at Kitty's funeral? Anyway, there must have been some trouble. At first Kay thought she might stay, but she wouldn't. I have no idea what it's all about.'

He was silent a second. 'I'm keen to accuse Kay of getting all high and mighty,' he said, thinking of her whirling round the skating rink hand in hand with Patrizia. 'But really, she's all right, I suppose.'

'You've known her all your life, Thomas. Of course she's all right. She's changed here in England. You've changed. You're pulling away from each other now.' Leonora stood up and poured the bitter dregs of the cocoa down the sink. 'And that's no bad thing if you ask me.' She smiled at Thomas. 'I hear that you had a splendid time skating?'

His head went up and he blushed. 'Wonderful. You should have seen Florence. Patrizia said she was a natural skater.'

'Did she? Well, I suppose she should know, shouldn't she?' She put her hand on his arm. 'You will be careful, Thomas, won't you, dear?'

Thomas looked into his mother's eyes and knew that she knew. Not about his mind-bending time in front of the fire in Patrizia's house; but she knew that he loved Patrizia. He longed for her to say that that was no bad thing either. But of course she wouldn't. Or couldn't. Why should she?

In his bedroom he wrote out a telegram to Harry explaining what had happened to his father, and left it on his dressing table ready for Leonora to send in the morning. Later he stretched out in his bed and thought of Hugh in his narrow hospital cot. The old man would hate it, being exposed there to strangers. And how would he take the news about the pit?

Thomas turned over and pulled the blanket under his chin. He would go and see him in the hospital tomorrow, straight after his short shift, seeing as it was Saturday. That was the least he could do.

[illegible]

[illegible]

[illegible]

[illegible]

[illegible]

[illegible]

[illegible]

[illegible]

[illegible]

[illegible]

[illegible]

Sixteen

A Sorting-out

Kay walked down the line and contemplated the surprising fact that the chance to work Saturday mornings at the Rainbow Works was always a welcome privilege for the women. They were paid time-and-a-half for their work and because they finished at twelve o'clock Saturday still felt like a special day.

As well as this most of the girls were 'dressed' under their overalls, they wore make-up, their hair, out of curling pins, gleamed from its Friday Amami shampooing. This was the morning they could show a bit more of their best, their public selves; after the shift they would go down to Priorton, or off to Darlington to shop. And they would treat themselves to a Carricks' tea and catch the bus home in time to get ready for Saturday-night pictures or dancing.

Only half the operators were in, so Kay was surprised to see Ginger's sleek auburn curls bent down over her task; an emerald-green blouse peeped out beneath her overall. She looked up and winked as Kay stopped beside her station.

'Now then, Mrs Fitzgibbon, gettin' a bit of overtime in, are you?' Her make-up was immaculate. The swelling on her lip had subsided.

'You too, Ginger? I'd have thought you'd have rested today.'

Ginger's face was lit by what seemed to be a genuine grin. 'I told you. I wouldn't give them the satisfaction. And the foreman says to us on Friday there's a rush on this lot of cookers for some reason.' Her glance strayed behind Kay, who turned to see Laurenz Gold strolling up the line.

Ginger leant past Kay to get a good view and winked at him. 'What now then, Buggerlugs? Been thrilling all the girls down in T block, have yer?'

Laurenz slowed down for a second, then quickened his step to get past them, his jaw tight. He was white with anger.

Kay turned back to Ginger, smiling slightly. 'You should go easy on him, Ginger. You got him in a state yesterday as well.'

Ginger's head was back down over her wiring. 'Go easy? That'll be the day.'

Kay made her way down the line, talking to one or two of the operators as she went. Saturday mornings afforded a little more time for this kind of thing; she always came into the Works even though Captain Marshall assured her that it was absolutely not necessary. Not on Saturday mornings.

The telephone was ringing when she got into her office. The crackle told her it was an inside line, but the caller rang off without saying anything. Then it rang again and it was Laurenz.

'Did you just ring?' she said.

'Ring? Me? No. Why?'

'Someone rang, then rang off.'

'Not me.'

'Do you want something?'

'You have forgotten.'

'Forgotten what?'

'Tonight we ride in the country. You promised.'

She hesitated.

'Kay? Are you still there?'

'Yes. I must talk to you.'

'We will talk tonight,' he said very coldly.

'Very well. Seven o'clock. At the bottom of The Lane. Laurenz, I—' But there was a crackle on the line as he rang off. She dialled his internal number, but put the phone down before it rang. There would be time enough to talk tonight.

That afternoon she went with Thomas to the hospital to visit

Hugh Longstaffe. The old man was sitting up in bed, a large cage supporting the blanket over his leg. He was spotlessly clean and his thick grey hair was brushed. He looked shrunken and almost frightened. Kay wondered if this could be the same fearless pitman who, without very much trouble, had stolen her brother from under her nose.

The nurse who walked them down the ward said Mr Longstaffe had been long-suffering but very miserable. 'Couldn't get a smile out of him nohow. Sometimes it takes the old miners that way. You'd think they'd be used to confinement down there under the earth. But no . . .'

Hugh brightened when he saw Thomas and was even happier when Thomas told him that his livestock had been fed, and that he had made a special visit this morning to let the hens out. And he would be going later that afternoon to feed and lock the hens up again. 'I've promised to take Peter and Florence. Will that be all right?'

But Hugh, reassured, was no longer really listening. He waved his hand towards the clean bare ward. 'D'you know this place was the workhouse once? They've cleaned it up, like,' he said miserably.

'You'll be out soon,' said Thomas, his eyes on the nurse who was talking to the patient in the next bed. 'Is that not so, Sister?'

'Mr Colman says it'll be a week at least. There was extra damage because Mr Longstaffe left it a long time before we got him.'

'Me own fault,' said Hugh. 'All me own fault. An' they say I'll not be back to work in a month. Sommat about the *liggiments*.'

He did not mention the seizure. Thomas wondered whether the doctors had not mentioned it to him, or whether Hugh was pretending he had not been told. The seizure was much more of a threat to his work than was the leg.

Kay poked in her bag. 'Leonora sends her best, and she sent some papers for you: the *News Chronicle*, the *Northern Echo*. And some dandelion and burdock. And Florence sent you her sweet ration.'

He smiled, but pushed the packet back at Kay. 'I can't take the bairn's sweets.'

She put the bag firmly back into his hand. 'You can't refuse them, Hugh. She would be really upset.' She took a brown envelope from her basket. 'And she sent you a drawing of your rabbits.'

He pulled out the sheet and held up the neat picture of two rabbits who looked as though they were having a tug of war with a very bright green lettuce leaf. The tension went right out of Hugh then, and he beamed. 'What it is to have a family,' he said. 'I count meself a lucky man.'

As they walked back down the ward, feet clattering, Thomas took Kay's arm. 'He's got a nice surprise in store. Do you know I sent Harry a telegram this morning? I'm sure he'll come. That'll make the old boy happy.'

The hotel dining room suffered from too much drapery which had hung around too much food for too long. But the cloth on their table was spotless; the silver was heavy and the service respectful. There was a degree of discreet interest in this rather handsome young couple. Most of the customers here were eating alone: businessmen in transit dining grandly at their company's expense. They munched their carrots and contemplated their long, boring evening, their night in a strange bed before the relief of an early morning call to catch their trains which chugged north to Edinburgh, or south to Birmingham, Manchester or London from Darlington's bustling railway station.

Kay pushed her lamb around her plate, eating one mouthful to Laurenz's three. He was at his most charming: he told her stories of his adventures before the war, when he escorted people away from their persecution in Austria through Switzerland. 'The problem, of course, was the passports. It wasn't long before people had to have their Jewish identity marked on their passport. And soon anyone whose passport was so marked was not allowed into Switzerland. The whole thing shut like a trap.'

'Couldn't you get special passports? Passports without the mark on?'

'For a while a man called Goldfarb in Vienna made them for me. Then he was taken.'

'Oh dear.'

He shrugged. 'It was a risk we all took.'

'So that was how you met Patrizia?' she said. 'Rescuing her.'

He laughed shortly. 'It was what you might call a matter of convenience. She was the last one I took through and I went all the way with her. Goldfarb was taken and they were on to me.'

'But you married her?' she persisted.

'We were in the camp. Everything was so transient there. Families were slipping apart. Peter was born. I did want a son.' He put his knife and fork carefully together. 'And it bound her to my side,' he said. It seemed brutally simple.

'But you loved her?' she pressed.

'Love, Kay? Love? That is the indulgence of those who are secure and do not worry about their survival. It is for people playing games and striking poses who have nothing better to do.'

She looked around the dark dining room. 'Is that what we're doing here? Striking poses?'

He leant over, took her hand and turned it over. With the tip of his finger he traced the lines on her hand, then he closed her hand over his finger. 'We do not talk of love here, Kay. Love is tame. It is security and the yoke of domesticity. You and I are about desire. Passion. Compulsion. These things keep us alive, remind us we are things of nature . . .'

She shivered. 'Beasts, you mean.'

He held tight on to her hand. 'No, Kay. That we are natural beings and must follow our desires.'

She rescued her hand and lifted her full wine-glass to her mouth. She took a long sip then breathed very deeply to get rid of the tingle of excitement which was trickling right through her body. 'So, what's Ginger been doing to you?'

He stared hard at his glass. 'Ginger? What has she been saying?'

'Nothing. But she seems to have made you very mad lately.'

'It is nothing. She knows I think her an insolent slut and she does not like it.'

Kay laughed. 'Can't say she looked very crushed this morning.'

'You laugh at me also,' he scowled.

'Oh Laurenz,' she said. 'You might be very handsome but you have no sense of humour.'

'Sense of humour!' he said sourly. 'You British think you are so funny!'

'They do say sense of humour and fortitude are what won the war for the British.'

'Do they? So they are not counting American dollars and American guns, American battalions and American aeroplanes?'

She threw her napkin on the plate. 'I'm not sitting here to listen to this.' Her feeling of outrage surprised herself. She hadn't thought she cared so much that she could feel such loyalty for this cold place.

He caught her hand in his. 'That is better! A bit of passion, a bit of power from the self-composed Mrs Fitzgibbon!'

'You talk about games. All you do is play games.'

He took her other hand in his. 'So let us play some more games. The room . . .'

She snatched her hand away and looked at the other diners who ate on stolidly through their jam sponge puddings.

'I have the room,' he repeated. 'Tonight we are Mr and Mrs Gold.'

'I need to talk to you. Seriously.'

'Let us talk upstairs. If it is serious we need to be in private.'

She found herself following him. She smiled faintly as the desk clerk greeted them, then stood uncomfortably beside Laurenz in the grinding lift. He produced the key with a magician's gesture and ushered her in. The room's wide windows looked on to the ornate town hall and the traffic grinding away along the street below. Laurenz lit a standard lamp which illuminated a table in the window, then closed the velvet curtains.

Kay was still hovering by the door, clutching her handbag. 'I just came to say, Laurenz, for once and for all, I can't do it, all this. Patrizia, she is so . . . nice. She showed me how to skate. Once I met her properly I knew all this is not right.'

He strode across the room, took her by the shoulders and shook them. 'You are so stupid. What about Patrizia! She betrays me already with your saintly brother.' He knew there was no truth in that, but it would soften Kay up.

'Thomas?' She remembered her mother's words. 'I don't believe it,' she said hesitantly.

He pulled her to him and started to kiss her cheek, then her brow below the hairline. 'I have tolerated all that just for you. In the camp I would have slit his throat. Here, I might make a divorce and she is deported.' He started to push the collar of her dress away from her neck. 'With no one do I feel this, Kay.'

The feeling of his lips at the base of her neck checked her protest. Her head, her body, seemed full of heat and she wanted his lips on hers to cool her down. So when his face came up she raised her lips to his and closed her eyes. She welcomed the power of his body as it locked onto hers, and their two figures made one. They rocked slightly before crashing together onto the bed. Their kissing went on and on, then his hand was on her breast and thigh over her dress. Then he knelt up astride her, and tore off his jacket and shirt and she glimpsed his narrow muscular chest before his lips were on hers again, drowning her senses and obliterating her common sense.

His lips moved to her ear. 'Turn over,' he whispered. 'Turn over.'

Obediently she lifted a shoulder and started to turn. He reached round and undid the back of her dress, and suddenly she was lying on her face and he was pulling her dress away, kissing her bare shoulder. His hand was on the back of her head now; he forced it down, half suffocating her in the pillow. At that moment in her ear, clear as a bell she heard Ginger's voice, as though her friend was standing beside her.

'*Go easy? That'll be the day.*'

When had Ginger said that? Last night? It seemed a year ago.

Her head swimming, Kay put her hands under her chest and forced her head and body back, throwing Laurenz off balance.

Still she struggled under him, ineffectually for a second, but then her brain cooled and she saw it all. She understood. She stopped struggling and went slack. 'Ginger. You did that to her. You . . . animal.'

He was still wrestling with her. 'Ginger? I tell you she is a slut,' he said through gritted teeth. 'I tell you to give her the sack but you do nothing. She needs a lesson.' He fought to hold her down again.

Kay's flailing hand somehow hit on her handbag which was lying on the bedside table. She brought it up hard against his cheek then smashed it back the other way over his eye. He howled and leapt back. She slid from under him and raced for the door, then into the lift where she pulled her dress back onto the shoulder and redid the zip. She ran her hand through her hair as the cage creaked its way to the ground floor.

Then she strode through the entrance looking neither right nor left and ran for the car. Beneath the panic and the anger, as she drove the winding way home, there was a degree of satisfaction that she had fended him off, had not accepted the inevitable.

But by the time she was drawing up at Blamire House her own guilt was rising to the surface. After all, without her, Laurenz would not have attacked Ginger. She was sure of it.

One thing for certain, she would sack Laurenz immediately. But first there was Ginger to see. The truth of the thing had to be open between them. Who was Ginger protecting? Herself? Kay? Certainly not Laurenz Gold. Closing over a wound without cleaning it was bound to make the poison flourish. That stood to reason.

She burst into the kitchen and wondered instantly what Thomas was doing there in army uniform. Then she looked again and it wasn't Thomas at all. It was a stranger, as tall as Thomas and as fragile-looking. But he wore no glasses and his hair was reddish brown rather than blackish brown.

He put a hand out towards her. 'You must be Kay. I'm Harry Longstaffe. Thomas found me at the hospital and swept me here for some supper before he deposits me back at Dad's house.' He shook her hand firmly. 'Good to meet you.'

'How is Hugh?'

A slight shadow fell across his face. 'Not so good, to be truthful. There is this thing about the blackout. Doctor's talking about blood poisoning. He's very groggy.'

'He's a strong man. He'll rally.' She wondered why she was beginning to care now about this old man whom she had so disliked at first. Perhaps it was an appropriate thing to say to his son.

'I hope so.'

She sat down and pulled off her gloves. 'I thought you were Thomas. The likeness is extraordinary.'

'It tickled my dad. Maybe that's why he took to Thomas at first.' He laughed. 'But anyone would like old Thomas.'

She warmed to this man who liked her brother so much.

'He tells me you are twins.'

It was her turn to smile. 'And you're about to tell me we're not much alike.'

His eyes narrowed. 'I wouldn't say that. Superficially yes, you are unlike. But you have a similar . . . aura . . . around you.'

'Aura, that's not a very military word!'

'You'd be surprised.'

'Aura? Perhaps you're right. After all we have breathed virtually the same air for twenty-six years, and have lived within yards of each other all that time. But actually, lately . . .' Her voice tailed off.

'Lately?' he said.

'Since we've come to England he's kind of gone right away from me. It's all your father's fault.'

'Poor old Dad. Now what's he guilty of?'

'He's taken my brother Thomas off into that world of coal seams and men's men. Changed him.'

Harry shook his head. 'Just showed him a side of himself which was there but sleeping. And he hasn't lost the nicer side of himself. My father talks of him with the children. You couldn't wish for a gentler soul.'

'Does he think that?' She stood up. 'Anyway, where is he? My mother too.'

'Thomas is upstairs reading "The Little Tin Soldier" to your daughter who woke up from a deep sleep and started to cry. Your mother went to bed after supper. She had a folder of papers in her hands and was talking about preparing for a meeting.'

At that moment Thomas bustled through the door. 'Asleep. The old magic works again!' His eye lit on his sister. 'Kay. This is early for you.'

'The band was really dreary and the company was poor. So we decided to make it an early finish.' She carefully didn't say who the *we* were. 'Anyway the car's here so you can run . . . Harry back. He must be tired after his long day. That train from London.' She threw Thomas the keys.

Harry leapt to his feet, protesting that he could easily make his own way home. Thomas reached for his coat. 'No, we'll call at the Royal George for a late drink. The old boys in there'll be wanting to know about Hugh. One of them stopped me by the allotments when we went across to lock up the hens.'

'Well then.' Harry put on his peaked cap which added another two inches to his height. He reached out and shook Kay's hand again. 'Hope we meet again soon, Kay.' Then he was gone after Thomas and she closed the door to shut out the cold night.

She put her head round her mother's door and told her not to worry about the noise from the boiler as she was going to have a late bath. Her mother looked at her over her glasses and asked if there was anything wrong.

'My bones are aching and I thought a bath might ease them. I just hope I'm not sickening for the flu.'

Her mother's eyes strayed back to her papers. 'Try some salt in the water, that always helps.'

Later, sitting in the steaming water, Kay decided she would go and see Ginger in the morning to open up this thing about Laurenz between them. Perhaps she had jumped to the wrong conclusion. Even if it weren't Laurenz, Ginger should talk about it, even if she told no one else. But Kay had this feeling in her bones about Laurenz Gold.

Then, even later, as she lay in her clean nightdress, between her clean sheets, she gave thanks that, willing or unwilling, she had not gone through with tonight's adventure. But even as she gave thanks she was consumed by a sense of being alone. Stephen was dead. Thomas was gone from her. Laurenz Gold, attractive and dynamic as he was, was no more trustworthy than a snake.

She dreamt of Laurenz, marching in the desert in British Army fatigues. She ran after him but when he turned it was with Thomas's face topped by this strange quiff of reddish-brown hair.

To find Ginger's address Kay had to get Jim Murton, the gateman, to let her into the Works and into the personnel room in the admin. block. The files were neat and well kept, so discovering that Ginger lived at number seven, Bridge Street, Priorton, was no problem. On the way out she asked Jim how she could find Bridge Street. 'Can't miss it, Mrs Fitzgibbon. Tucked away there under the viaduct on the way down to the river. So steep you'd need a pulley to get you back up. Folks that live there must have legs like hosses. On a windy day, you can lie on the wind as you walk down.'

Fortunately number seven was only a little way down the bank but Jim was right, the houses did cling to the bank at an improbable angle, dwarfed by the great viaduct looming above them.

The man who came to the door, white-faced and sandy-haired, was younger than her, a younger, uglier version of Ginger. His arms were short and his shoulders were immensely strong. He kept her at the door and bellowed behind him, 'Ginger!'

There was a clattering on the stairs and Ginger appeared, a green velvet dressing-gown over her nightie and three steel curlers in the front of her hair. 'Bloody hell,' she said, 'a royal visit.' She pulled her brother to one side. 'Where's yer manners, Ed? Invite the lady in. Don't worry about him, Kay, he's in shock. Nobody except the police come the front way down this street.'

The front door led straight into a chill front room furnished with a utility couch and chairs. On the wall were pictures made of fragments of mother of pearl set on black velvet. 'You sit down here, Kay, an' I'll scrounge us a cup of tea.' She opened the connecting door and a gale of heat and talk wafted through before she closed it. The talk stilled a second; obviously Ginger was explaining the identity of her visitor. Then the chatter started again.

Ginger's mother, Mona, put her hennaed head round the door. 'Didn't realise it was you, Mrs Fitzgibbon. Are yeh all right?'

'I'm fine, Mrs Simpson. How's the cooker doing?'

Ginger's mother looked uneasy. 'Nice. Very nice. Very smart. Of course, I'm more used to my range.'

Ginger was elbowing her way through the door; in her hands were two very decent cups and saucers. 'Her puddings were flat, Kay, her cakes sank in the middle and her meringues burnt to a crisp,' she said briskly. 'She's back on the fire oven now.'

'I do use the rings,' protested her mother. 'They're very handy. Problem is I don't know timings and things. I know it with me own oven, like. Been cooking in a coal oven since I was eleven years old. You get a feel for it. How the oven really works. For this thing you need a special cookery book or sommat.'

Kay took her tea from Ginger. 'Should be possible to make some kind of cookbook of our own,' she said thoughtfully. 'What's your name? Your Christian name?'

Ginger's mother frowned. 'Mona. Mona Simpson.'

'That'll do,' said Kay, her enthusiasm growing. 'We'll get somebody down here, say, a commercial cook? And you and she can work some of your recipes on the new cooker. Get the timing and the temperatures right. We'll call it *Mona Simpson's Northern Cookbook* and give one away with every cooker.'

'I don't know about that,' said Mona. Her head vanished and the door slammed behind her.

'Don't worry about her,' said Ginger, settling down in the high-backed chair beside the empty fireplace. 'She's embarrassed.' She put her own cup and saucer on the high mantelpiece and started to unwind her hair from the curlers. 'So what do we owe this honour to? You're not just here for the time of day, I take it?'

'I came to tell you I'm going to sack Laurenz Gold.'

Ginger stopped unwinding her hair, then continued. 'Are yeh now? Now why would you do that?'

'It was Laurenz who . . . attacked you, wasn't it?'

Ginger looked her in the eye. 'The word you're looking for is rape, flower. Now what made you think that?'

Kay stayed silent.

Ginger took a hairbrush from her dressing-gown pocket and started to pull it through her hair. Her face was grim. 'I see now. The sleazy devil tried it with you. Did he . . . ?'

Kay shook her head. 'I got away.'

Ginger laughed bitterly. 'Quicker off the mark than me. He's dangerous, that snake.'

'I don't know how I got taken in, Ginger. Crikey! I'm so stupid.'

'You? You're just out of the egg, and he's a devious snake. So where's the surprise? But me! I've been around and I was already wary of him. Didn't I warn you against him? And I still went with him. So, who's the most stupid?'

'We should go to the police, Ginger. There's two of us.'

'Don't make me laugh. They'd have us down for sluts. Even you.'

'I'll certainly sack him. But that's not enough. It was a terrible thing. He might have killed you. He'll get away with it.'

Ginger shook her head. 'No he hasn't. I sent our Ed after him. Got his name out of me yesterday. He waited half the night for him but he got him.'

Kay frowned. 'Got him?'

'Gave him a bloody good hiding.'

Kay felt a flood of satisfaction and relief flow through her. 'You told Ed what happened?'

Ginger shook her head. 'Nah. We don't talk about things down here. Squawking all over the place'd just embarrass them. But to be honest, our Ed knew sommat was wrong. He's the only one here with any nous. He asked me if I wanted sommat doing. I said yes, I wanted Laurenz Gold giving a good hiding. So he did it. No questions asked.'

'And do you feel better now?'

'You bet I do. Do you?'

'Do you know, I think I do.'

An hour later a nervously welcoming Patrizia Gold opened the door to Kay. She noticed that Patrizia looked behind her and knew she was disappointed that Thomas, or even Florence, was not with her. Kay smiled at her, a deceptively open smile. 'I wondered if I might have a word with Laurenz? It's about work and it's rather urgent.'

Patrizia opened the door wider. 'Come in. Come in. He's still in bed. Something terrible happened, you know, someone attack him very badly, last night. No. Early hours of morning. Very bad attack.'

Five minutes later Laurenz came down wearing immaculate trousers, a bright Fair Isle pullover over his shirt. The whole of one side of his face was black and blue and his immaculate hair was awry. He came down the stairs one at a time: there was obviously some difficulty with one of his legs. He smiled painfully at her. 'Kay, how very nice of you to call.' He turned to his wife. 'Is that Rebeka I hear, calling for you in the kitchen,

Patrizia? Kay and I have some business. We'll talk in the sitting room.'

Ushering Kay in he shut the sitting-room door behind him and stood with his back to it watching her. 'Is it you I have to thank for this . . . treatment?'

She shook her head. 'I wish it was me, really. But no. It was another injured party. I just came to tell you you are sacked. I don't want you again in my factory, under any pretext.'

'Oh, so powerful, aren't you, Mrs Fitzgibbon?'

'Well, I can't punch you, which is what I'd like to do, so this is the next best thing.'

He opened the door wide and stood back to let her through. 'Well, then. There is nothing more to say, is there?'

She turned at the front door to face him. 'You know if I . . . if we . . . went to the police they would deport you.'

His thick lashes veiled his eyes then he looked at her. 'They would not believe you. They would see you for the sluts you are.'

He closed the door carefully behind her and turned to see Patrizia coming from the kitchen to the hall, Rebeka on her hip. 'Did she go? That was not very long.'

He shrugged. 'She was very angry. I told her on Friday I was leaving and she came to beg me to stay.'

'Leaving? I have not heard this before.'

'I am going to Coventry to work on the cars with Mikel. I am sick of this little town with its little people.' Last night one of those little people had made him repeat ten times, between kicks in the ribs, that yes, yes, he would go. Even worse, he'd had to repeat that he was an animal, not fit to walk on two legs. He had shrieked the words then and had sweated all night at the thought of his own crawling, scrabbling collapse.

'I will not stay in this town,' he barked now at Patrizia. 'Mikel says there is money to be made down there. Decent jobs too.'

Her face was stricken. Would he uproot her again and drag her to some other strange town? She thought of Thomas and the liberating tenderness that now infused her life. 'What about me? About the children?'

He looked at her absently. 'You? You have a job have you not? And a house. You stay here. There is only lodgings down there. I will send you money when . . . when there is some spare.'

She turned away a second to hide the relief on her face. 'When will you go?'

'Tomorrow, first thing. I will need a map. I don't know how long it will take to get there on the bike.' His brow furrowed. 'Where will I get a map? No shops open on Sundays?'

'Perhaps Thomas has one?' she said eagerly. 'There are many books and such things in that house.'

'Thomas?' He raised a brow. 'Ah, Thomas. He would give you anything. Is that not so? Yes, you can go and get a map from him. But first . . .' He lifted Rebeka from her arms and set her on the floor beside Peter who was drawing a picture of the viaduct with a train chuffing across it. 'You take care of your sister, Peter. Do not let her out of the kitchen. Do you hear?'

Peter did not look up from his drawing. 'Yes, Papa,' he said.

Back in the hall he indicated the stairs with his chin. 'Now then, *liebling*, let's just make it clear to you where your loyalties lie, shall we?'

Trudging up the stairs before him, Patrizia thought that one day she would say no to him. And on that day she would be truly free. Free not just of him but of the nightmare which had been her life for the last eight years. But even in the middle of her weariness she had the inkling, the nugget of knowledge that things were changing. Truly they were not as they were.

Seeing Laurenz haul his battered body through the door in the early hours of the morning had been a revelation for her. Even as she had bathed his bruises she felt little sympathy for him and less gratitude for him being there at all.

Seventeen

On the High Plains

On Sunday afternoon Kay went with Thomas to visit Hugh. They picked up Harry Longstaffe on the way. At the hospital they had a sobering discussion with the Sister who said Mr Longstaffe had endured a very disturbed night and was now in a deep sleep. They were not to talk to him. The doctors feared that there was some poisoning in the system which was making him very low. Nursing and rest would be the key. 'He is not a young man,' she said almost too firmly, as though to pre-empt hope. They could not rule out the problem of a further seizure.

On the way back both Kay and Thomas, in the front of the car, felt some of the misery which was emanating from the back seat where Harry Longstaffe sprawled, his long legs half across the next seat.

Kay turned round, then turned back quickly at the sight of tears coursing down Harry's cheeks. When she turned back he had pulled out a khaki handkerchief and was blowing his nose. 'Can't think what this is. I never cry. He's all I've got, the old man, you know,' he said simply. 'I came through the war. I had one or two scrapes but always I worried about how he would do without me. I never thought how I would do without him.'

'He'll be all right, you'll see. He's a tough man. A colossus.' But Kay felt much less sure than she sounded.

'A colossus?' He smiled faintly. 'I hadn't quite thought of him as that.'

Thomas made an unexpected left turn and pulled the car to a

stop in the middle of the raw new council estate, beside a flourishing oak tree. Kay's heart sank as she recognised the road where Laurenz lived. 'What do we want here?' she said, too sharply.

'I just want to leave something with Patrizia,' said Thomas. Patrizia was on his mind all the time these days: when he went to sleep, when he woke up; down under the earth he could see her shape, that distinct inward-line of her waist, in the very curve of the seam cut into the ancient stone by men such as Hugh Longstaffe. Thomas had thought at first the pit was a place to escape the world of women. But now the deep earth seemed the very distillation of woman, its deep places yielding warmth and sustenance, a sense of inclusion.

In the car he turned round to Harry. 'This is the family I told you about. You met young Peter, didn't you? I've just translated this thing his mother did. Her own story of her family. She calls herself the last witness. She took it down in German and I've translated it into English for her, so young Peter can read it one day. That's what she hopes, anyway.'

'Perceptive woman,' said Harry, putting away his handkerchief and straightening his jacket. With Kay he watched as Thomas knocked on the narrow door and Patrizia answered it, one child on her hip, the other behind her skirts. She put a hand in Thomas's and looked up at him. Kay thought uneasily that Laurenz might not after all have been lying when he talked about there being something between these two.

'Thomas tells me you spent the war in Alexandria?' Harry interrupted her thoughts.

She nodded. 'He tells me that you were with the Eighth Army there?'

'Briefly. They moved me around. The air raids you had down in Alexandria must have been quite something. All that naval hardware – what a target!'

'You got used to the raids. They just really targeted the harbour.' She was trying to make up her mind whether she liked this man or not. She had definitely disliked his father, right to the point where he was cast down in hospital, even if she liked him more now. But the son was different. He was not his father after all.

'I miss it,' she ventured.

'The bombing?'

'Alexandria. The dry heat. The people. The colour. The light.' It all flooded back into her. Just the thought of it warmed her.

'All this must be very different.'

'Different?' she laughed. 'It's so cold here. And black.'

'Well, I'll grant you that we've had the coldest winter for I don't know how long,' he agreed. 'But it's June now. A lovely day.'

She shivered.

Thomas popped his head through the car window. There was a warmth about his face. A satisfaction. 'Patrizia is insisting we go in for a cup of coffee. She's cock-a-hoop about something.'

Peter was at the door. He looked directly at Kay. 'Is no Florence?' he said.

'Florence is at home with her grandma, Peter,' said Kay. 'She will see you at school tomorrow.'

Patrizia beamed from one to the other. 'Come in, come in! I have much to tell you!'

Thomas followed her through. 'As I said, Patrizia, I've brought you the last witness translation. I made two copies, one for you and one for Peter.'

She took them from him and smoothed the covers with her palm. 'Peter, in time, he will know how important is that story, those people. The names that are named. Now we will have some coffee.' She sensed both Thomas and Kay looking for Laurenz.

She shook her head. 'No Laurenz.'

'He has gone?' said Thomas.

She spoke in German directly to him. 'He went to join Mikel in Coventry. He packed his panniers with the things from under the bed, all stolen, of course. It seems he is bored with Priorton. Something has happened here. Someone frightened him. I do not know who, but it has made him go.'

For a second, Thomas wished he had been the one who had frightened Laurenz Gold. He translated Patrizia's words roughly for Kay and Harry.

Patrizia smiled at them. 'So, you may all come in and all will be peace.' She threw out her arm in a wide arc. 'Come in, come in. This is my house.'

As they sat down in the sitting room Patrizia remarked on the likeness between Thomas and Harry. '*Brüder*,' she smiled.

'She says we are like brothers,' said Thomas.

Harry nodded. 'I know. If you remember . . .'

'I forgot. You were in Germany.'

'Austria too.'

Patrizia lifted her head. 'You were in Vienna?'

Harry nodded. She stared at him for a moment but asked no more questions. She turned to Thomas. 'Anyway, Laurenz has gone,' she said. 'As I say. Gone to work with Mikel.'

He frowned. 'For good?'

She shrugged. 'He was in a hurry as I tell you. Someone beat him.'

'Who?'

'I tell you I don't know who. An angry husband perhaps? It has happened before but I have never seen him so frightened.'

'Will he be back?' said Kay, thinking of the power and menace of Ed Simpson.

She nodded slowly. 'Oh, he'll be back. Sometime he'll be back.'

Before they came away Thomas had promised Peter that he would return and take him to Hugh's allotment later with Florence, to lock up the hens. As they drove back Thomas asked Harry if he would like to help at the allotment.

'Do you need me?' said Harry.

Thomas shook his head. 'More hands than we know what to do with. Patrizia said she might come too.'

'Well, in that case I'll cry off, if you don't mind. What I'd really like to do is show Kay the Priors' Park. Just to show you

Priorton's not all slaughterhouses and pit heads. I bet you haven't been in the park, have you, Kay?'

Kay shook her head. 'I've seen the gates from the car and that's just about it.'

'I loved it there when I was young. Have you got a bathing suit?'

'A bathing suit?'

'Yes. We can swim. It's a lovely day.'

'It'll be freezing,' said Kay gloomily.

'Don't be a spoilsport,' said Thomas, very glad that Harry wasn't coming with him to clutter up the space between him and Patrizia. 'Give it a go, Kay.'

So she ended up dashing into the house for her costume and towel and changing into low shoes while Thomas collected Florence, and Harry talked to Leonora about his father. Then, under Harry's direction, Thomas dropped them, not at the great gates, but a mile further on, where a stile gave on to a narrow path through a field which edged a great swathe of woodland.

Harry jumped about with enthusiasm, anxious to be off. 'This is the best way in, fewer people up here.'

They waved Thomas away and set off over the stile down towards the first set of trees which marked the boundaries of the park. There was no sun but the sky was very blue and the leaves had just about unfurled their summer brightness. They walked down a broad grassy way between two stretches of woodland.

Harry stamped the ground with his foot. 'See this? This was the original road into Priorton. The priors would ride down to the Priory in their carriages, fat from feasting with the Bishop.'

He went and leant against one of the great trees which lined the route. 'See this? This tree could very well be five hundred years old. Our grandparents and our shared great-grandparents, and great-great-grandparents could have played under it, raced round it.'

Kay went up and put her hands on the bark and closed her eyes. Her palms itched and she could feel the touch of other hands, of other times, just as she used to in Alexandria. But there she felt the single person, the maker of the pot. Here she could feel many hands, like the chattering of a crowd rather than a single voice.

'What are you thinking?' Harry Longstaffe's voice sounded beside her.

She told him about the pots; how she could feel the individual maker. And here in the Priors' Park, how she could feel the people who had touched the tree.

He put his hand beside hers, his long fingers furrowing in the bark. 'I envy you that,' he said. 'That way of knowing.'

She had missed it since she settled here; that sense of inhabiting more than one realm. In some ways, though, the factory layers of time and resonance were equally satisfying.

She said nothing of this to Harry then, although she remembered his reference to the aura which surrounded both her and Thomas. For a soldier, he was certainly unusual.

They walked on in silence, then he said, 'I'm sorry I haven't seen you with your pots. I'd have liked to hear you talk about them.'

'I have some here in England.' The words were out of her mouth before she could stop them.

'Where? Blamire House?'

She shook her head. 'No. They're in a little place set up by my grandmother Kitty. It's more a kind of reading room or museum. We put the pots there for safekeeping. It's all locked up now. Shut before the war and never really opened up again.'

'Can we get in there?'

'I suppose so.'

'Will you show me your pots?'

'There are more interesting things there than my pots. My grandfather Scorton collected them. Roman fragments from around here. Things from his own life too, as an engineer.'

'Could you show me those too?'

'I don't see why not.'

Harry led the way through the trees. They were starting to

move upwards now but even so the canopy of green closed over them and they lost sight of the town for minutes on end. In one place a silence of ages stuck to them like dandelion seeds, invading their senses and sealing their mouths. Then, as quickly as it had dropped about them, the silence lifted, blown away in the crisp breeze that was filtering its way through the trunks of the ancient trees. Harry glanced down at her. 'Now how was that for an aura?' he murmured softly.

She nodded, and walked on without speaking. Now the trees thinned out a little, and they were on a high plateau. Below them, like a toy village, Priorton was laid out, almost enclosed by the massive arches of the viaduct. The spires of the churches and chapels thrust themselves up into the bright sky like fingers poking out from the regular rows of the streets and terraces of the town which was so neatly dissected by its long, straight High Street. To their right, as if to counterpoint this busyness, the lacy curtain wall of the Priory protected the simple power of the fortress-like Priors' Chapel.

'What a view!' said Kay. 'I never realised.'

'I've heard my father say the High Street is the straightest in England because it follows exactly an old Roman Road.' He put a casual arm round her shoulder and led her forward to the edge of the plateau. 'Now be careful!'

Down there, way below them, was the park. A river meandered right under the escarpment, rendered almost invisible by the angle of the stone and the tangle of protruding tree roots.

'That's the Lawless,' said Harry. 'Tributary of the Gaunt. You can see the two rivers joining, down there through the trees.'

On the other side of the river on flat greensward little knots and clusters of people lounged on the grass. Families sat on rugs and tattered blankets. Small children played ball. Groups of young men and women played some kind of chasing game. Some of them were still in bathing suits, towelling themselves vigorously and calling to the others who were swimming and splashing in a turn of the river, which was obviously deep enough for swimming.

Kay turned to Harry. 'What a lovely place.'

He grinned at her pleasure. 'When you've only got a back yard, you need somewhere to go on a sunny day. This was the place to go. I was always here when I was a boy. Either up here on the High Plains with my friends climbing the escarpment and imagining we were heroes, or down there playing cricket or football, or swimming. I thought it was Heaven. My dad had to come and find me at nightfall.' He laughed. 'He had a bellow like a bull.'

'What did you call this place?'

'Up here? It's called the High Plains. And down there? Well. That's just the Priors' Park.' He put down his khaki rucksack. 'Now. What about a swim?'

She peered down over the steep escarpment. 'I suppose we dive?' she said drily.

He laughed. 'No. We get changed up here because it's very private. Then I'll show you a pathway down to the deepest bit of the swimming pool.'

He went to the side of the clearing. 'I'll have this clump of bushes and you have that one. No one can see us up here except the birds.'

Five minutes later she was standing shivering on the edge of the pool and Harry was swimming strongly upstream. She braced herself and slipped into the water, shuddering as the cold hit all her senses at once. She trod water for a minute, then, seeing Harry's head bobbing ahead of her, she struck out and swam her tentative breaststroke in his direction. He found a foothold and stood and waited for her. His hair, darkened by the water, was slicked down and he looked more like Thomas than ever. He pulled a hand down his face to get rid of the water and smiled at her. 'There, that's not so bad, is it?'

She stood beside him, her teeth chattering. 'It's f-f-freezing,' she spluttered. 'I d-d-don't know what I'm trying to prove here, but I'm g-g-going back and putting my clothes on.'

She turned and swam away at speed to their part of the bank. She climbed up the escarpment, hanging on to the protruding roots of trees to haul herself up the steep bank. Once on the High Plains she raced behind her clump of bushes, took off her suit and rubbed her poor freezing body with her towel before dragging her clothes on, her teeth chattering like castanets all the while.

Then Harry was there, fully dressed. 'Give me your towel,' he said. Obediently she handed it over. Then he pulled her head towards him and started to rub her hair very hard till her head rang and her blood sang.

She pulled away. 'Enough! That's enough.'

'Now we run home,' he said. 'That'll warm you up and stop you getting a chill.'

And run she did. Whenever she slowed down he chivvied her on and she started again. By the time she got to Blamire House she was so warm she was sweating and her hair was dry, lifting in the wind. She looked up at him. 'I bet you're merciless with those recruits of yours.'

'Never lost one yet,' he said cheerfully. 'Now then, do you think that Leonora would have a hot cup of tea for two weary soldiers?'

Overtaken by darkness, Laurenz Gold had to lay up overnight in a barn before setting off again the next morning for Coventry. In the afternoon, he stopped at a transport café on the edge of Coventry and drank thick brown tea and ate Spam sandwiches to warm himself up before he ventured into the city to hunt for Mikel. He smoothed out Mikel's letter on the worn American cloth and read the address. He looked up at the woman behind the narrow counter. 'Where will I find this place? Cheylesmore?'

She removed her cigarette from her mouth and peered at him more closely. If it weren't for all that bruising this one had almost film-star good looks. Even the bruising gave him a kind of glamour. She frowned. 'Cheylesmore?' Then her brow cleared. 'Oh. *Charlesmore*!'

He looked at Mikel's letter. 'It does not look like this.'

She took a drag at her cigarette and creased her eyes against the smoke. 'Tha's how you say it. How things are and how they look is two different things, duck. Where are you from, then? Foreigner, ain't yer?'

He smiled his best smile. 'I am Swiss. I hope to find work in Coventry.'

She nodded sagely. 'You and a thousand others. Coventry, it's like a blessed league of nations. A shrine to the future. Pouring in, they are. Not that there isn't work. World's gunna go car mad and that's where Coventry'll cash in. That's what a feller said in here the other day anyway. And he drove a transporter so he should know.'

'So can you tell me how to get to this place?' He pushed his letter under her nose again.

She peered at the creased paper through the smoke. ''S easy. Down here two mile. Turn right after another quarter of a mile. Cheylesmore is on your left. Then ask anyone for the street.'

Laurenz found Cheylesmore as easily as she had said. Then, before he asked the whereabouts of the particular street, he returned and went for a ride round the city. The city centre was like a building site, awash with scaffolding and the impedimenta of the building trade. New buildings stood out like scars against the fragments of medieval stone which still remained. Weed-ridden bomb-sites still flourished behind sketchy hoardings and substantial shop fronts were tacked on to temporary pre-fabricated buildings. Then Laurenz rode on further from the centre to a sprawling area pockmarked with patched-up factory buildings and work-shops with dusty windows. The whole place had an energy that excited him. This place, this city, was more his speed. There would be so much more for him here than in the sleepy town of Priorton.

Back in Cheylesmore, informed of his cousin's arrival, Mikel bounded down the stairs of the small suburban house where he lived squashed together with five other single men. He frowned when he saw Laurenz. 'What has happened to your face, Lau?

I hardly recognise you. You look as though you have been through a meat-grinder.'

Laurenz shrugged. 'What is it always? A jealous husband, maybe? Am I too ugly to be welcomed by my only cousin?'

Mikel laughed and drew him to his chest in a big bear hug. Yes, he was welcome; yes, he could sleep on his floor tonight till they found a room for him tomorrow. And yes, they were taking people on at the Jag, and anyway how were Patrizia and the children?

'Patrizia is fine. She is working. And the children are well. Peter is making much progress with his English. He has been put up a class.'

Mikel rubbed his fat hands together. 'Good. Good. Soon you will be making much money here, and they can come here to live.'

Laurenz hesitated. 'We will wait and see about this. Patrizia is content there.'

'But a man must have his family!' insisted Mikel.

'Leave it alone, Mikel. She is settled there.' Laurenz crouched down to get some of the more precious items from his saddlebags. 'Will you help me with these, Mikel?'

Later, nursing a mug of coffee made on his single gas ring, Mikel told Laurenz about the Goldfarbs. 'They have a paper shop near the city centre. One brother saw me once and followed me. They came together here and asked for you. Pushed me around the room a bit. I just kept saying we lost touch in the DP camps. They said if ever I saw you, to tell you their uncle died in Auschwitz and they haven't yet been able to trace their sisters.'

Laurenz glanced up at the room. 'They know you live here?'

Mikel nodded.

'I'll stay here tonight only then, and find another place in another part of the city.'

'We could go together,' said Mikel eagerly. 'Stay in Radford, near the factory.'

Laurenz shook his head. 'No, we are safer separate. We will

see each other at work. That will be good, will it not?'

He remembered how Mikel had hardly recognised him. It was not that difficult to change your appearance. He had done it before. He would grow a beard, bleach his hair. Who would recognise him then?

On Monday morning Kay caught up with Ginger when she was parking her bike in the long bicycle rack. 'How are you, Ginger?'

'Me, Kay? Never better.'

'You're sure?'

Ginger glanced at her almost kindly. 'Listen, flower, what happened to me was rotten. Never worse. But if yer let things like that get inter you, right inside, it seems to me that the bad lads win. As it was, our Ed knocked the lights out of him so I'm all right. An eye for an eye.'

'Did Ed really not know what happened?'

'Like I said to you, we don't spell things out. But we know about each other. Especially our Ed and me.'

'Well, Ed really did the trick. I went down there to tell him he was sacked. Then half a day later the bird had flown. Run away.'

'Good riddance to bad rubbish.' They stopped at the head of the cooker line. Ginger looked up at her curiously. 'Hard for you, like, seeing you had a bit of a soft spot for him.'

'Me? No. He was good dancer, that's all. But dancing isn't everything. Like you, I say good riddance to bad rubbish. Anyway, I've met someone . . .'

'Attagirl! More fish in the sea.'

'But what about Patrizia? She'll be working down near you again. I can get her moved, you know.'

'No need for that. That little shrimp? Doesn't worry me. I'm sorry for her, that's all. Seems to me we're more sisters under the skin than ever. She's had years of that to put up with, poor little bugger.'

The Captain greeted Kay's news about Laurenz Gold with a

grim satisfaction. 'Fly-by-night,' he said briefly. 'But you weren't to know, Mrs Fitzgibbon. Takes experience.' He put his fingertips together. 'Now, will you tell John Harkness, or shall I?'

'I will.' She wasn't looking forward to telling the news to the tool-room manager.

The Captain then took pity on her. 'Well, that aside, marketing have made great leaps with the spillage tray cookers. They say it's a good selling point. I have to admit that was a very good idea, Mrs Fitzgibbon.'

She nodded. 'We should get those older women back in. See how they've got on with their cookers.' She stood up. 'And I've got another idea.'

He sighed. 'Oh dear. Have you?'

'I talked to one of the women yesterday. She's using the surface rings but can't get the hang of the oven. Timing and things.'

'The sooner the Coal Board takes those black monsters out of the houses and puts nice little tile fireplaces in the better,' growled the Captain. 'They jolly well won't learn till they have to.'

'Anyway, I thought we could get a commercial cook to work with this lady and evolve recipes for all the traditional dishes. Recipes which give detailed temperatures and times, so they can get the same effect with our cookers as they do on those black monsters, as you call them. I've got the title. *Clean Cooking*. Subtitled *Mona Simpson's Northern Cookbook*.'

'Who's Mona Simpson?'

'Mona Simpson's the woman I talked to on Sunday. The mother of one of our operators. I'd write a foreword to it, saying how much less work there is in electric cookers, how mothers and wives need not be a slave to the stove. And we'll give one book away free with every cooker.'

He stroked his chin. 'Now that is a good idea. You could use Mrs Morpurgo who cooks at the Gaunt Valley Hotel. I eat there every Saturday and Sunday. It's very good.'

'And we could have a cooking competition to launch it,' she rushed on. 'The best Sunday dinner . . .'

'Whoa! Whoa!' He put up a podgy hand as though fending off a blow. 'Slow down, Mrs Fitzgibbon. One thing at a time! First you'd better go and reconcile the tool-room manager to the loss of our fine Swiss – or near Swiss – toolmaker.'

'Reconcile?' Kay raised her brows. 'He'll be cock-a-hoop. He'll be laughing all over his face. *I told you so* won't be in it.'

She was proved to be wrong. John Harkness raised his brows and looked miserable. 'Sound idea of yours, that was. Laurenz was a bit of fancy work but he knew his stuff. Brought a bit more investment into development here. And it's been a useful addition to the training of the apprentices. Brought the whole place into trim.' He looked her in the eye. 'You'll have to replace him. Advertise. You'll want somebody with good skills.'

She smiled inwardly. So it had been a good idea. And, of course, John Harkness would not want to lose his extra pay or his extra status. She came away from the tool room quite satisfied. What she had thought of as a humiliating reversal had been, in fact, a partial success.

That night she did not get back from the Works until seven and was followed into the house almost immediately by a grim-faced Thomas and Harry Longstaffe.

'Are you on your way to the hospital?' she asked.

'We've been there,' said Harry briefly. 'And he's gone.'

Kay frowned. 'Gone?' Her brain raced. Surely Hugh was not dead?

'Came round from this deep sleep that was to do him so much good, put on his clothes and his cap and escaped. Taken two crutches and made off,' said Harry.

'He must be feeling better,' suggested Leonora.

'The Sister said that wasn't the case. Says it was only willpower that would move him.'

'He'll be at his house. Go straight down there,' ordered Kay.

Thomas shook his head. 'Been there. It was empty. Locked up tight as a drum.'

'We left the back door open, just in case he gets there,' said Harry miserably.

'Well,' said Kay, 'I think you need to go to the police . . .' She was interrupted by an almighty banging on the door. They raced to open it and there on the doorstep was old Hugh's friend from the reading room at the club. Beside him was a massive younger man who held in his arms, as gently as a baby, the bulky figure of Hugh Longstaffe. Hugh's face was chalk-white and his blue-veined lids were closed over his eyes.

The old man spoke. 'Hughie here made his way to the club an' collapsed in the doorway. We wus ginna tek him home, like but he ses ter tek him here. Blamire House on The Lane. Ses he has family here.'

'So he has.' Leonora took charge. 'Bring him in, up here, up here.' She led the way upstairs to her own bedroom. Over her shoulder she told Thomas to go and get the doctor. 'Dr Fairless, four doors down. Tell him I told you to come for him.'

Kay stayed downstairs and thanked the men who brought him. The old man shook his head. 'We're old marrahs, me and Hugh.' He took up a sentinel position on a straight-backed chair in the hall. 'Ah'll have a bit sit down here, if yer dinnet mind. Just wait till the doctor's had his say. The lads down the club'll wanter know.' He looked up at his young companion. 'Yeh can make yer way back now, Arthur. Ah'll get down there as soon as Ah hear.' He refused Kay's offer of tea, coffee or even brandy. 'Nah, hinney. Like Ah say, Ah'll wait here till the doctor says owt. Just sit quiet, like.'

'Good of you to take the trouble to bring him here,' said Harry miserably.

'Nae trouble, son. Hugh's an old marrah of mine. Started at the pit alongside me. Done me many a favour. Queer old business tonight. He dragged himself to the club on crutches. Good thing it's nae distance from the infirmary, like. Anyway, he collapsed in the hall and asked for me, then telt us he didn't want to gan hyam, but come up here to The Lane. Said he has family here.'

'So he has,' said Kay, repeating her mother's words.

In two minutes Thomas was back with Dr Fairless, a grizzled man with his dinner napkin still attached to his top waistcoat button. He bustled upstairs and spent half an hour with Hugh and then came down to talk to Harry.

'Surprisingly, he's quite stable.' He glanced at Leonora. 'He is conscious and talking. Adamant that he will not return to hospital. So we won't move him as yet.'

'He can stay as long as he needs to,' she said.

'I'll go to the hospital and acquaint them of his whereabouts, and talk to his doctor there. And I'll return later tonight to check on him: in the morning as well, if necessary.' At that point he noticed his dinner napkin and unlooped it from his waistcoat, folded it neatly and put it in his medical bag. 'I'll leave him in your hands, Mrs Scorton. You have nursing experience, I believe?'

Leonora stared at him. 'Many years ago, yes. But how would you know?'

'In my distant youth in the Great War I was on the staff of a military hospital. Purley Hall, just outside Priorton. You served there, I believe?'

Leonora nodded. 'Yes, so I did.'

'So I have faith that you can care for Mr Longstaffe, Mrs Scorton. He needs the best of nursing. He says you are his cousin and will take care of him.'

'I can take care of him,' said Harry.

The doctor turned to him. 'You must be his son?'

Harry nodded.

'He also says he wished you to return to the army, that your leave must be overdue.' He smiled slightly. 'He says you have more important things to do than chase after an old man. He also says it is not to be discussed. He will not be persuaded. I am to say he will be perfectly well with Mrs Scorton. He is a man of authority, your father. A remarkable man.'

Hugh's old friend from the club stood up. 'Well, Ah'll be gettin' on then. Old Hughie's settled. The lads'll down the club'll wanter know.'

When the door banged behind him and the doctor, the others stood in the echoing hallway and looked at each other.

Leonora looked at Harry. 'He'll be all right here, Harry. And welcome.'

Kay looked at Harry, wishing he would not rush away to his raw recruits so soon, when they had just begun to know each other. She thought of him up on the High Plains, eager to make her like his park, his town.

Thomas looked at Kay, recognising that her interest in Harry was more than just cousinly. Perhaps now she would not dismiss Hugh out of hand, perhaps she would see him as important in all their lives.

Harry turned from Leonora to look directly at Kay. 'If that's what Dad wants I will go. But just to fix up a proper, longer leave. I need to be with him. We've missed so much of each other in the last seven years. I'll get back as soon as I can. See to his convalescence. He's very weak. It might take some time, I suppose.'

'Yes,' said Thomas, glancing at his sister. 'I suppose it might.'

Eighteen

Cooking up a Storm

Despite or perhaps because she had never cooked in her life Kay became fascinated by the cookery book project. After doing a deal with Mona with regard to the cost of the ingredients, the pooling of food coupons and factory rates for the hours spent, she and Mrs Morpurgo passed a week at the Simpson house just watching Ginger's mother, Mona Simpson, cook.

Mona knew the idiosyncratic ways of her cast-iron range as a sailor knows his boat. 'Every one of these beasts is different,' she told Kay. 'I started on me grandma's and it took two hours to get that set right. The left-hand middle of the oven was the hottest. But once it was set, that old beast would hold steady for hours, really reliable. Now me mother's was different again. It would light and draw in ten minutes. With hers, right-hand top was the place you'd set things away, give them a headstart. But then sometimes the wind'd change and it'd cool too fast and the pastry went to leather and the cakes would collapse. It made her cry more than once. Bad as dropping a line of washing in the lane.'

They watched Mona light her fire with the hot cinders from the night before, get a hot centre going, then throw a whole bucket of coals on the stone shelf behind the fire, raking it down judiciously to get the heat just right.

They tried stews and dumplings; meat and potato pies; leek pies and Lancashire hotpot. They tried apple pies and plum pies; steamed fruit puddings made from Mona's last year's bottling; and steak and kidney pudding which melted in the mouth and which depended on Mona's special relationship with the butcher. They had fruit cake, orange cake, lemon cake and Bakewell tarts. They had jam tarts and lemon curd tarts, butterfly cakes and queen cakes. The food was tasted, tried, then shared out among the other houses in the pit rows near where the Simpsons lived. Some of the coupons for the extra ingredients for this extravaganza were supplied by the Captain, who had contacts at the Ministry.

Mona managed all this while catering for her husband and sons coming off fore shift and back shift, all expecting their 'breakfasts' in a staggered fashion, just when they came in from work. During these times Kay and Mrs Morpurgo were banished to the cluttered front room. Mona had to admit that the cooking experiment had to be achieved without the wholehearted cooperation of her husband and three sons. It was sufficient that Mona had persuaded them to have their tin baths in front of the fire of her neighbour, who was grateful for the two bob a time Kay was paying even while protesting she would have done it for nowt and wasn't it time White Leas had baths like other decent pits anyway?

While she was exiled to the front room, in consultation with Mrs Morpurgo, Kay filled pages and pages of her notebook with heat levels and ingredients, quantities and times. She starred special tricks which Mona used to get around the depressing constraints of rationing.

Mrs Morpurgo shook her head at the difficulty of the task. So much that was going on was about feel – a handful of this, a pinch of that. But Kay said she must have her own recipes which approximated to these. They would make a selection; adapt them; Mrs Morpurgo could try them out on a Rainbow cooker; and they would bring them back and get Mona to try them on her new cooker. It had to be easier than the old range.

Mrs Morpurgo shook her head again. 'There's no saying it'll be better. Easier perhaps, but not better.'

Ginger's brother Ed, newly bathed, came across Kay getting

a breath of fresh air in the back yard. 'All right then?' he said, civil enough.

Kay nodded. 'Fine.'

'Me ma's havin' the time of her life, like, messing about with youse lot.'

'Good,' she said. 'I'm pleased.'

'Tells us she's gunna use the money towards her holiday in South Shields. Her and me da that is.'

'Smashing,' she said.

'She'd 'a gone anyway, like. Not short of a copper or two, me ma.'

'Mmm.'

He hesitated by the heavy back door. 'Seems like you and me saw off the Austrian, between us. Our Ginger says you sacked him as well.'

'There was no need. He was on his way.'

He nodded. 'Damned near killed him.'

She shrugged.

'He's a bad lot.' His curious, light-grey eyes met hers. 'Seems like you cottoned to that as well as our Ginger.' The door clicked behind him.

For a second Kay was visited by the panic she had felt as she thrust her bag upwards under Laurenz's chin to get him off her. Then very purposefully she breathed deeply and let the panic trickle out of her. It was Ginger who said that if you let it affect you, you let the bad lads win. And she was right.

Mona Simpson enjoyed her week. There was extra money which was welcome even in this affluent household which had five pay packets coming in. She had company, which she enjoyed. And she was curious about the lively young Kay Fitzgibbon who had taken such a fancy to their Mavis, now called Ginger by everyone except Mona herself.

While they were waiting for the dishes to cook she got Kay to help her change the beds and polish the brasses, beat the mats on the line and mop the lino surrounds. She shared her glee with Kay that the chore of getting the men bathed was transferred to one neighbour; the greater chore of the weekly wash was transferred, for payment again, to another neighbour. The neighbours would have done this for nothing, but Mona liked to spread out her good fortune.

At three o'clock on the Friday the three of them sat round the kitchen table to enjoy a last butterfly cake and cup of tea. Beside the door were the baskets of goodies Mona had packed for them to take home. The room was hot and smelt of vanilla and baked fruit.

'Well, that's about it. I can't think of anything else to cook,' said Mona, tossing her hennaed head. 'So what happens next?'

'Well, we've got our recipes. Mrs Morpurgo here will juggle them about a bit so they can be done on the Rainbow electric cooker. I'll get Mrs MacMahon, a friend of my mother's, to try them. Then we'll be back and ask you to try them on your cooker.'

Mona nodded. 'There is one thing you haven't thought of.'

'What's that?'

'Fuel. The coal that we cook by comes free. Concessionary coal from the pit. Part of the men's wages. The electric we'll get a bill for.'

'I'll pay for your electricity this time, while we're doing this experiment.'

'So you will. But if you want to get all them women out there to use your cooker, you'll need to keep this in mind.'

Making her way back to the factory Kay thought this fuel problem was unanswerable locally for the time being. Nationally, it didn't matter. According to the Captain, most other areas of Britain, where coal was not immediately plentiful, had already moved on to electric or gas cookers. And here, before long the coal ranges would come out. Already they were seen as cumbersome and labour intensive. And the miners were earning decent money. They would put in tiled fireplaces and pay the electricity bills if the wives were keen enough.

She had welcomed the preoccupation of the cookery project

as it kept her mind off Harry Longstaffe. He had held her hand in both of his when she dropped him off at the station, and told her to keep in touch, without giving her an address. She had assumed he would do the keeping in touch, because he did know where she lived. But there had been no letter.

Later, back at home, Leonora sent her with a tea tray and some of Mona's butterfly cakes in to Hugh Longstaffe. He was sitting in the small front sitting room watching the world from the window. With Leonora's careful nursing, the poison in his leg had now subsided and he had insisted that he should get dressed and come downstairs. He had told Leonora that old men died in their beds and he had no intention of dying just yet.

He smiled when he saw Kay, and asked her to sit down with him while he had his tea. She hesitated, then did so, unsure of what he was about. There was no doubt that Leonora was his favourite. She often took her papers in there and worked quietly while he commented to her about the people who passed the window. If he didn't know them, he knew their brother or father, and there was always a tale to tell.

'Leonora says you've been cooking today again.'

'Not really. More watching somebody else cook. We're going to make a cookbook for the cookers we sell. Trying to make it possible to cook all the things you can in a kitchen range. I think you should be able to cook them much more easily on our cooker.'

He nodded. 'Good idea. Them black things is more trouble than they're worth. All right if you have a wife at home all day to stoke and fiddle with it. But me and Harry were working shifts and fettling for ourselves. D'you know how we managed?'

'No.'

'We set broth away on a Mondah, with good pot stuff in it and mebbe a bit of lamb. Then heated it up every day and threw a bit more fresh in it. Then on a Sundah a neighbour took pity on us and we had our dinner there. Your Rainbow cooker, with a book to tell us how to do it, would've been a Godsend to us then, me and our Harry.'

She smiled. Pleased at his endorsement, and more pleased at his mention of Harry.

'I got a letter from our Harry,' he said.

'Did you?'

'You seem to have made a big impression on him. Says here . . .'

She waited an age while he took the letter out of one pocket and his glasses out of another. 'Says here, *Is a very clever woman, but like Thomas in other ways*. I don't know that that would suit Thomas, like. Not too flattering on him. He's clever in his own way.'

He put away the letter and the glasses. 'So what do you think of him? Our Harry?'

She took a breath. 'Nice man. I like him.'

'Good,' he said. 'Now will you pour the tea or shall I pour me own?'

Without Hugh's quiet, intense presence the long hours underground dragged for Thomas. He was put to fill for Len Simpson, one of Ginger's older brothers, whose own marrah had gone down with pneumonia after he got soaked on a fishing trip up the dale. Len was a dour, hardworking man who was obsessed with his output, keen to keep his tally up and fill his wage packet. Unlike Hugh, he did not match his working rhythm with Thomas, who caught the sharp end of Len's tongue more than once because he wasn't filling fast enough. It dawned on Thomas that Hugh must have been losing money in the months they had been working together, rather than make Thomas feel feeble.

At bait time Len called to other acquaintances crouching over their sandwiches in the lamplit twilight. A small group of them played cards, others talked of piece-work rates and pubs, and speculated whether the new National Coal Board would really make a real difference to their job. They talked of horses and dogs and of men whom Thomas didn't know, doing things he did not care about.

Thomas munched on in silence, thinking of Patrizia, whom he saw as much as he could now, using the children as a benevolent pretext. He was fond of young Peter and Rebeka but the moments he lived for were when they went to bed and he and Patrizia would have an hour or so together. Sometimes they made love, but sometimes they just sat in the firelight holding hands, making plans for what they would do when they had solved the problem of Laurenz.

Once at bait time he came out of his Patrizia-laden reverie to hear a man talking to Len Simpson about the pleasures of breeding budgies. 'Why, man, they're like flying flowers.'

Thomas caught up with the man on the walk down to Priorton from the pit. 'Did you say you bred them, these budgies?'

'Why aye, man. Ah breed them for the satisfaction, like, but Ah sell a few so Ah can pay for the feed.'

'Can I buy one?'

The man looked at him then, up and down. 'Foh thesel'?'

'No, not really. For a friend.'

The man cackled. 'Foh a woman, I bet.'

Thomas walked on silently.

'Ah tell yeh what!' said the other man. 'Come hyam with me now, and you can tyek a look. If yeh fancy a one Ah'll give yeh a fair price. They'll not be ready for a week or so, like but yeh can tek yer pick.'

Three days after she talked to Hugh Kay had a short letter from Harry Longstaffe.

> I am still tangled up with red tape here, but I have been doing some serious thinking and am making arrangements to be up there for longer. The old man seems very content with Mrs Scorton's expert care, and he says he has been holding court for all his old friends up at Blamire House. However, I know the minute he is really well he will want to be in his own home and I must be there then. He tells me that you have been learning to cook. Now that is a

surprise, as I had you down for the big businesswoman who would not soil her hands with a saucepan. I have been thinking a lot about our afternoon on the High Plains and am very keen to show you other places of interest, to convince you that though our land cannot boast the heat of Egypt, it has other delights. And I am very keen now to see your museum and your pots. There'll be a lot to do when next I am home. If you can find a minute in your busy day I would welcome a letter.

She waited five long days before she replied. When she did her letter was newsy and lighthearted. She reported on Hugh's progress, assured Harry she wasn't learning how to cook – *I leave that to the experts* – and told him that Thomas was caring for Hugh's allotment, taking Florence and Peter, even little Rebeka now, down there every night to feed and shoo the hens back into their cree, harvest early potatoes and weed and hoe the few vegetables which had survived.

Sometimes Hugh has them sitting in a line in front of him, and the children have to tell him all they have done. Young Peter's English is just about indistinguishable now from the way Florence speaks, which now shows she is from round here. Hugh is sad he was unable to do the planting this year but we talk of next year.

She wrote of events at the factory and plans afoot for the celebration of the Royal Wedding. *They all see it as a fairy tale, but I don't quite see it that way. I am pleased she has found him but it will be no picnic for either of them.* She signed it, *Yours sincerely, Kay Fitzgibbon.*

That night she went to the allotment with Thomas and the children. Thomas asked if she was sure she wanted to go. 'It's very muddy down there, you know.'

'It's a fine evening, I feel like some fresh air to get the smell of rubber and wire out of my nostrils.' She also felt that it would give her something concrete to talk to Hugh about, and write to

Harry about. 'If I didn't know better I'd think you didn't want me to go,' she said.

'No. No,' said Thomas. 'The more the merrier.'

Peter was ready, wearing his wellingtons when they arrived. Patrizia's warm smile extended from Thomas to Kay.

'How's the job going?' asked Kay.

Patrizia nodded. 'It is fine. At first I thought I would never keep up with Ginger. But soon I did. Then her friend Janet came back and I thought my job had gone, but they set up a new line and she's training some new ones.' Then she laughed. 'But you know all this, of course.'

'Sort of.' Kay smiled, her nerves tingling a little at the intimacy between Patrizia and Thomas which danced like gauze in the air.

Patrizia waved them off. 'I will have coffee and biscuits ready for you when you return,' she called.

They were less than an hour, but when they came back the door was open and there was no smiling welcome. They could hear sobs coming from the little sitting room. Thomas thrust Rebeka into Kay's arms. 'Take them into the kitchen.'

Kay did as she was told, looking around for Laurenz. It must be him. She sat the children round the table and poured some milk for them. Then she made a cup of tea and ventured into the sitting room with it. Thomas was sitting on the sofa with Patrizia in his arms. She was shuddering and moaning.

'What is it?'

Thomas shook his head helplessly.

Kay kneeled down beside Patrizia. 'What is it, Patrizia? What's happened?' She touched the other girl's arm. 'What is it? Is it Laurenz?'

Patrizia looked up at her from a wrecked face and shook her head. She took a deep sobbing breath. 'Willem, my friend, the old Dutchman at the camp. He died this afternoon. In his chair. Judith found him. She came here to tell me.'

Thomas stroked her hair.

'Oh dear. I am so sorry.' Kay made her take a sip of tea. 'What an awful shock.'

Patrizia rubbed her face with her hand. 'I was all right when Judith told me. He was an old man after all. Then she went back and I started to think about him. About him being the last witness for that family as I am for mine. Then I thought of my mother and my stepfather and my uncles. You know Laurenz would not let me . . . he was impatient when I talked of my mother. I have not cried.' She started to cry again, letting out ugly strangled cries of despair. Thomas looked up at his sister, willing her to do something.

'I tell you what,' said Kay. 'Give me the key to the car, Thomas. I'll take all the children to Blamire House and they can sleep there in Florence's room.' She looked directly at her brother. 'You take care of Patrizia. She needs you at the moment.'

She made a game of collecting the night things with the children. Patrizia pulled herself together enough to kiss her children goodbye and tell them to be good as they were very lucky to have such a treat.

She shut the door behind them and looked up at Thomas again, her eyes filling up with tears. He took her in his arms and stroked her face and her hair. 'There now, sweetheart, you cry till there are no tears left. Then you'll feel better. Don't you think it's time you wept?'

Three days after the death of Willem, Thomas walked up to the estate, carrying a battered bird cage covered by an old curtain. He received some odd looks but he was used to those.

Patrizia, enveloped in a big black apron, a dripping sheet in her arms, came to the door.

'What is this?' she said, smiling confidently up at him. The time for timidity between them was past.

He whipped the curtain off the cage like a magician and the little blue bird jumped on its perch and chirruped.

'A bird!' she said.

'A budgerigar!' he said solemnly. 'We call them budgies. They sing and sometimes, if you teach them how, they talk.'

'A budgie. Come in, come in! How the children will love him. But first will you help me to get this dratted sheet through the mangle?'

Earlier that day Kay had stopped by Patrizia on the line and asked how she was.

'How is she?' Ginger answered for her from the next bay. 'She's bloomin' marvellous. Got me on the run already.'

Patrizia nodded. 'I am fine now, thank you, Kay. Though I miss the old man. You were so kind. I thank you.'

'It was nothing. The children had a fine time but I am afraid they had little sleep. They woke up at three o'clock in the morning and decided it was time for school. It took us all our time to get them out of their school clothes and back into bed.'

Patrizia looked anxious. 'Peter, he . . .?'

Kay laughed. 'He was fine. Led astray by Florence, I'm afraid.'

Later, as Kay walked home, Ginger caught up to her on her bike. She slowed down then jumped off to walk alongside her. 'What's this, Miss Boss, no limousine?'

Kay laughed. 'Duggie informs me we've run out of petrol coupons for the month. So, in his terms, Shanks's pony is called for. It's no problem on a fine day like this.'

'Fine day? Never thought you'd say that 'bout the weather round here.'

'Neither did I.'

'I'm pleased I've seen you, anyway, like.'

'Why's that?'

'I need to ask you about something.'

'Anything.'

'To tell you the truth, Kay, I'm in a bit of a pickle.'

Kay's heart dropped at Ginger's sober tone. 'What is it?'

'Well, to be very plain, I'm only having that bastard's bastard.'

'Ginger!'

'Well, that's exactly how I feel about it.'

'Oh, Ginger, what will you do?'

'Well, for one thing, you're the only one I'm telling.'

'They'll find out. They'll all have to find out.'

'They needn't.'

'What does that mean?'

Ginger slowed down to a stop. 'What's been made can be unmade. There's a woman in New Morven who can—'

Kay was horrified. 'No, Ginger, no!'

'It's his kid. That bastard's kid.'

'It's an innocent.'

'Well, I was going to ask your advice and you've given it now.'

They stopped where their ways must part. Kay put a hand on Ginger's arm. 'Don't do anything . . . anything . . . in haste, Ginger. And don't do anything without telling me. Promise?'

'I suppose I have to. Go on then, I promise.'

Every night after work Laurenz and Mikel had a meal together in a café, one of seven shops on a newly built crescent which stood on a site where a bomb shelter had taken a direct hit. The food was substantial, given the constraints of rationing, and it beat concocting God knew what stuff on a single gas ring.

Laurenz was making an impression at this factory, as he knew he would, by dint of hard work, charm and insightful, intelligent engineering suggestions. In time he knew he would make his way up this ladder. There were things happening on the side too: delivery wagons with excess stock; storerooms with vulnerable padlocks. And he had got his hands on some petrol, which surprised even him.

Heartily tucking into his greasy meal, Laurenz knew that he could settle in this city: it was hard, and going forward fast. It had something to offer him.

The steamed-up mirror, set in green tiles on the café wall, reflected a very different Laurenz from the man who had escaped from Priorton those weeks back. The bruises and cuts had healed cleanly and his well-cut beard, naturally a rusty grey, covered the bottom part of his face. He had bleached his black hair to a similar colour and all in all had changed his appearance entirely. He looked less glamorous, craggier and ten years older. It was a wonder Mikel himself recognised him at all now.

One night, they were just finishing with a second cup of thick brown tea when the bell on the shop door clanged. Mikel kicked Laurenz under the table. Two men marched in and stood by their table. Their strong features and dark hair crammed under woollen working caps proclaimed them foreigners. The older one, who wore steel-rimmed spectacles, spoke in German. 'Good evening, Mikel.'

Mikel put down his cup. 'Good evening, Mr Goldfarb.'

The man removed his leather gauntlets. 'My brother and I made a special trip across here to see you tonight. We saw you come from the factory. We note that you do not go straight home now, that you come here to eat.'

'It was very kind of you to keep an eye on me,' said Mikel easily.

'We wondered whether that cousin of yours had been in touch. Laurenz Gold. As I said, we need to see him urgently.'

'Yes. Yes, Viktor. I told you I would let you know.'

The two men looked across at Laurenz. 'And whom have we here, Mikel?' said Viktor Goldfarb.

Laurenz took a drink of his tea and looked at Mikel over the rim of his cup. 'An' who might this lot be when they're at home?' he said in his best Durham accent. 'Talk English, will yer? Ah canna understand a word ye're saying.'

In careful English Mikel explained that these men were looking for a cousin of his, with whom he had now lost touch. He looked up at Viktor. 'This is John Davies, whom I work with. He comes from up North.'

Viktor nodded briefly then leant over and lifted Mikel to his feet by the front of his jacket. 'If ever you do come across that murdering, lying pig of a cousin of yours, Mikel, will you tell him my brother and I are seeking him?' He shook Mikel till his head rang. 'Do not frighten him. We just wish to check a few facts with him. Do you understand?'

'Yes, yes.' Mikel struggled away from Viktor's grasp. 'Do not worry, Viktor. I will tell him.'

They waited a good time after Viktor and his brother had left, paid their bill and strolled out of the café.

'Phew!' said Mikel. 'That was what the English call *a close shave*.'

Laurenz put his arm through Mikel's. 'They are numskulls, *Dummköpfe*,' he said. 'Now I will take you home.'

Later, as they walked together into his rooming house, Mikel looked nervously behind and ahead of them. 'This will not work, Lau. This will not work.'

Laurenz was more jaunty. 'Of course it will. They did not recognise me. You could see that.'

'But they are determined. You saw that.'

At the door, Laurenz watched Mikel fiddle with the lock. 'Do not worry, cousin. Your worry creates more danger than Viktor Goldfarb.'

They walked into the shabby room and, like a magician, Laurenz produced a sauce bottle from the inside of his pocket. The bottle was spotlessly clean and contained a clear liquid. 'Vodka!' He thumped Mikel on the shoulder. 'Tears of Heaven!'

'Where in Heaven itself did you get that?'

'The same places I get my petrol. People leave things around. Now then, we will drown your fears and make some toasts to the future!'

They were on to their third glass when Mikel asked his question. 'So what is it, this thing about the Goldfarbs, Lau? I thought you did business with old Goldfarb. Good business.' He had never enquired too closely into Laurenz's affairs. He had learnt many years ago to leave his cousin's dark side strictly alone. He felt powerless in the face of it and his own family's responsibility in creating that brutal part of Laurenz had always troubled him. As his own father acknowledged, they could never make up for that. The fact that they had spoilt and indulged him when he finally came to them might sop their own consciences, but it only made it worse.

Laurenz drained his glass. 'I did good business with him,' he said. 'As you know he was very good with ink and paper, Mr Goldfarb. Passports, permits. Thousands of marks he had from me, from the people I took through. Lined his pockets. Then near the end he asked me to take his nieces out.' His voice acquired a sulky tone. 'They were bad girls. Moody, ill prepared, ill disciplined. They ran from me near one of the passing places and just about fell on a patrol, four men in a jeep.' He paused.

'The soldiers took them to the police? They were put on to a transport?'

Laurenz poured himself another glass of the liquor. 'They didn't get that far. Well, they . . . you know what those bastard soldiers do! When I finally found the girls they were dead. In the end all they were was target practice. I buried them there in the woods. I didn't leave them.' He said this in praise of himself.

Mikel closed his eyes a second. 'So why didn't you go back and tell Mr Goldfarb?'

'That would have been stupid. Who would have come with me after that? I would have lost all my business.'

'So what did you say to him?'

'I told him that I had watched them run over the border and enter the first house in the chain. Then an army transport came and I had to flee.'

'Did he swallow it?'

'He did at first, but when he didn't hear from them he grew suspicious. Started to question me. Then he stopped doing papers and passports for me. Patrizia's was the last one he did. I could see betrayal in his face, Mikel. I was for it.'

'So . . .'

'So I moved first. A little note to the *Polizei* about the false wall in his workshop and all the forgery gear behind it.'

'Lau.' Mikel put his hand over his eyes. 'Have you no conscience? I can't believe that you . . .'

'Sharks. We are all sharks, Mikel. Some of us are bigger and better sharks than others, that is all.'

* * *

Later that night, Laurenz took many side turnings this way and that, finally ending up at his own lodgings. As he closed the front door his landlady plodded out in her slippers to hand him his post: a single letter in a thin white envelope.

He sat down in his untidy, cluttered room to learn from Patrizia's neat writing that she and the children were well, although that friend of Thomas, the miner, had been ill. And her own old Dutch friend had died, which had made her sad. He had been kind to her, although Laurenz did not know him. But Thomas and his sister Kay had been so kind. The work at the factory was fine. In fact she was as quick as anyone now. She would not give up the job now for the world. Would he ever find time to come home? If he did he was to be sure to let her know as she would make sure she was there. She sent love to their father from Rebeka and Peter.

Laurenz threw down the letter and stamped on it. 'Thomas and his sister Kay . . .' he muttered. 'His sister Kay . . .'

He reached again for the vodka.

The following night when he returned to his room after his meal at the café, there was a surprise waiting for him. His room was immaculately tidy. The mirrors and furniture were polished, the bed neatly made. A small chill touched the centre of his being. He raced downstairs to ask his landlady if she had cleaned his room. She shook her head vigorously. 'Now, Mr Gold, that is not in our agreement. We agreed—'

'Then who cleaned it? It has been cleaned.'

She smiled, showing her ragged teeth. 'That would be your friends. Such nice men.' The crisp ten-shilling note had proved that to her. 'They came earlier, waited a while, then went off when you didn't come.'

He was livid. 'Friends? I have no friends!'

She bridled. 'Surely you must be wrong, Mr Gold. Everyone has friends.'

He was getting into bed when he found it under the clock: a piece of paper folded in two. On it, in a very fine hand, was written in German:

* * *

> Sir. Do you have a daughter? Do you have a son? You must watch them closely or you may lose them. It is very common, these days, to lose one's children.

The note was unsigned.

He looked around for the letter from Patrizia. It was nowhere to be found.

Nineteen

Mothering

Down at the factory Kay kept a discreet eye on Ginger. Any girl would be sweating at the thought of the inevitable exposure as the weeks went by. But Kay knew Ginger better, these days, than to look for signs of breakdown or despair. Ginger seemed no different; she worked as quickly as ever, laughed and teased both boys and girls in the same old way.

In the end Kay could not bear the tension. She stopped by the production line and asked Ginger if she would be so kind as to come to her office after the shift. Ginger winked across at Patrizia. 'I'll be chargin' overtime for this, Patsy.'

Patrizia nodded and smiled at Kay, her hands still busy. She was pleased that Thomas's sister was less distant with her these days. 'Peter asks if we can go to skate again, Kay. Perhaps Friday?'

'Yes, fine,' said Kay. She wondered if Harry Longstaffe would be back by the weekend. 'I'm sure Florence would like it.'

'Skating?' said Ginger contemptuously. 'I'd 'a thought it was too bloody cold for a desert flower like Merle Oberon!'

'It was all right,' said Kay. 'The children loved it, but Patrizia here's the expert. You should see her whiz around.'

Ginger grinned. 'I forgot she was from the Alps. You're a funny pair. Desert flower and Snow Queen.'

'It is not cold in Vienna,' protested Patrizia, all laughing indignation. 'In summer it is hot. Hot enough to grow grapes and make wine.' It was only when she put her head down and got on with her work that she realised she had said the name of the city of her birth for the first time without having to endure a rippling surge of pain and despair.

Two hours later, Ginger hitched her bottom on to Kay's work-table. 'So what is it? Not the sack, I hope.'

Kay offered her a cigarette and took one herself. 'I don't know how you can be so calm. How are you? What's happening inside that head of yours?'

Ginger drew hard on her cigarette and looked at Kay through the veil of smoke. 'How am I? Sick as a dog on a morning. Fit as a lop aside from that. Me mother's looking at us queer but no one else has twigged.'

'So what will you do?'

Ginger shrugged. 'Whatever I do, it'll have to be soon.'

'But have you decided what?' Kay persisted.

'It's your fault. I'd have had it all sorted days back, if you'd not said that thing.'

'Said what thing?'

'Said that it . . . this bairn . . . was an innocent. The minute you said that, it became, like, a person. Not sommat to do with that bastard. That piece of Brylcreemed rubbish.'

'So . . .'

'Well, look at it my way. If I do have this bairn, I'll lose me job here that I bloody love. And my family, that I love nearly as much as the job, well, they'll chuck me out on me ear. It's true that me mam might wear it . . . but the lads'll not. Free as birds in their lives, but they've always been so bloody sanctimonious about their little sister. And then there's this bloody town. I like it, mek no mistake, but this poor little bugger inside me'll have to be a good fighter from day one. He'll get "called" from one end of the town to the other.'

'So,' asked Kay again, 'what will you do?'

'Well, seeing as you ask, I'm having this baby and all that stuff will happen, make no mistake. And I won't give a damn. Except I'll take the face off anyone who "calls" my bairn. In front of my face, like.'

'What! You *are* going to have it?'

'Gotcha!' Ginger was grinning all over her face.

Kay came round the table and hugged her. 'Your job's safe here whenever you want it, Ginger. Blast it, I'll make sure you get paid right through.'

Ginger squirmed away from her grasp. 'Proper little fairy godmother aren't we?'

Kay laughed. 'That's it. I'll be its godmother and Florence'll be its godsister.'

'Godmother! Not *the* Mrs Fitzgibbon, surely. People from The Lane don't get to be godmothers to bastards.'

'Ha! Little you know! There's a long tradition of bastards in our family, although we don't call them that.' She counted them off on her fingers. 'There's my grandmother Kitty, my mother, my Auntie Mara, my Uncle Tommy, though he's dead and past caring. The fact that me and our Thomas were born in wedlock is entirely due to my mother's eccentricity.'

Ginger roared with laughter and buttoned her overall which was pulling a bit now. 'Well, then, it an't such a big decision, is it? So what about you? Recovered from that passion for the Viennese waltz, have you?'

'The dancing's all I miss,' said Kay, pulling on her own coat. 'And I haven't much time for that at present. I'm learning so much here that even the Captain doesn't scowl at me any more. And . . .' She was thinking about Harry Longstaffe.

'And?' said Ginger.

'Nothing.'

'Suit yourself. Now then, can I walk you to the corner?' said Ginger as she opened the door. 'I'll have to practise walking. The bike'll be uncomfortable before long.'

'Don't mind if I do,' said Kay, and linked her arm as they walked down the deserted shop floor, still humming and settling after a long day's work.

Just before their ways parted Kay said, 'I've got to come and see your mother with the draft cookery book. She needs to try the recipes out on the cooker to test them. I wonder whether you'd like me to be around when you tell her about this other thing? The cookery book would be a good excuse.'

For a second Ginger looked her soberly in the eyes. 'Do you mean that?'

'Absolutely.'

'Right! Eight o'clock tonight. The lads'll be at the club and we'll have her to ourselves.'

Hugh Longstaffe decided he was better. Yes, he still had the plaster on, but he only used one stick now. And it wasn't as though it had been bone that was broken. 'Just *liggiments* after all.'

He made sure they all knew he meant it when he started to get up at the crack of dawn and present himself in the kitchen to help, washed and shaved, a clean pullover on top of his collarless shirt. Mrs MacMahon tolerated two mornings of this before she went to Leonora. Leonora sought out Hugh. 'I think Mrs MacMahon thinks it's unmanly for a man to wash up or lay the table. Says Duggie wouldn't dream of it.'

Hugh looked miserable for a second. 'And what does she think I did all those years when there was just me and our Harry, when I washed, fed and cared for him all on me own? And was quite good at it, though I say it myself. There's nowt to housework, nowt. Women make a big fuss o't.'

Leonora laughed. 'You must be feeling better, Hugh, to get so cross.'

'I feel as useless as a hen that canna lay, and as near to the chop. I feel ten year older every week. I've gotta stop it or I'll never get back to the pit.'

Leonora bit her lip. It was very clear to her and to Dr Fairless, who had paid a lot of attention to Hugh, that her cousin could never go underground again, never again wield his miner's pick. However well he got, the time was past for that. Kay called him a colossus. Well, he was that no longer. Leonora felt she couldn't say this to him. She compromised with, 'I'd not be in any hurry if I were you.'

'And I need to get back under my own roof,' he said stubbornly.

She shook her head. 'Dr Fairless says no. There is a danger of the poison reintroducing itself. He won't take the responsibility, and neither will I.' She did not mention the seizure. Although Hugh knew about it, he never mentioned it, and ignored people who did.

Hugh slumped back in his seat. Leonora searched wildly in her mind for something, some project that would satisfy his restlessness, make him feel useful. 'I've got it! The museum!'

'What?' he said.

She explained to him about the building, all under wraps now, which Kitty had set up as a kind of family memorial. 'Some old things from the family are there. There's a small library. Pots that young Kay brought back from Egypt. Kitty left some money in her will to open it up as a kind of public reading room.'

'There already is one. At the club.'

'But women can't use that one, neither can children. It'd be kind of optimistic to open it again just now. The war's over. We've got the Education Act, and they're working on a National Health Service, but everything seems so drab. I suppose the Royal Wedding'll brighten things up a bit. But this would be in our town. Something for the future.'

'What needs doing to it?'

'It needs opening up, cleaning, dusting, arranging. We can all help with that. And then when it opens it'll need a kind of warden. Someone to watch it while it's open.'

'I could only do that until I'm properly fit for the pit.'

'Yes, yes, we'll find someone else then. Will you think about it, Hugh?'

'Aye, I'll think about it. Better than sittin' here like some old racehoss put out to grass.'

Mikel insisted on travelling North with Laurenz. He came across to his cousin's lodgings with his case, and lounged back on the bed watching Laurenz pack his things. 'Moving again, Lau? Will you never settle down in one place?' he said.

'Those Goldfarbs will chase me here anyway now, sooner or later, Mika. And they know where Patrizia and the children are now because of that stupid letter she sent me.'

'Do you think they will be in danger, she and the children?'

Laurenz stared at his cousin a little too long before he shook his head. 'These men are not killers, Mikel.' His lip curled.

Mikel shrugged. 'They frightened me. They have reason . . .'

Laurenz reached across and took his cousin by the throat, then threw him back on the bed. 'That was the war. Difficult things happened,' he said sulkily. 'If it were still the war, I would kill them and there would be an end of it. But here it is not so easy.'

'That's crazy talk, Lau. Crazy.'

'It is crazy they imagine they could kill me.' Laurenz was scowling at the back of his hand, flexing the fingers one by one.

It dawned on Mikel that this time, for the first time in many years, his cousin was scared. In fact this situation was no worse than many things they had been through together. Easier, in fact, because here they were in peacetime England. The war was over.

But something had happened to Laurenz in County Durham: perhaps that beating which had made such a mess of him. Whatever it was, it had budged Laurenz from his shelf of certainty.

'To the Goldfarbs it was not just the war. It was their uncle, their sisters. Their family just like yours. Do not deceive yourself. They mean business,' said Mikel.

Laurenz shrugged. 'They do not have the stomach for it. They wish to frighten me where they think I must be weak. They wish me to worry, that I have a family at all. But my so-called family does not trouble me. I can get another wife, other children.'

Mikel frowned. 'I would believe that crazy talk if you weren't here, giving up your job again, and racing back up to Priorton!

Why move them off to London, if that's what you're planning?'

Laurenz shrugged. 'Both Peter and Patrizia speak English now. There is sympathy with women and children. That could be useful. And perhaps London is big enough. I do not choose to live where I look over my shoulder all the time. I have done that for fifteen years now.' He buckled his rucksack and sat back on the bed. 'Perhaps I get old.'

Mikel flicked a finger at Laurenz's grizzled beard. 'You certainly look like an old man.'

Laurenz grinned suddenly, his depression falling off him like an old cloak. 'You're right. First thing, this beard comes off. Old men don't get jobs.' He leapt to his feet. 'The barbers. Then I go to a certain place and obtain some petrol. Then we buzz up and collect Patrizia and the children and off we go.'

'Shall we stay in Priorton?'

Laurenz scowled. 'No. Did you not listen? We cannot stay there, fool. What were we saying? This is why I talk about London. A big place. A man could get lost there. There must be things for a clever man to do in London.'

Mikel laughed at the return of his cousin's fizzing optimism, but underneath he felt uneasy. He wondered how long they would have to keep moving to get out of the way of the people Laurenz had offended.

He wondered too how long he himself could take it. His own sense of guilt for what his family had done to Laurenz, his own sense of obligation to his cousin, was wearing thin. One day he would have to say stop, that he would not join in the game; he would have to live his own life. Then Laurenz would turn on him, he was sure of it.

So he was talking as much about himself when he said, 'What if Patrizia does not want to come? She sounds settled there, as though she is putting down roots.'

'I am rescuing her from the Goldfarbs.'

'But you said yourself she's not in danger from them.'

'She will have no choice. She will have to come. Or she will suffer. And she knows it.'

And Mikel knew that this was a clear message for him. Laurenz had an animal's instinct for threat, wherever it came from. Which was not surprising, considering.

Mona Simpson was pleased to note the progress on the cookery book. Kay handed her the hardbacked, lined book filled with Mrs Morpurgo's neat cramped script.

'See, the ingredients are what we took down when we were here, and the timings and temperatures are how Mrs Morpurgo's adapted them for the Rainbow cooker.' Kay laid down an envelope with money and coupons in it. 'The money's there for the ingredients, with extra coupons from the Captain. What we want you to do is try these recipes on your Rainbow cooker and write down any differences of opinion you have with Mrs Morpurgo. She has left the opposite pages clear so we can make changes. Whatever you go for, we'll allow to stand for the final book. And your name will be on the front of course.'

'Nice of yer!' Mona raised a brown-painted brow.

Kay took her disdain on the chin. 'Credit where credit's due,' she said cheerfully.

There was a silence while Mona turned the pages of the book and peered at recipes that she had only ever had in her head and never seen on paper.

Kay coughed. 'Now, Mona, there's something Ginger . . . Mavis has to tell you.'

Mona turned four more pages before she looked up at her daughter, her face tight. 'Yer gunna tell us yer've fallen wrong, aren't yer?'

For once, Ginger looked worried. 'Ma . . .'

Mona shook her head. 'I need no tellin'.' She paused. 'I canna think what yer da'll say. Or the lads.'

'It's not them I'm worried about. What you think's the only thing, Ma.'

Mona shook her head. 'I canna stand on any pedestal meself. I fell wrong with Len before your da and me got married. It's human nature, after all, having babies.'

'There's no question of marryin' the bloke, Ma.'

'Am I allowed to ask who it is?'

Ginger shook her head. 'A bloke. That's all.'

Mona started to crease the cloth in front of her. 'I knew you were leaving it too late to find a man of your own. What are you? Twenty-eight? I had four of you by then. You've left it too late, bin seeing too many lads. Yer dad always said—'

Ginger's laugh was not as hearty as usual. 'I've heard him. "She'll come to nee good, that lass." Well, now it seems he's right, doesn't it?'

Kay was relieved to see Ginger getting angry.

'Well, yes,' said Mona. 'Seeing as you mention it. He's said it every Friday night for the past five years.'

'And do you think I'm a slut too?'

'I wouldn't go so far as saying that, Mavis.'

Kay intervened at last. 'But it's not Ginger's fault, Mona! Not at all, he . . .'

Ginger shot a warning look at her and she shut up.

'What's this? What's this?'

'Tek no notice of her. She knows nowt.'

Mona smoothed out the creases she had just made in the tablecloth. 'So you're determined to have the bairn? There are ways, you know.'

'She's having it,' said Kay. 'She's decided that.'

Mona turned to Kay. 'For someone who knows nowt about it, you seem to know quite a lot, Mrs Fitzgibbon.' She turned back to her daughter. 'So you're going to have this bairn, then?'

'Yes.'

'Where? Your da'll have you the other side of the door as sure as shot. Lads as well. Mebbe not Ed, but the others.'

'Then me da's a bloody hypocrite. And the rest of them.'

Mona laughed. 'They all are, men. Isn't that why you're having this bairn without gettin' married?'

'Do you think he'll really chuck us out, Ma?'

'Sure as shot, like I say,' said Mona with grim certainty.

They all looked at the fire, their brains foraging around

for any solution to this intractable problem.

'You can go to London,' put in Kay suddenly. The faces of mother and daughter, as they turned to look at her, were eerily similar, their expressions mingling surprise and dawning hope.

'What're you talking about?' said Ginger.

'You can go and stay with my Auntie Mara. You saw her at Kitty's funeral, remember? She's expecting a baby too, a few months earlier than you, but . . .'

'She wouldn't want me hanging around.'

'She wouldn't worry a bit. She's really easygoing, is Mara.'

'Well, you could go on another month here,' said Mona hesitantly. 'You shouldn't show for a while.'

'And then you could go to London, have the baby and decide what you want to do. Like I say, your job'll be here when you get back.'

Ginger glanced at her mother. 'Well, I . . .'

'It sounds all right to me. People round here can be very cruel. Even people with plenty of skeletons in their own cupboard.'

'Starting with me own brothers, like.'

'Mmm, you might be right there.' Mona looked at Kay. 'I have to say it's kind of you, doing this for our Mavis, Mrs Fitzgibbon.'

Kay laughed. 'Now then, Mona, if I'm going to be godmother to your grandchild I think you'd better call me Kay.'

'Well, Kay, I have to thank you.'

'Don't. It's nothing.'

Ginger shot up. 'Ooh. I have to go for a wee! How I'm gunna keep this a secret another month I don't know.' She charged out of the back door.

Mona watched the door click and turned to Kay. 'There's more to this, isn't there?'

'She's told you what she wants you to know,' said Kay.

'Kind of her. It's not that brother of yours, is it?'

Kay shook her head. 'No. I promise you.'

'Is our Mavis all right?'

'You can see she is. She's much better now she's actually told you. She was worried about that.'

'She had a good right to be worried.' The sneck rattled again. Mona held up the recipe book and when Ginger got back in she was talking about that.

Kay stood up. 'I'll have to go.'

Mona stood up and grasped her tightly by the forearm. 'You can be sure I'll do a bloody good job on these recipes.'

Kay smiled down at her. 'I knew that from the very beginning, Mona,' she said.

Ginger walked to the back gate with Kay on her way out. She held the gate closed. 'Me mother's as baffled as I am about all this help, Kay. Pleased as I am about it, I can't really think why you're doing all this for me.'

'Well, thank you very much. I thought we were friends.'

'Well, I suppose . . .'

'And anyway, this wouldn't have happened to you if I hadn't been carrying on – well, refusing to carry on – with that snake.'

'You don't know that. He's a bad bugger. Bad for the sake of being bad. Mebbe you're flattering yourself.'

'I know it. I know it very well, Ginger. If I hadn't slipped into that tangle with Laurenz Gold, none of this would have happened.'

Twenty
Family Matters

When Laurenz and Mikel arrived only Rebeka was at the council house, in the care of old Judith. Laurenz strode through the immaculate rooms, shivering and rubbing his hands and arms to get some feeling back into them after the long drive. 'Where is Patrizia, where is Peter?' he demanded.

Judith sat on placidly in her chair. 'Frau Gold is at the factory, and Peter will be at the house of Mrs Leonora Scorton, playing with Florence. Frau Gold collects him on the way home from the factory.'

Laurenz picked up Rebeka who howled her objection at such rough handling.

'Laurenz!' warned Mikel.

Laurenz put his daughter down quite gently and she went to hide behind Judith's skirts. 'When will my wife be back home?' he said.

She looked at the clock on the mantelpiece. 'Another hour at least.'

'Has anyone called here? Any strangers?'

Judith shook her head, then suddenly she smiled. 'Yes, there was one, such a nice man. He could speak our language. He asked about Patrizia and the children. He knew her mother, apparently, in the old days.'

Laurenz knelt by her chair then and clasped her arm in his cold hand. 'If you are here, Grandmother, in my house, you will answer the door to no one. Do you hear? Never.'

Judith yelped with pain. 'I hear you, *mein Herr*. There is no need . . . have we not had enough of that where we have been?'

'Laurenz!' Mikel warned him again.

Laurenz loosened his grip and stroked her arm. 'I'm sorry, Grandmother, but I worry about my wife and my children. Do you see?'

Outside the house Laurenz turned to Mikel. 'I will go to the factory and get her. The Goldfarbs could be there now. You stay here and watch Rebeka.'

Mikel, relieved to escape Laurenz's intense presence even for a short while, stood at the door. 'You are an odd one, Lau. When you are with Patrizia and the children it is clear you care nothing for them, but here you are charging round the country like some rescuing knight.'

Laurenz tied his scarf round his neck and stood astride the bike. 'You are so stupid, Mikel. How can you be so stupid? Don't you see? I do this because they are mine. Only mine.' His face twisted then. 'And Peter must never, must not be left alone.' Then he set off down the lane, engine roaring, scarf flying in the air behind him.

Mikel stared after him and thought of the evil seeds sewn in a child who until the age of eight had only a shred of clothes for his back and dog food for his stomach; whose greatest effort was rewarded by a boot in his face or a buckled belt for his back. A boy too intelligent and cunning to be cowed by such treatment, who stored the evil deeds like a camera stores images, to project them back on those weaker than himself as soon as he was the stronger one.

Leonora made Hugh sit on a chair in the middle of the floor while he got back the breath lost on the long walk down from The Lane to the museum.

He put both hands on his stick and looked round. 'This place must have been a chapel at one time,' he said. 'Look at that pew. Don't see carving like that nowadays.'

'I believe so.' Leonora started to pull off the white dust-cloths. 'Whew! These are dusty, but the cases underneath are not so bad. Look, here are my father's tools and the workings of some of his watches. And his mechanical toys! Florence would have a field day here. And these Roman coins and pottery fragments. And axe heads from even further back. Before the Romans.'

Hugh pointed with his stick. 'And what are those?'

She smiled. 'Oh, those are Kay's. Her bowls that she brought from Egypt. Kitty and she came down here with them not long after we arrived.'

'So what are your plans for this place, Leonora?'

'Well, there is this little endowment in Kitty's will to open it again. So it can be a public reading room, as it was before. A place where children can come to do their homework, for instance. Houses are so crowded now. Where can a clever child get peace and quiet?'

'And what do you see here for me, Leonora? Some kind of caretaker?'

'Well, yes I suppose.'

He shook his head and pulled himself to his feet. 'Well, flower, Ah'll willingly help you to get the place into some kind of good fettle. But caretakin's not for me. Once a pitman always a pitman. Ah'll get back into the pit even if they only let me sort coal from stone on the bank. And you don't just need a caretaker here. You need someone who can label all this stuff, answer the children's questions. Mind you, I do know the very man.'

'So who might that be?'

'Well, your Thomas has made a right good hand of the pit. A brave hand, more than a good hand, given his constitution. An' he's survived these months down there from sheer cussedness. They took him on because of some regard for me. But he's strugglin' now, brave as he is. Bless us, he's not cut out for it, Leonora.' He put a hand on one of the showcases to steady himself. 'In time, mebbe he could do it if he had to, if were the only thing and he had bairns to feed. Many have done it and grown miserable and shrunken in the process. But it's not the only thing, is it? There's not that deep need, is there? He might be Freddie Longstaffe's grandson, but he's your son as well, and Kitty Rainbow's grandson, after all. Now this place, this museum, with a free hand, he'd make sommat of this. See how good he is with bairns! He'll make this the place it could be. He'll have them flockin' here in droves. I promise you that.'

Leonora was leaning against one of the cabinets, staring at him, her arms folded.

'Now what're yer starin' at?' he grumbled.

'I was thinking. Funny how we don't see what's under our noses, isn't it, Hugh?'

Jim Murton watched idly as the clean-shaven, dark-haired man chugged through the Rainbow Works' gates on his dusty motor cycle. Jim reflected that security at the Works did not compare now with that job in wartime. Nowadays all it consisted of was signing wagons in and out and cranking the telephone to inform Goods Inwards that they had a delivery.

During the war, of course, the Home Guard took security very seriously. Everyone passing through was questioned, his – or her – name noted. Every worker had their bags and pockets searched on their way in and on their way out.

These days, all the other Home Guard lads had gone on to other, better jobs and there was only himself, daytime, to manage the gates. He moaned very publicly about this, but with no spies and no explosives there was less need for a heavy hand. And his job was easier, there was no denying it.

The lad on the motor bike was vaguely familiar: good-looking feller, foreigner. He worked here a while back. Perhaps he was getting set on again. Jim waved him through.

'You've got company,' Ginger said grimly to Patrizia.

Patrizia looked up and her smile froze as she saw Laurenz marching down the line, his silk scarf swinging over his flying jacket. She glanced at him and went on with her wiring.

He went and put his hand on her shoulder. 'You must come, Patrizia. There are things we have to do.'

'She can't,' said Ginger. 'Shift's not over.'

He ignored her and shook Patrizia hard. 'Come, Patrizia.'

She looked up at him, her fingers still busy. 'I cannot come. As Ginger says, the shift is not over.'

'You take no notice of women like her.' He lifted Patrizia bodily from her stool. Ginger jumped up and caught hold of the two ends of his scarf and yanked him back away from Patrizia. He turned and pulled a fist back to punch Ginger, but Patrizia grabbed his arm. Other women leapt off their stools and came towards him. They started to pull at his jacket and his hair. He fought back ruthlessly but sheer weight of numbers meant that in a minute he was on the dusty concrete with Janet's sturdy weight on his chest. Ralph, the progress lad, came to the edge of the crowd and whistled.

'On top of the job, aren't yer, ladies? I'll give yer that.'

'Stop bloody sniggering, will yer? And go and get Duggie, or Kay Fitzgibbon,' said Ginger, carefully tightening Laurenz Gold's scarf till it was just short of choking him. 'This bugger's slowing us down. Me and Patsy here'll miss out on our bonus if we don't watch it.'

Ralph raced to Duggie's office to recount the spectacle. Before setting off himself Duggie picked up the phone and told Jim Murton to get down to the cooker line as there was a bit of a kerfuffle down there. In his little hut, Jim finished his tea and walked briskly to the site, pleased at the diversion.

In the end it took five men to get Laurenz Gold out of the Works; four to carry his swearing, kicking body, and Ralph to wheel the motor bike. They stood in a semicircle round the bike and watched him mount it, start it up and roar off.

Jim rubbed his hands together. 'Well, that got shot of him, lads.'

'Good riddance to bad rubbish,' said Ralph sourly. 'That's what I say. Bliddy Nazzy.'

'You missed a bit of a show this afternoon,' Ginger told

Kay as they walked out of the factory later that afternoon. 'Buggerlugs was in. The Austrian. Came to drag young Patrizia off to his lair.'

'Duggie told me.'

'Janet just about flattened him.'

'I heard,' said Kay. 'Good thing too. So how's things, Ginger? How are you feeling?'

'All right in the main. Had a bloody big belly ache this morning, but it soon went off.'

'So how yeh doin' with Len Simpson then?' said Hugh to Thomas who had come into the sitting room and thrown himself on to the chair beside him.

'All right,' said Thomas briefly.

'Are yeh?' Hugh cocked an eye at him. Thomas's skin, which had been golden when he arrived last year, was now white-blue where it was pitted here and there with coal dust, despite the bath he had had the second he came in from work. Behind his glasses his eyes were red-rimmed and sore, both from the poor sleep that working shifts afforded him and the perpetual incursion of gritty coal and dust fragments which adhered like glue to the moister parts of the body. These sometimes embedded themselves right into the flesh if one got too near the blast as the shot firers did their work.

Thomas's nails were split and broken, two of them black where they had been crushed under stone or caught between prop and coal. And Hugh knew that the younger man's back, under its neat check shirt, would be scored by scars, fresh and healing, acquired in the process of squeezing and wriggling, snake-like, through spaces too narrow for any man. 'All right, eh?'

'That Len Simpson has no patience.' The words cracked out of Thomas. 'He had me by the throat at five o'clock this morning because I wasn't filling fast enough.' Thomas had been terrified, leapt on by the big man in the narrow space because, despite his undeniable strength, he would not, could not, work like an automaton, shovelling coal on to an endless, endless conveyor which creaked and grumbled like a crotchety old man as it swept the coal away from the working.

'Allus was greedy, was Len,' Hugh said thoughtfully. 'But can yer blame him? It's a terrible way to make a living, and the money is all you have to show for it, when push comes to shove.'

'But you said you liked it,' said Thomas. 'The wonderful miracle of the silver coal, working in the folds of the earth . . .'

'Now, now, son, no call to be bitter. Ah've spent a workin' life down there. If Ah couldn't find beauty Ah'd be no better than an animal. We all has our own ways of making silk out of slack.'

'It's not the same without you there,' said Thomas simply.

'Getaway!' Hugh's modest disclaimer was interrupted by bumps and screams above their heads. Hugh smiled. 'That's the bairns up in Florence's room, back from school.'

Thomas looked at the clock. Just an hour now till Patrizia would come to collect Peter. Now he could count the minutes and not the hours.

'So you're thinking of coming out of the pit?'

Thomas looked at him sharply. 'I didn't say that.'

'Well, you're a fool if you don't. You know it now. You've shown some grit, an' that's no bad thing. An' there's no denying yer a strong lad. Get out of it now, and do sommat more suited to you.'

'But you . . .?'

'I'm just an old pitman. I knaa nae better. Canna wait ter get back, tell you the truth. Ah must be crackers.'

'Can you really see yourself back in the pit with that leg?'

Hugh stared at him for a second. 'Well, mebbe that's a bit of an old man's dream. But if Ah didn't go to the pit where would I go? Ah live on me own, marrah, the pit connects me to things. It meks me important. Otherwise I'm just another old codger like those geezers down the club. Snoring and drinking away the bright days. Man, Ah'd rather be down the pit.' He shot Thomas a piercing glance. 'Or six feet under.'

The door burst open and Florence bounded in, followed by Peter. 'Is it time to go to do the hens, Thomas?' said Florence.

'We have had tea,' said Peter in his deep voice. 'Very good. Corned-beef hash.'

Hugh reached for his stick. 'Ah'll come down with yer. Here's me talkin' about goin' back down the pit and I'm too idle to feed me own hens.'

'There's no need—' began Thomas.

'Ah'm comin',' said Hugh. And there was no further argument.

Five minutes after they had all left for the allotment Leonora answered a ring on the doorbell to find a handsome, well-set-up young man in a flying jacket on her doorstep. His smile was charming. 'I am Laurenz, perhaps you will remember. Husband to Patrizia. I am told that my son is here with you?'

She opened the door wide. 'Oh, come in, come in. They have just gone off with our old friend Hugh to feed the hens. They will be back soon. Perhaps in half an hour.'

As she led the way to the sitting room Leonora felt a little uneasy. She knew that this man had been away from Priorton for a while. She had eyes in her head. Thomas was clearly more than fond of little Patrizia.

But as Laurenz chatted airily to her Leonora did not get the sense of a man with a grudge. He asked after Thomas, and her daughter, Mrs Fitzgibbon.

She told him how well Peter was settling into school. He was back up in Florence's class now and was astonishing them all with his cleverness. 'Perhaps he gets it from you, Mr Gold? When you were at the factory my daughter told me you were a fine engineer. Did you do well at school?'

He waited so long to answer her that she looked at him sharply, wondering if she had, after all, mistaken his mood.

Then he shook his head. 'As far as I know I did not go to school until I was eight, Mrs Scorton. At that time I went to a country school with my cousin Mikel. I made great progress but it was a poor school. The teachers were cretins. Once I could read, everything I learnt I taught myself.'

She frowned. 'That's a late start. Did Austrian schools . . .'

He cut through the air with his hand, as though he would physically cut the conversation short. 'You will forgive me, Mrs Scorton. I do not remember, before I was eight, where I went to school.' He stood up and peered out of the window. 'Did you say half an hour? I have no time to wait. My daughter is at the house being watched by an old witch. I must rescue her.' He clicked his heels, took Leonora's hand and bent over it. '*Gnädige Frau*,' he said. 'Thank you for your kindness.'

When Laurenz got back to his house the old woman Judith had gone. Mikel was there, sitting on the floor with his head pulled back into the lap of the younger Goldfarb, Heini, who was holding a knife to his throat. His brother, Viktor, was sitting by the table with Rebeka on his knee. She was playing with the carved ebony handle of another knife while, delicately, he held on to the sharp blade.

Viktor nodded at Laurenz with a sharp duck of the head. 'So much better without the beard, Mr Gold. It made you into such an old man.' He waved the knife at him. 'Sit down, won't you? It is your house after all.'

'What do you want?'

'I want to know about my daughters and my brother. He paid you to get them out, I believe?'

'You know everything I know.'

'We know nothing except that after we were taken my uncle paid you a great deal of money to take my sisters to safety. We know that my wife did not survive and my brother Heini and I alone survive from my family. And more recently we have come to know some more, from something which came to us after the war, in a bundle of our uncle's effects, hidden under the floorboards in his workshop. A miracle. An unopened letter speaking to me over the years.' He grunted, took the knife from Rebeka and turned the blade inwards against her chest. 'And from this we find that my uncle was betrayed and what was left of him was carted off, eventually, to die.'

Laurenz looked steadily into the older man's eyes. 'I promise you I dealt fairly by your sisters. They were lively girls, thought it all a game.' He injected a note of severity into his voice. 'They were undisciplined. They would not do as they were ordered. Such indiscipline is dangerous.

'I reprimanded them.' He could not tell Viktor that he beat one of the girls, with the other one watching, to try to instil discipline. 'But still they ran away.'

'And . . .'

Laurenz bit his lip, he made tears come to his eyes. 'They ran off.'

'And . . .'

'Into the arms of a small patrol.'

'You saw it?'

'I had followed them.'

'But you did not save them?'

'There were eight soldiers and only one of me.'

'Only two of them, my sisters,' said Heini Goldfarb, pressing his knife more closely on Mikel's throat.

'Laurenz!' squeaked Mikel.

'I waited. I did not run away.'

'And watched?'

He did not say anything.

'What about after?' said Goldfarb.

'I buried them.' He veiled his eyes. 'I said the old prayer.'

'Why did you tell my uncle they had got away?'

'I thought the truth would hurt him, and you.'

'And you thought you would not get the second part of the money? My uncle wrote that you were eager for payment.'

'I had done as much of the job as I could. I needed the money for the next exit.'

'But you knew my uncle suspected you?'

Laurenz shook his head. 'I had no idea.'

'And you didn't denounce him?'

'I promise you, hand on heart, I did not.'

'In his letter to me my uncle said he suspected you. That you would betray him.'

'He was confused. They made us all suspect each other at that time.'

Mikel, watching Laurenz, marvelled at the sheer innocence on his face. Guilt made no more mark on him than a finger does on flowing water. What was new, though, was the fear that had taken root in him, where before there was no fear. This new fear had driven him from Priorton down to Coventry, and had now driven him back again. And would drive them all on from here. For all his play-acting here, he was scared.

Mikel tried to reckon when it had all started. Was it with the beating he had received from that man in Durham? But he had had beatings before and had just thrown them off as though they were the pecking of an importunate fly. Then there was the appearance of the Goldfarbs which made him look to the past, to the years when it was his secret custom to cheat vulnerable people who trusted him. But now Mikel could feel his cousin travelling further back to when he himself was vulnerable. Perhaps back to those childhood years, the years sealed off, shut out. Perhaps it was something to do with Peter, the same age now as . . .

'Hey, get up, will you?' Mikel stopped his dreaming. Heini had lifted the knife from his throat and was hauling him to his feet. Viktor Goldfarb handed Rebeka over to her father. Rebeka started to cry.

'I don't believe a single word you say. You are a cretinous liar,' Viktor said. 'But this is not the time or the place. This is a law-abiding country. We should not import the terrible anarchy here.' Casually, the Goldfarbs made their way towards the door. 'But there will be a time and a place. You will have no peace, I promise you. There is balance in all things. I had little peace in the camp where they left me to rot. But I've had less peace since I came out and discovered that my sisters were not safe, as I had thought. I lie awake enduring their agony. But you? If you were a real man you too would suffer such agonies. You have them on your conscience and the many others whom you must have tricked, who slipped from your hands into the hands of murderers during those years. You will have no rest, I assure you. Because one day it will explode back on to you. I might light the touch-paper, or it could be Heini here. Or some other soul with a right to justice.'

Then the Goldfarb brothers were gone and the only sound in the room was Rebeka whimpering. Then Laurenz laughed. 'See?' he said exultantly to the pale-faced Mikel. 'They are craven cowards. They could never do anything to me. They do not have the belly for it.'

Rebeka started to scream. Laurenz stopped laughing and put her roughly down on the couch. 'Shut up, child. Shut up, you whining wretch!' He picked up a cushion and Mikel lunged at him and flicked it from his hand.

'Are you entirely mad, Laurenz?' he demanded.

At that point the door was flung open by Patrizia who raced in, picked up Rebeka and faced Laurenz. 'What are you doing?' she cried.

Thomas followed her in, hand in hand with Peter. Both their faces were strained and anxious.

Laurenz smiled. 'Doing, *liebling*? I am trying to get our little daughter to calm down. That witch of a woman, Judith, left her screaming, didn't she, Mikel? You should not leave her with such a woman.' He turned to Thomas. 'Ah, Thomas? I see you have been keeping an eye on my little family while I have been away. Well, you will be pleased to hear that your heavy duties are at an end.' He leant across and, taking Peter by his trembling shoulders, brought his son in front of him like a shield. 'We are to leave this backwater. I have a job in London.' He looked contemptuously round the room. 'I will get a decent house, unlike this slum. We will go tomorrow.'

Patrizia, soothing Rebeka in the corner, looked up. 'I will not leave. I have work. I will stay.'

Laurenz smiled again at Thomas. 'Thank you for bringing my wife and child home, Thomas. Perhaps you will leave us? I am very tired and very hungry. Patrizia will make me a meal, won't you, Patrizia?' He moved to the corner where the budgie was chirruping in his cage. 'And what have we here, Peter?'

'It is a singing bird,' said Peter. 'Thomas brought it.'

Laurenz lifted up the cage and swung it round, dislodging the budgie from his perch. 'He did, did he? Well, if you forgive me, Thomas, a caged bird is a bit of a ridiculous thing to give Patrizia who has spent the last few years behind wire.' He swung the cage again and the budgie squawked its protest.

'Laurenz, no!' pleaded Patrizia.

Thomas's jaw hardened. Mikel moved towards him and put a friendly hand on his arm. 'Wait!' He went across to Laurenz and unclasped his fingers from the handle of the cage. He handed it to Thomas. 'It is all right, Mr Scorton. I will watch for them. For Patrizia and the children,' he said. He knew now that he should never have gone away. It was vain to think that he could break away from them. Patrizia needed him, as did Laurenz in his own twisted fashion.

'Go,' said Patrizia. 'It will be all well. Laurenz and I will eat, and we will talk about this.'

Thomas went out into the street, and hesitated. He did not want to leave her there, but he would make more trouble if he stayed. Yet he didn't trust Laurenz Gold, not an inch, even when Mikel was guarding Patrizia and the children like some great lumbering sheepdog.

Further down the street a girl and a boy were playing hopscotch on a chalked pitch on the pavement.

'Hey!' Thomas called out to them.

They approached him, curiosity overcoming their apprehension.

'What is it, mister?' said the girl, a heavy child with her elbows out of her jumper.

'Do you want a budgie?' he said, holding up the cage. Very obligingly the budgie started to chirrup and to hop from perch to perch.

'You kidding us, mister?' said the girl.

'No. Honestly. This budgie is without a home.' He fished in

his pocket and pulled out a two-shilling piece. 'There's a shilling there for taking him and a shilling to get birdseed. They sell it at the pet shop in the High Street.'

'What's his name?'

'Er . . . Peter.'

'All right, mister.' The girl took the cage, the boy took the money.

'Thanks, mister,' she said.

He watched them go back down the street towards their house, the hopscotch forgotten. They chattered together, occasionally holding up the cage to get a better look at the bird. The budgie would be safer with them than with Laurenz Gold. He could only hope that they didn't drown it and pocket the money.

Thomas turned up his collar, stuffed his hands in his pockets and leant against the lamppost beside the Golds's gate. This might prove to be a long wait.

When Patrizia had come after work to collect Peter she had blanched at the news that Laurenz had been at the house. At first she refused Thomas's offer to walk her home, but when he steadily insisted she gave in.

Leonora watched them walk down The Lane, each of them holding hands with Peter, then made her way up to Kay's bedroom. She sat on the bed and watched while Kay changed out of her tight smart work clothes into more casual slacks, inherited from Mara, and an old Fair Isle jumper which had belonged to Thomas. She pulled the pins out of her hair; brushing it hard relieved some of the strain of the day.

'Patrizia seemed quite afraid of her husband,' said Leonora.

'He is not a nice person,' said Kay.

'I thought you were impressed with him.'

'So I was, at first. He is a clever man and can use his wits.'

'And handsome, in a flashy sort of way.'

Kay looked at her mother through the mirror. 'Why do you say that?'

Leonora shrugged. 'I might be forty years older than you, Kay, but that does not insulate me from masculine charm.'

Kay blushed. 'I'm sorry, Mother. In fact you did hit a bit of a nail on a bit of a head. I thought at first he was, well, interesting. The charm, the self-confidence, but there is something . . .'

'I felt it too,' said Leonora. 'Just today. He was politeness itself but . . . but it was as though you were watching a film. And it was as though he was watching it too. And we were both admiring his performance.'

It was on the tip of Kay's tongue to tell her mother just how vicious Laurenz really was, but she resisted. She might end up telling about Ginger, and that would be a real breaking of confidence. It would also underline her own weakness and stupidity. She would take a leaf from Ginger's book on that. The more you care, the more the bad lads win.

'Here, give me the brush,' said Leonora. 'Let me do it. It's a long time since I did your hair. A long time since we've really talked at all. You seem to be perpetually rushing in and out, these days.' As she brushed the thick hair she told Kay about the museum, how she and Hugh would be putting work in to straighten it up.

'Hugh?'

'Yes. He's feeling better now. It does him no harm to feel helpful.'

'Good idea,' murmured Kay, almost asleep now with the hypnotism of the brush. 'I hope you're giving my pots pride of place. Kitty and I took them there. One of the last things I did with her.'

'Oh yes, pride of place.' Leonora gathered all Kay's hair in her hands and pulled it neatly behind Kay's shoulders. Then she sat on the chair beside the bed. 'I want to ask you a very delicate favour, Kay.'

'Delicate? I suppose normally I'm very crude?'

Leonora shook her head. 'Don't talk such tosh, Kay. But you can be very direct. It is one of your charms in the ordinary way of things. But Thomas, nowadays . . .'

'Ah, Thomas!' Kay could not stop the note of sarcasm in her voice.

'See what I mean?' said Leonora with some asperity.

Kay sat up straighter. 'So what have I to be delicate about?'

Leonora told her of the plans for the museum, and Hugh's proposal that Thomas should be curator. 'Now can you see the need for delicacy?'

Kay shook her head. 'It would be good for him. He would be good at it. Much more suitable for someone like him than going down the pit. It was a hare-brained scheme imagining he would survive down that hole in the ground in the first place.'

Leonora let a silence develop, then she said again, 'See what I mean? I know from Hugh that Thomas is finding it hard to endure the pit. I don't think we can imagine, really, how hard it is. But do you ever imagine he would give it up under those terms? Under that humiliation? With you busy saying I told you so?'

'No,' Kay said slowly. 'You're right, I suppose.'

'He'd die down what you call that black hole first. He has a stubborn streak, has our Thomas.'

Kay started to tidy the muddle on her dressing table. 'We could . . . I suppose we'd have to imply it couldn't happen without him.'

'It would be true, after all,' said Leonora eagerly. 'And we can say how much benefit the pit has done him. Those men he talks about. The hundred tasks it takes to get coal out of the earth. How he did it, how they do it. It takes such grit. What you simply must show is respect.'

'Well, I grant you it has certainly strengthened his resolve; made him see something through to the end.'

'And he knows more about the way the mines work, that's archaeology in its own way. Sam would see that, using the clues to decode people's way of life. Their attitudes.'

Kay thought about how she could hold the pots, to get just such a sense of real lives lived. There was less of that feeling now in her life, and she missed it. She thought again of her time with Harry Longstaffe on the High Plains. He knew so little of her, but he still knew that; how she could feel through time. 'There could be fossils from the mine, I suppose,' she said. 'Ancient flora and fauna.'

'What about a working model of a mine? The miners and their families could come and see it, if only to tell us where we had gone wrong.'

'It's a shame Kitty isn't here. She'd have made one herself. She'd have a stab at anything. Did you see her mending the toy railway for Florence just before she died?'

'Why not Thomas and Hugh together?' said Leonora. 'They could find a way of building one between them, and perhaps it will keep Hugh from mourning the pit. I cannot . . . cannot see them letting him go underground again.'

Mona Simpson was enjoying the rare treat of feeding three of her family at once. Charlie had had his meal when he came in off night shift at eight o'clock. Len had his at three when he got in from his early shift. But now in one go, around her table, she had Ed, who had had 'one off' today to go to the races, her husband Toller, who had done a day shift, and Ginger just in from the factory.

Mona gave the men a meat and potato pie each and split one between her and Ginger. They ate in silence, as was their custom. Mona reflected that she must have got the timing right on these pies. They weren't half bad, even if they were cooked on the shining cooker squashed into her scullery rather than the good old coal range.

Suddenly Ginger made a harsh noise, half grunt, half scream, and arched back in her chair. The men stopped eating; Mona was at her daughter's side, an arm round her waist. She looked at Ed. 'Will yer help us get her upstairs, son?' she said.

Ed lifted Ginger easily and Mona went ahead and opened the door which hid the stairs, then the door to the tiny front bedroom where Ginger slept. Just as he was laying her on the bed she screamed again and shuddered with pain. Mona took his shoulder and shoved him out of the bedroom. 'Gerrout of here,' she said. 'Go and get Mrs Cotherstone.'

When Ed got back downstairs, his father, stolidly demolishing the rest of his pie, cocked an eye at him. 'What's up there?' he demanded.

'I have to get Mrs Cotherstone,' said Ed.

Toller put down his fork. 'Why, that's the midwife,' he growled.

'Aye. I knaa.'

'I knew it. Fuckin' women,' Toller grunted, picking up his fork. 'I'll swing for that lass. I'm tellen yer.'

Leonora went downstairs to put the tea on the table, saying she could wait for Thomas no longer. Neither she nor Kay mentioned Thomas's special relationship with Patrizia despite the fact that it was on both their minds at that minute.

Kay tied back her hair with some ribbon and went into the sitting room to see Hugh. 'I see you've been plotting with my mother, Mr Longstaffe.'

'Plotting, hinney? Me?' He took a long draw on his pipe. 'Now what meks yer say that?'

'Setting my brother up in a new job so you can expel him from your pit.'

'Naebody's chuckin' him outa the pit, hinney. He's makin' a fair fist of it. Started out strong, ended up brave. Lads down there have some time for him, and that's a compliment. They can be ruthless when it suits them.'

She peered out of the sitting-room window and watched a weary horse pull a heavy Co-op delivery wagon up The Lane. 'I don't think I appreciated . . .'

'What was that, hinney?'

'What a big job it is, working down there. Skilled, I should think.'

'Skilled? There's *clivorer* men down there than you'll see in any factory.'

She smiled at him. 'Now you can't expect me to agree with that.'

'Maks nae matter, it's true.' He looked at her soberly. 'But still it's not the place for young Thomas. It'll brek him. He's brave but a bit of a tender bough.'

'Well, between us we'll have to make him want to do this museum thing.' She paused. 'I think it'll only work if you and he do it together. It'd mean you'd have to give up the pit.'

'Aye, that's what I've been worrying about. But, to be perfectly honest they wouldn't have let us do much if I'd gone back. Some sweeping-up job on the bank. That's all I'd be good for.'

'Well, you don't need to do that now. You and Thomas can make a go of the museum. It'll be worth while.'

'Well.' He shot her a sidelong glance. 'It's not that I'll lose the connection at the pit now. There's always Harry.'

She turned towards him. 'Harry?'

He shrugged. 'Silly bugger's . . . sorry foh the language . . . he's talking now of coming out of the army. A letter today. Resigned his commission, coming home and talking about going back in the pit. Can yer credit it? Bloody hell, what's that?' His musing was shattered by a great hammering on the door. Kay looked sideways through the bay window.

It was Ginger's brother Ed Simpson, in his shirtsleeves, using both his fists to batter the door for all he was worth. Behind him was Patrizia, Rebeka in her arms. Her face was white and she too was breathing hard with the effort of recent running.

Twenty-One

Pursuit

Laurenz had been genial over supper. He made them all sit down at the table, although only Mikel ate with him. Laurenz was quite ravenous; he wolfed down his meal without any show of manners, food spitting out of his mouth as he talked. And he did talk a great deal. He talked about the hundreds of people whom he had saved on his courier route; of his employer in Switzerland who had said he was the most brilliant young man he had ever met. 'It is true that he was something of an invert but he was respected, very respected. He was known to have good judgement.'

And then there was that Harkness fellow, the tool-room manager here at the Rainbow Works. He had loathed Laurenz at first, but he too had to admit the sheer brilliance of his ideas and proposals. The jealousy and ignorance of Kay Fitzgibbon was the problem there. He had thought she would be useful at first, but that was a rare misjudgement on his part. It was ridiculous that a woman should have such power. 'But I forget, Patrizia! You are intimate with this family. They take you skating. They treat you and my children like pets. They give you birds to play with. They walk hand in hand with my children. And you are the object of worship for that great eunuch, Thomas Scorton.'

'Laurenz!' warned Mikel.

Patrizia looked Laurenz in the eye. 'Thomas is a good friend to this family, Laurenz. And he is no eunuch.'

Peter tugged at his mother's sleeve. 'Mama, Mama, what is eunuch?'

Laurenz finished his meal, pushed his plate away and wiped his mouth with the back of his hand. Mikel, not yet finished with his meal, watched him carefully.

Patrizia moved to pick up Laurenz's plate and he struck away her hand. 'Leave it,' he said. 'Sit down.' He reached across and pulled Peter round towards him. He placed his hands on Peter's rigid shoulders and brought his face close to his. 'Now then, Peter. Have you been a really good boy for your mama while Papa has been away?'

The boy nodded.

Laurenz shook him. 'What? Have you no tongue?'

'Yes, Papa. I have been good.'

'What about school? Are you still being taught with babies?'

'No, Papa. I am in the next class with Florence. And I am in the top section also. Miss Plumstead says—'

'Florence Fitzgibbon? You must not play with her. She is a very bad girl. Do you hear me?'

'But Papa . . .' The hands on his shoulder gripped him like a vice. 'Yes, Papa!' he said sorrowfully.

'You know your papa has worked and slaved for you in this damned country. To give you a life. Are you happy?'

Peter was not happy at this moment, with his senses invaded by his father's smell of brilliantine and motor oil, with his mother's wide-open eyes imploring him to bear up under this assault. 'Yes, Papa,' he said resignedly, 'I am happy.'

Laurenz clutched his son closely to him. 'I am glad.' His chin was digging now into Peter's head so Peter could feel as well as hear the voice. 'I once knew this little boy, Peter, who was not so happy. His life was full of dark shapes, screaming voices and heavy blows, foul smells and the pain of great hunger. He was a very unlucky boy, was he not?' Tears stood in his eyes.

'Yes, Papa.' Peter's voice was muffled by his father's coat. 'Yes.'

Patrizia put Rebeka on the floor and came towards them.

'Laurenz!' There was pity in her voice. Somehow she had to get Peter from him.

Laurenz stood up and took a step backwards, hauling his son with him. 'Get away from me!' he sobbed.

She put a hand out towards them, both palms out.

He reached into his pocket and pulled out a stick. There was a click and a blade snaked out, transforming the stick into an evil-looking knife. 'I said get away, will you!'

'Peter!' shrieked Patrizia.

'Don't worry about Peter!' he said. 'Peter will be safe with me. He is my son. A boy must be with his father. Peter will come to London with me. You can stay here with your eunuch and your girl-bastard if you want. A boy must be with his father.' He put the knife at Peter's throat. 'Mikel, get her away from me or . . .'

Mikel put gentle hands on Patrizia's shoulder. 'Come. Pick up the little one. It will be best.' He put his arms round her and Rebeka and pulled them into the corner of the room. 'There now, Lau,' he said quietly to his cousin. 'We do as you wish. Be careful with the boy.'

Laurenz pushed his son towards the door. 'Go upstairs and put on your thickest jumper and coat then come straight back here. And find a hat. It is cold on the bike. Now do it quickly or your mama will be very cross.' He waved the knife at Patrizia. 'Tell him!' he said.

'Do as Papa says,' said Patrizia, nodding to Peter. 'Quickly.'

In minutes Peter was back in his thick jumper and coat. On his head he had the little red woolly hat he had last worn when they went skating with Florence and her family. Patrizia gulped but this did not prevent the tears coming.

Laurenz took him by the wrist, backed out of the room and shut the door behind him. They ran across to try to open it, but it stuck.

'He has put something behind it,' sobbed Patrizia. 'A chair or something.'

Mikel started to put his shoulder against the door but Patrizia pulled him away. 'The front door! The front door!' They raced into the hall, then out of the rarely used front door. Patrizia spotted Thomas who was still standing shivering under the lamppost. 'Thomas, Laurenz has Peter!' she shouted.

He ran towards her and as he did so Laurenz came careering round from the back on the motor bike, Peter crouching in front of him. Thomas launched himself towards the bike and Laurenz steered straight at him and through the open gate. The front wheel and the handle caught Thomas and flung him ten yards along the bare garden where he grunted and then lay very still.

Mikel said, 'See to the Englishman,' and galloped past Patrizia in pursuit of his cousin.

Patrizia put Rebeka on the step and dropped on to her knees beside Thomas. There was blood over his face where he had scraped over the stones and his leg was under him at a strange angle. She touched his hand. He groaned, and opened his eyes. 'Peter?' he said faintly.

'Mikel will get him. Don't worry,' she said before he passed out again. Rebeka ran towards her and she put out an arm and cuddled her close. She was still there, kneeling on the ground, when Mikel returned.

He shook his head. 'Lost him at the corner of the estate,' he gasped. 'But the Goldfarbs were there. They have been hanging round. Motor bike and sidecar. They followed him.'

'Oh, Mikel! Peter's sitting in front! He could crash!'

Mikel looked miserable. 'What can we do?'

Patrizia closed her eyes for a second, then took a deep breath. 'First we must get Thomas inside on to the couch. Can you lift him?'

When Mikel staggered into the house with the groaning Thomas Patrizia realised the couch would be too short so she raced upstairs for blankets and pillows so he could be laid on the floor. She pulled a blanket under Thomas's chin, then she ordered Mikel, 'You stay with Thomas. I'll run for Leonora. She'll know how to help him. And Kay will help me to find Peter with her car. Just talk to Thomas, keep talking to him.'

She put her coat on and picked up Rebeka. 'Keep talking to him.'

The two men watched the door shut behind her.

'She is so lovely,' muttered Thomas through gritted teeth. 'A lovely woman.'

'Yes, she is,' said Mikel quietly. 'I thought so from the day Laurenz brought her to the farm. But she was just a girl then. I think like me, you love Patrizia also. I should not have left her here with him.'

'Mmm.' Thomas closed his eyes as a wave of pain hit him. When it receded he opened them again. Then he spoke in German. 'What is the matter with that man? With Laurenz? He is crazy.'

'I think perhaps you are right.'

'So why have you stuck with him? All these years?'

'I love him and I feel responsible for him. That's why.'

'Love him? That animal?'

'It is strange that you say that.' Mikel sighed. He hesitated, then he spoke. 'There was a time, when Laurenz was very young, a bad time. I thought he had forgotten it. But it has been on my mind lately, and then tonight, he said some things to Peter. Perhaps he is remembering. Perhaps this is what makes him lose his . . . power to control things in these days. He was always so good at that. The control.'

Thomas stirred a little under his blanket, closed his eyes against the pain and said through gritted teeth, 'What was this bad time, then?'

'Lau would kill me for telling you, but perhaps that does not matter now.' He sighed. 'Laurenz is my cousin. His mother was my father's most favourite sister, a very beautiful woman whose husband was loathed by her father, my grandfather. Perhaps he hated the husband most because he was a Jew. She died when Laurenz was born and her husband died when Lau was about three. My grandfather, not wanting this child of a Jew in his house, sent him to a relative in Vienna, a butcher who had no children.

'After that, the child was just forgotten about for five years. There were the seasons on the farm, much hard work. Then one day my father had to go to Vienna on some matter to do with the purchase of land. On a whim, he called on the butcher to ask after the child of his favourite sister. The butcher told him the child was not there. Said he had died of diphtheria two years back.

'Well, my father was a shrewd man, and there was something about the butcher's demeanour, and the attitude of the woman who helped in the shop, which made him persist. He asked to see the certificate of death, and the butcher started to prevaricate. That was when the woman who helped in the shop told him to go out the back, and look in the dog kennel.'

Mikel took out his handkerchief and blew his nose. 'Lau was chained in this little shed like a dog. Filthy. No clothes on. Straw. Scraps of food. A tin dish of water like you would give a dog. He was wild. He howled like a dog and fought, even when my father tried to take him from there, to help him.'

'What a tale,' grunted Thomas. 'So your father brought him home?'

'He brought him home, and we took care of him. Under the crust of dirt he was so bright, so beautiful, so quick. Luckily he seemed to lose those bad years from his mind and we thought that a good thing. My father was riven with guilt over him, and indulged him too much, I think. We all did. My father made me promise to take care of him, always. And that is what I have tried to do.' He sighed. 'But I closed my eyes too much, even though I have tried to protect Patrizia. The bad years were echoing inside Laurenz, lying in wait for him like a wolf in the woods. Now, as Peter is passing through those years of Laurenz's own suffering, the bad years seem to have come back to the surface for Laurenz and he is a wild dog again.'

'What happened to the butcher? Was he prosecuted?'

'He? Oh no, Thomas. The butcher was not a *he*. It was a *she*. And she was not prosecuted. She ran off, to Hungary I think. We did not hear of her again.'

* * *

The vibration and noise of the motor bike between Peter's short legs mingled with the thud of his father's heart, which was beating into Peter's back like a great thumping drum. His ears were filled with the roar of the engine. As the motor bike raced and swerved through the streets of Priorton there was no room inside his small body for feelings of fear.

His father's voice was screaming into his ear. 'We will be safe, Peter. Do not be afraid. There will be no harm.'

Within minutes Laurenz had to wrench the bike to a halt behind two buses which were parked abreast, faced in opposite directions, their drivers exchanging the time of day. Laurenz sounded his horn. He shrieked on and on at them in German. 'Get out of the way! Get out of the way, you dumb pig-dogs!'

Peter screamed as the Goldfarbs drew up alongside them. Viktor, who was driving, leaned towards Laurenz, his face obscured by his black leather helmet. 'Let the child go,' he shouted. 'Our quarrel is not with him.'

'You threatened him, you *Dummkopf*! You threatened him and his sister!'

Pedestrians, hearing the altercation in that still distrusted language on their own streets, stopped silently to watch, their eyes suspicious. Peter screamed again as Viktor's gauntleted hand grasped his shoulder. Laurenz's fist shot out to punch Viktor in the face and the older man fell to one side, releasing his grip on Peter.

The bus ahead ground its gears and started to draw away and Laurenz's engine roared. He set away again, squeezing through the widening gap between the buses. Peter could hear and feel his father laughing. 'There, Peter,' he shouted into Peter's ear. 'That is how you do it.'

Laurenz bent his head sideways to see behind him. 'And still the pigs come,' he yelled.

He swerved into a small road and stopped at a stone arch and great iron gates, one of which stood open. Peter could hear the roar of the other bike as it missed them and passed by. His father lifted him off the bike and planted him in the road. 'They will be back. Walk away,' he said. 'Walk away and you will be safe.' He pushed Peter on the shoulder. 'Go to your Uncle Mikel.'

Peter started to walk.

'Peter!'

He stopped and turned round.

'Remember, Peter. Be the shark! Only the shark!' He revved up the engine and, the dust rising under his wheels, he drove through the open gateway.

When Patrizia got to Blamire House a red-haired man was already on the doorstep, pounding at the door. They both virtually fell into Kay's arms as she opened the door.

'It's Ginger,' Ed gasped. 'She's real bad with . . . she's losing the bairn. That bastard. I'll kill him. I knew it. I knew there was more to it than . . .'

'Kay,' said Patrizia determinedly. 'Thomas is harmed. Laurenz ran into Thomas with the motor bike and he has taken Peter away.' She looked up at Leonora who was hovering behind Kay. 'You must go to Thomas, Leonora. You will know what to do.'

'Who's taken Peter?' said Florence from her place on the stairs.

'Florence,' said Kay firmly, 'go across the yard and ask Duggie if Momma can have the car. And ask Mrs MacMahon if she will come here. Go!' She turned to Ed. 'How is Ginger?'

'She is poorly. Me father is livid. She was asking for you.'

Kay closed her eyes a second, then took a deep breath. 'We will have to deal with this other thing first. This man, the man who's run off with his son is the man whom' – she glanced at Patrizia – 'you gave that beating to.'

'My son is with him,' said Patrizia. 'I think he is in danger.'

'Would you like to help us find him?' Kay asked Ed.

'Give us half a chance,' said Ed.

In the end Leonora went off on her own to find Dr Fairless

and take him to see to Thomas. Kay and Patrizia left Rebeka with Florence and Mrs MacMahon, under the eye of Hugh Longstaffe, and drove with Duggie through the streets of Priorton looking in every direction. They searched right to the edge of town but there was no sign of Laurenz, or of his bike and small passenger.

They were just talking about taking the search further out on the main road when they saw a small figure trudging before them head down, face scowling. 'Peter! There he is, my Peter!'

Duggie stopped the car. Patrizia leapt out and swept her son up into her arms. '*Liebling*, dearest boy. Are you all right?' She brought him to the car and he sat between her and Kay. 'He is all right,' said Patrizia happily. 'He is all right.'

'What happened?' said Kay. 'Peter, where is your father, Peter?'

Peter raised his face from his mother's shoulder. 'Papa left me near some very big gates. Some nasty men chase us on another bike. So Papa stop beside the big gates and make me jump off. Tell me to go home to Uncle Mikel. To run fast, or the nasty men will get me.'

'And what happened then?'

'I go in a corner and watch. The bike stops. Papa he cannot make the bike start again and the bad men are nearly up to him. He jumps from bike and runs through the big gates. And they follow him. So I come to find you, Mama. And Uncle Mikel. Papa says they will kill him. Will they kill him? I don't want the nasty men to kill my papa.' For the first time he started to cry.

Ed Simpson stirred in his back seat. 'I want to get after him,' he said grimly. 'We're wasting time here.'

'We've got Peter now,' said Patrizia. 'Leave him. Leave Laurenz.'

Kay thought quickly. There was no way Ed would be put off, she knew that. She would need to be there with him. Vengeance on Laurenz could and would blight Ed's life. That would, in Ginger's terms, be a case of a bad lad winning. Even if he were dead.

'It's the gates to Priors' Park,' she said. 'That's what Peter saw. The big gates on the way into the park. Duggie, could you drop Ed and me there, then take Patrizia home with Peter? Then come back to the park gates and wait?'

They passed Laurenz's bike at a narrow inner gateway in the park. Further on, past the Priory itself, beside a wall they came to another abandoned motor bike and sidecar.

The park, on this late summer evening, was deserted; the broad stretches of greensward were eerie, haunted by the absent picnickers and swimmers and children playing kiss-and-tell. The river lapped in a sullen fashion at the foot of the escarpment. Kay lifted her eyes to the High Plains soaring over the river where she and Harry Longstaffe once – it seemed a long time ago – had played their own game of not kissing and not telling.

She and Ed Simpson were half walking, half running along the narrow path. She wondered vaguely what they were about to do. Were they about to kill Laurenz Gold, or save him? From the look on Ed's face he would happily kill him. She was not so sure about herself. What she did know was that she wanted him sorted out, exorcised in one way or another. He was unfinished business for her as well as Ed Simpson. But they must not ruin their lives as they finished this business.

So she padded on.

They followed the pathway round through the trees. Then they were approaching a bridge which would allow them to cross the river and go up towards the High Plains. They slowed at the sight of two figures coming towards them. The older one was wearing steel-rimmed glasses, a leather helmet pushed back onto his neck.

Kay stopped before them. 'Is that your bike and sidecar at the gate?' she asked.

Viktor Goldfarb took off his glasses and nodded cautiously. 'That is our vehicle,' he said.

'Were you chasing Laurenz Gold?'

'The bastard!' put in Ed Simpson.

Viktor looked at him quizzically. 'You also, sir?' He paused.

'Well,' he said, 'your bastard is up there somewhere. We were chasing him. But it is getting dark among the trees and we kept losing our way. We heard a scream' – he said this with some satisfaction – 'so we left it. How do you say it? We called it a day.' He clicked his heels and bowed his head. 'So I will say good evening, madame.'

They watched the two Austrians march away then Ed said, 'Now we'll get him. Come on, Kay, come on!'

He started to run and she followed him across the bridge and up, always up through the trees. They ran on for a while before they found the edge of the escarpment. Then they started to walk along, feeling their way through the trees in the dense dusk. They started to run again and Kay almost fell through the roots of a tree, where the soil had come away from the edge of the escarpment.

'Here,' she said. 'He must have fallen here.'

'Let me go first,' said Ed.

She saw the murder in his eyes and she said firmly, 'No. Let me.'

So she found her way downwards, hanging on to roots and overhanging branches, just as she had done on that day with Harry.

In five minutes she had found him, draped across some ancient roots, hanging out over thin air, his legs at a strange angle. He was clutching a root with both hands. His eyes were closed and she thought he was unconscious. She wedged herself beside him. 'Laurenz,' she said.

His eyes opened and a faint smile crossed his face. 'I had a little fall, *liebling*. And now you have come to help me.' His gaze shifted as he caught sight of Ed behind her. 'But no, I think you have come to kill me.'

'No,' she protested, her mind made up. 'Here, take my hand.' She put out her hand. 'I promise you, Laurenz.'

He loosened one hand from the root and reached out towards her, a wide smile on his face. '*Mutti*,' he said.

Her blood froze.

'*Mutti!* Little mother. You come with me. Stay with me. Don't leave me.' He grasped her arm in an iron clasp and fell another foot, pulling her with him. She tried to shake him off, then forced the hand clasping her arm over another root, trying to wrench her own arm down to free it.

'Bitch!' he muttered and brought his other hand up to hit her. As he reached towards her, there was a crackling and scrambling behind her and a single 'Cer – Christ!' from Ed, who missed his footing. The tree root which Laurenz was hanging onto groaned and broke and he went hurtling down the escarpment, battered from branch to branch, root to root like a rag doll. Kay hung on for her own dear life, her ears filled with his long strangled scream which ended in a splash as Laurenz hit the water, in the deepest part of the river where only the best swimmers ventured.

Clinging helplessly to the roots, she watched the spreading rings of water which showed where Laurenz had been catapulted into the water, and at the bubbles which gushed up once, twice, three times.

Then there was nothing.

'That's it then.' Ed's voice came from up above her, where he too was clinging to a root although his was as big as a tree trunk. 'Good riddance to bad rubbish. Saves us the bother, anyway.'

Kay felt a wave of irritation at his tone. 'Oh, for God's sake, get us back up, will you? If we don't get a move on I'll end up in the drink with him. Perhaps that'll save you the bother as well.'

Ed moved very cautiously, first to improve the stability of his own position, then to hang down and lift Kay to safety by holding her round her waist and helping her walk up two thick tree roots. Her remark had hit home. 'Can't see why you're being narky,' he complained. 'He's the bad'n, not me.'

She sat on a branch further up the bank to get her breath back. 'But you would have been the bad'n if you'd done what you wanted to do to him. Don't you see that? He'd have won then, or his badness would have. Your Ginger knows that.'

'Ginger!' he said. 'We need to get to her.'

'We need to get off this escarpment and tell the police before we do anything else.'

'Right. Then we'll get to Ginger.'

They went straight to the Simpson house from the police station. Ginger was tucked up in her bed looking half her usual size. Her face, small and pinched, lit up when she saw Kay. 'What cheer, flower,' she said. 'Haven't we been in the wars?'

Kay sat on the bed. 'How are you, Ginger?'

'All right. I was leaking blood like a colander at first, so I had them worried. Red hair, see? But that's stopped now. I feel as weak as a kitten, sorry for the bairn that's lost.' She laughed drily. 'I had just got used to thinking about it as an innocent.'

'I'm sorry,' said Kay.

'Don't tell me it's all for the best, I've had enough of that from my mother. All she's relieved about is that my father might not – just *might* not – throw me out. And our Ed's baying for the Austrian's blood—'

Kay interrupted her to deliver an edited version of the events of the last two hours. Ginger whistled. 'Blo-ody hell.' She paused. 'Nobody deserves to die before their time, like. In that or any other way.'

Kay squeezed Ginger's hand. 'You're such a generous person.'

Ginger snatched her hand away. 'Oh, gerroff, you. Allus mekkin' a fuss.' She smoothed the bed cover. 'Now I think you'd better get yersel' home and have a bath. Yer look like a bliddy scarecrow.'

Kay was at the bedroom door when Ginger called her back. 'What is it?'

'I'll need a shift off tomorrow, mebbe the next day. But I should be back on Monday.'

'Don't be silly, Ginger. Take as long off as you need.'

'I'll be there,' said Ginger. 'Would you like to be stuck in this house for weeks on end? Be reasonable.'

Mona looked up from her fireside chair as Kay came into the kitchen. To Kay's relief the room was otherwise empty. 'I've sent them all down to the club,' said Mona. 'Pleased to get rid of them. I even give them me own club money fer this week to give me a bit o' peace and quiet.' She paused. 'Our Ed telt us what happened to the lad. Just deserts, I suppose.' She looked Kay in the eye. 'It was a forced job, our Mavis getting like that, wasn't it?'

Kay nodded.

'Just as well, then.' Mona reached underneath her cushion and produced the recipe book. 'Finished your recipes for you,' she said. 'Just tried the last one today. Meat and tatie pie. Your Mrs Morpurgo got the timing right but not the temperatures. They're all right now, like.'

Kay took the book from her. 'Thanks, Mona. Very good of you to do this. It'll help sell the cookers, I'm sure of it.'

'No bother, Kay. A pleasure to do anything for a friend of our Mavis.'

Twenty minutes later Mrs MacMahon met Kay in the hallway of Blamire House to inform her that Mrs Scorton was at the hospital with Thomas, as was Mrs Gold and Mr Mikel Schmidt. The news was that Thomas was not too bad and should soon be on the mend. The children were all in bed in Florence's room, Rebeka in the long drawer taken out of the big press. The police had been, and would be coming back later. And Duggie was going down the fish-and-chip shop, did she fancy a packet?

Kay shook her head. 'No, thank you, Mrs M. Couldn't eat a thing.'

'Well, in that case will you go in and see Hugh Longstaffe? The old feller says he wants to see you the second you get in.'

Kay was too tired to see anybody, but this was a royal command. She knocked on the sitting-room door and walked in. Hugh, as usual, was sitting in the bay window. And there, standing with his back to the fire, looking boyish in flannels and soft shirt, was Harry Longstaffe. He looked at Kay long and hard, then burst out laughing.

'What?' she said crossly. 'What is it?'

He came towards her and took both her hands in his. 'What on earth have you been doing to yourself?' he said. 'You look like Worzel Gummidge.' Still holding her hands he led her to the overmantel mirror. 'Look!'

Her face was smudged with dirt and her hair was awry, braided in an entirely random fashion with twigs and leaves. She nodded. 'Worzel Gummidge!' she agreed wearily.

He pulled her round to face him. 'Now then,' he said, 'how on earth did you get into this state?'

She looked at him with a very faint smile. 'Now that is a very long, long story.'

He released one of her hands in order to disentangle a twig from her hair. 'Isn't that a coincidence? Now that the army has finally freed me from its greedy grasp, I have a long, long time to listen!'

Twenty-Two

Epilogue

'It's a ceremony!' announced Florence.

'In a church?' asked Peter. 'My papa had a ceremony in a church before they put him in the ground. My Uncle Mikel cried.' He shuddered. 'My mama cried. I did not like the church. It was very cold.'

'It's not in a church,' said Florence. 'It's in two places. It's in the factory first, to see this special cooker they've made. Then it's the tea party at the museum. You know, where Thomas and Uncle Hugh go when they're not down the allotment?'

'Will there be jelly?'

'Sure to,' said Florence with more confidence than she felt. Adults seemed pretty keen on sour things, like pickled onions and sausage rolls.

Report in the *Priorton Courier*, November 1st 1947

Today's ceremony at the Rainbow Works, Priorton, took place on the shop floor at the end of line one, where, at twelve noon, the first completed cooker with the innovatory no-spill ring and spillage tray slid off the line on schedule. The operators were wearing their new overalls, in a brilliant shade of ice-green which set off the auburn hair of the new line leader, Miss Mavis Simpson (see picture left), known as Ginger to her close associates. The ceremony was presided over by the Managing Director, Captain Marshall, and the owner, Mrs

Kay Fitzgibbon (pictured above with her mother, Councillor Leonora Scorton). Mrs Fitzgibbon is grand-daughter of the founder of the Rainbow Works, Miss Kitty Rainbow, a well-known figure in Priorton until her death last year. Also present were the Chairman and members of the Priorton District Council (see picture left). In his speech the Chairman said the future in this area would depend more and more on these so-called light industries rather than the more familiar traditional industries of coal and steel. In addition, the launch gave him extra pleasure as this particular cooker would be packaged this very day and sent on behalf of Priorton District Council as a wedding present for Her Royal Highness Princess Elizabeth and Lieutenant Mountbatten on the occasion of their forthcoming marriage. There was a chuckle of appreciation all round when the Chairman said that there was no guarantee that Her Royal Highness would be cooking on it herself. However, if she did venture down that road she could find no better guide than the new Rainbow Cookery Book *devised by Mrs Fitzgibbon and Mrs Mona Simpson, mother of Miss Mavis Simpson, mentioned above.*

The whole party, including the women from the cooker line, were then transported in coaches to the Rainbow Memorial Museum, reopened today for the first time in ten years. Visitors were welcomed by the Museum Curators, Mr Thomas Scorton (shown left with his wife Patrizia), and Mr Hugh Longstaffe (shown right with his son Captain Harry Longstaffe, recently appointed under-manager of White Leas Colliery). Refreshments, taken from the new recipe book, were served. Complimentary copies of the recipe book were given to guests. The Courier *has three complimentary copies of the cookery book which will be sent to the first three readers' requests received.*

'No jelly,' said Peter gloomily.

'Just pickled onions and sausage rolls,' nodded Florence.

'Just as I expected. I know! Let's go and see that colliery thing that Thomas and Uncle Hugh made. Have you seen how the winder winds them all the way to the top? And all those miners squashed in there?'

'Uncle Hugh says they are called pitmen,' said Peter.

'Same thing,' said Florence nonchalantly.

Across the room Kay and Ginger munched on their sausage rolls and watched Peter and Florence race down the long hall. 'The kids seem to be having a nice time,' said Ginger.

'Aren't you?'

'I'd rather be back at work doing a bit of wiring. All this standing round – bit po-faced if you ask me.'

'Rather be jitterbugging?'

'Chance'd be a fine thing,' said Ginger gloomily.

'Not much dancing lately?'

'Well, Janet's gone off and married a bliddy dog-man and the rest seem young somehow. Or I'm getting old.'

'You and I should go dancing again. In Darlington. Then you can find yourself a soldier boy.'

'I see you've got one for yourself. Captain bliddy Longstaffe, no less!' Ginger nodded across at Harry Longstaffe who was now in earnest conversation with his father. 'He's a looker, no doubt about it. I tell you what, he looks like . . .'

'My brother Thomas. I know. Funny that, isn't it?'

'Would your man come dancing too?'

Kay laughed. 'If I ask him.'

'Oh, it's like that, is it? Got him eatin' out of yer hand?'

'Well, not as far as work's concerned. I tried to stop him going back down the pit and he took not a blind bit of notice.'

'Manager. It's not the same. You ask our lads.'

'Anyway, Ginger, what about going dancing?'

'Well, flower, I might just take you up on it.' She paused. 'I was watching the proud parents.' She nodded across at Kay's Aunt Mara and Dewi Wilson who were showing off their new son John-Paul to Mikel Schmidt. Mara looked younger than ever, but the portly Dewi looked more like a grandfather than a father.

Kay said cautiously, 'Do you think of your . . . of the baby, Ginger?'

Ginger laughed. 'I get some bloody silly stirrings sometimes, but nothing that can't be cured by a bit of overtime, or scrubbing the kitchen floor. My time for that'll come, you watch. Mebbe I will get me a soldier boy.'

'It's no excuse, Ginger, but Thomas did tell me a terrible tale about what happened to Laurenz when he was little.'

'Like you say,' said Ginger drily, 'it's no excuse. His wife and your brother look happy enough.' She gestured towards a corner where Thomas was opening a cabinet and showing Patrizia the contents. 'Look, Kay, I'll just go across there and rescue the Captain from my mother. She looks as though she's trying to tell him how to run his factory – and he's had enough of that from you.'

Kay stood very still for a minute, looking round at all the people. Harry came up and put an arm through hers. 'Queen of all you survey?' he said.

She shook her head.

'So what were you thinking?'

'I was thinking how I love them all. How I came here a year ago and hated this place. Called it cold and dark. I wanted to go back to Egypt straight away. Back to the heat and the bright skies. My grandmother said there was heat and warmth here but you had to dig for it, nurture the land and make that land produce it for you. She challenged me then to stay two years and then go. If I wished.'

'And do you wish?'

She shook her head. 'She knew me like she knew herself. I'm caught now. I've done some nurturing and I want to see it all flourish.'

'So you can stay and marry me then.'

Slowly she shook her head. 'Did you not know, there's a strong tradition in this family of staying out of wedlock? I was thinking of giving it a try.'

He kissed her very thoroughly then, ignoring the light patter of ironic applause around them. 'Now then!' he said. 'Am I to take that as a threat or a promise?'

A Coffin for Two

Quintin Jardine

After cracking their first case together as a private investigation team, Oz Blackstone and Primavera Philips find themselves simultaneously in love and in the money. And where better to lie back and contemplate life than the picturesque village of St Marti, on the rugged Costa Brava.

But is their new home quite so idyllic as it looks? Some very dark secrets begin to emerge as the inhabitants draw them into the intrigue which bubbles away beneath the surface, until suddenly, faced with a mysterious skeleton and an unauthenticated Dali masterpiece, Prim and Oz stumble across one of the century's most amazing stories . . .

'Entertaining . . . keeps you intrigued'
Carlisle News & Star

0 7472 5575 X

HEADLINE

Written in Blood

Caroline Graham

It is clear to the more realistic members of the Midsomer Worthy's Writers' Circle that asking best-selling author Max Jennings to talk to them is a little ambitious. Less clear are the reasons for secretary Gerald Hadleigh's fierce objections to seeing the man – a face from his past – again. But, astonishingly, Jennings accepts the invitation and before the night is out, Gerald is dead.

Summoned to investigate, Chief Inspector Barnaby finds that Gerald's solitary life was as much of a mystery to his well-heeled neighbours as his violent death. The key is surely their illustrious guest speaker – but where is he now?

Now part of the major television drama series, *Midsomer Murders*, starring John Nettles as Chief Inspector Barnaby.

'Plenty of horror spiked by humour, all twirling in a staggering *danse macabre*' *The Sunday Times*

'Very funny, with a brilliant cast of eccentrics' *Yorkshire Post*

'Enlivened by a very sardonic wit and turn of phrase, the narrative drive never falters . . . a most impressive performance' *Birmingham Post*

0 7472 4664 5

HEADLINE